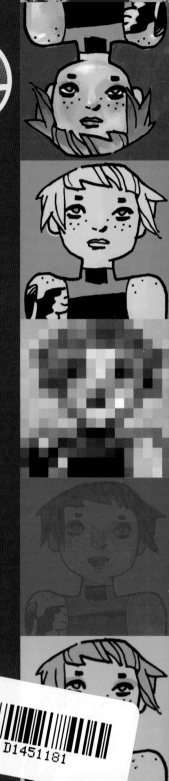

eve stranger

"...the artwork is all kinds of stylish ...reads like a lightning bolt of pure fun to the face. 10/10."
—*Comics Bookcase*

"It's got intrigue, character, action and clever wit. Like a pill that guarantees creativity and adventure in healthy doses, you'll be instantly hooked."
—*PopCult HQ*

"Visually stunning and engaging."
—*The Super Powered Fancast*

"Equal parts Memento and The Jason Bourne Identity, writer David Barnett and artist Philip Bond create a compelling heroine."
—*Newsarama*

"...one of this year's most intriguing original characters."
—*Broken Frontier*

"The art from Philip Bond has that perfect, pop-punk feel to it. It's a great, fun, funny, gorgeous to look at book ...I want more of it. I NEED more."
—*Bleeding Cool*

"A mod heroine...from one of the best imprints in the la EVE STRANGER was inevit
—*Doom*

"Philip's art is full of joy, style, character and vim. These adventures of an amnesiac assassin are enormously entertaining... feisty...UNFORGETTABLE."
—*Hero Collector*

BLACK CROWN HQ

Shelly Bond, Editor • **Megan Brown,** Assistant Editor • **Arlene Lo,** Proofreader
Philip Bond, logo, publication design and general dogsbody • **Chris Ryall, President**/Publisher & Chief Creative Officer

BLACK CROWN is a fully functioning curation operation based in Los Angeles by way of IDW Publishing. Accept No Substitutes!

For international rights, contact **licensing@idwpublishing.co**

ISBN: 978-1-68405-600-2

23 22 21 20 1 2 3

Chris Ryall, President & Publisher/CCO • **Cara Morrison**, Chief Financial Officer • **Matthew Ruzicka**, Chief Accounting Officer • **David Hedgecock**, Associate Publishe • **John Barber**, Editor-in-Chief • **Justin Eisinger**, Editorial Director, Graphic Novels and Collections • **Scott Dunbier**, Director, Special Projects • **Jerry Bennington**, VP New Product Development • **Lorelei Bunjes**, VP of Technology & Information Services • **Jud Meyers**, Sales Director • **Anna Morrow**, Marketing Director • **Tara McCrilli** Director of Design & Production • **Mike Ford**, Director of Operations • **Shauna Monteforte**, Manufacturing Operations Director • **Rebekah Cahalin**, General Manager

Ted Adams and Robbie Robbins, IDW Founders

IDW
www.IDWPUBLISHING.com

Facebook: **facebook.com/idwpublishing** • Twitter: **@idwpublishing** • YouTube: **youtube.com/idwpublishing**
Tumblr: **tumblr.idwpublishing.com** • Instagram: **instagram.com/idwpublishing**

eve stranger

"RETROGRADE"

Written by David Barnett
Art by Philip Bond & Liz Prince
Colored by Eva de la Cruz
Lettered by Jane Heir
Publication Design by Philip Bond
Editorial Assistance by Megan Brown
Edited by Shelly Bond

EVE STRANGER is created by David Barnett & Philip Bond

blackcrown.pub

part one:
RESCUE ME

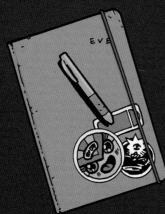

"THIS ALWAYS HAPPENS."

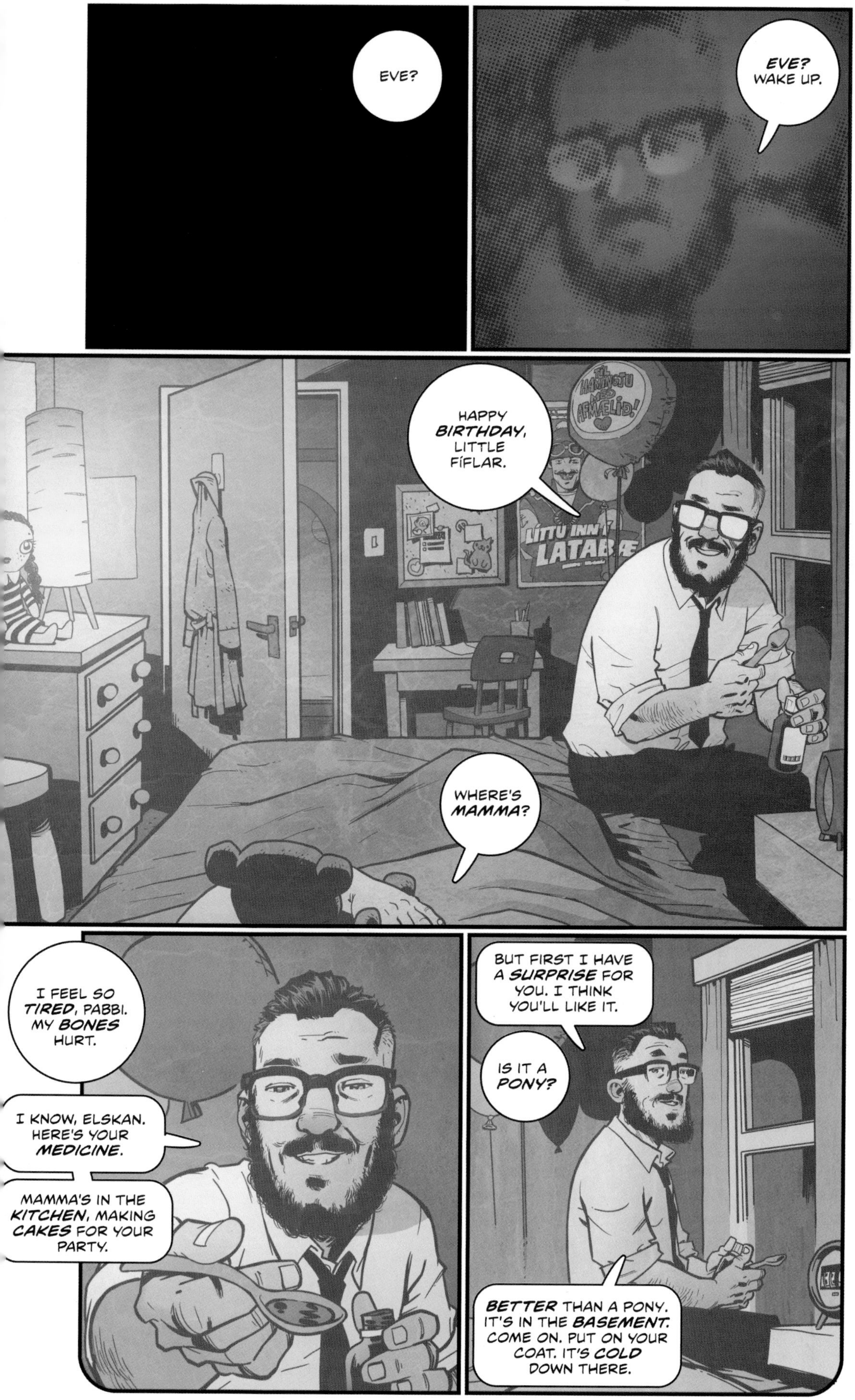
EVE?
EVE? WAKE UP.
HAPPY BIRTHDAY, LITTLE FÍFLAR.
TIL HAMINGJU MEÐ AFMÆLIÐ!
LÍTTU INN Í LATABÆ
WHERE'S MAMMA?
I FEEL SO TIRED, PABBI. MY BONES HURT.
I KNOW, ELSKAN. HERE'S YOUR MEDICINE.
MAMMA'S IN THE KITCHEN, MAKING CAKES FOR YOUR PARTY.
BUT FIRST I HAVE A SURPRISE FOR YOU. I THINK YOU'LL LIKE IT.
IS IT A PONY?
BETTER THAN A PONY. IT'S IN THE BASEMENT. COME ON. PUT ON YOUR COAT. IT'S COLD DOWN THERE.

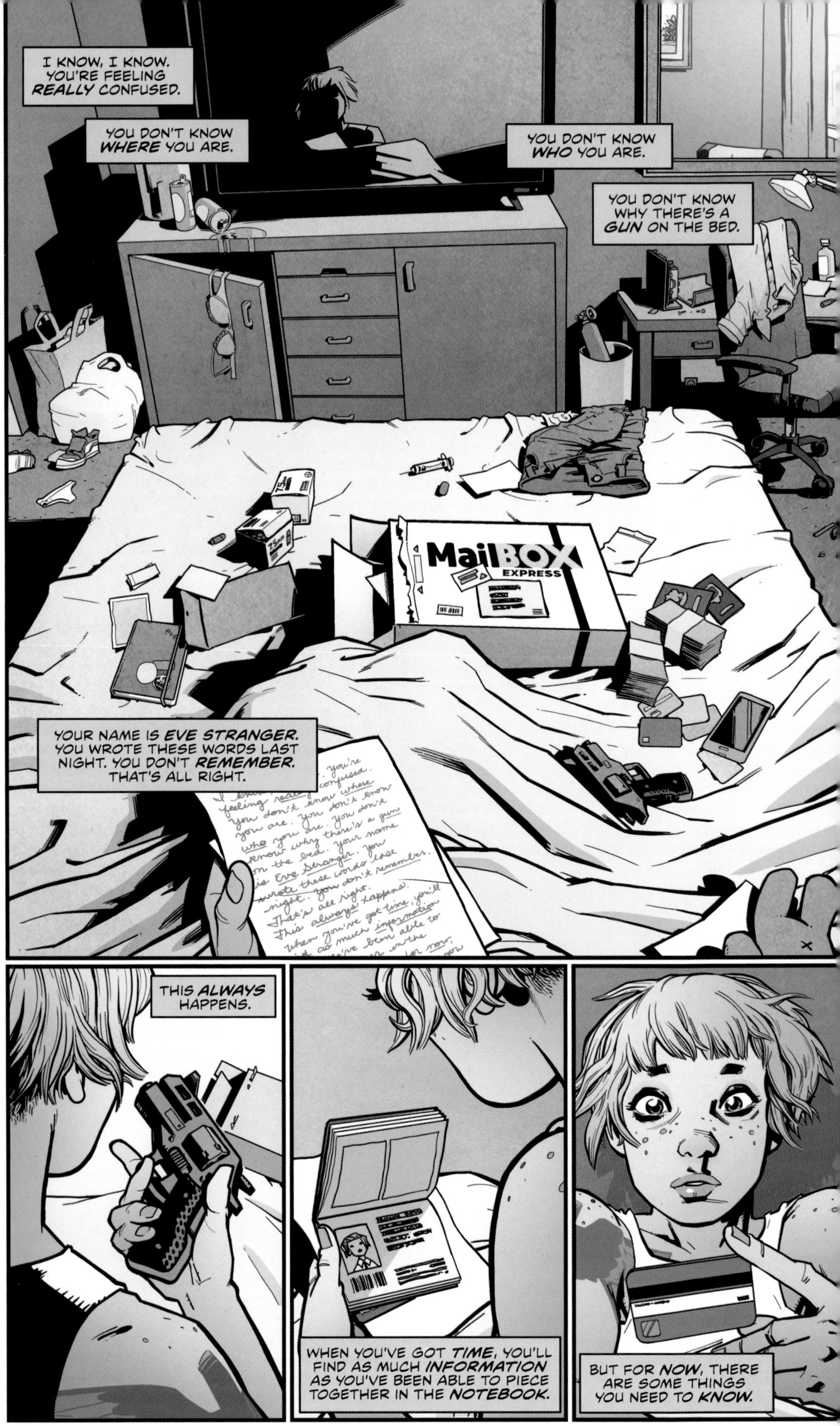
I KNOW, I KNOW. YOU'RE FEELING REALLY CONFUSED.
YOU DON'T KNOW WHERE YOU ARE.
YOU DON'T KNOW WHO YOU ARE.
YOU DON'T KNOW WHY THERE'S A GUN ON THE BED.
MailBOX EXPRESS
YOUR NAME IS EVE STRANGER. YOU WROTE THESE WORDS LAST NIGHT. YOU DON'T REMEMBER. THAT'S ALL RIGHT.
THIS ALWAYS HAPPENS.
WHEN YOU'VE GOT TIME, YOU'LL FIND AS MUCH INFORMATION AS YOU'VE BEEN ABLE TO PIECE TOGETHER IN THE NOTEBOOK.
BUT FOR NOW, THERE ARE SOME THINGS YOU NEED TO KNOW.

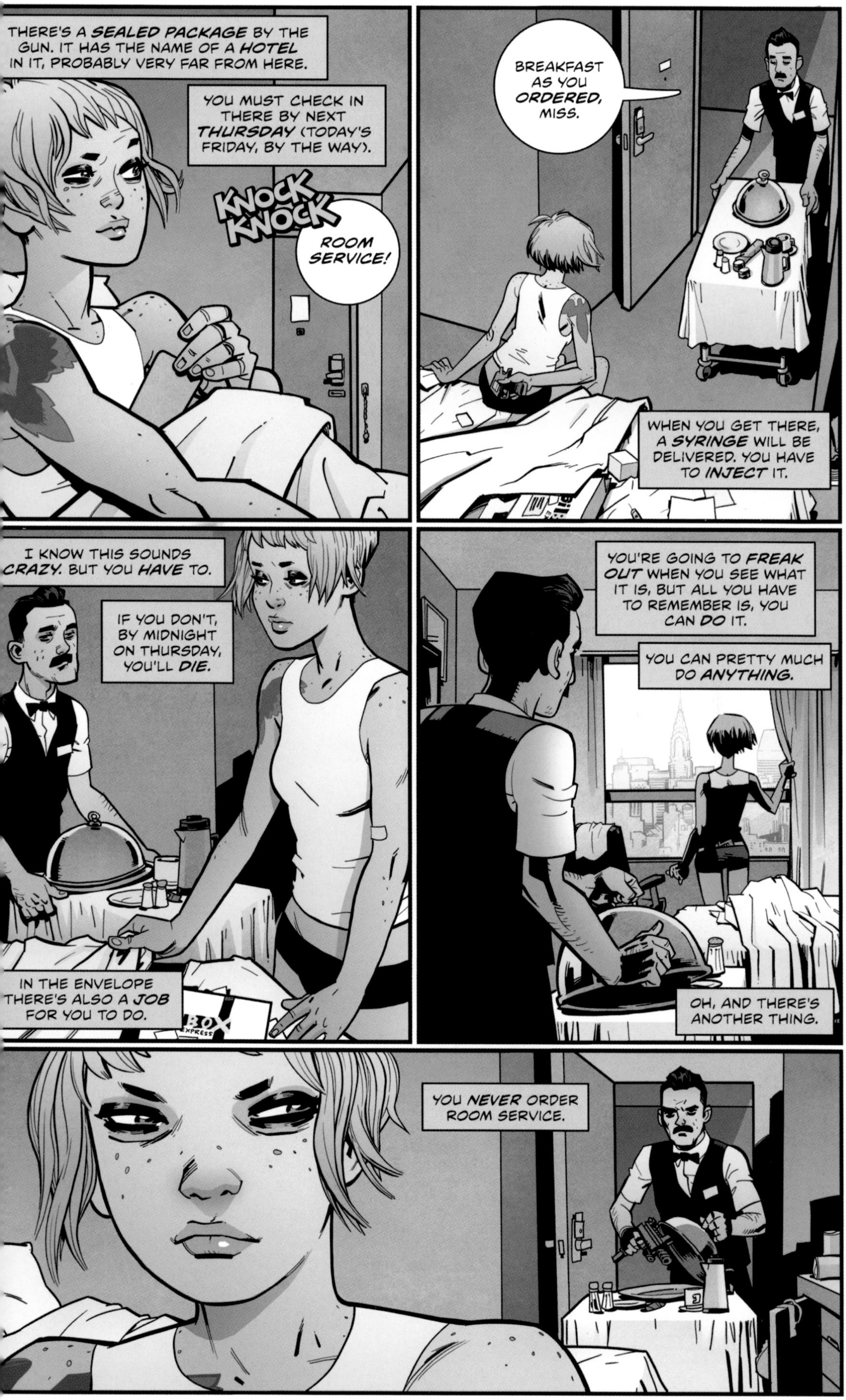

THERE'S A SEALED PACKAGE BY THE GUN. IT HAS THE NAME OF A HOTEL IN IT, PROBABLY VERY FAR FROM HERE.
YOU MUST CHECK IN THERE BY NEXT THURSDAY (TODAY'S FRIDAY, BY THE WAY).
KNOCK KNOCK
ROOM SERVICE!
BREAKFAST AS YOU ORDERED, MISS.
WHEN YOU GET THERE, A SYRINGE WILL BE DELIVERED. YOU HAVE TO INJECT IT.
I KNOW THIS SOUNDS CRAZY. BUT YOU HAVE TO.
IF YOU DON'T, BY MIDNIGHT ON THURSDAY, YOU'LL DIE.
IN THE ENVELOPE THERE'S ALSO A JOB FOR YOU TO DO.
BOX EXPRESS
YOU'RE GOING TO FREAK OUT WHEN YOU SEE WHAT IT IS, BUT ALL YOU HAVE TO REMEMBER IS, YOU CAN DO IT.
YOU CAN PRETTY MUCH DO ANYTHING.
OH, AND THERE'S ANOTHER THING.
YOU NEVER ORDER ROOM SERVICE.

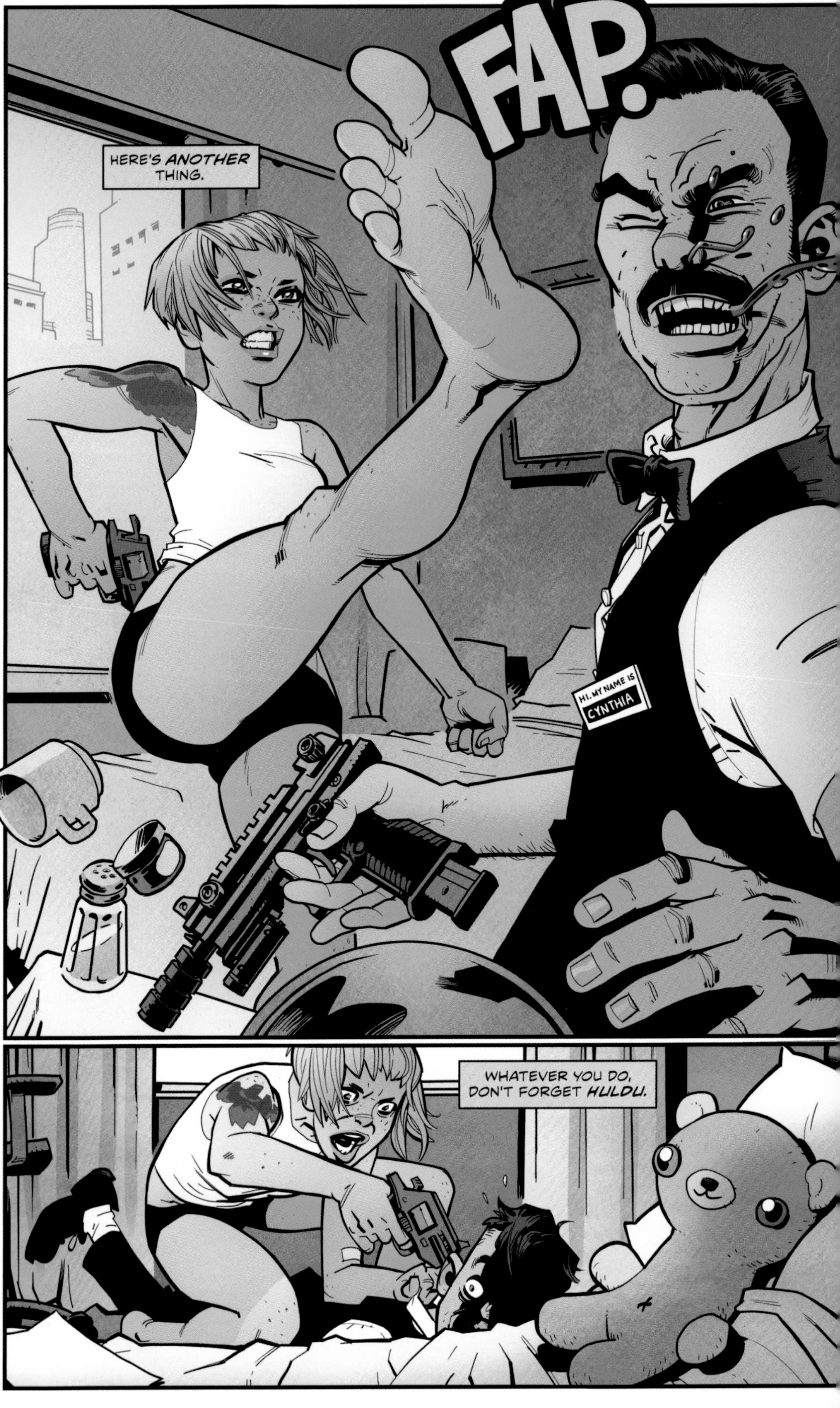
HERE'S ANOTHER THING.
FAP.
HI, MY NAME IS
CYNTHIA
WHATEVER YOU DO, DON'T FORGET HULDU.

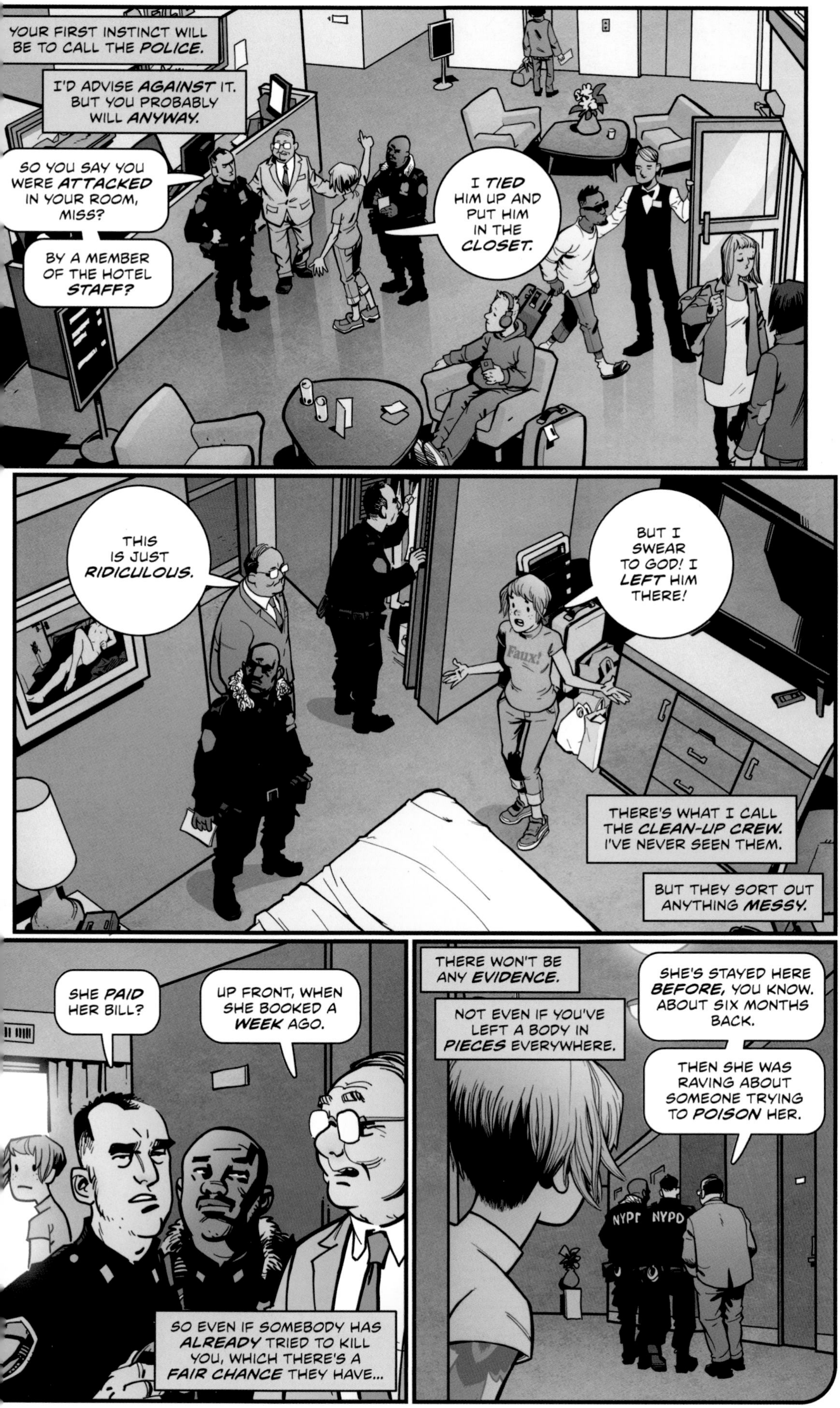
YOUR FIRST INSTINCT WILL BE TO CALL THE POLICE.
I'D ADVISE AGAINST IT. BUT YOU PROBABLY WILL ANYWAY.
SO YOU SAY YOU WERE ATTACKED IN YOUR ROOM, MISS?
BY A MEMBER OF THE HOTEL STAFF?
I TIED HIM UP AND PUT HIM IN THE CLOSET.
THIS IS JUST RIDICULOUS.
BUT I SWEAR TO GOD! I LEFT HIM THERE!
Faux!
THERE'S WHAT I CALL THE CLEAN-UP CREW. I'VE NEVER SEEN THEM.
BUT THEY SORT OUT ANYTHING MESSY.
SHE PAID HER BILL?
UP FRONT, WHEN SHE BOOKED A WEEK AGO.
SO EVEN IF SOMEBODY HAS ALREADY TRIED TO KILL YOU, WHICH THERE'S A FAIR CHANCE THEY HAVE...
THERE WON'T BE ANY EVIDENCE.
NOT EVEN IF YOU'VE LEFT A BODY IN PIECES EVERYWHERE.
SHE'S STAYED HERE BEFORE, YOU KNOW. ABOUT SIX MONTHS BACK.
THEN SHE WAS RAVING ABOUT SOMEONE TRYING TO POISON HER.
NYPD NYPD

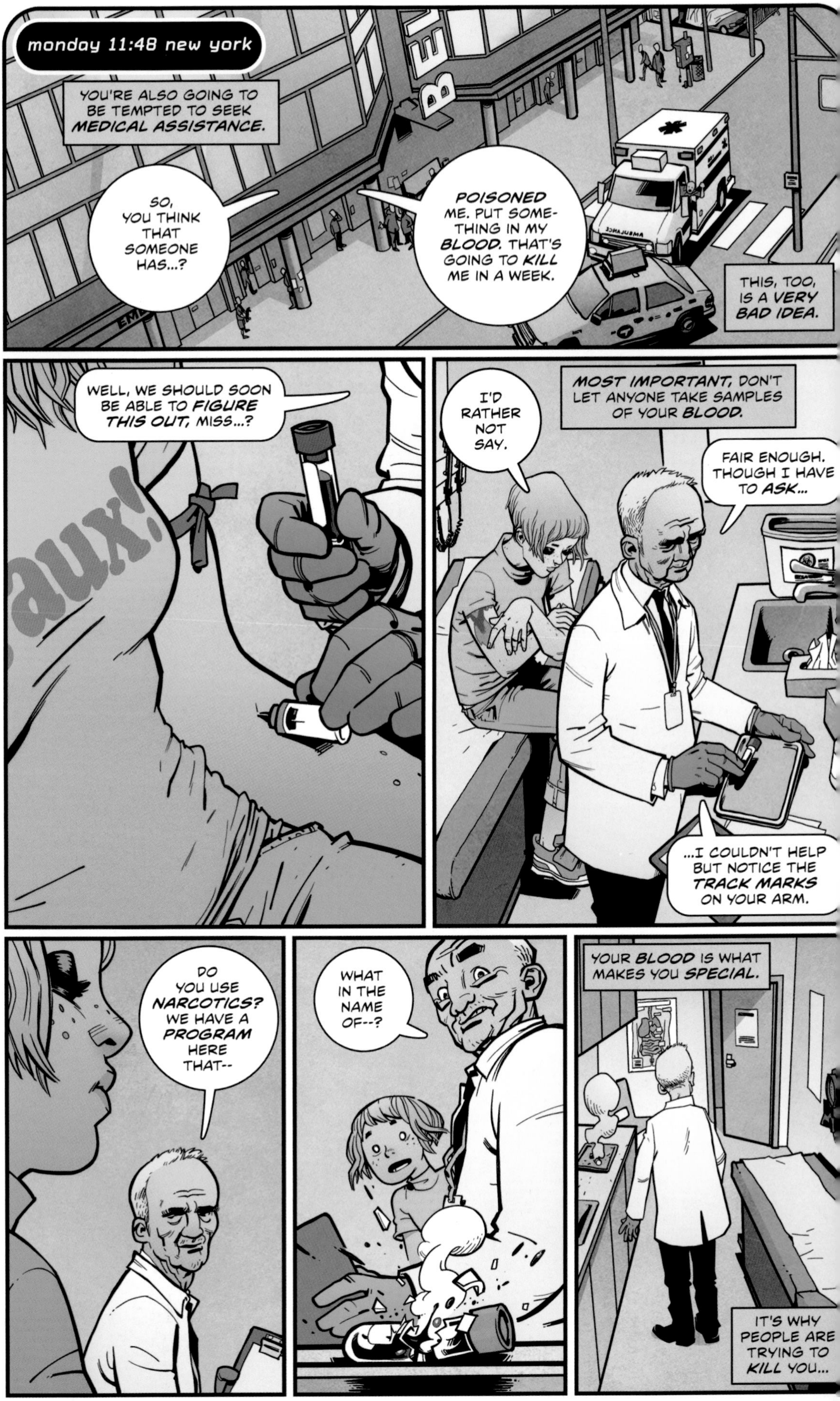
monday 11:48 new york
YOU'RE ALSO GOING TO BE TEMPTED TO SEEK MEDICAL ASSISTANCE.
SO, YOU THINK THAT SOMEONE HAS...?
POISONED ME. PUT SOME-THING IN MY BLOOD. THAT'S GOING TO KILL ME IN A WEEK.
THIS, TOO, IS A VERY BAD IDEA.
WELL, WE SHOULD SOON BE ABLE TO FIGURE THIS OUT, MISS...?
MOST IMPORTANT, DON'T LET ANYONE TAKE SAMPLES OF YOUR BLOOD.
I'D RATHER NOT SAY.
FAIR ENOUGH. THOUGH I HAVE TO ASK...
...I COULDN'T HELP BUT NOTICE THE TRACK MARKS ON YOUR ARM.
DO YOU USE NARCOTICS? WE HAVE A PROGRAM HERE THAT--
WHAT IN THE NAME OF--?
YOUR BLOOD IS WHAT MAKES YOU SPECIAL.
IT'S WHY PEOPLE ARE TRYING TO KILL YOU...

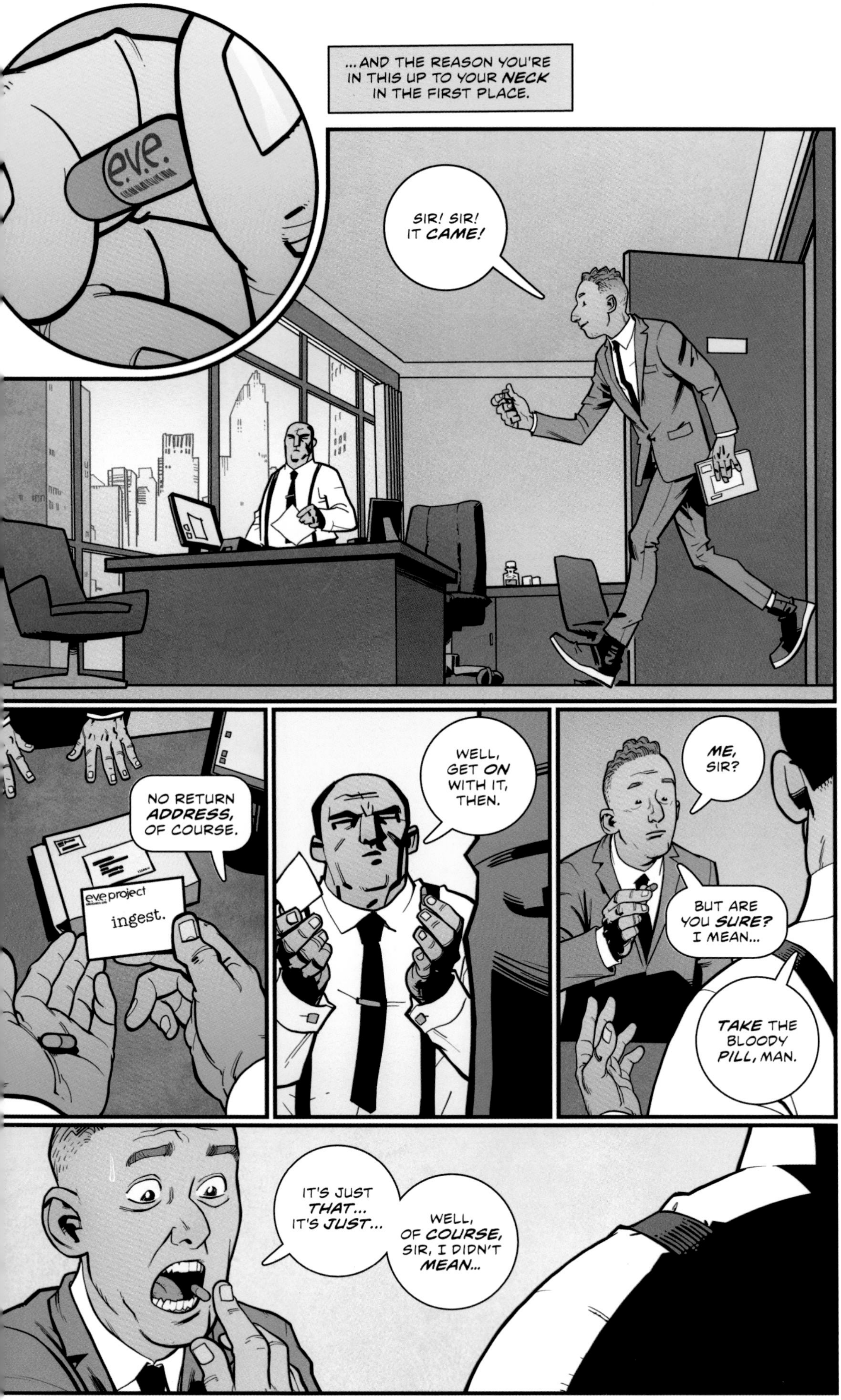
e.v.e.
...AND THE REASON YOU'RE IN THIS UP TO YOUR NECK IN THE FIRST PLACE.
SIR! SIR! IT CAME!
NO RETURN ADDRESS, OF COURSE.
eve project
ingest.
WELL, GET ON WITH IT, THEN.
ME, SIR?
BUT ARE YOU SURE? I MEAN...
TAKE THE BLOODY PILL, MAN.
IT'S JUST THAT... IT'S JUST...
WELL, OF COURSE, SIR, I DIDN'T MEAN...

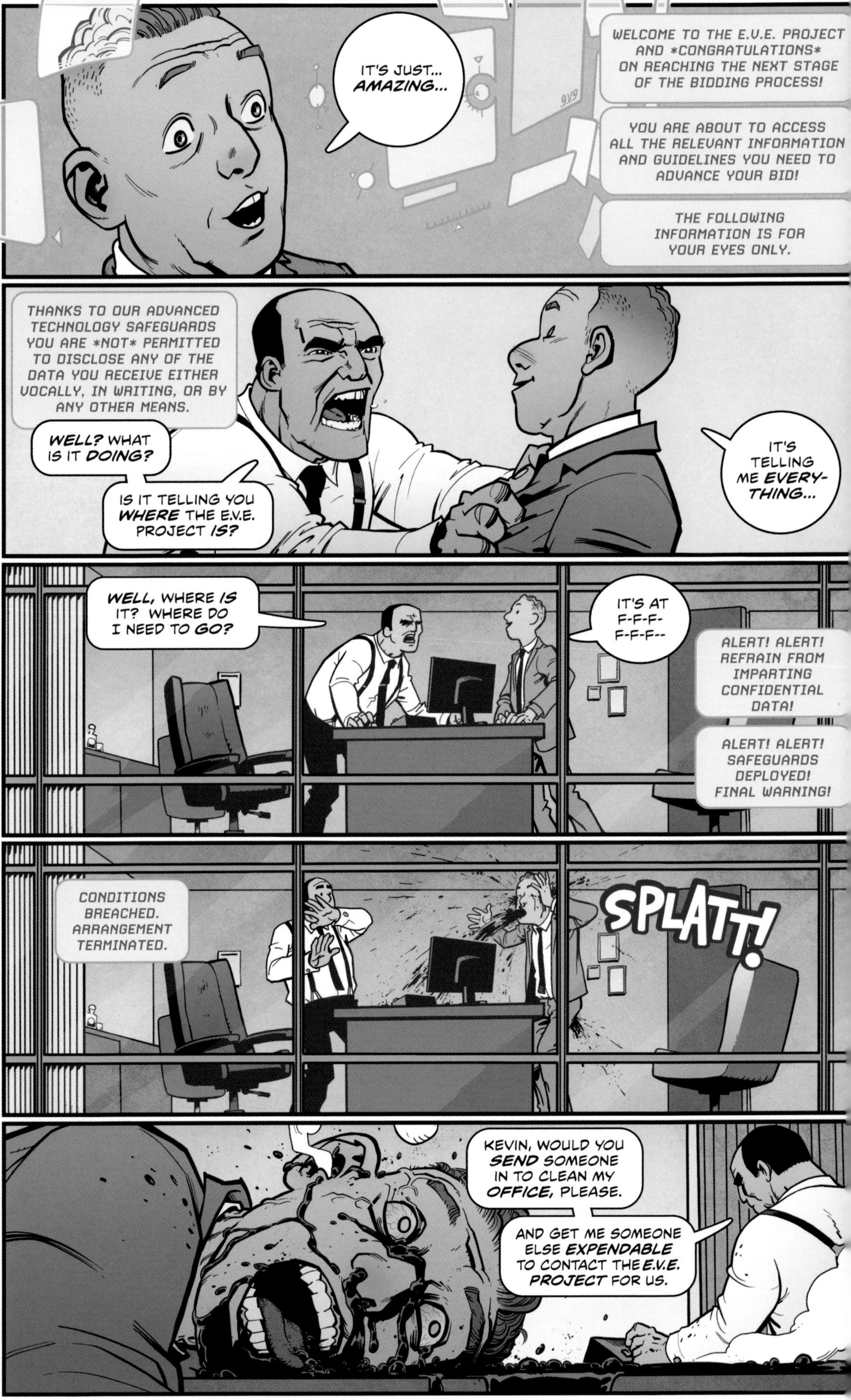
IT'S JUST... AMAZING...
WELCOME TO THE E.V.E. PROJECT AND *CONGRATULATIONS* ON REACHING THE NEXT STAGE OF THE BIDDING PROCESS!
YOU ARE ABOUT TO ACCESS ALL THE RELEVANT INFORMATION AND GUIDELINES YOU NEED TO ADVANCE YOUR BID!
THE FOLLOWING INFORMATION IS FOR YOUR EYES ONLY.
THANKS TO OUR ADVANCED TECHNOLOGY SAFEGUARDS YOU ARE *NOT* PERMITTED TO DISCLOSE ANY OF THE DATA YOU RECEIVE EITHER VOCALLY, IN WRITING, OR BY ANY OTHER MEANS.
WELL? WHAT IS IT DOING?
IS IT TELLING YOU WHERE THE E.V.E. PROJECT IS?
IT'S TELLING ME EVERY-THING...
WELL, WHERE IS IT? WHERE DO I NEED TO GO?
IT'S AT F-F-F-F-F-F--
ALERT! ALERT! REFRAIN FROM IMPARTING CONFIDENTIAL DATA!
ALERT! ALERT! SAFEGUARDS DEPLOYED! FINAL WARNING!
CONDITIONS BREACHED. ARRANGEMENT TERMINATED.
SPLATT!
KEVIN, WOULD YOU SEND SOMEONE IN TO CLEAN MY OFFICE, PLEASE.
AND GET ME SOMEONE ELSE EXPENDABLE TO CONTACT THE E.V.E. PROJECT FOR US.

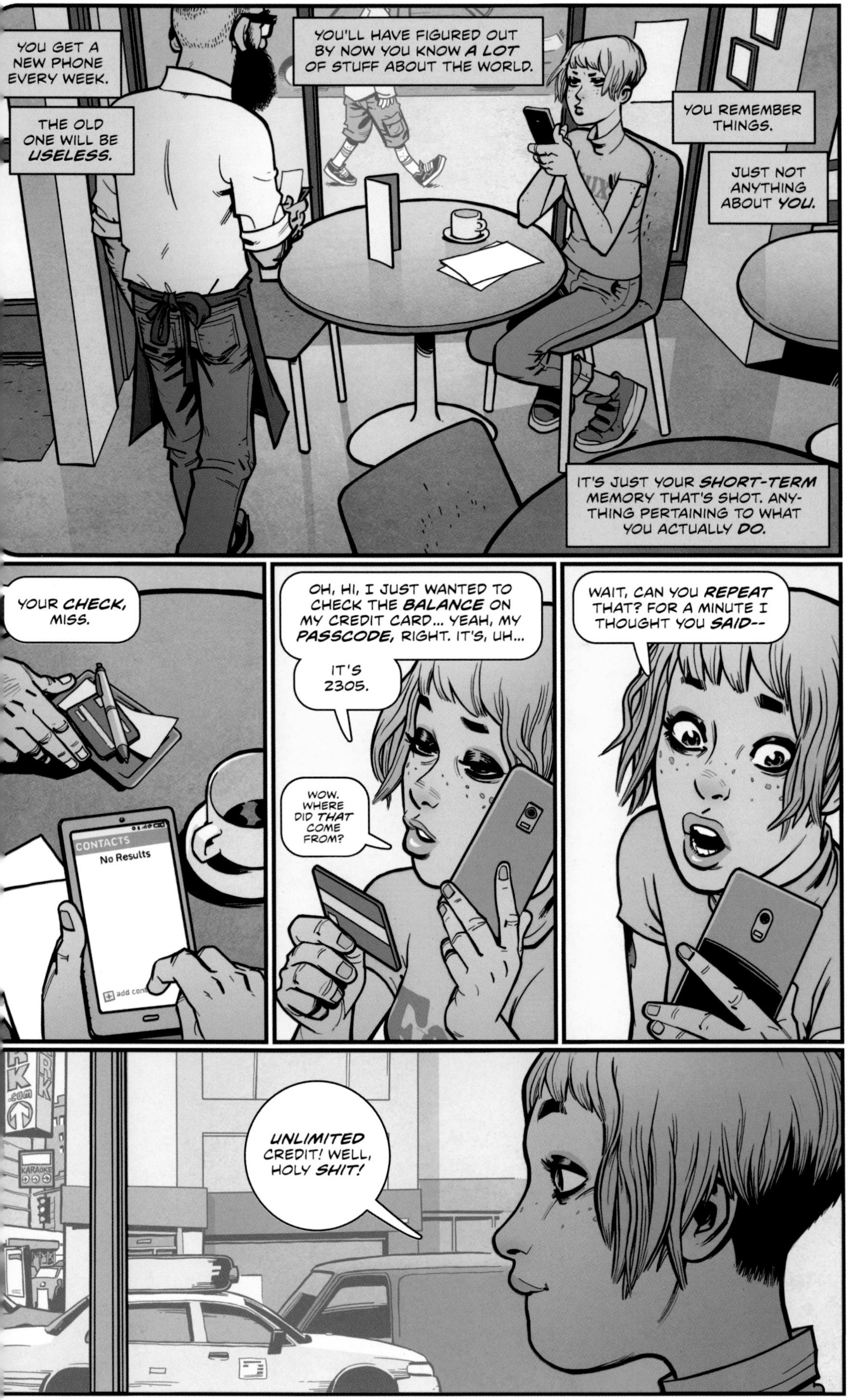
YOU GET A NEW PHONE EVERY WEEK.
THE OLD ONE WILL BE *USELESS.*
YOU'LL HAVE FIGURED OUT BY NOW YOU KNOW *A LOT* OF STUFF ABOUT THE WORLD.
YOU REMEMBER THINGS.
JUST NOT ANYTHING ABOUT *YOU.*
IT'S JUST YOUR *SHORT-TERM* MEMORY THAT'S SHOT. ANYTHING PERTAINING TO WHAT YOU ACTUALLY *DO.*
YOUR *CHECK,* MISS.
CONTACTS
No Results
add con
OH, HI, I JUST WANTED TO CHECK THE *BALANCE* ON MY CREDIT CARD... YEAH, MY *PASSCODE,* RIGHT. IT'S, UH...
IT'S 2305.
WOW. WHERE DID *THAT* COME FROM?
WAIT, CAN YOU *REPEAT* THAT? FOR A MINUTE I THOUGHT YOU *SAID--*
.com
KARAOKE
UNLIMITED CREDIT! WELL, HOLY *SHIT!*

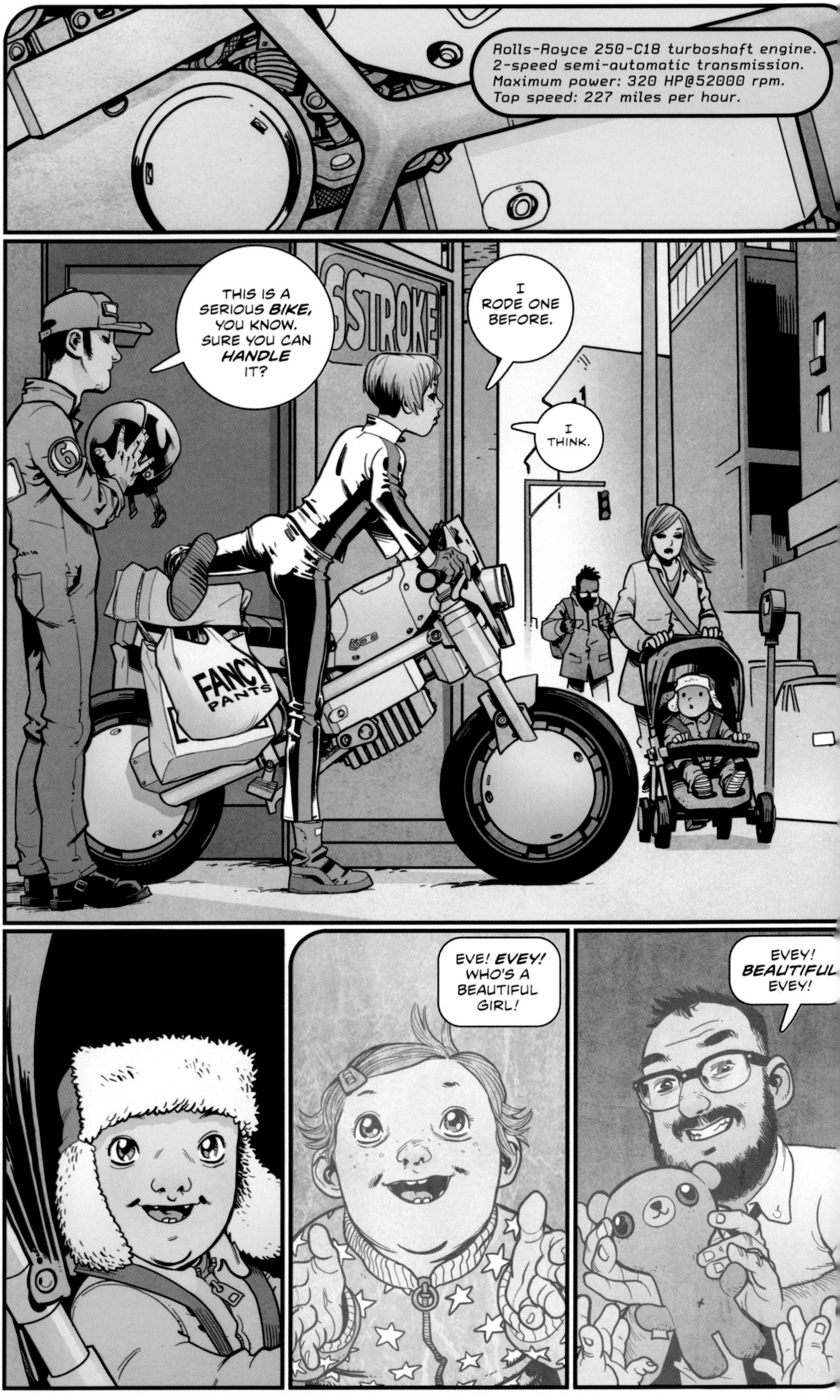
Rolls-Royce 250-C18 turboshaft engine. 2-speed semi-automatic transmission. Maximum power: 320 HP@52000 rpm. Top speed: 227 miles per hour.
THIS IS A SERIOUS BIKE, YOU KNOW. SURE YOU CAN HANDLE IT?
I RODE ONE BEFORE.
I THINK.
STROKE
FANCY PANTS
EVE! EVEY! WHO'S A BEAUTIFUL GIRL!
EVEY! BEAUTIFUL EVEY!

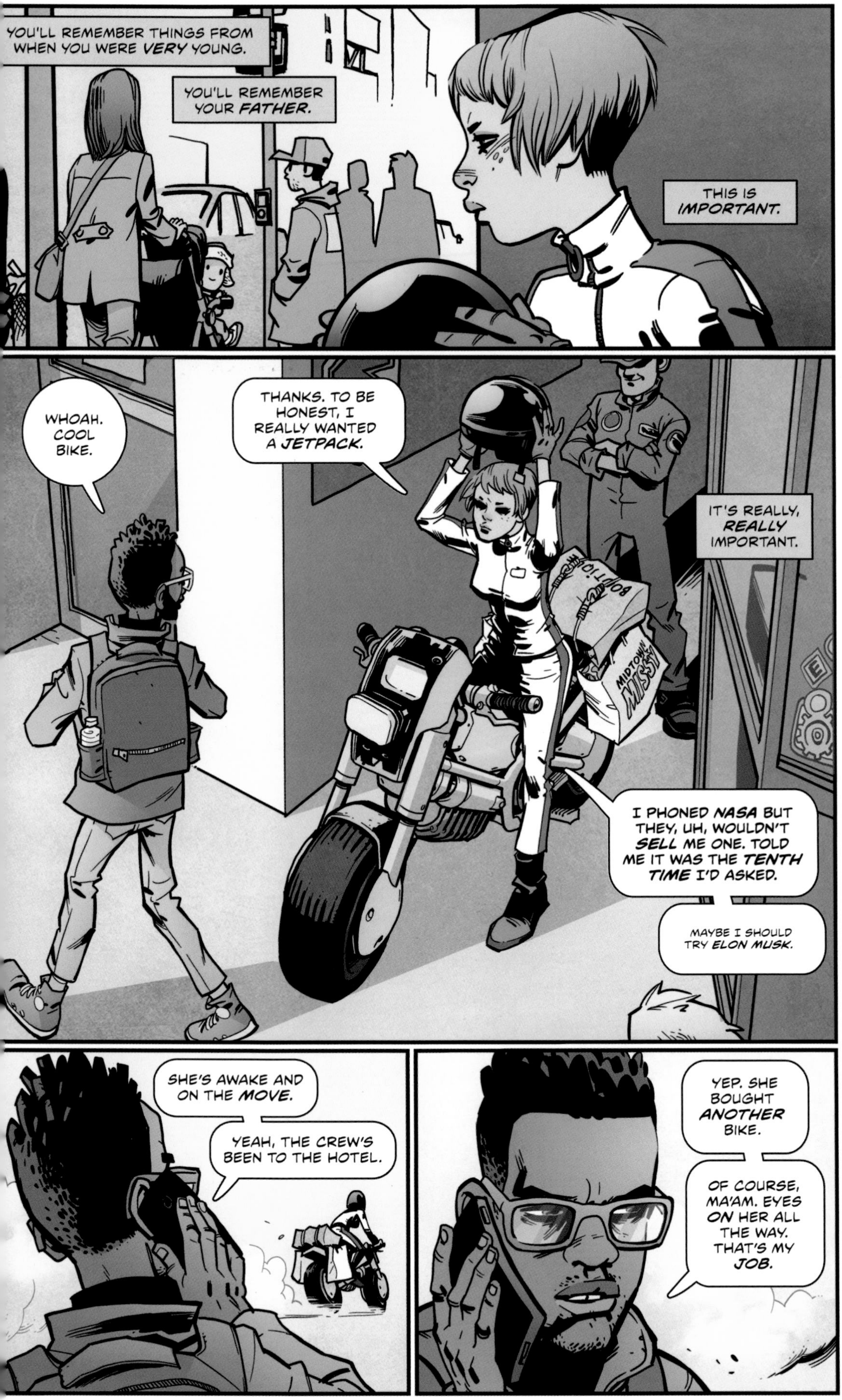
YOU'LL REMEMBER THINGS FROM WHEN YOU WERE VERY YOUNG.
YOU'LL REMEMBER YOUR FATHER.
THIS IS IMPORTANT.
WHOAH. COOL BIKE.
THANKS. TO BE HONEST, I REALLY WANTED A JETPACK.
IT'S REALLY, REALLY IMPORTANT.
I PHONED NASA BUT THEY, UH, WOULDN'T SELL ME ONE. TOLD ME IT WAS THE TENTH TIME I'D ASKED.
MAYBE I SHOULD TRY ELON MUSK.
MIDTOWN MISSY
SHE'S AWAKE AND ON THE MOVE.
YEAH, THE CREW'S BEEN TO THE HOTEL.
YEP. SHE BOUGHT ANOTHER BIKE.
OF COURSE, MA'AM. EYES ON HER ALL THE WAY. THAT'S MY JOB.

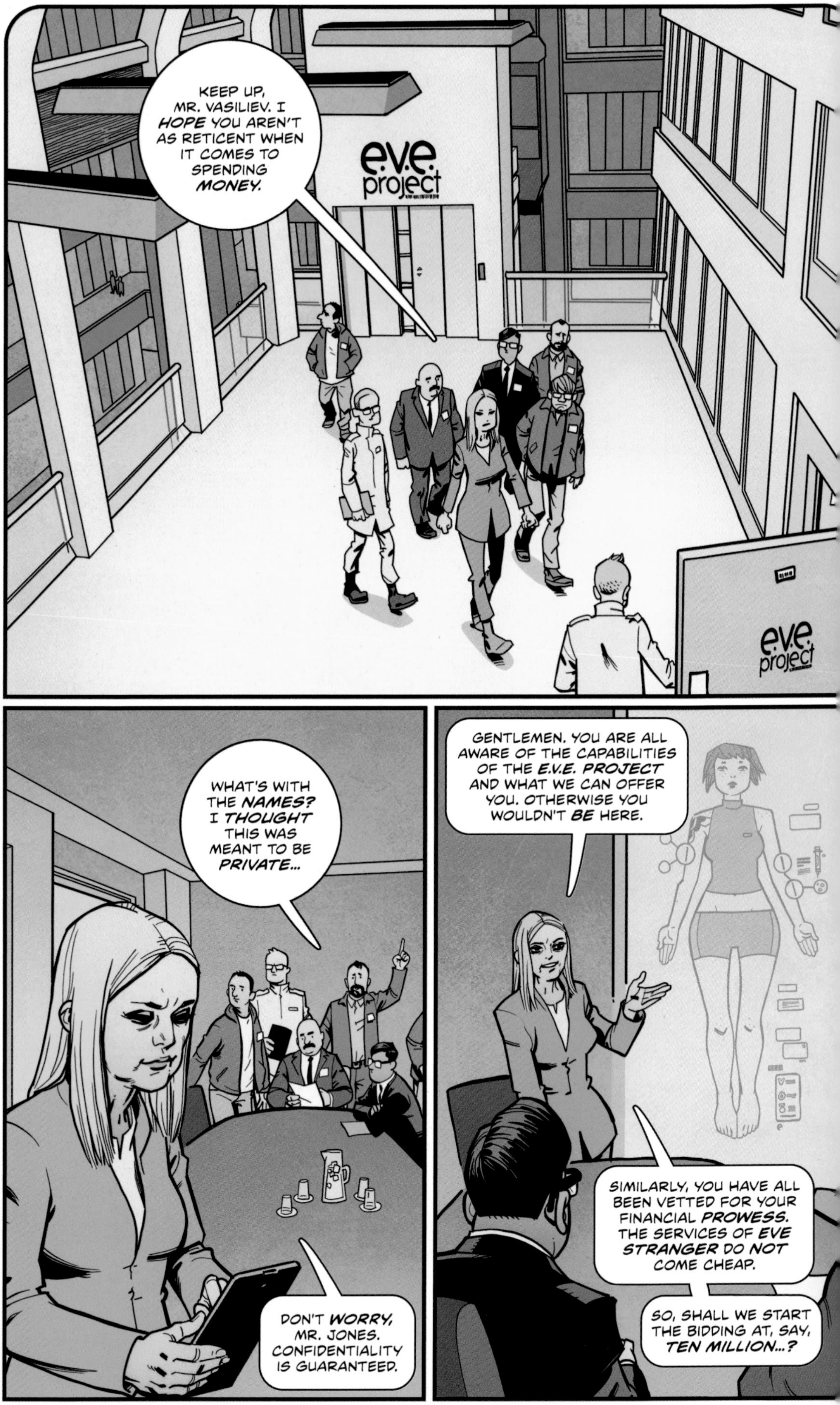
KEEP UP, MR. VASILIEV. I HOPE YOU AREN'T AS RETICENT WHEN IT COMES TO SPENDING MONEY.
e.v.e. project
WHAT'S WITH THE NAMES? I THOUGHT THIS WAS MEANT TO BE PRIVATE...
DON'T WORRY, MR. JONES. CONFIDENTIALITY IS GUARANTEED.
GENTLEMEN. YOU ARE ALL AWARE OF THE CAPABILITIES OF THE E.V.E. PROJECT AND WHAT WE CAN OFFER YOU. OTHERWISE YOU WOULDN'T BE HERE.
SIMILARLY, YOU HAVE ALL BEEN VETTED FOR YOUR FINANCIAL PROWESS. THE SERVICES OF EVE STRANGER DO NOT COME CHEAP.
SO, SHALL WE START THE BIDDING AT, SAY, TEN MILLION...?

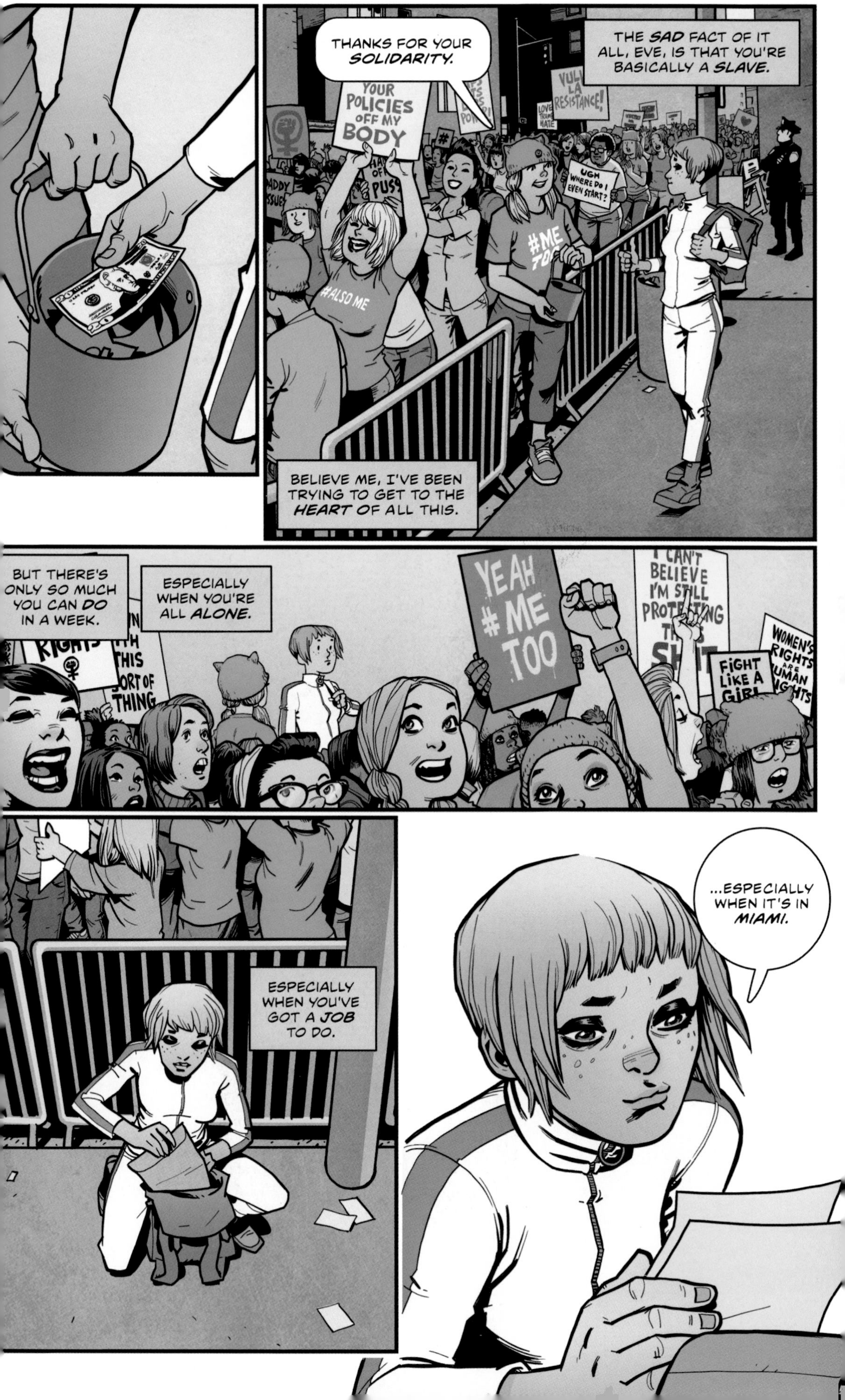
THANKS FOR YOUR *SOLIDARITY.*
THE *SAD* FACT OF IT ALL, EVE, IS THAT YOU'RE BASICALLY A *SLAVE.*
YOUR POLICIES OFF MY BODY
VULVA LA RESISTANCE!
UGH WHERE DO I EVEN START?
#ALSO ME
#ME TOO
BELIEVE ME, I'VE BEEN TRYING TO GET TO THE *HEART* OF ALL THIS.
BUT THERE'S ONLY SO MUCH YOU CAN *DO* IN A WEEK.
ESPECIALLY WHEN YOU'RE ALL *ALONE.*
YEAH #ME TOO
FIGHT LIKE A GIRL
WOMEN'S RIGHTS ARE HUMAN RIGHTS
ESPECIALLY WHEN YOU'VE GOT A *JOB* TO DO.
...ESPECIALLY WHEN IT'S IN *MIAMI.*

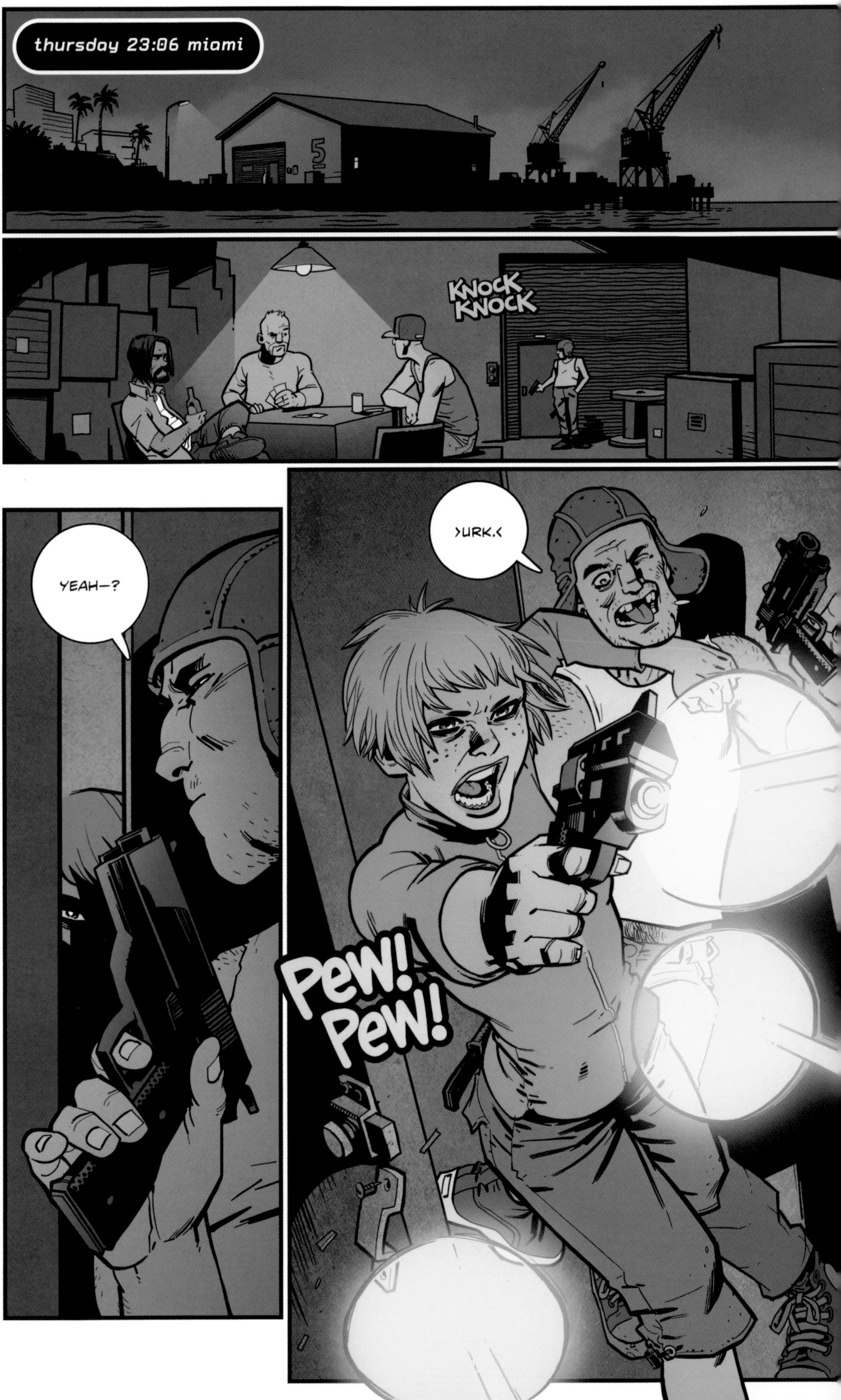
thursday 23:06 miami
5
KNOCK KNOCK
YEAH—?
>URK.<
Pew! Pew!

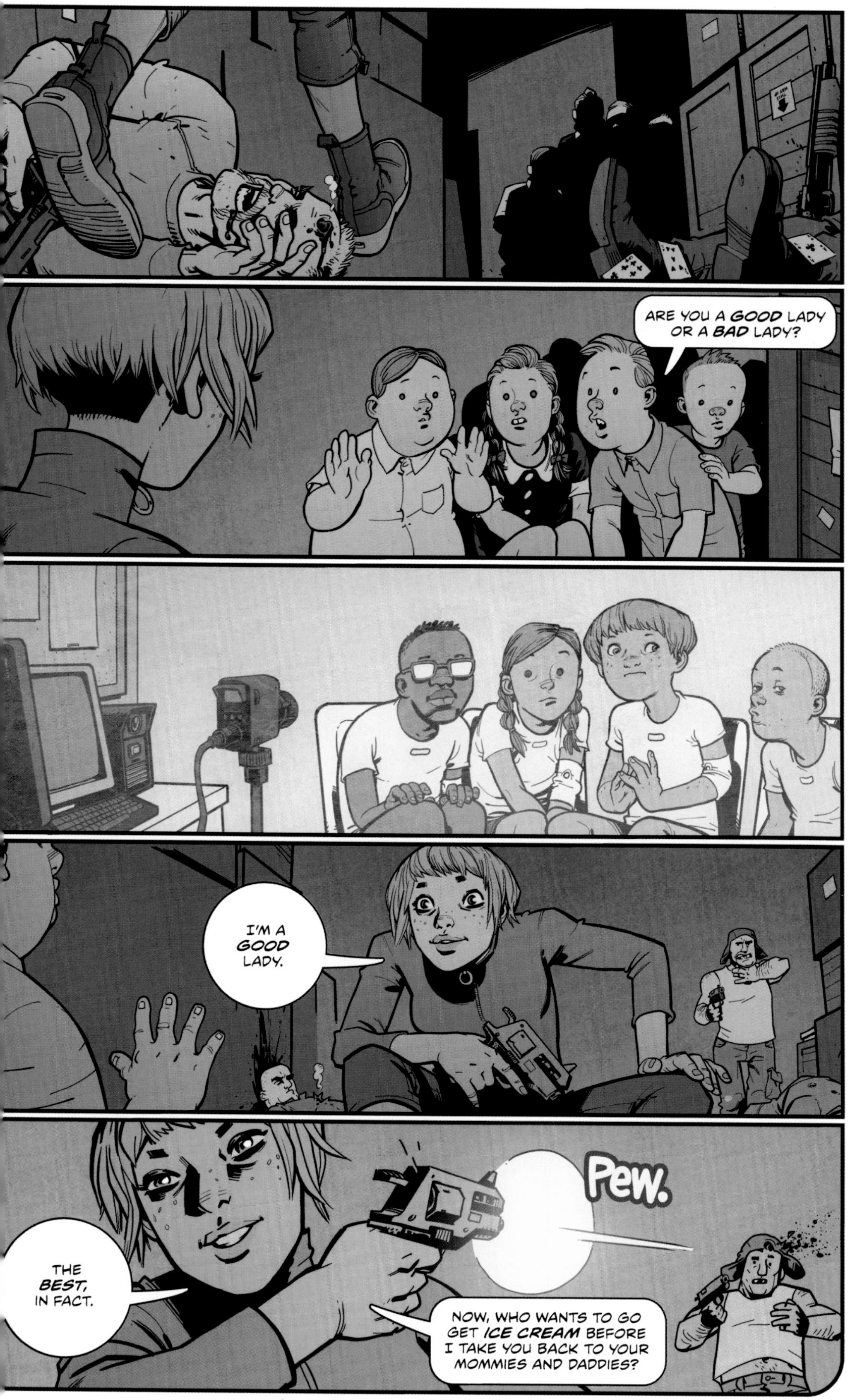
ARE YOU A GOOD LADY OR A BAD LADY?
I'M A GOOD LADY.
THE BEST, IN FACT.
Pew.
NOW, WHO WANTS TO GO GET ICE CREAM BEFORE I TAKE YOU BACK TO YOUR MOMMIES AND DADDIES?

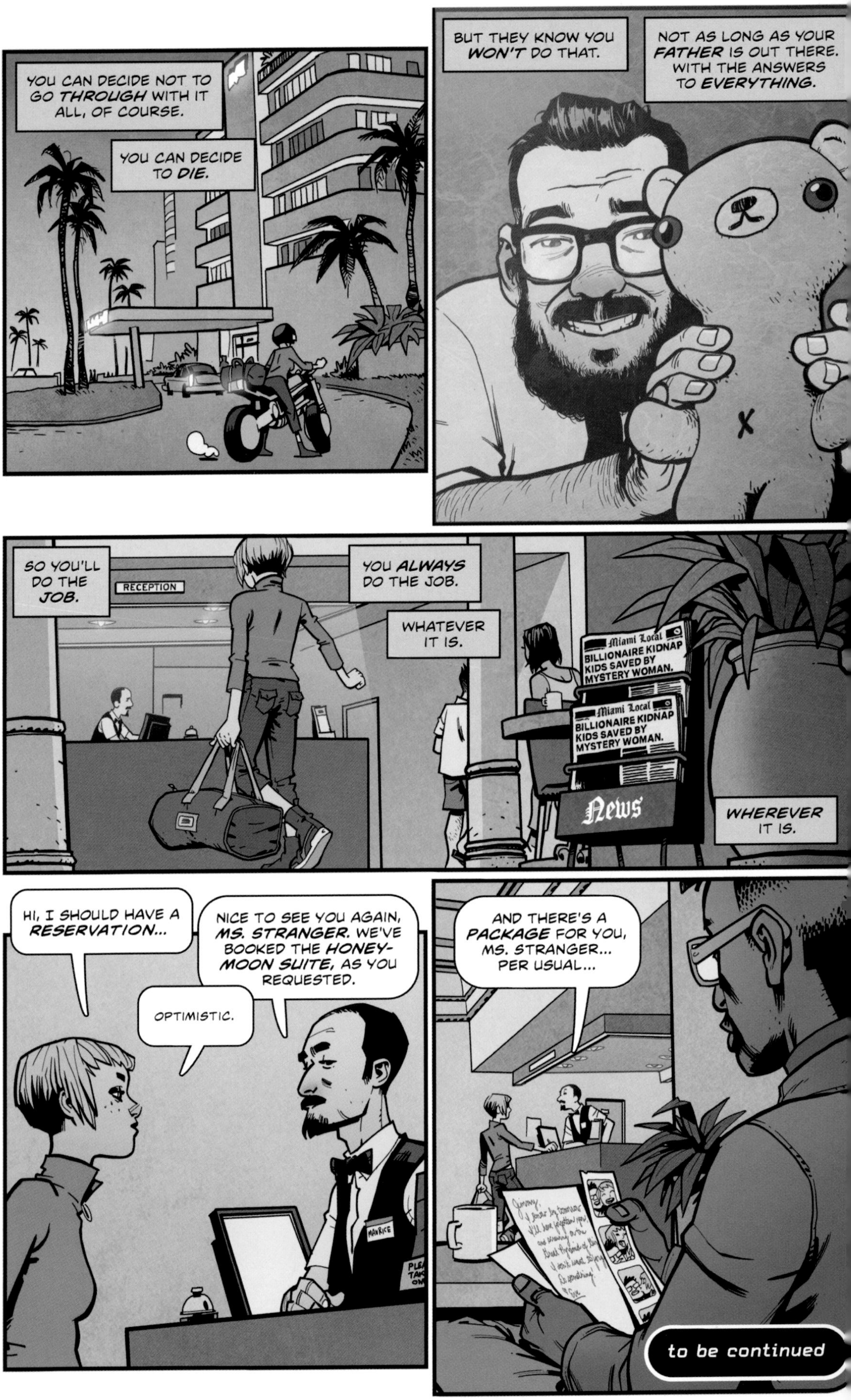

YOU CAN DECIDE NOT TO GO THROUGH WITH IT ALL, OF COURSE.
YOU CAN DECIDE TO DIE.
BUT THEY KNOW YOU WON'T DO THAT.
NOT AS LONG AS YOUR FATHER IS OUT THERE. WITH THE ANSWERS TO EVERYTHING.
SO YOU'LL DO THE JOB.
RECEPTION
YOU ALWAYS DO THE JOB.
WHATEVER IT IS.
Miami Local
BILLIONAIRE KIDNAP KIDS SAVED BY MYSTERY WOMAN.
Miami Local
BILLIONAIRE KIDNAP KIDS SAVED BY MYSTERY WOMAN.
News
WHEREVER IT IS.
HI, I SHOULD HAVE A RESERVATION...
NICE TO SEE YOU AGAIN, MS. STRANGER. WE'VE BOOKED THE HONEY-MOON SUITE, AS YOU REQUESTED.
OPTIMISTIC.
MAURICE
AND THERE'S A PACKAGE FOR YOU, MS. STRANGER... PER USUAL...
to be continued

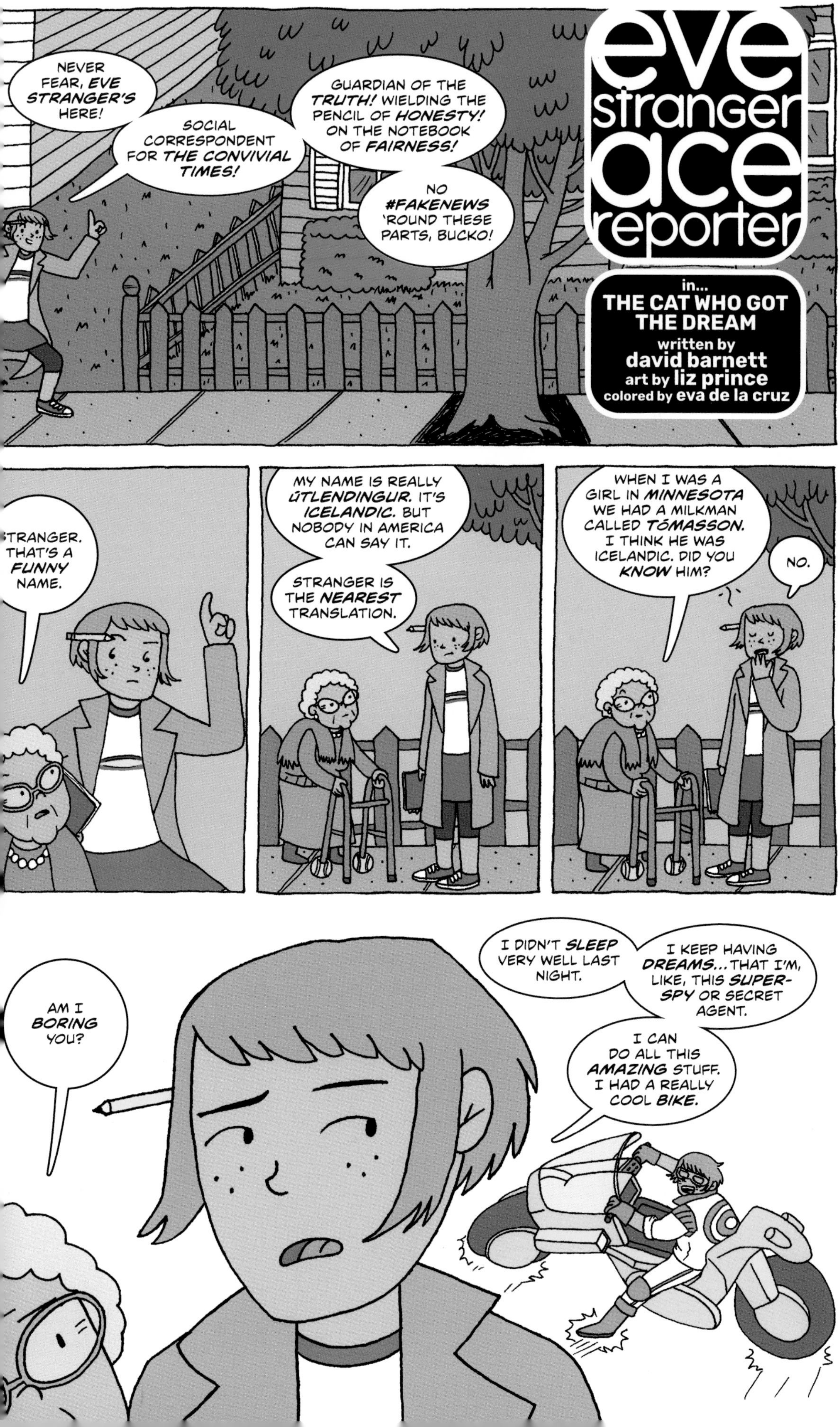
eve stranger ace reporter
in... THE CAT WHO GOT THE DREAM
written by david barnett
art by liz prince
colored by eva de la cruz
NEVER FEAR, EVE STRANGER'S HERE!
SOCIAL CORRESPONDENT FOR THE CONVIVIAL TIMES!
GUARDIAN OF THE TRUTH! WIELDING THE PENCIL OF HONESTY! ON THE NOTEBOOK OF FAIRNESS!
NO #FAKENEWS 'ROUND THESE PARTS, BUCKO!
STRANGER. THAT'S A FUNNY NAME.
MY NAME IS REALLY ÚTLENDINGUR. IT'S ICELANDIC. BUT NOBODY IN AMERICA CAN SAY IT.
STRANGER IS THE NEAREST TRANSLATION.
WHEN I WAS A GIRL IN MINNESOTA WE HAD A MILKMAN CALLED TÓMASSON. I THINK HE WAS ICELANDIC. DID YOU KNOW HIM?
NO.
AM I BORING YOU?
I DIDN'T SLEEP VERY WELL LAST NIGHT.
I KEEP HAVING DREAMS... THAT I'M, LIKE, THIS SUPER-SPY OR SECRET AGENT.
I CAN DO ALL THIS AMAZING STUFF. I HAD A REALLY COOL BIKE.

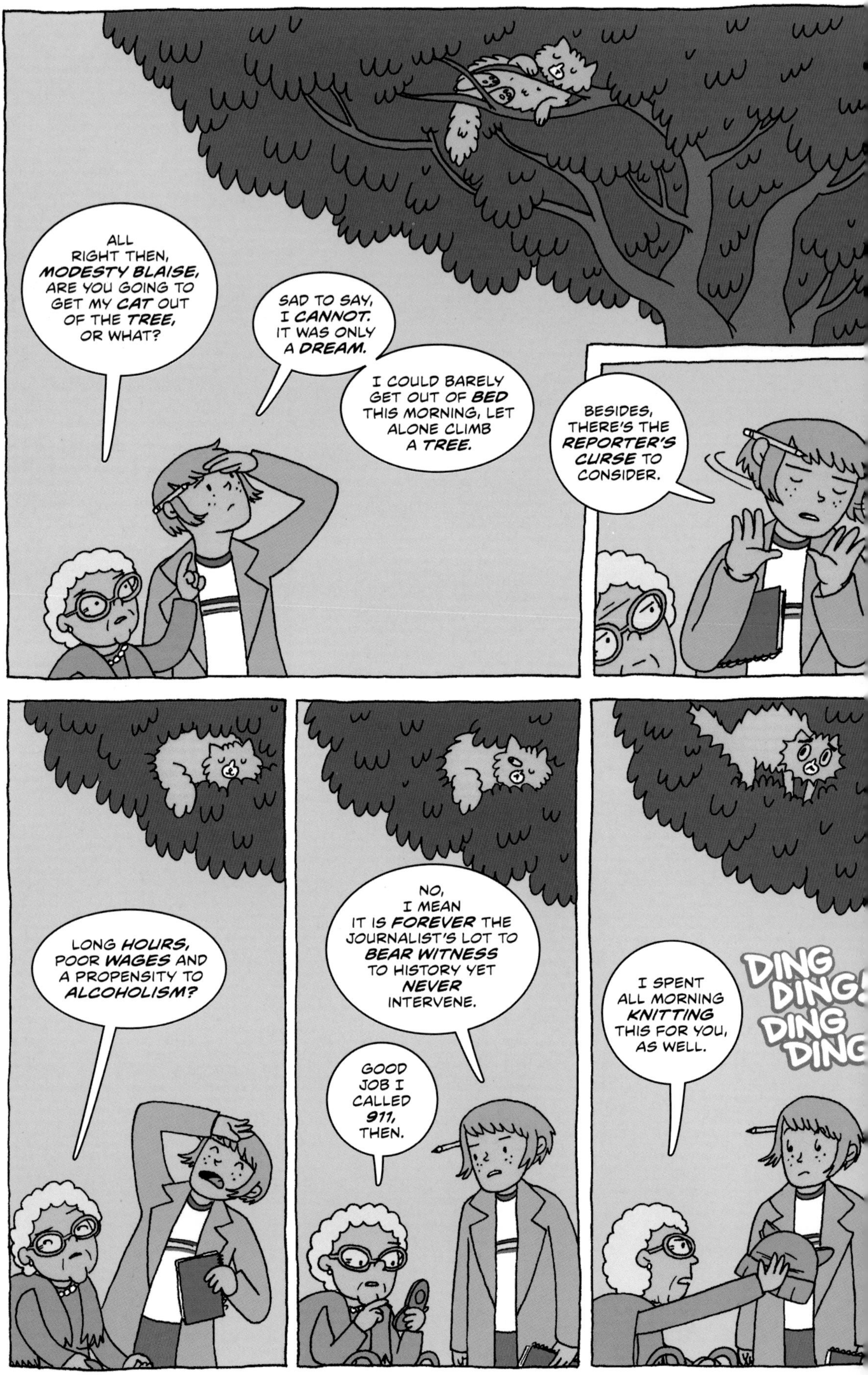
ALL RIGHT THEN, MODESTY BLAISE, ARE YOU GOING TO GET MY CAT OUT OF THE TREE, OR WHAT?
SAD TO SAY, I CANNOT. IT WAS ONLY A DREAM.
I COULD BARELY GET OUT OF BED THIS MORNING, LET ALONE CLIMB A TREE.
BESIDES, THERE'S THE REPORTER'S CURSE TO CONSIDER.
LONG HOURS, POOR WAGES AND A PROPENSITY TO ALCOHOLISM?
NO, I MEAN IT IS FOREVER THE JOURNALIST'S LOT TO BEAR WITNESS TO HISTORY YET NEVER INTERVENE.
GOOD JOB I CALLED 911, THEN.
I SPENT ALL MORNING KNITTING THIS FOR YOU, AS WELL.

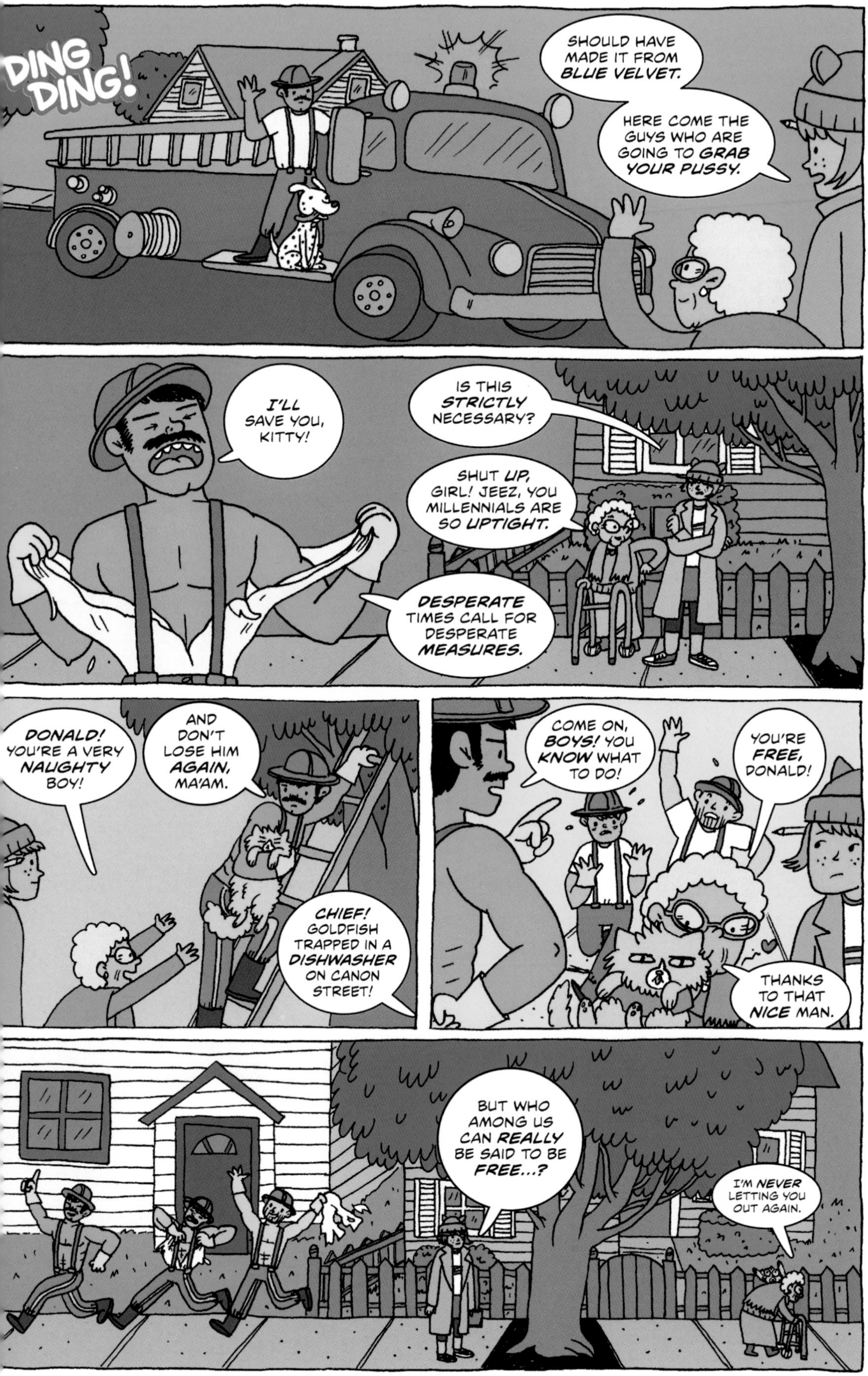
DING DING!
SHOULD HAVE MADE IT FROM BLUE VELVET.
HERE COME THE GUYS WHO ARE GOING TO GRAB YOUR PUSSY.
I'LL SAVE YOU, KITTY!
IS THIS STRICTLY NECESSARY?
SHUT UP, GIRL! JEEZ, YOU MILLENNIALS ARE SO UPTIGHT.
DESPERATE TIMES CALL FOR DESPERATE MEASURES.
DONALD! YOU'RE A VERY NAUGHTY BOY!
AND DON'T LOSE HIM AGAIN, MA'AM.
CHIEF! GOLDFISH TRAPPED IN A DISHWASHER ON CANON STREET!
COME ON, BOYS! YOU KNOW WHAT TO DO!
YOU'RE FREE, DONALD!
THANKS TO THAT NICE MAN.
BUT WHO AMONG US CAN REALLY BE SAID TO BE FREE...?
I'M NEVER LETTING YOU OUT AGAIN.

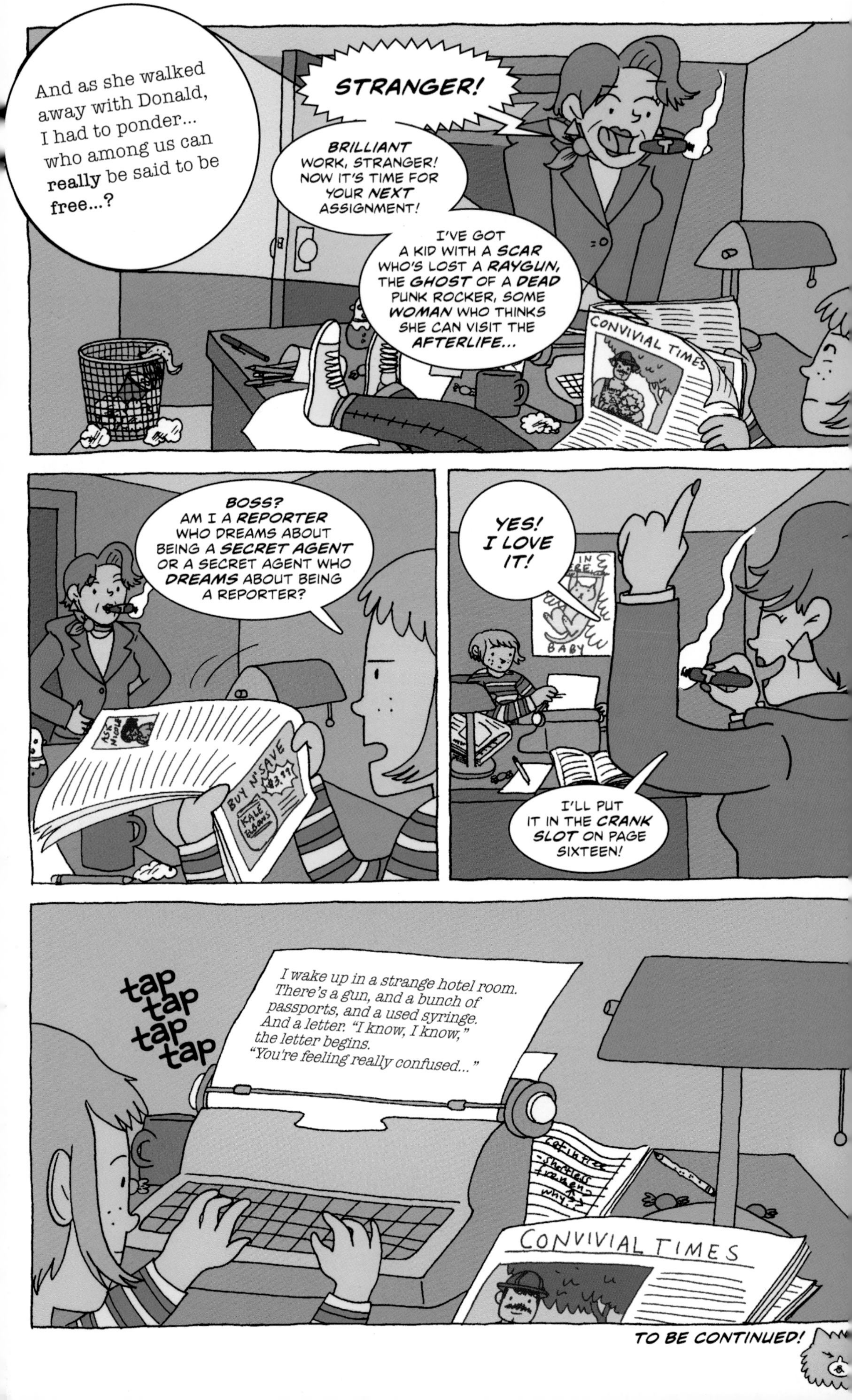
And as she walked away with Donald, I had to ponder... who among us can really be said to be free...?
STRANGER!
BRILLIANT WORK, STRANGER! NOW IT'S TIME FOR YOUR NEXT ASSIGNMENT!
I'VE GOT A KID WITH A SCAR WHO'S LOST A RAYGUN, THE GHOST OF A DEAD PUNK ROCKER, SOME WOMAN WHO THINKS SHE CAN VISIT THE AFTERLIFE...
CONVIVIAL TIMES
BOSS? AM I A REPORTER WHO DREAMS ABOUT BEING A SECRET AGENT OR A SECRET AGENT WHO DREAMS ABOUT BEING A REPORTER?
BUY N' SAVE
YES! I LOVE IT!
I'LL PUT IT IN THE CRANK SLOT ON PAGE SIXTEEN!
tap tap tap tap
I wake up in a strange hotel room. There's a gun, and a bunch of passports, and a used syringe. And a letter. "I know, I know," the letter begins. "You're feeling really confused..."
CONVIVIAL TIMES
TO BE CONTINUED!

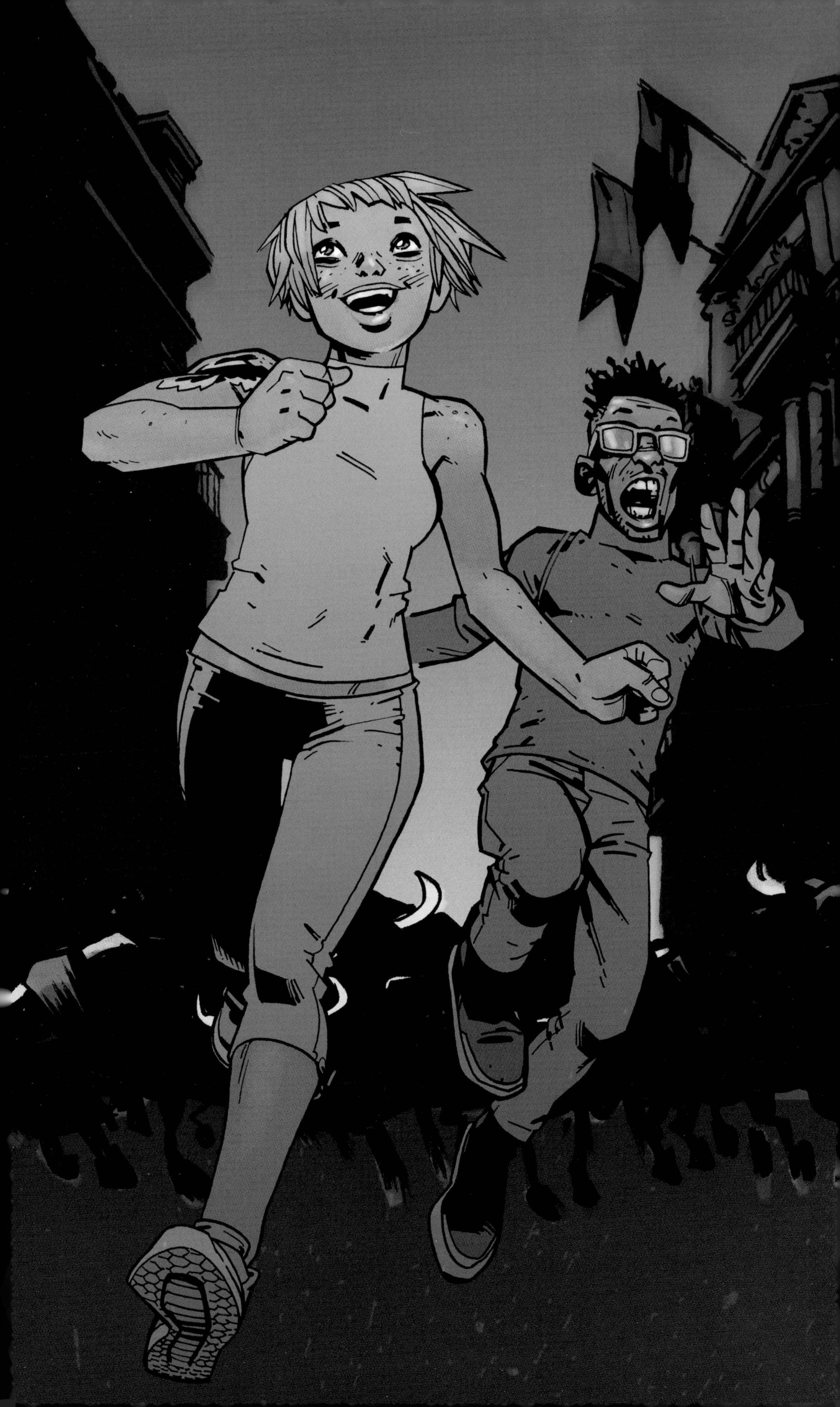

part two:

NOWHERE TO RUN

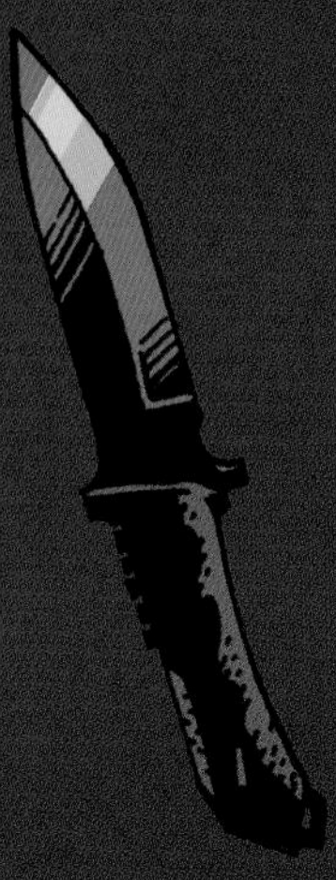

"...SHALL WE
SEE THE COLOR
OF YOUR MONEY?"

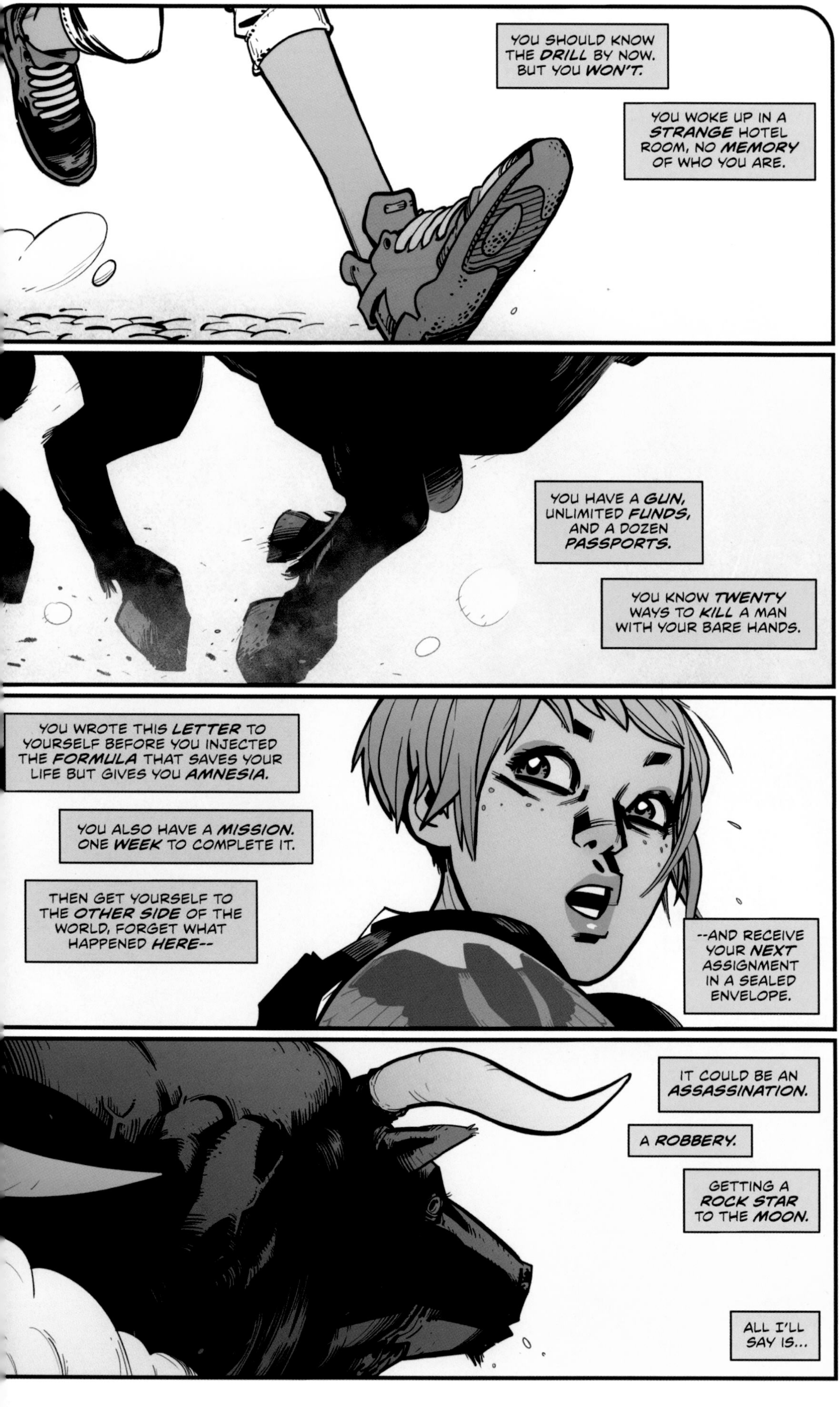
YOU SHOULD KNOW THE DRILL BY NOW. BUT YOU WON'T.
YOU WOKE UP IN A STRANGE HOTEL ROOM, NO MEMORY OF WHO YOU ARE.
YOU HAVE A GUN, UNLIMITED FUNDS, AND A DOZEN PASSPORTS.
YOU KNOW TWENTY WAYS TO KILL A MAN WITH YOUR BARE HANDS.
YOU WROTE THIS LETTER TO YOURSELF BEFORE YOU INJECTED THE FORMULA THAT SAVES YOUR LIFE BUT GIVES YOU AMNESIA.
YOU ALSO HAVE A MISSION. ONE WEEK TO COMPLETE IT.
THEN GET YOURSELF TO THE OTHER SIDE OF THE WORLD, FORGET WHAT HAPPENED HERE--
--AND RECEIVE YOUR NEXT ASSIGNMENT IN A SEALED ENVELOPE.
IT COULD BE AN ASSASSINATION.
A ROBBERY.
GETTING A ROCK STAR TO THE MOON.
ALL I'LL SAY IS...

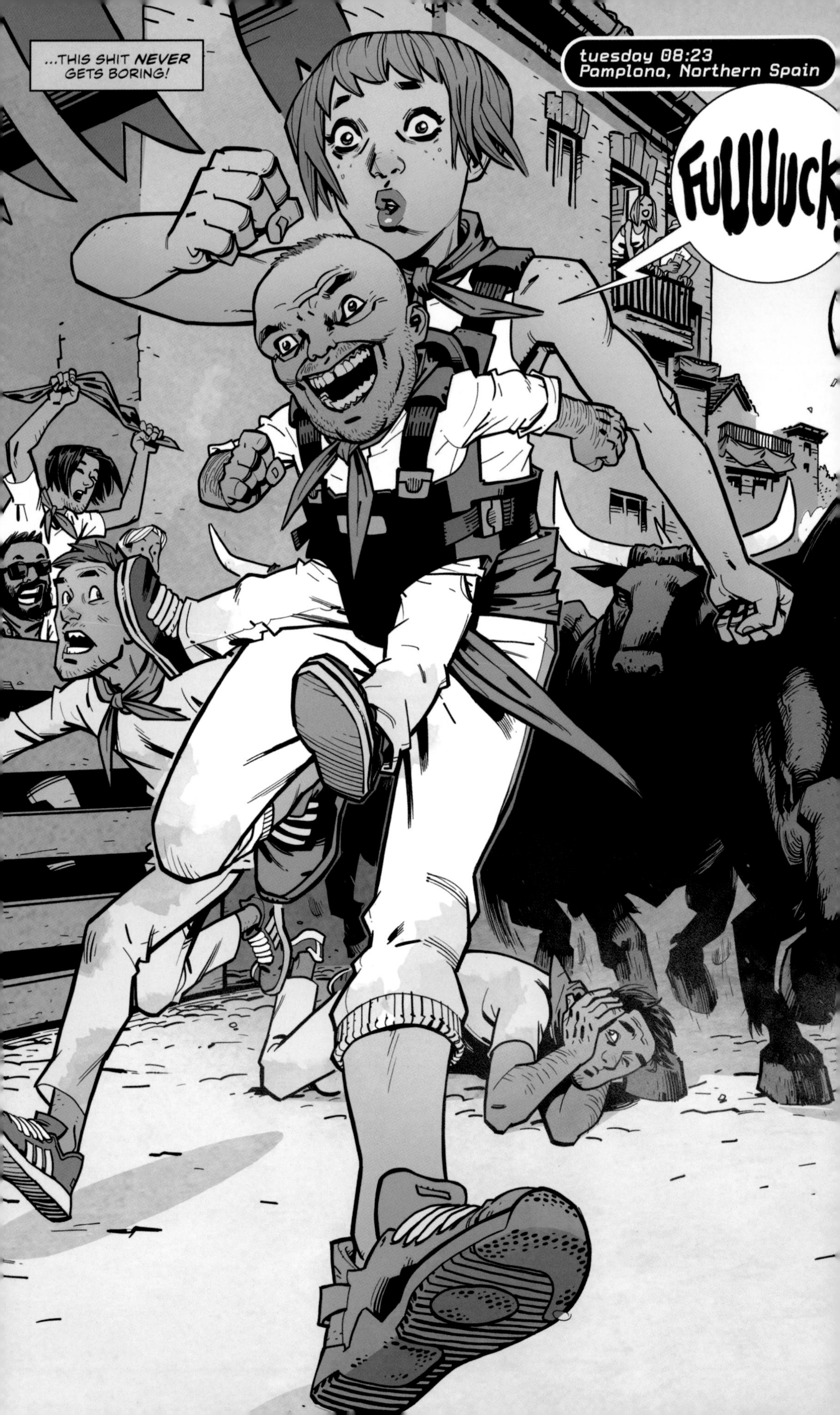
...THIS SHIT NEVER GETS BORING!
tuesday 08:23
Pamplona, Northern Spain
FUUUUCK

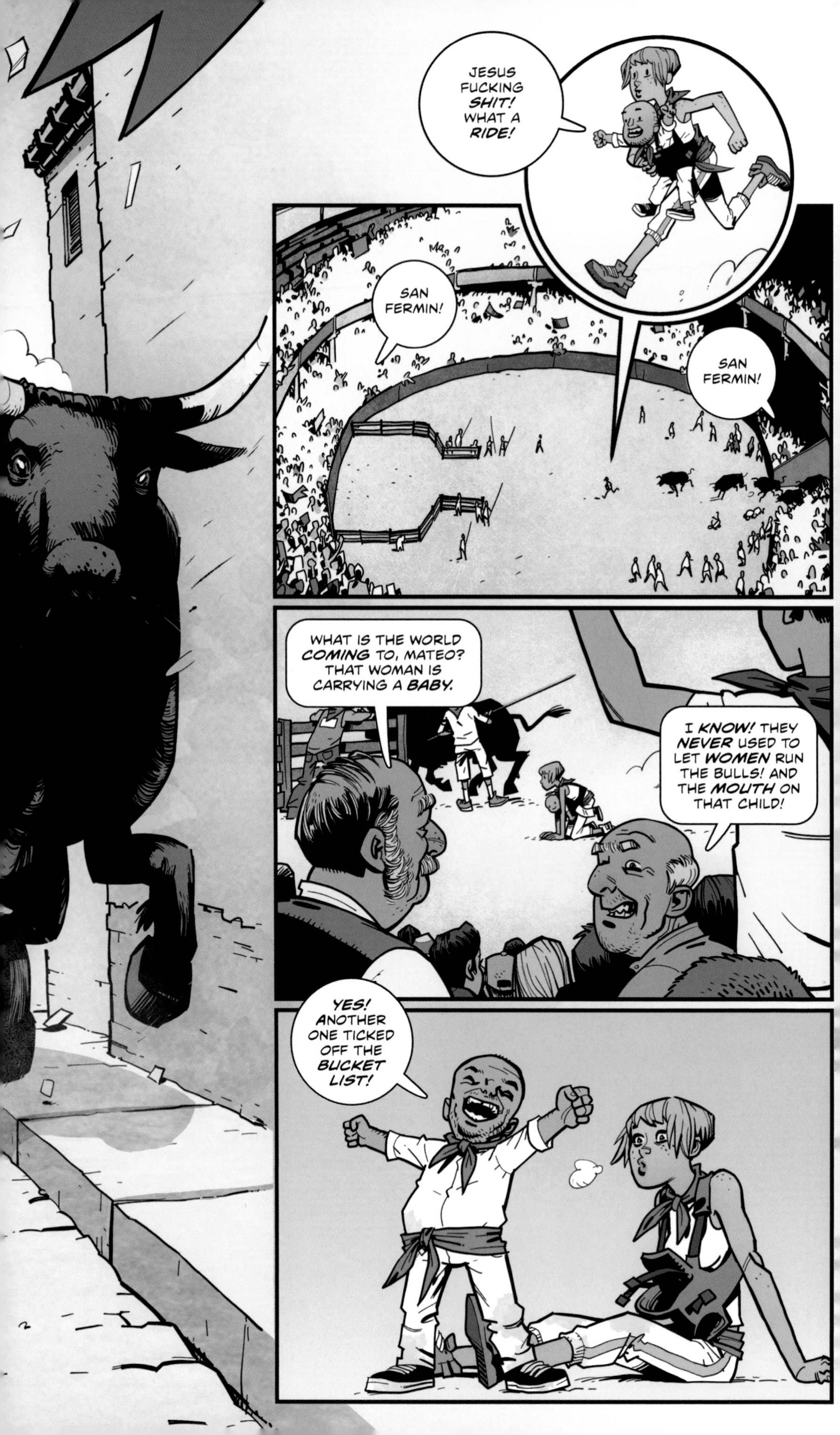
JESUS FUCKING *SHIT!* WHAT A *RIDE!*
SAN FERMIN!
SAN FERMIN!
WHAT IS THE WORLD *COMING* TO, MATEO? THAT WOMAN IS CARRYING A *BABY.*
I *KNOW!* THEY *NEVER* USED TO LET *WOMEN* RUN THE BULLS! AND THE *MOUTH* ON THAT CHILD!
YES! ANOTHER ONE TICKED OFF THE *BUCKET LIST!*

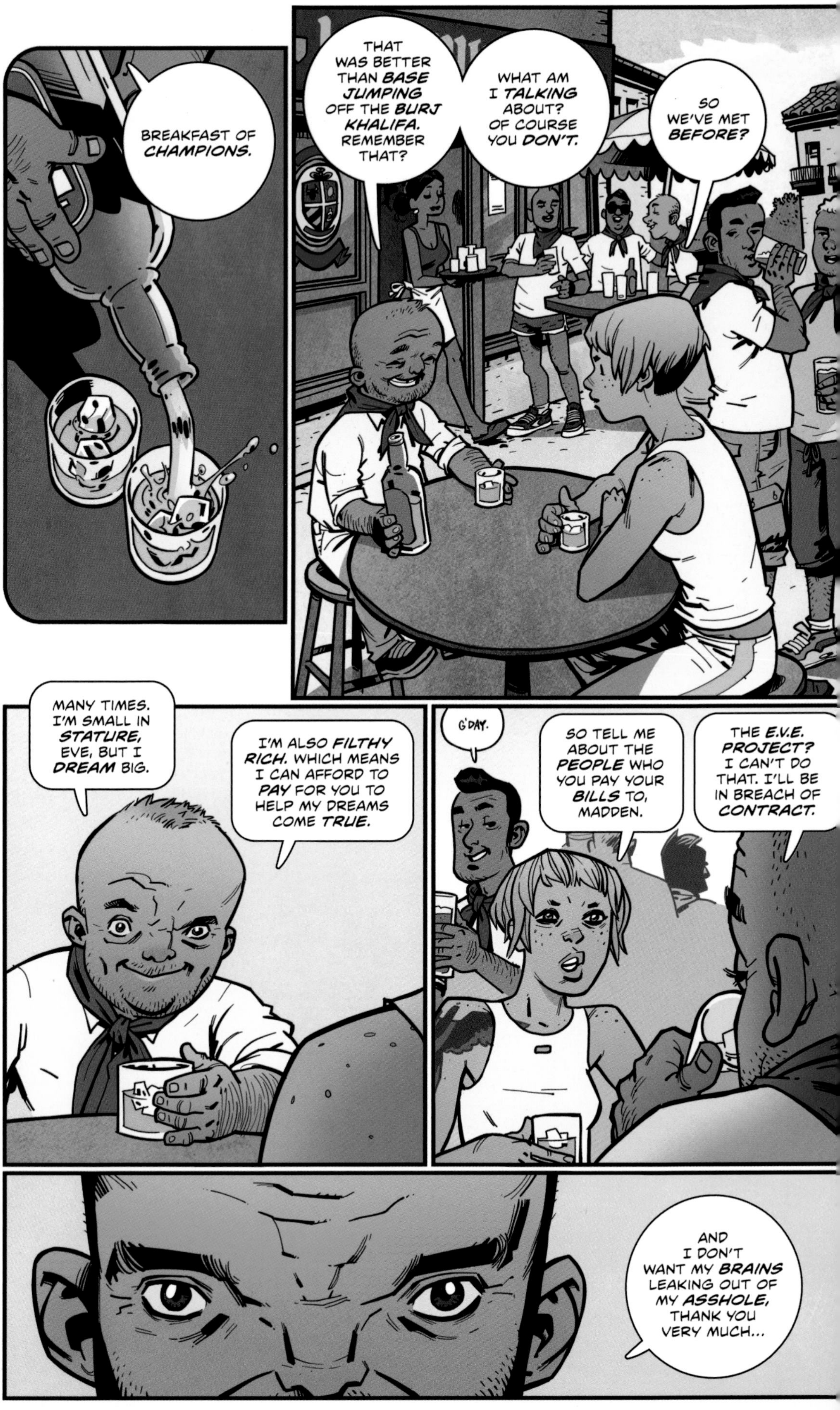
BREAKFAST OF CHAMPIONS.
THAT WAS BETTER THAN BASE JUMPING OFF THE BURJ KHALIFA. REMEMBER THAT?
WHAT AM I TALKING ABOUT? OF COURSE YOU DON'T.
SO WE'VE MET BEFORE?
MANY TIMES. I'M SMALL IN STATURE, EVE, BUT I DREAM BIG.
I'M ALSO FILTHY RICH. WHICH MEANS I CAN AFFORD TO PAY FOR YOU TO HELP MY DREAMS COME TRUE.
G'DAY.
SO TELL ME ABOUT THE PEOPLE WHO YOU PAY YOUR BILLS TO, MADDEN.
THE E.V.E. PROJECT? I CAN'T DO THAT. I'LL BE IN BREACH OF CONTRACT.
AND I DON'T WANT MY BRAINS LEAKING OUT OF MY ASSHOLE, THANK YOU VERY MUCH...

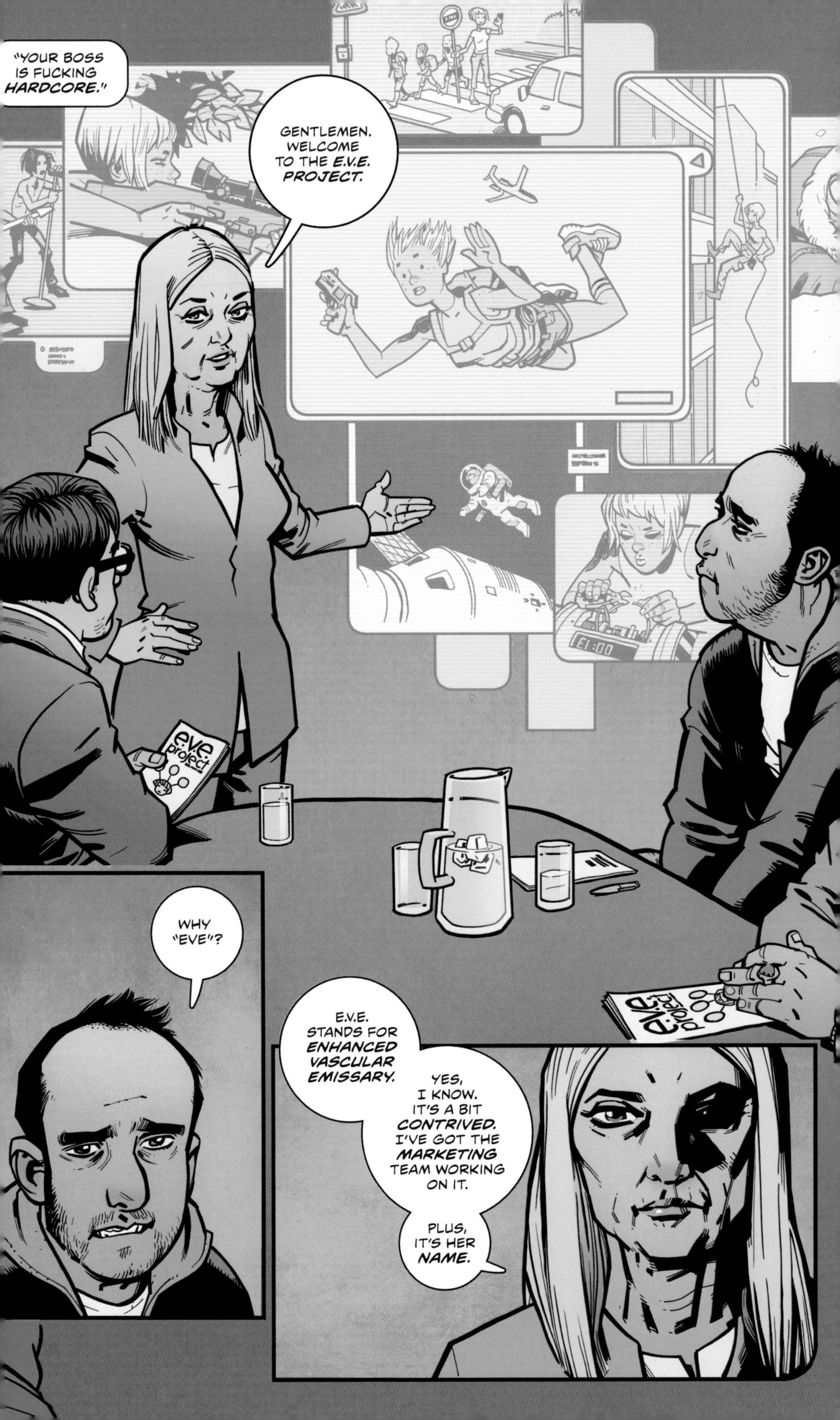
"YOUR BOSS IS FUCKING HARDCORE."
GENTLEMEN. WELCOME TO THE E.V.E. PROJECT.
e.v.e. project
WHY "EVE"?
E.V.E. STANDS FOR ENHANCED VASCULAR EMISSARY.
YES, I KNOW. IT'S A BIT CONTRIVED. I'VE GOT THE MARKETING TEAM WORKING ON IT.
PLUS, IT'S HER NAME.

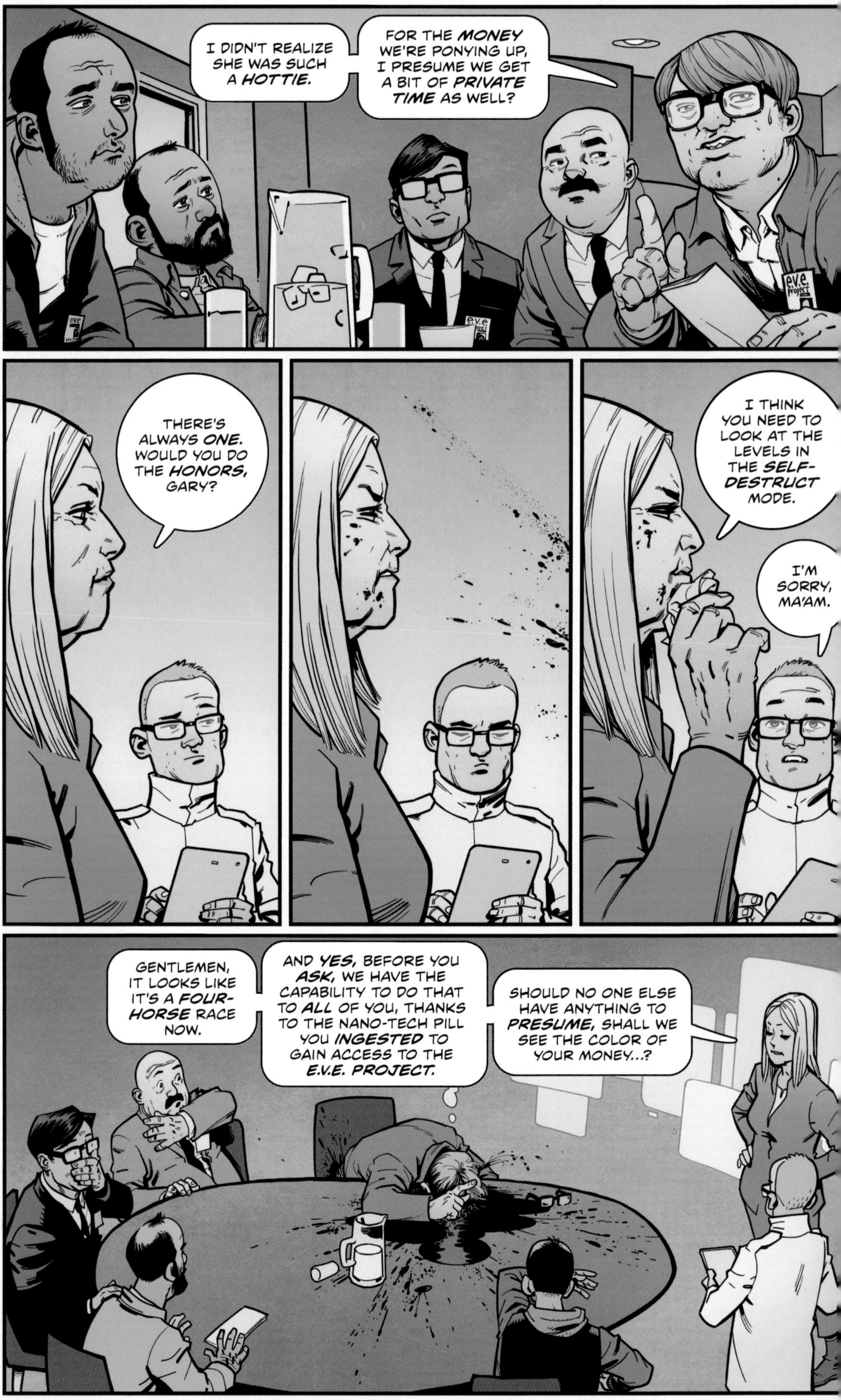
I DIDN'T REALIZE SHE WAS SUCH A *HOTTIE.*
FOR THE *MONEY* WE'RE PONYING UP, I PRESUME WE GET A BIT OF *PRIVATE TIME* AS WELL?
THERE'S ALWAYS *ONE.* WOULD YOU DO THE *HONORS,* GARY?
I THINK YOU NEED TO LOOK AT THE LEVELS IN THE *SELF-DESTRUCT* MODE.
I'M SORRY, MA'AM.
GENTLEMEN, IT LOOKS LIKE IT'S A *FOUR-HORSE* RACE NOW.
AND *YES,* BEFORE YOU *ASK,* WE HAVE THE CAPABILITY TO DO THAT TO *ALL* OF YOU, THANKS TO THE NANO-TECH PILL YOU *INGESTED* TO GAIN ACCESS TO THE *E.V.E. PROJECT.*
SHOULD NO ONE ELSE HAVE ANYTHING TO *PRESUME,* SHALL WE SEE THE COLOR OF YOUR MONEY...?

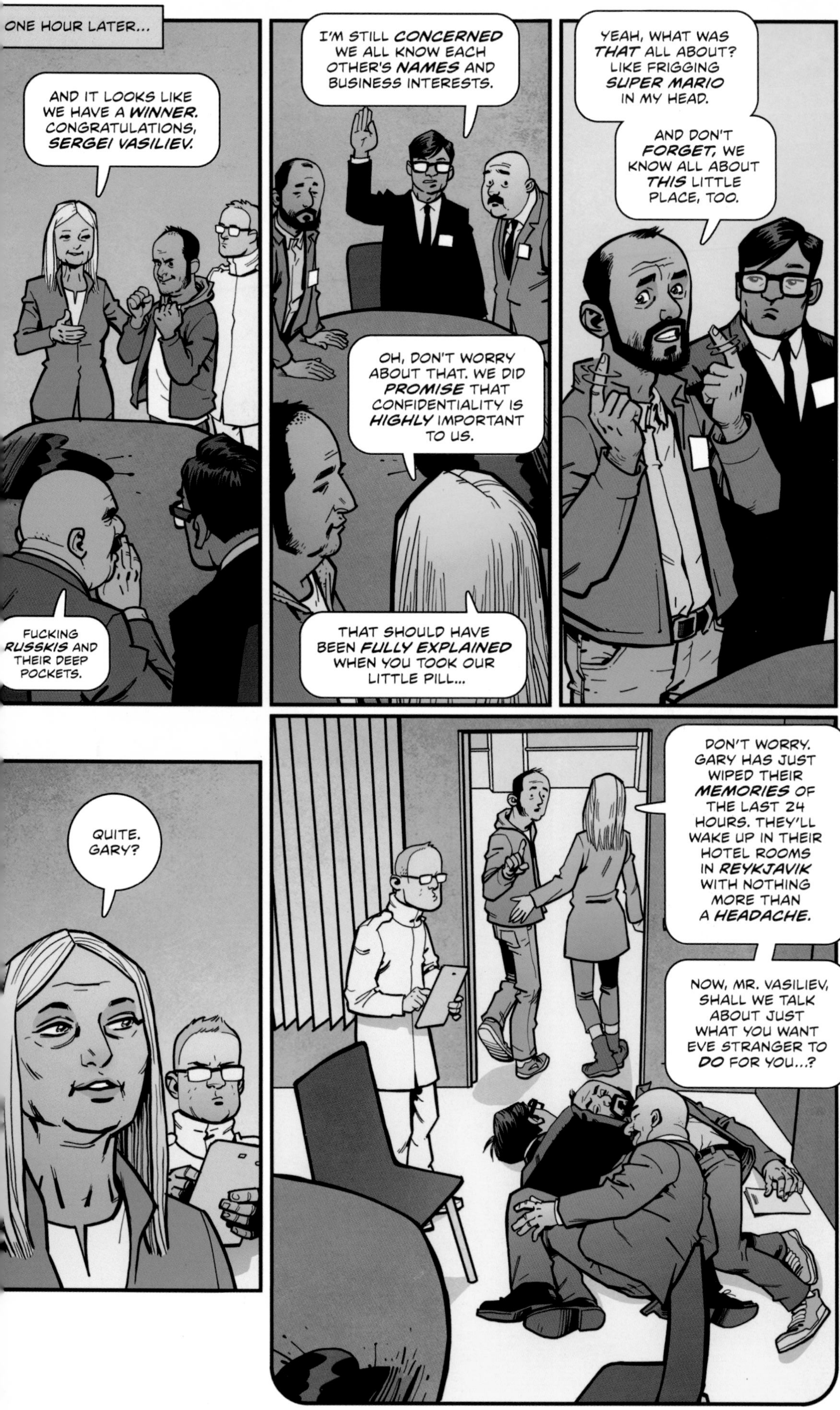
ONE HOUR LATER...
AND IT LOOKS LIKE WE HAVE A WINNER. CONGRATULATIONS, SERGEI VASILIEV.
FUCKING RUSSKIS AND THEIR DEEP POCKETS.
I'M STILL CONCERNED WE ALL KNOW EACH OTHER'S NAMES AND BUSINESS INTERESTS.
OH, DON'T WORRY ABOUT THAT. WE DID PROMISE THAT CONFIDENTIALITY IS HIGHLY IMPORTANT TO US.
THAT SHOULD HAVE BEEN FULLY EXPLAINED WHEN YOU TOOK OUR LITTLE PILL...
YEAH, WHAT WAS THAT ALL ABOUT? LIKE FRIGGING SUPER MARIO IN MY HEAD.
AND DON'T FORGET, WE KNOW ALL ABOUT THIS LITTLE PLACE, TOO.
QUITE. GARY?
DON'T WORRY. GARY HAS JUST WIPED THEIR MEMORIES OF THE LAST 24 HOURS. THEY'LL WAKE UP IN THEIR HOTEL ROOMS IN REYKJAVIK WITH NOTHING MORE THAN A HEADACHE.
NOW, MR. VASILIEV, SHALL WE TALK ABOUT JUST WHAT YOU WANT EVE STRANGER TO DO FOR YOU...?

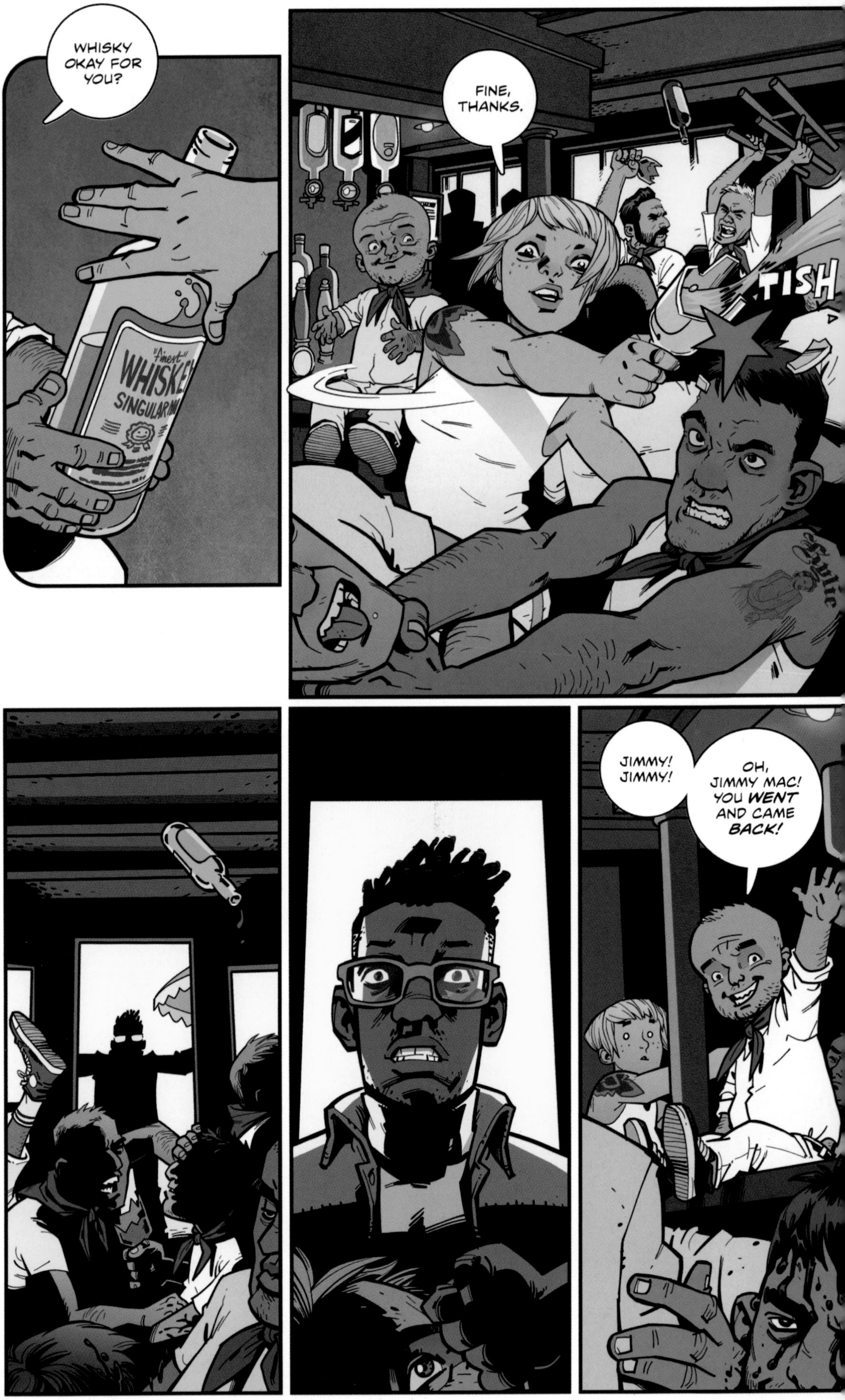
WHISKY OKAY FOR YOU?
"Finest" WHISKEY SINGULAR
FINE, THANKS.
TISH
JIMMY! JIMMY!
OH, JIMMY MAC! YOU *WENT* AND CAME *BACK!*

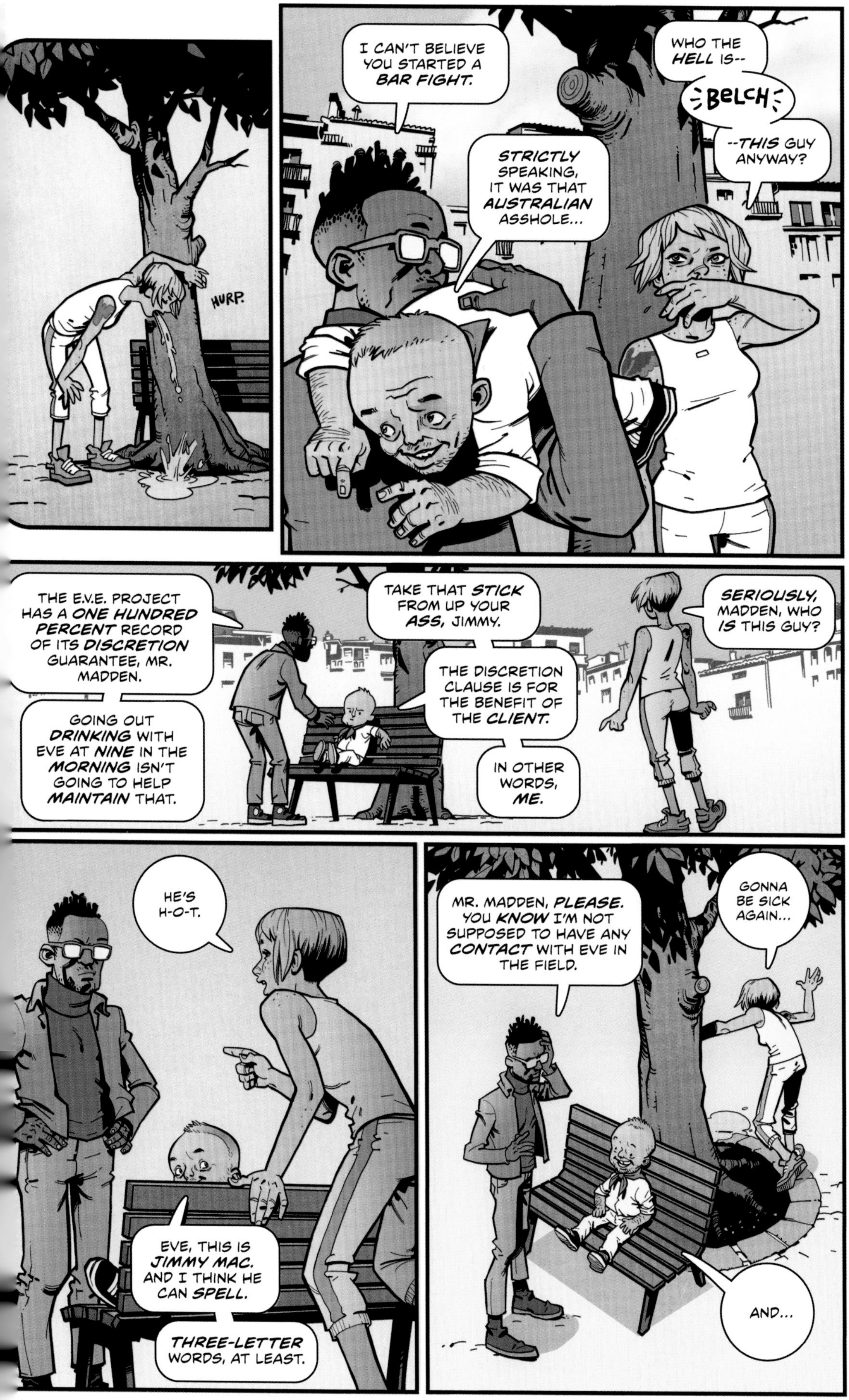
HURP.
I CAN'T BELIEVE YOU STARTED A BAR FIGHT.
STRICTLY SPEAKING, IT WAS THAT AUSTRALIAN ASSHOLE...
WHO THE HELL IS--
BELCH
--THIS GUY ANYWAY?
THE E.V.E. PROJECT HAS A ONE HUNDRED PERCENT RECORD OF ITS DISCRETION GUARANTEE, MR. MADDEN.
GOING OUT DRINKING WITH EVE AT NINE IN THE MORNING ISN'T GOING TO HELP MAINTAIN THAT.
TAKE THAT STICK FROM UP YOUR ASS, JIMMY.
THE DISCRETION CLAUSE IS FOR THE BENEFIT OF THE CLIENT.
IN OTHER WORDS, ME.
SERIOUSLY, MADDEN, WHO IS THIS GUY?
HE'S H-O-T.
EVE, THIS IS JIMMY MAC. AND I THINK HE CAN SPELL.
THREE-LETTER WORDS, AT LEAST.
MR. MADDEN, PLEASE. YOU KNOW I'M NOT SUPPOSED TO HAVE ANY CONTACT WITH EVE IN THE FIELD.
GONNA BE SICK AGAIN...
AND...

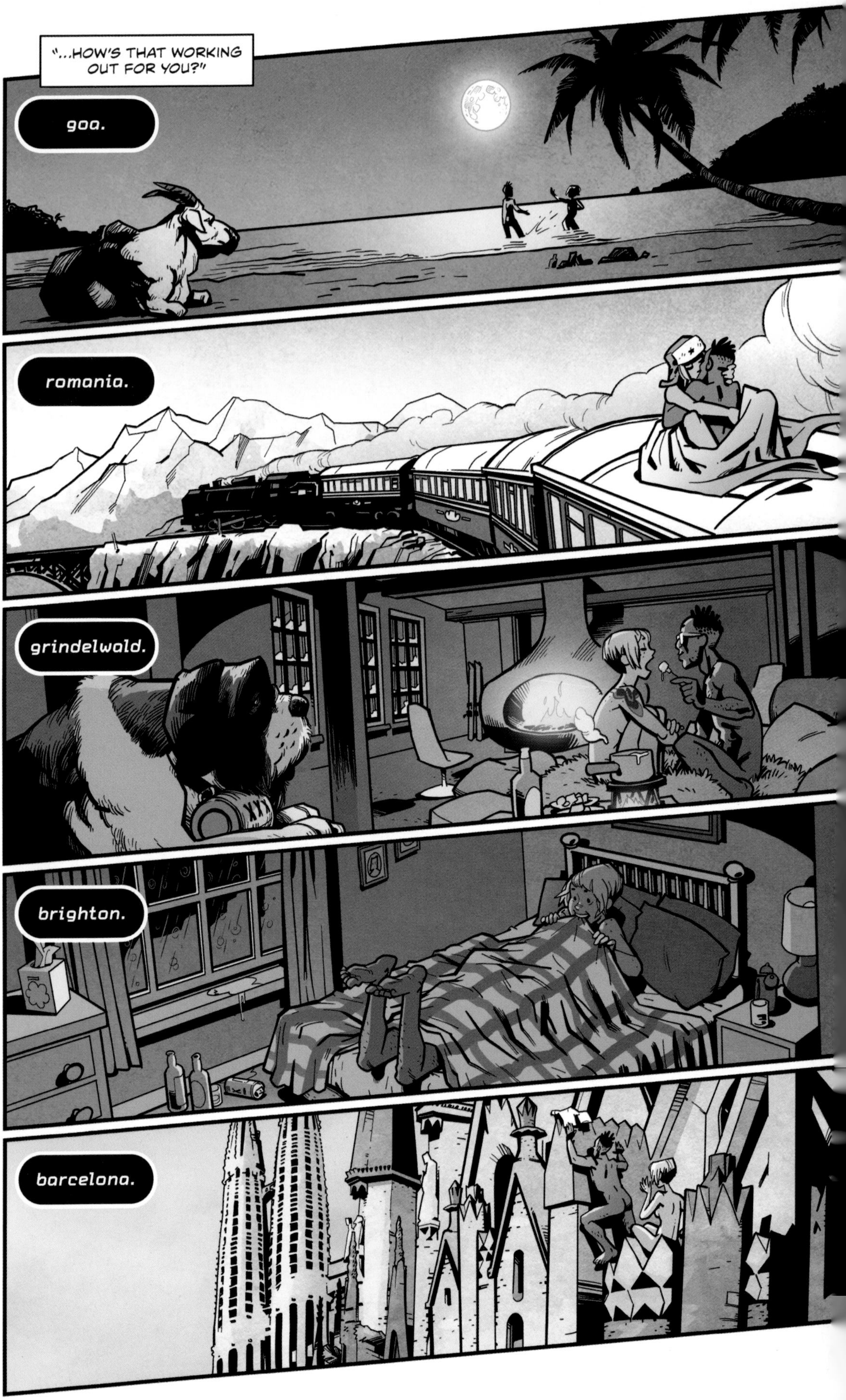
"...HOW'S THAT WORKING OUT FOR YOU?"
goa.
romania.
grindelwald.
brighton.
barcelona.

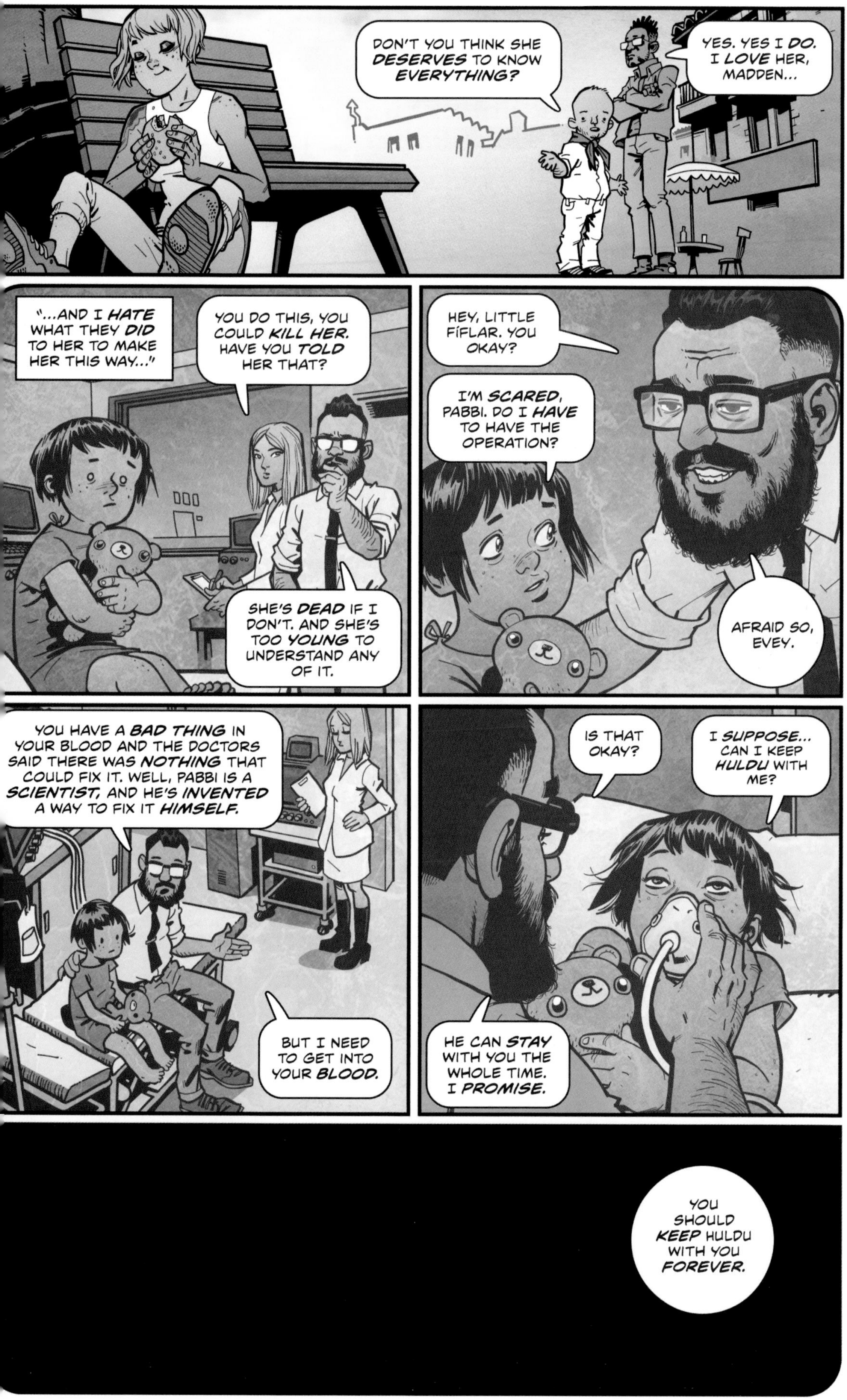
DON'T YOU THINK SHE DESERVES TO KNOW EVERYTHING?
YES. YES I DO. I LOVE HER, MADDEN...
"...AND I HATE WHAT THEY DID TO HER TO MAKE HER THIS WAY..."
YOU DO THIS, YOU COULD KILL HER. HAVE YOU TOLD HER THAT?
SHE'S DEAD IF I DON'T. AND SHE'S TOO YOUNG TO UNDERSTAND ANY OF IT.
HEY, LITTLE FÍFLAR. YOU OKAY?
I'M SCARED, PABBI. DO I HAVE TO HAVE THE OPERATION?
AFRAID SO, EVEY.
YOU HAVE A BAD THING IN YOUR BLOOD AND THE DOCTORS SAID THERE WAS NOTHING THAT COULD FIX IT. WELL, PABBI IS A SCIENTIST, AND HE'S INVENTED A WAY TO FIX IT HIMSELF.
BUT I NEED TO GET INTO YOUR BLOOD.
IS THAT OKAY?
I SUPPOSE... CAN I KEEP HULDU WITH ME?
HE CAN STAY WITH YOU THE WHOLE TIME. I PROMISE.
YOU SHOULD KEEP HULDU WITH YOU FOREVER.

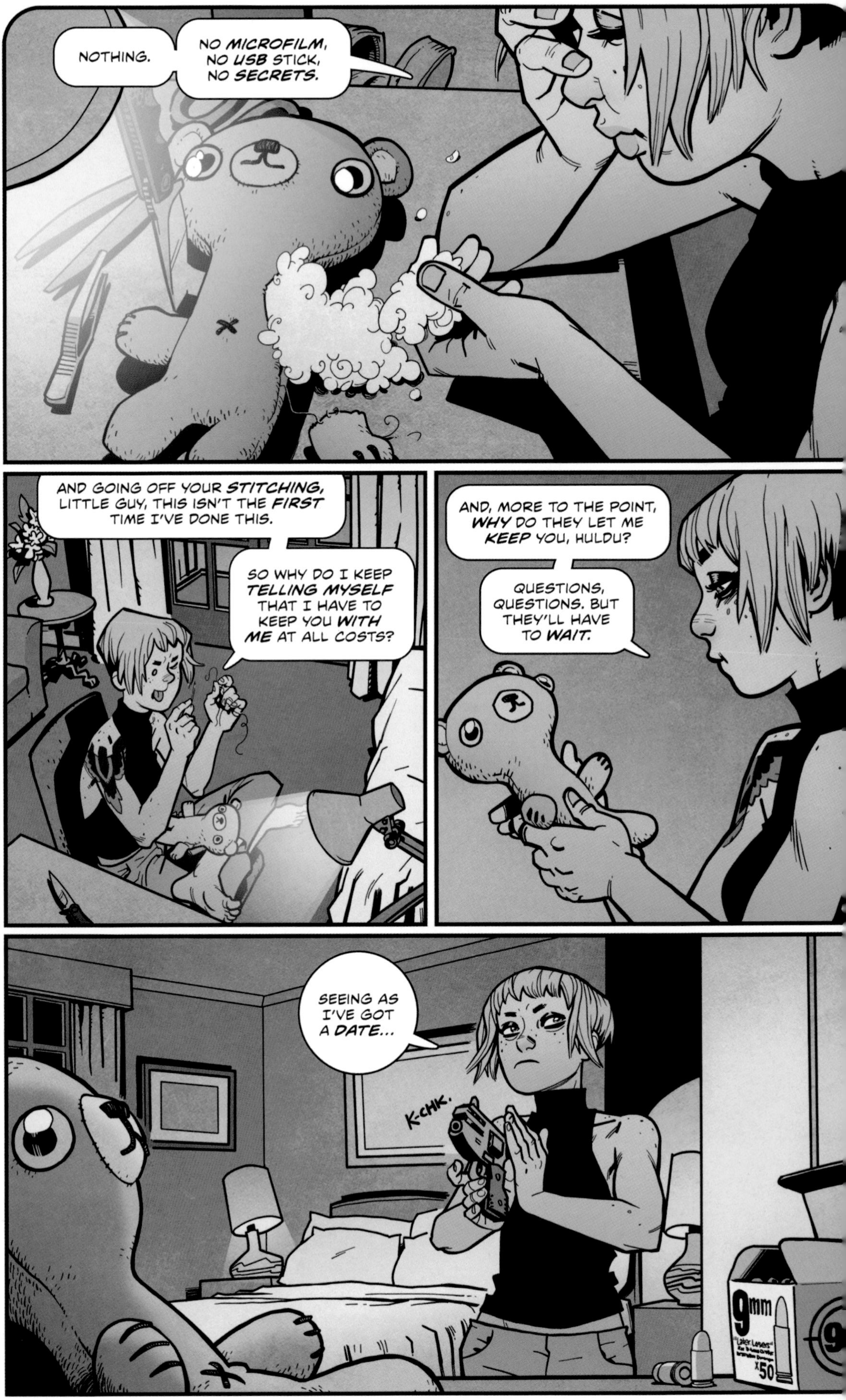
NOTHING.
NO MICROFILM, NO USB STICK, NO SECRETS.
AND GOING OFF YOUR STITCHING, LITTLE GUY, THIS ISN'T THE FIRST TIME I'VE DONE THIS.
SO WHY DO I KEEP TELLING MYSELF THAT I HAVE TO KEEP YOU WITH ME AT ALL COSTS?
AND, MORE TO THE POINT, WHY DO THEY LET ME KEEP YOU, HULDU?
QUESTIONS, QUESTIONS. BUT THEY'LL HAVE TO WAIT.
SEEING AS I'VE GOT A DATE...
K-CHK.
9mm
x50

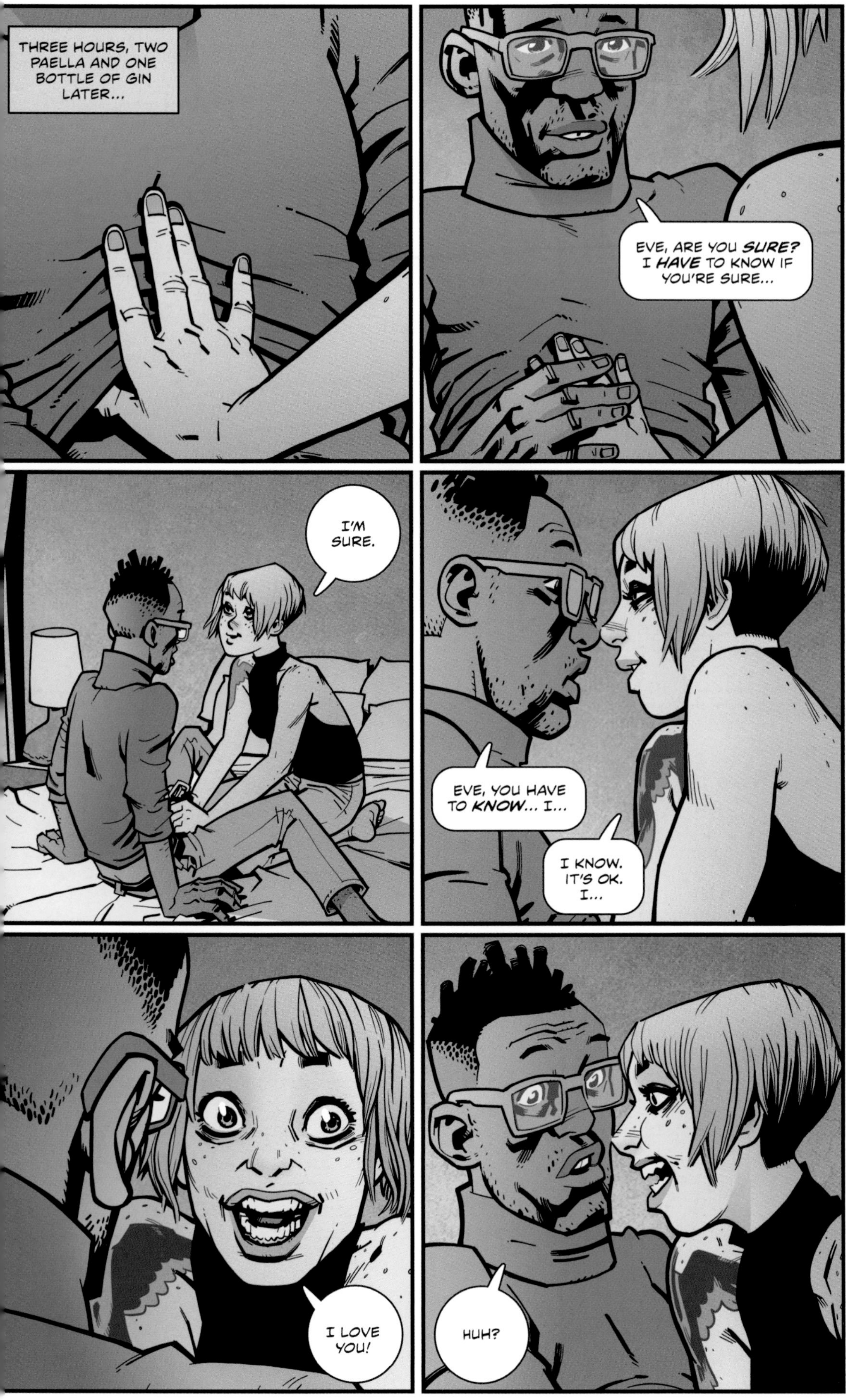
THREE HOURS, TWO PAELLA AND ONE BOTTLE OF GIN LATER...
EVE, ARE YOU SURE? I HAVE TO KNOW IF YOU'RE SURE...
I'M SURE.
EVE, YOU HAVE TO KNOW... I...
I KNOW. IT'S OK. I...
I LOVE YOU!
HUH?

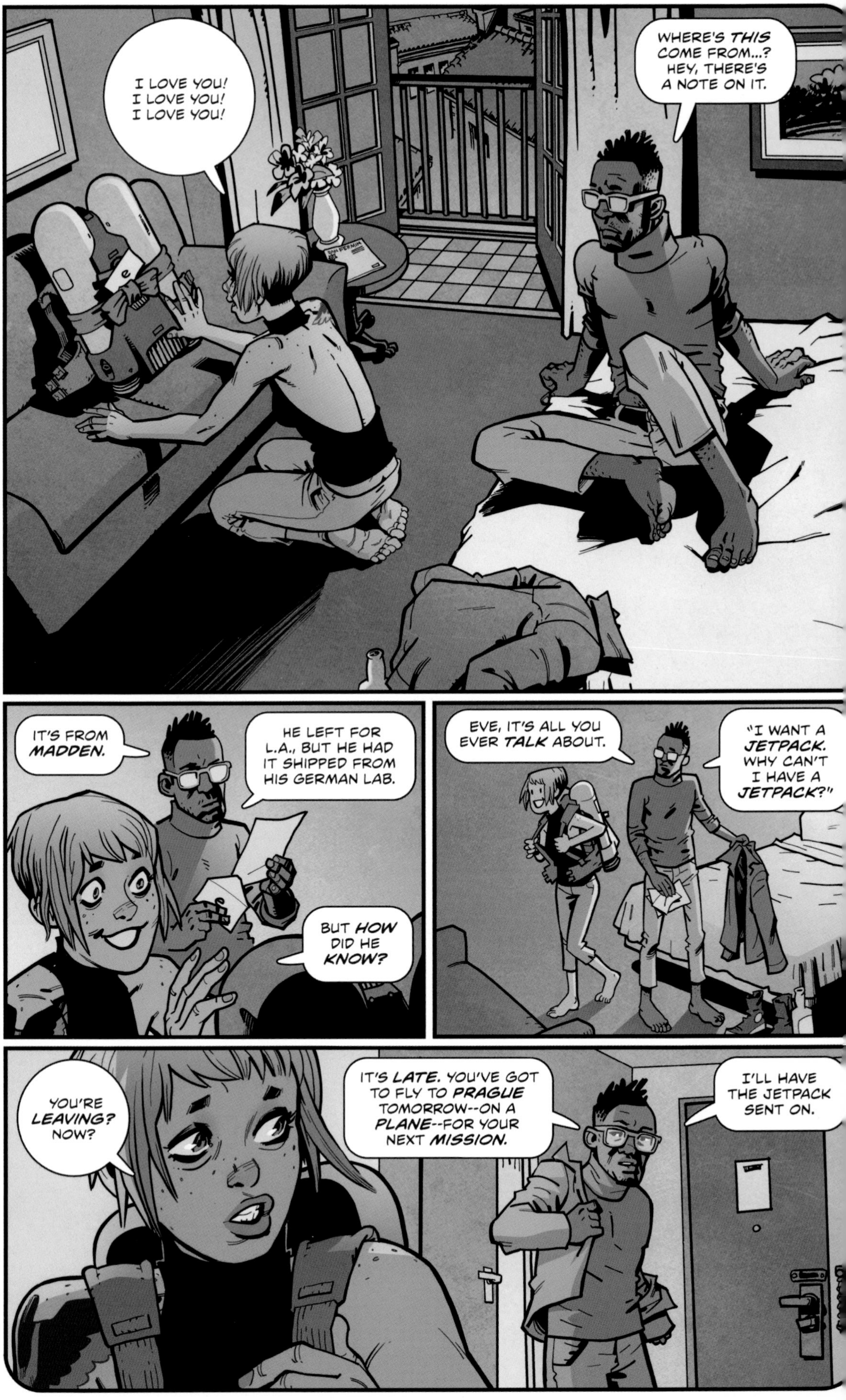
I LOVE YOU! I LOVE YOU! I LOVE YOU!
WHERE'S *THIS* COME FROM...? HEY, THERE'S A NOTE ON IT.
IT'S FROM *MADDEN.*
HE LEFT FOR L.A., BUT HE HAD IT SHIPPED FROM HIS GERMAN LAB.
BUT *HOW* DID HE *KNOW?*
EVE, IT'S ALL YOU EVER *TALK* ABOUT.
"I WANT A *JETPACK.* WHY CAN'T I HAVE A *JETPACK?*"
YOU'RE *LEAVING?* NOW?
IT'S *LATE.* YOU'VE GOT TO FLY TO *PRAGUE* TOMORROW--ON A *PLANE*--FOR YOUR NEXT *MISSION.*
I'LL HAVE THE JETPACK SENT ON.

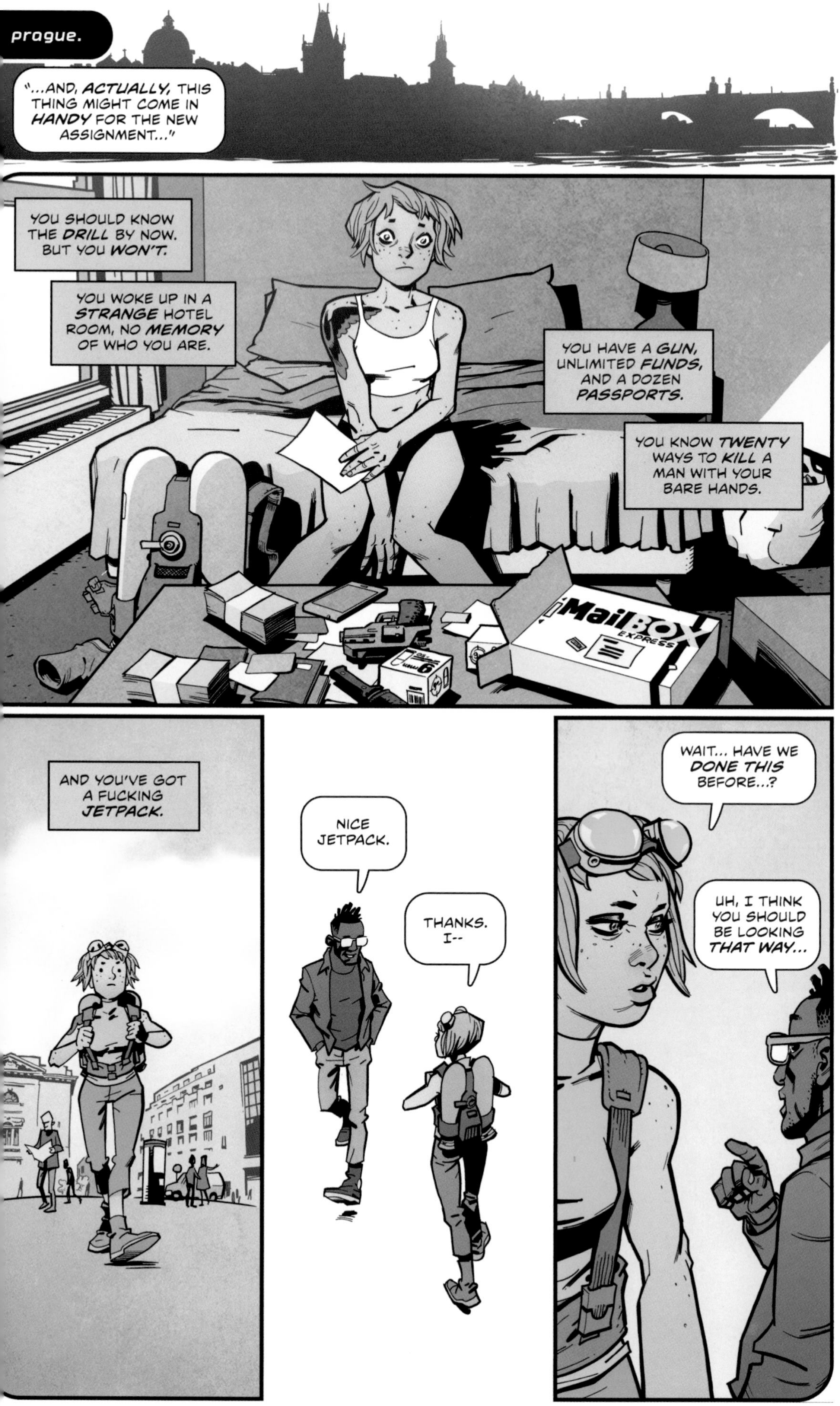
prague.
"...AND, ACTUALLY, THIS THING MIGHT COME IN HANDY FOR THE NEW ASSIGNMENT..."
YOU SHOULD KNOW THE DRILL BY NOW. BUT YOU WON'T.
YOU WOKE UP IN A STRANGE HOTEL ROOM, NO MEMORY OF WHO YOU ARE.
YOU HAVE A GUN, UNLIMITED FUNDS, AND A DOZEN PASSPORTS.
YOU KNOW TWENTY WAYS TO KILL A MAN WITH YOUR BARE HANDS.
MailBOX EXPRESS
AND YOU'VE GOT A FUCKING JETPACK.
NICE JETPACK.
THANKS. I--
WAIT... HAVE WE DONE THIS BEFORE...?
UH, I THINK YOU SHOULD BE LOOKING THAT WAY...

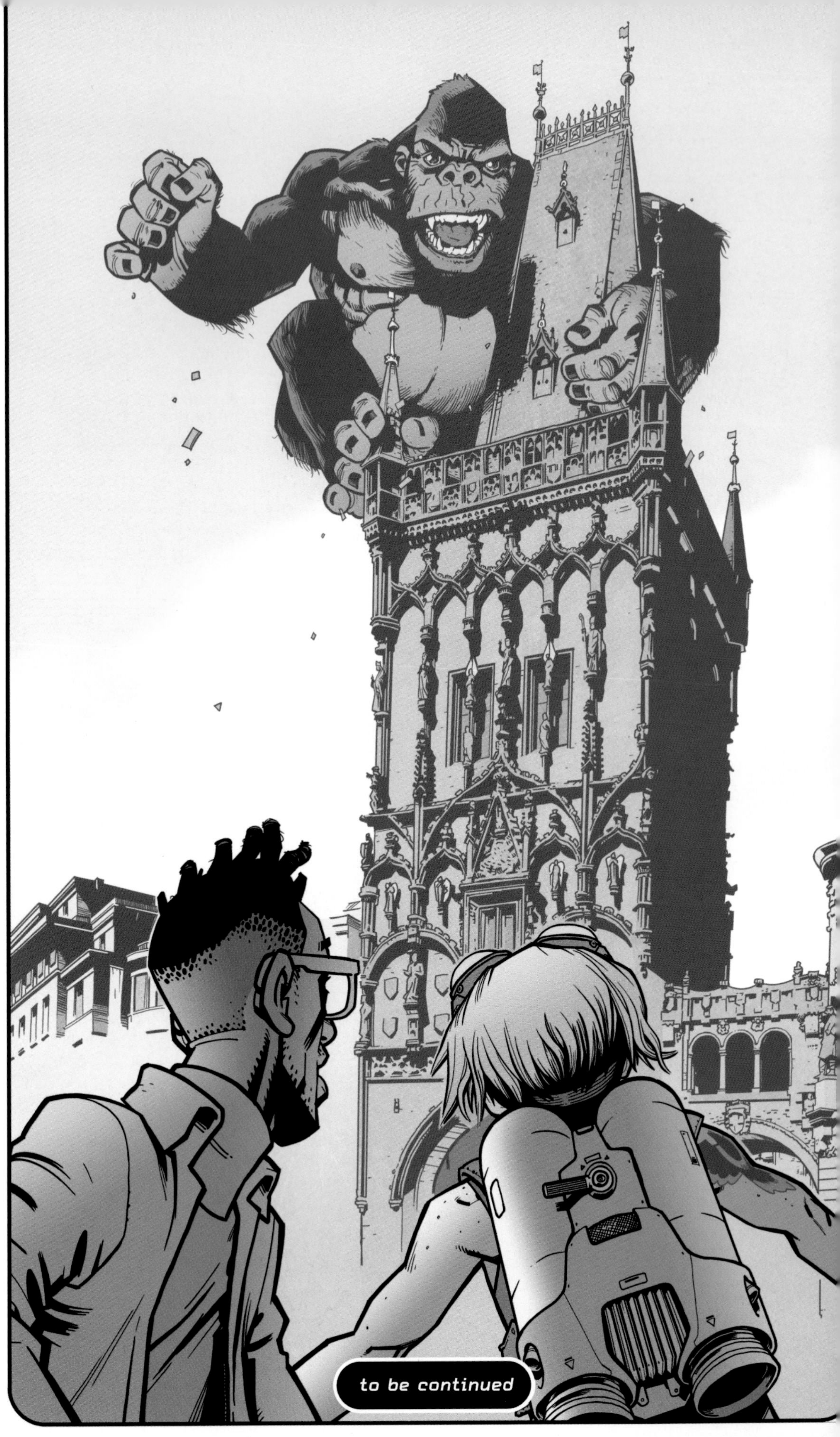
to be continued

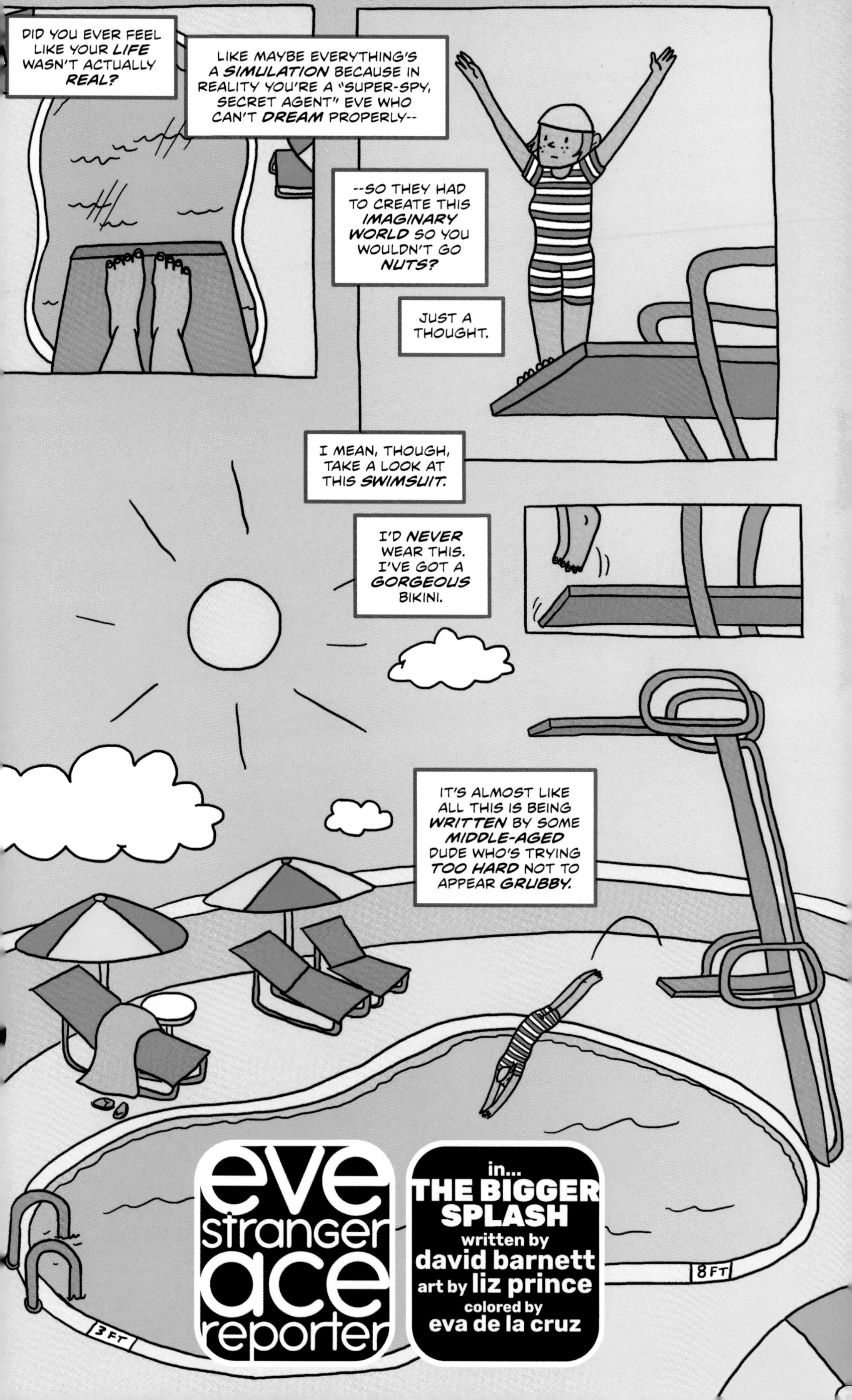
DID YOU EVER FEEL LIKE YOUR LIFE WASN'T ACTUALLY REAL?
LIKE MAYBE EVERYTHING'S A SIMULATION BECAUSE IN REALITY YOU'RE A "SUPER-SPY, SECRET AGENT" EVE WHO CAN'T DREAM PROPERLY--
--SO THEY HAD TO CREATE THIS IMAGINARY WORLD SO YOU WOULDN'T GO NUTS?
JUST A THOUGHT.
I MEAN, THOUGH, TAKE A LOOK AT THIS SWIMSUIT.
I'D NEVER WEAR THIS. I'VE GOT A GORGEOUS BIKINI.
IT'S ALMOST LIKE ALL THIS IS BEING WRITTEN BY SOME MIDDLE-AGED DUDE WHO'S TRYING TOO HARD NOT TO APPEAR GRUBBY.
8 FT
3 FT
eve stranger ace reporter
in... THE BIGGER SPLASH
written by david barnett
art by liz prince
colored by eva de la cruz

SPLASH!

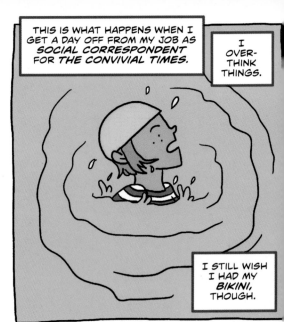

THIS IS WHAT HAPPENS WHEN I GET A DAY OFF FROM MY JOB AS *SOCIAL CORRESPONDENT* FOR *THE CONVIVIAL TIMES.*

I OVER-THINK THINGS.

I STILL WISH I HAD MY *BIKINI,* THOUGH.

ESPECIALLY SINCE THAT *AMAZING* GUY IS HERE AGAIN.

THAT WAS *INCREDIBLE.* I'M JIMMY.

WHAT, THE *DIVE?* OH, THAT WAS *NOTHING.* I'M EVE.

I COULD PROBABLY GO OFF THE *HIGH BOARD* IF I WANTED...

NOBODY GOES OFF THE HIGH BOARD!

THEY SAY IT'S SO *HIGH* YOU BEND *TIME* AND *SPACE* ON THE WAY DOWN.

THERE ARE PEOPLE WHO HAVE GONE OFF THE HIGH BOARD WHO WERE *NEVER* SEEN AGAIN.

PISH!

I'M GONNA DO IT *RIGHT NOW!*

OH MY GOD. ALL THIS TO *IMPRESS* SOME BEAUTIFUL BOY?

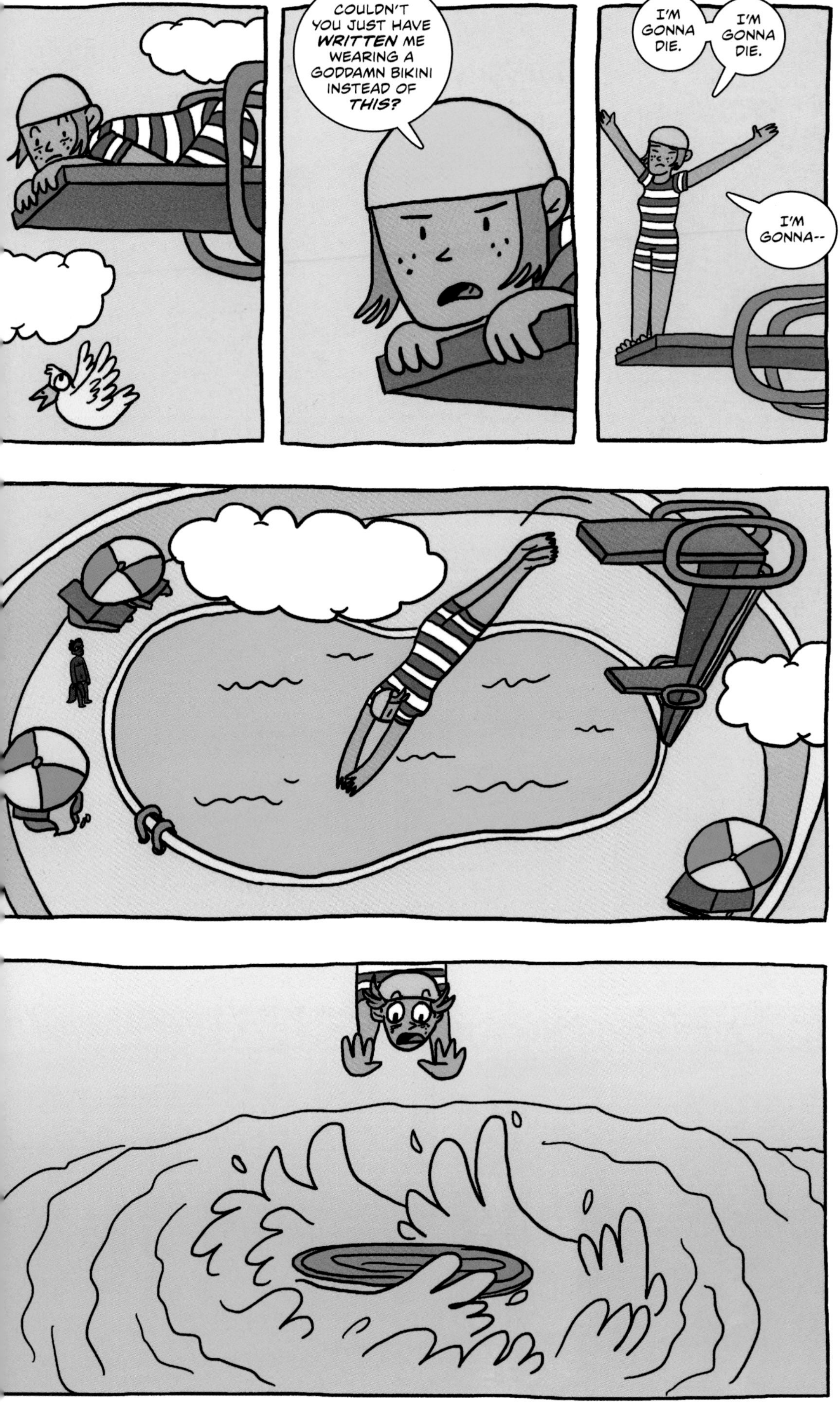
COULDN'T YOU JUST HAVE WRITTEN ME WEARING A GODDAMN BIKINI INSTEAD OF THIS?
I'M GONNA DIE.
I'M GONNA DIE.
I'M GONNA--

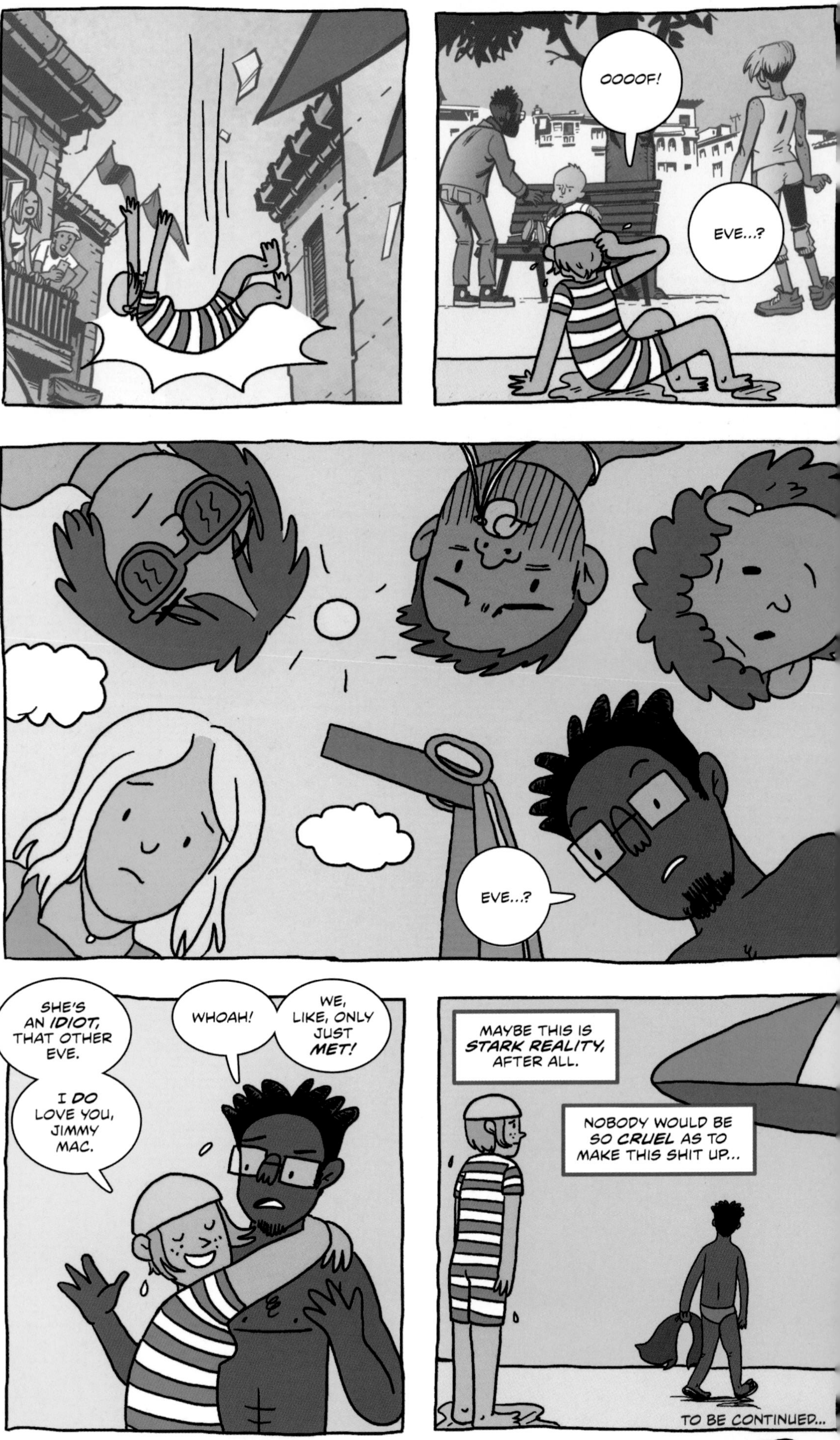
OOOOF!
EVE...?
EVE...?
SHE'S AN *IDIOT,* THAT OTHER EVE.
I *DO* LOVE YOU, JIMMY MAC.
WHOAH!
WE, LIKE, ONLY JUST *MET!*
MAYBE THIS IS *STARK REALITY,* AFTER ALL.
NOBODY WOULD BE SO *CRUEL* AS TO MAKE THIS SHIT UP...
TO BE CONTINUED...

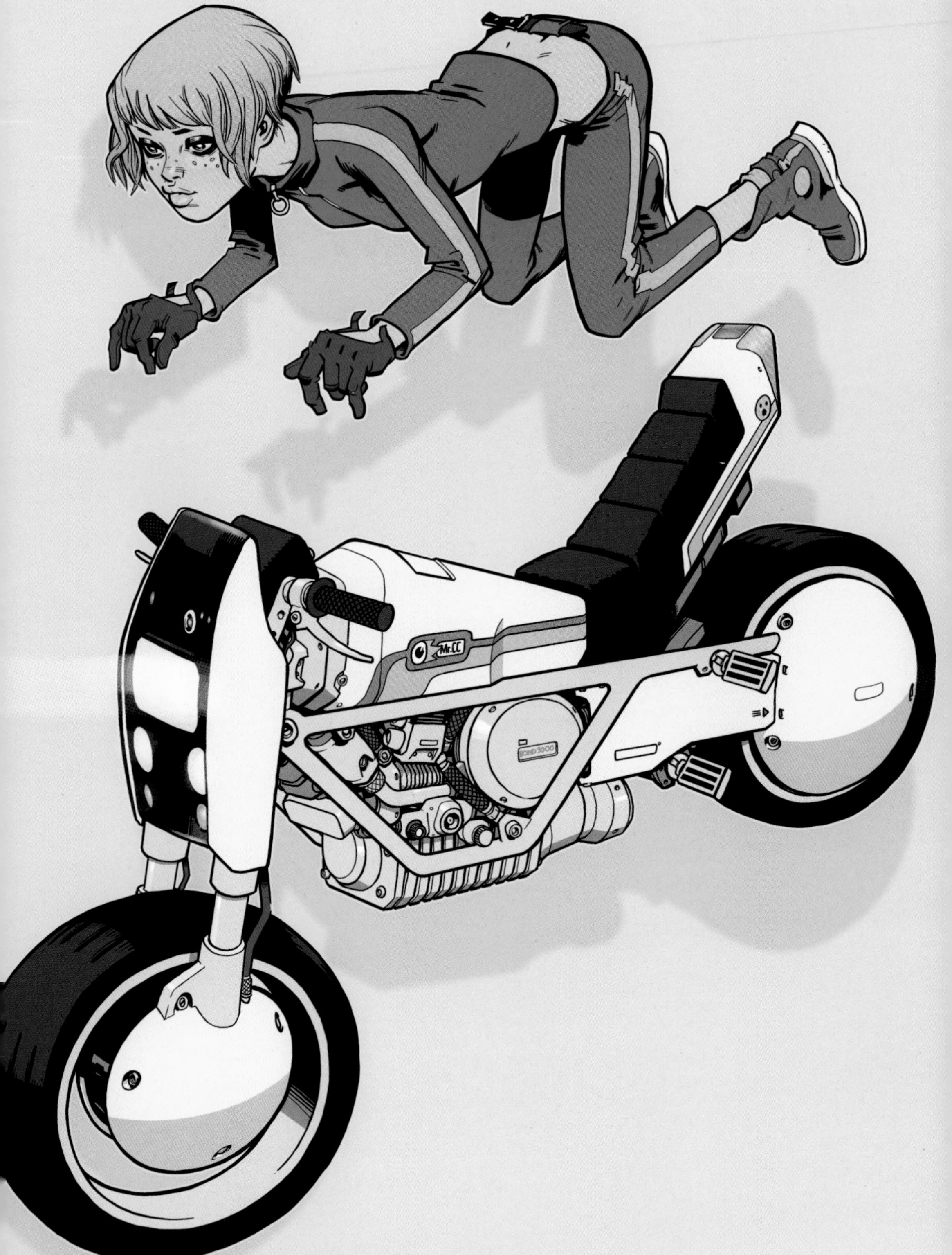
Mr.CC

part three:
SEVEN DAY LOVER

"I'M COVERED IN
SHIT AND BLOOD,
AND ONLY ONE OF
THOSE IS MINE."

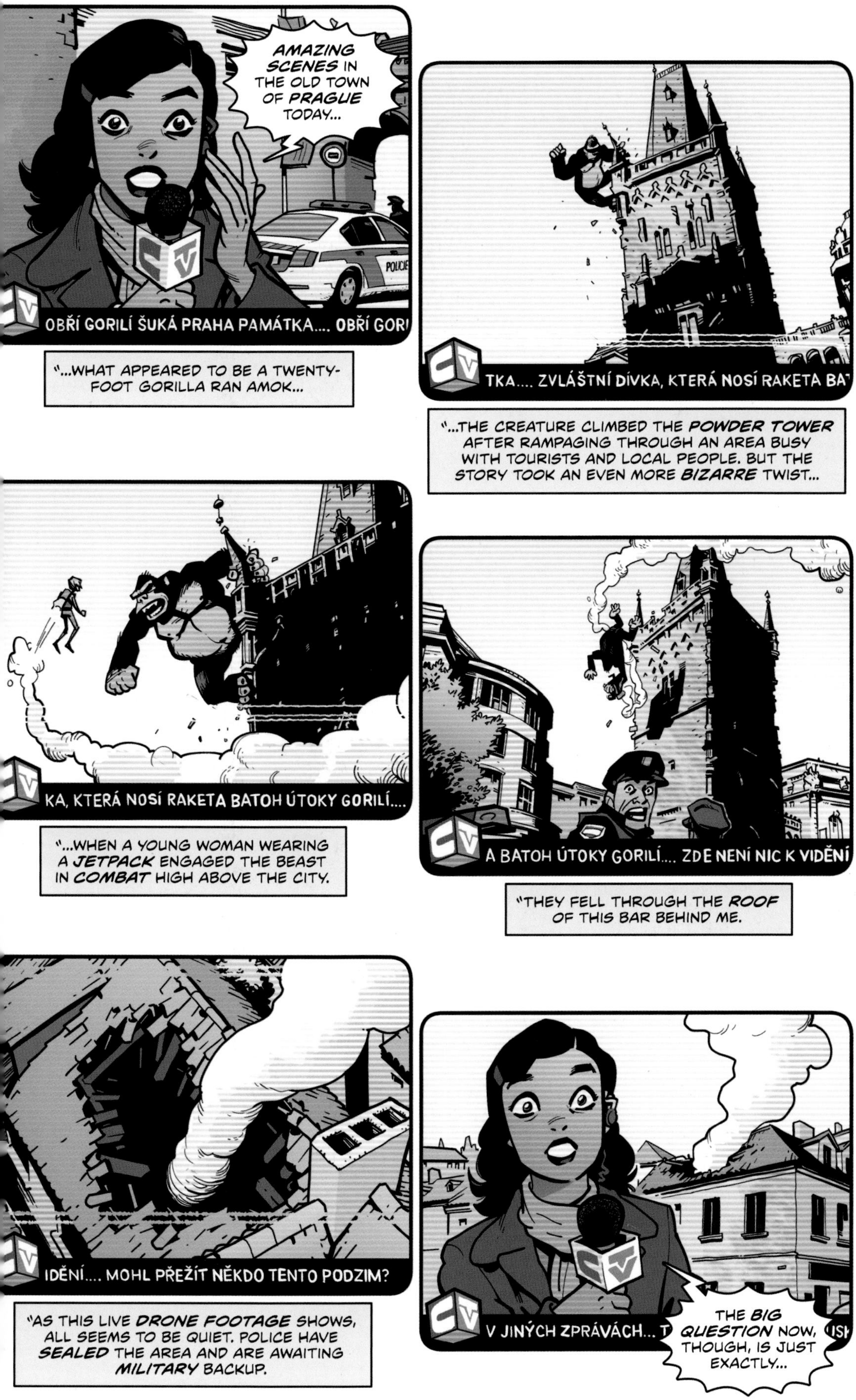
AMAZING SCENES IN THE OLD TOWN OF PRAGUE TODAY...
POLICIE
OBŘÍ GORILÍ ŠUKÁ PRAHA PAMÁTKA.... OBŘÍ GORI
"...WHAT APPEARED TO BE A TWENTY-FOOT GORILLA RAN AMOK...
TKA.... ZVLÁŠTNÍ DÍVKA, KTERÁ NOSÍ RAKETA BAT
"...THE CREATURE CLIMBED THE POWDER TOWER AFTER RAMPAGING THROUGH AN AREA BUSY WITH TOURISTS AND LOCAL PEOPLE. BUT THE STORY TOOK AN EVEN MORE BIZARRE TWIST...
KA, KTERÁ NOSÍ RAKETA BATOH ÚTOKY GORILÍ....
"...WHEN A YOUNG WOMAN WEARING A JETPACK ENGAGED THE BEAST IN COMBAT HIGH ABOVE THE CITY.
A BATOH ÚTOKY GORILÍ.... ZDE NENÍ NIC K VIDĚNÍ
"THEY FELL THROUGH THE ROOF OF THIS BAR BEHIND ME.
IDĚNÍ.... MOHL PŘEŽÍT NĚKDO TENTO PODZIM?
"AS THIS LIVE DRONE FOOTAGE SHOWS, ALL SEEMS TO BE QUIET. POLICE HAVE SEALED THE AREA AND ARE AWAITING MILITARY BACKUP.
V JINÝCH ZPRÁVÁCH...
THE BIG QUESTION NOW, THOUGH, IS JUST EXACTLY...

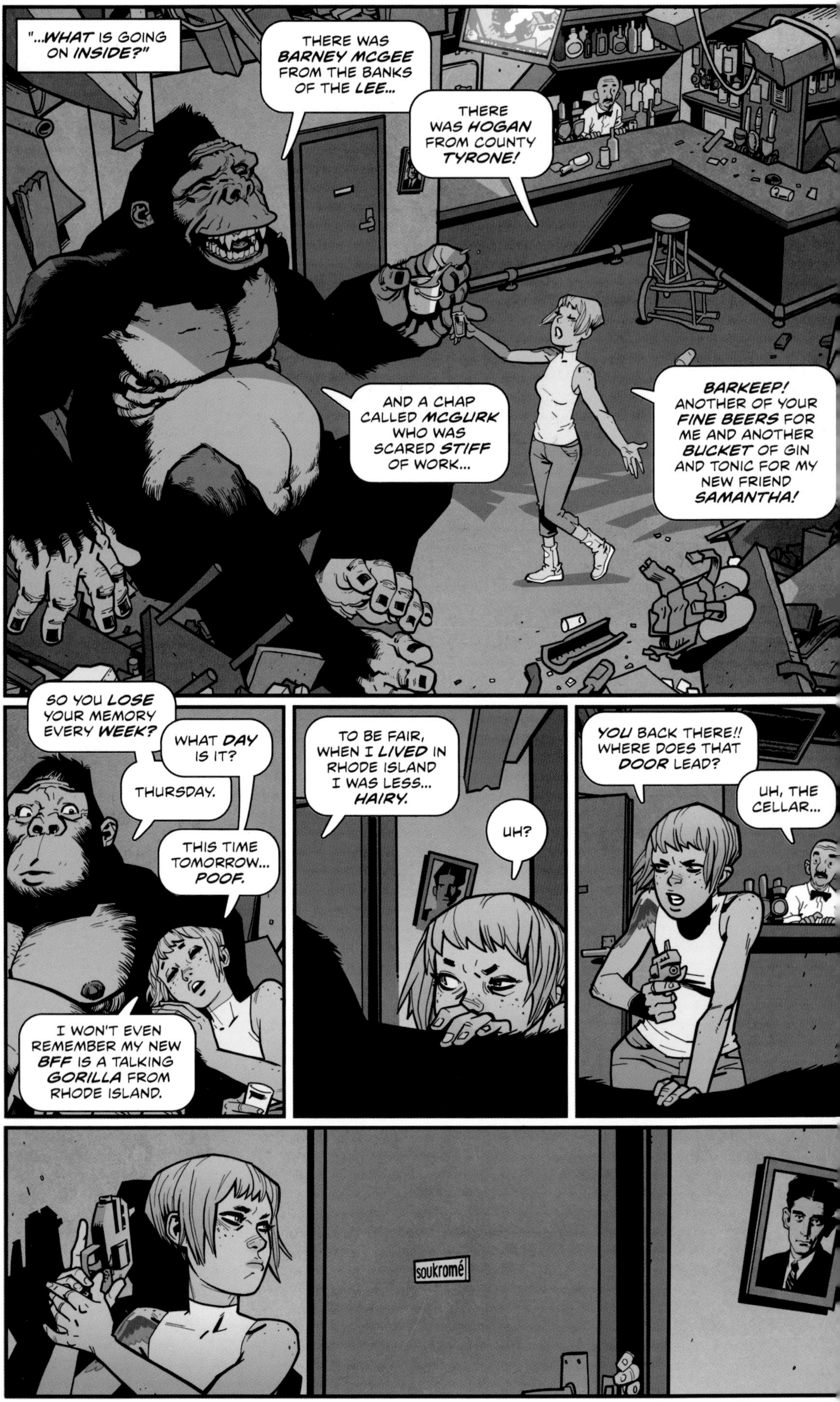
"...WHAT IS GOING ON INSIDE?"
THERE WAS BARNEY MCGEE FROM THE BANKS OF THE LEE...
THERE WAS HOGAN FROM COUNTY TYRONE!
AND A CHAP CALLED MCGURK WHO WAS SCARED STIFF OF WORK...
BARKEEP! ANOTHER OF YOUR FINE BEERS FOR ME AND ANOTHER BUCKET OF GIN AND TONIC FOR MY NEW FRIEND SAMANTHA!
SO YOU LOSE YOUR MEMORY EVERY WEEK?
WHAT DAY IS IT?
THURSDAY.
THIS TIME TOMORROW... POOF.
I WON'T EVEN REMEMBER MY NEW BFF IS A TALKING GORILLA FROM RHODE ISLAND.
TO BE FAIR, WHEN I LIVED IN RHODE ISLAND I WAS LESS... HAIRY.
UH?
YOU BACK THERE!! WHERE DOES THAT DOOR LEAD?
UH, THE CELLAR...
soukromé

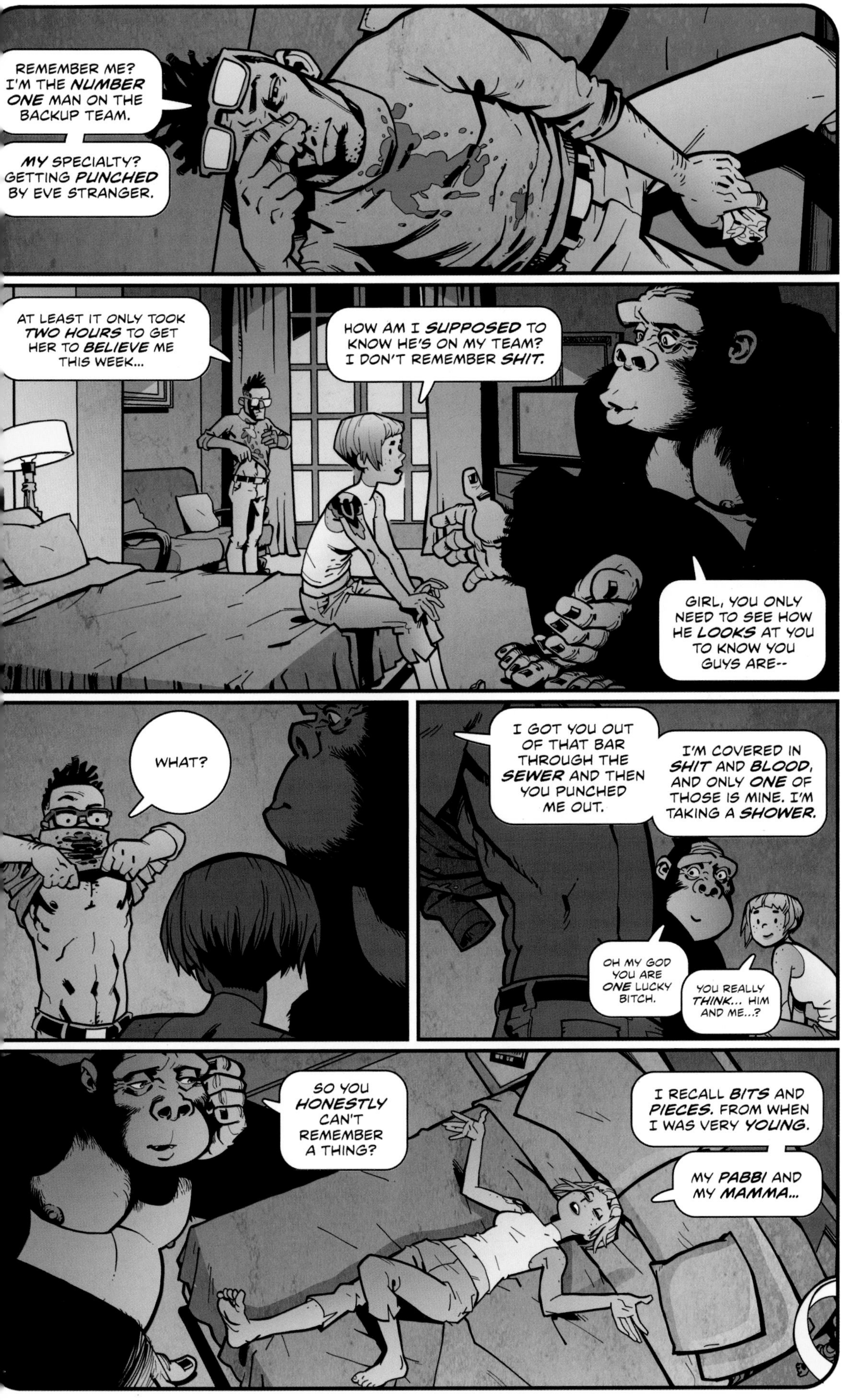
REMEMBER ME? I'M THE NUMBER ONE MAN ON THE BACKUP TEAM.
MY SPECIALTY? GETTING PUNCHED BY EVE STRANGER.
AT LEAST IT ONLY TOOK TWO HOURS TO GET HER TO BELIEVE ME THIS WEEK...
HOW AM I SUPPOSED TO KNOW HE'S ON MY TEAM? I DON'T REMEMBER SHIT.
GIRL, YOU ONLY NEED TO SEE HOW HE LOOKS AT YOU TO KNOW YOU GUYS ARE--
WHAT?
I GOT YOU OUT OF THAT BAR THROUGH THE SEWER AND THEN YOU PUNCHED ME OUT.
I'M COVERED IN SHIT AND BLOOD, AND ONLY ONE OF THOSE IS MINE. I'M TAKING A SHOWER.
OH MY GOD YOU ARE ONE LUCKY BITCH.
YOU REALLY THINK... HIM AND ME...?
SO YOU HONESTLY CAN'T REMEMBER A THING?
I RECALL BITS AND PIECES. FROM WHEN I WAS VERY YOUNG.
MY PABBI AND MY MAMMA...

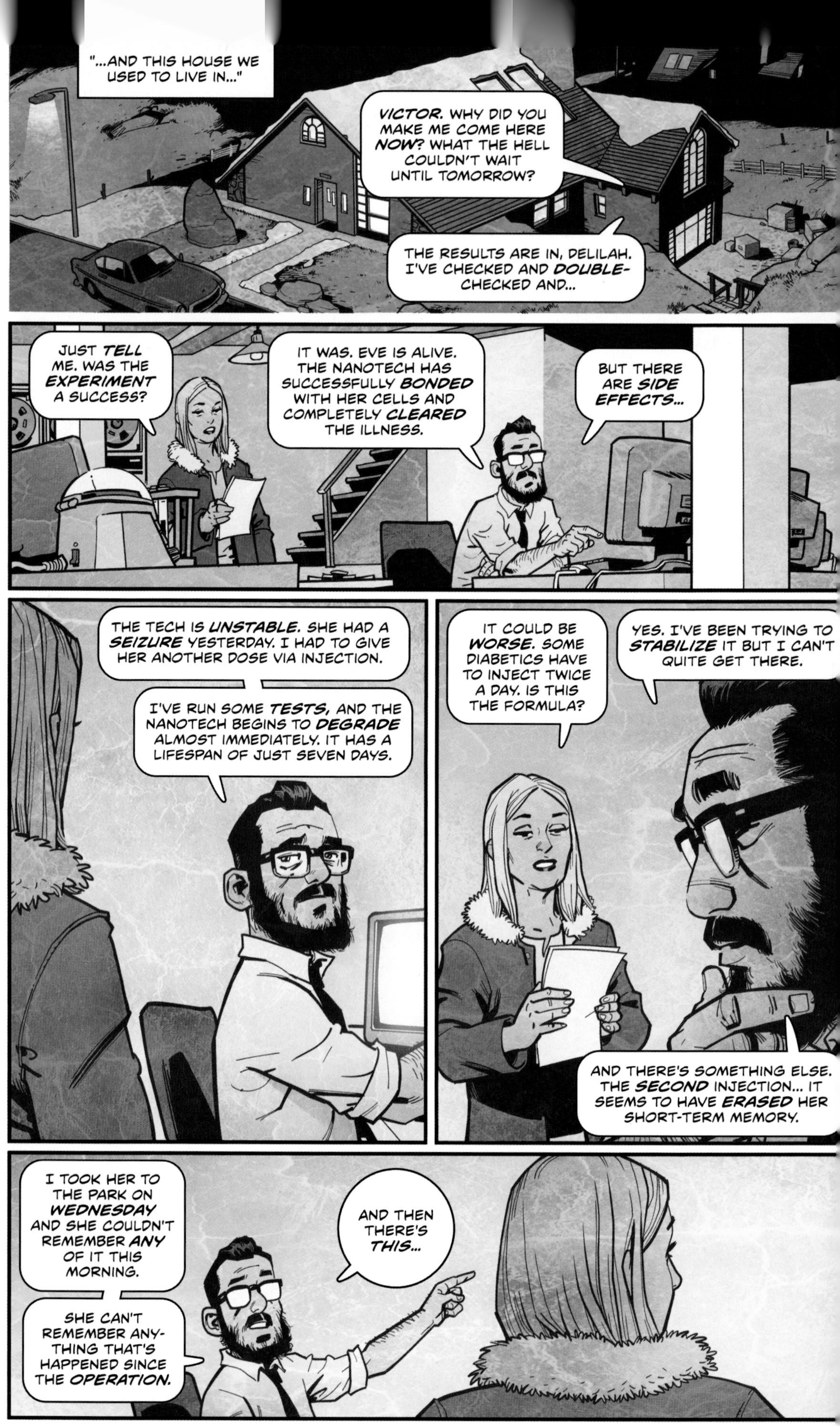
"...AND THIS HOUSE WE USED TO LIVE IN..."
VICTOR. WHY DID YOU MAKE ME COME HERE NOW? WHAT THE HELL COULDN'T WAIT UNTIL TOMORROW?
THE RESULTS ARE IN, DELILAH. I'VE CHECKED AND DOUBLE-CHECKED AND...
JUST TELL ME. WAS THE EXPERIMENT A SUCCESS?
IT WAS. EVE IS ALIVE. THE NANOTECH HAS SUCCESSFULLY BONDED WITH HER CELLS AND COMPLETELY CLEARED THE ILLNESS.
BUT THERE ARE SIDE EFFECTS...
THE TECH IS UNSTABLE. SHE HAD A SEIZURE YESTERDAY. I HAD TO GIVE HER ANOTHER DOSE VIA INJECTION.
I'VE RUN SOME TESTS, AND THE NANOTECH BEGINS TO DEGRADE ALMOST IMMEDIATELY. IT HAS A LIFESPAN OF JUST SEVEN DAYS.
IT COULD BE WORSE. SOME DIABETICS HAVE TO INJECT TWICE A DAY. IS THIS THE FORMULA?
YES. I'VE BEEN TRYING TO STABILIZE IT BUT I CAN'T QUITE GET THERE.
AND THERE'S SOMETHING ELSE. THE SECOND INJECTION... IT SEEMS TO HAVE ERASED HER SHORT-TERM MEMORY.
I TOOK HER TO THE PARK ON WEDNESDAY AND SHE COULDN'T REMEMBER ANY OF IT THIS MORNING.
SHE CAN'T REMEMBER ANY-THING THAT'S HAPPENED SINCE THE OPERATION.
AND THEN THERE'S THIS...

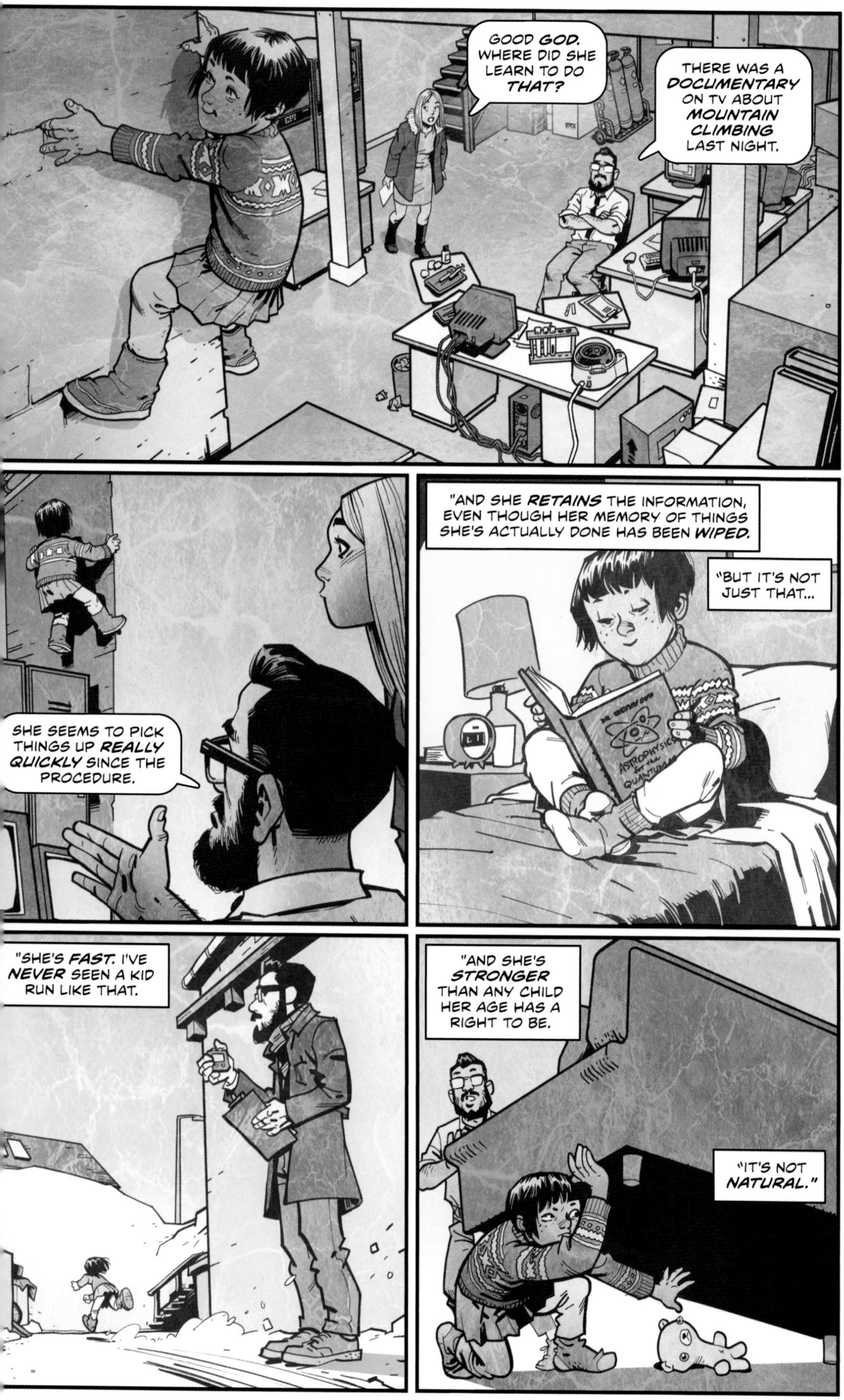

GOOD GOD. WHERE DID SHE LEARN TO DO THAT?
THERE WAS A DOCUMENTARY ON TV ABOUT MOUNTAIN CLIMBING LAST NIGHT.
SHE SEEMS TO PICK THINGS UP REALLY QUICKLY SINCE THE PROCEDURE.
"AND SHE RETAINS THE INFORMATION, EVEN THOUGH HER MEMORY OF THINGS SHE'S ACTUALLY DONE HAS BEEN WIPED.
"BUT IT'S NOT JUST THAT...
ASTROPHYSICS for the QUANTUM...
"SHE'S FAST. I'VE NEVER SEEN A KID RUN LIKE THAT.
"AND SHE'S STRONGER THAN ANY CHILD HER AGE HAS A RIGHT TO BE.
"IT'S NOT NATURAL."

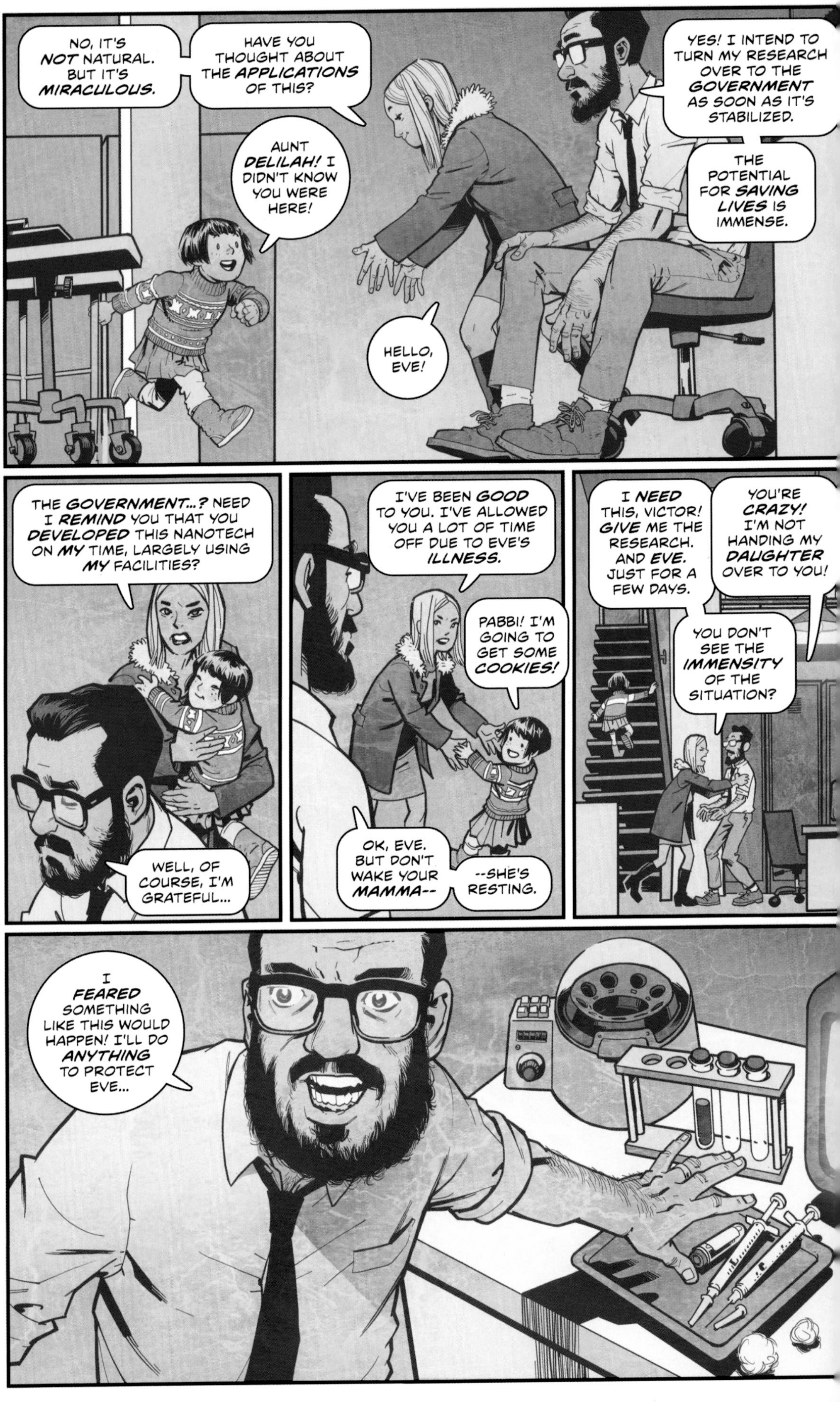
NO, IT'S NOT NATURAL. BUT IT'S MIRACULOUS.
HAVE YOU THOUGHT ABOUT THE APPLICATIONS OF THIS?
YES! I INTEND TO TURN MY RESEARCH OVER TO THE GOVERNMENT AS SOON AS IT'S STABILIZED.
THE POTENTIAL FOR SAVING LIVES IS IMMENSE.
AUNT DELILAH! I DIDN'T KNOW YOU WERE HERE!
HELLO, EVE!
THE GOVERNMENT...? NEED I REMIND YOU THAT YOU DEVELOPED THIS NANOTECH ON MY TIME, LARGELY USING MY FACILITIES?
WELL, OF COURSE, I'M GRATEFUL...
I'VE BEEN GOOD TO YOU. I'VE ALLOWED YOU A LOT OF TIME OFF DUE TO EVE'S ILLNESS.
PABBI! I'M GOING TO GET SOME COOKIES!
OK, EVE. BUT DON'T WAKE YOUR MAMMA--
--SHE'S RESTING.
I NEED THIS, VICTOR! GIVE ME THE RESEARCH. AND EVE. JUST FOR A FEW DAYS.
YOU'RE CRAZY! I'M NOT HANDING MY DAUGHTER OVER TO YOU!
YOU DON'T SEE THE IMMENSITY OF THE SITUATION?
I FEARED SOMETHING LIKE THIS WOULD HAPPEN! I'LL DO ANYTHING TO PROTECT EVE...

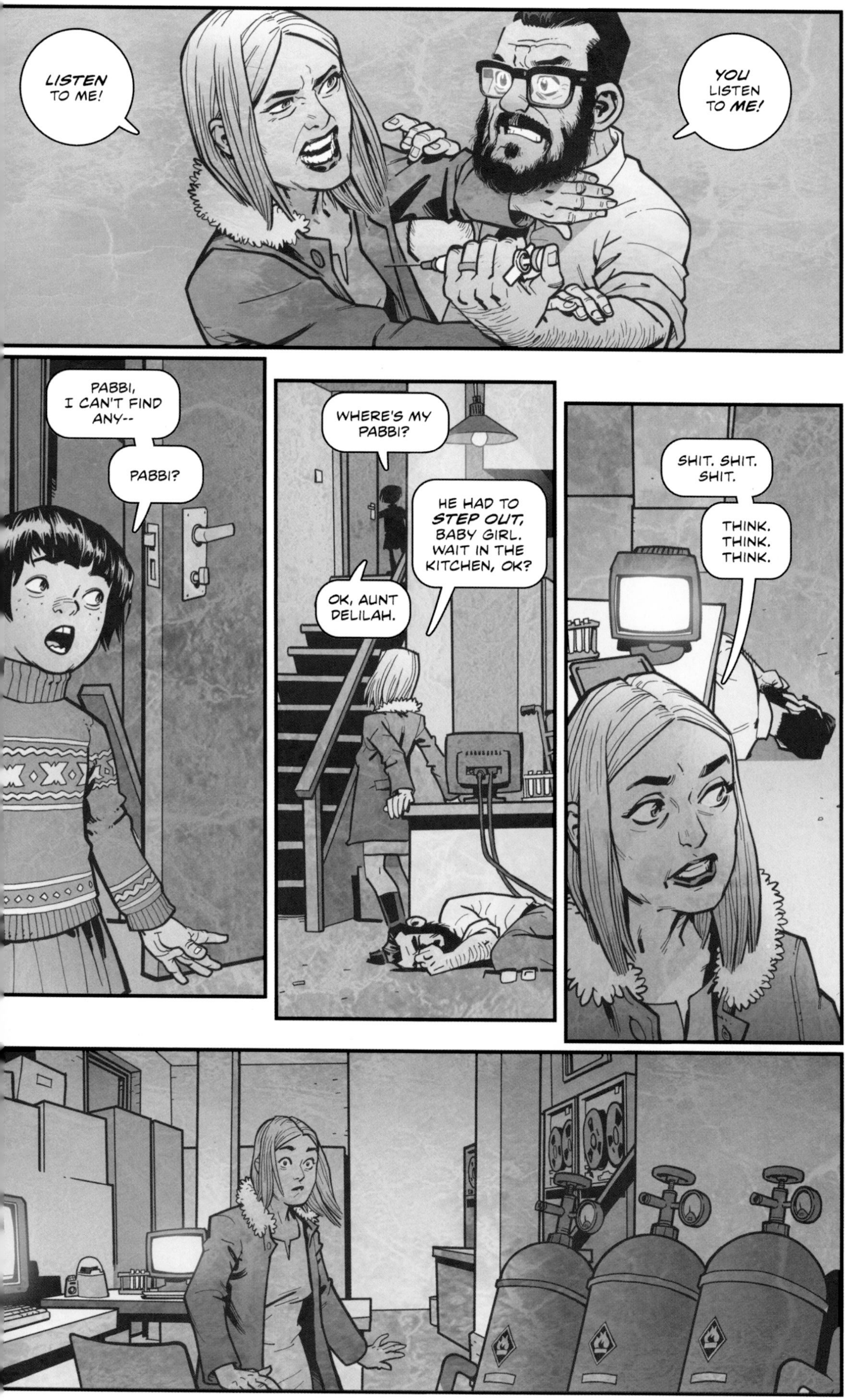
LISTEN TO ME!
YOU LISTEN TO ME!
PABBI, I CAN'T FIND ANY--
PABBI?
WHERE'S MY PABBI?
HE HAD TO STEP OUT, BABY GIRL. WAIT IN THE KITCHEN, OK?
OK, AUNT DELILAH.
SHIT. SHIT. SHIT.
THINK. THINK. THINK.

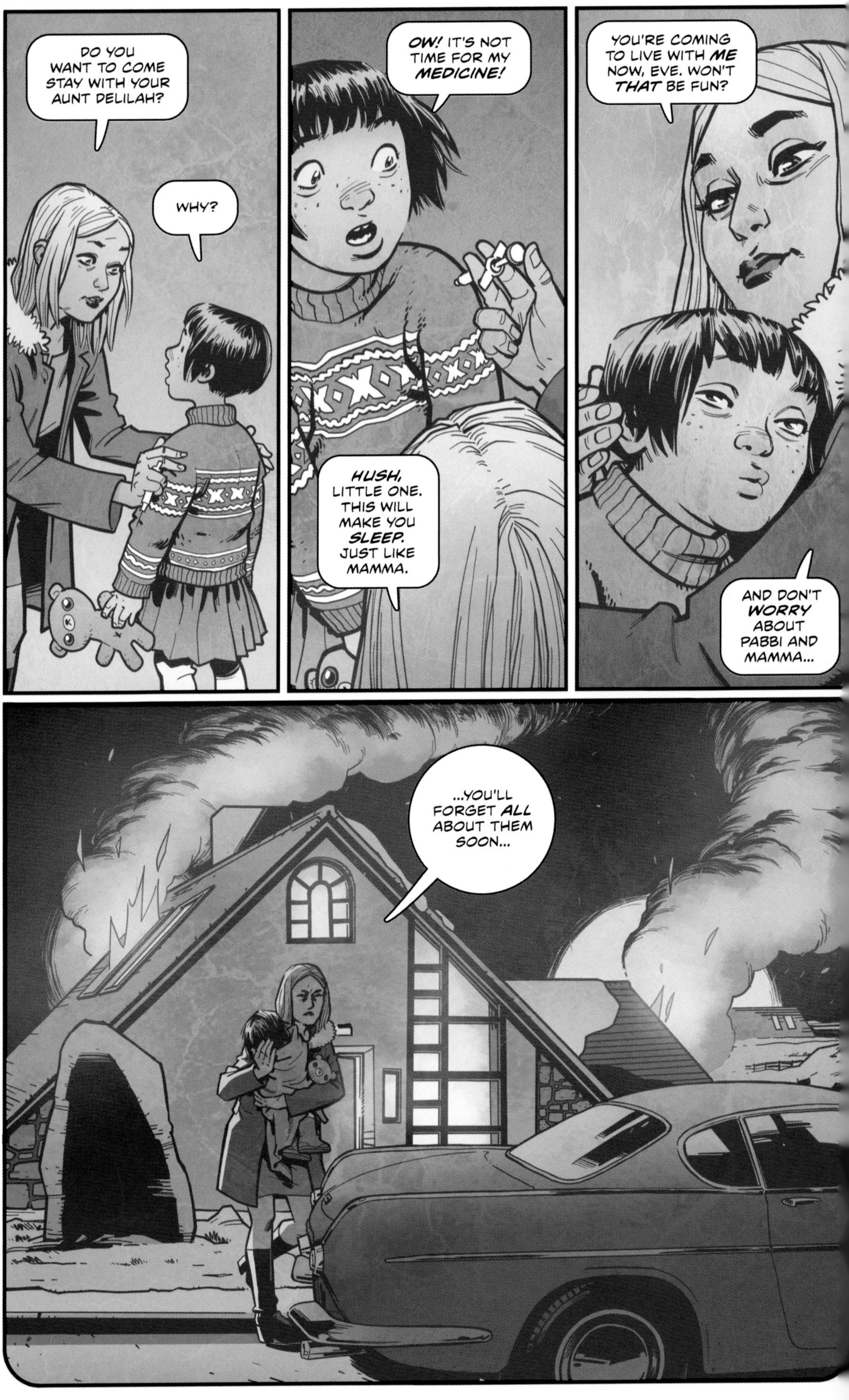
DO YOU WANT TO COME STAY WITH YOUR AUNT DELILAH?
WHY?
OW! IT'S NOT TIME FOR MY MEDICINE!
HUSH, LITTLE ONE. THIS WILL MAKE YOU SLEEP. JUST LIKE MAMMA.
YOU'RE COMING TO LIVE WITH ME NOW, EVE. WON'T THAT BE FUN?
AND DON'T WORRY ABOUT PABBI AND MAMMA...
...YOU'LL FORGET ALL ABOUT THEM SOON...

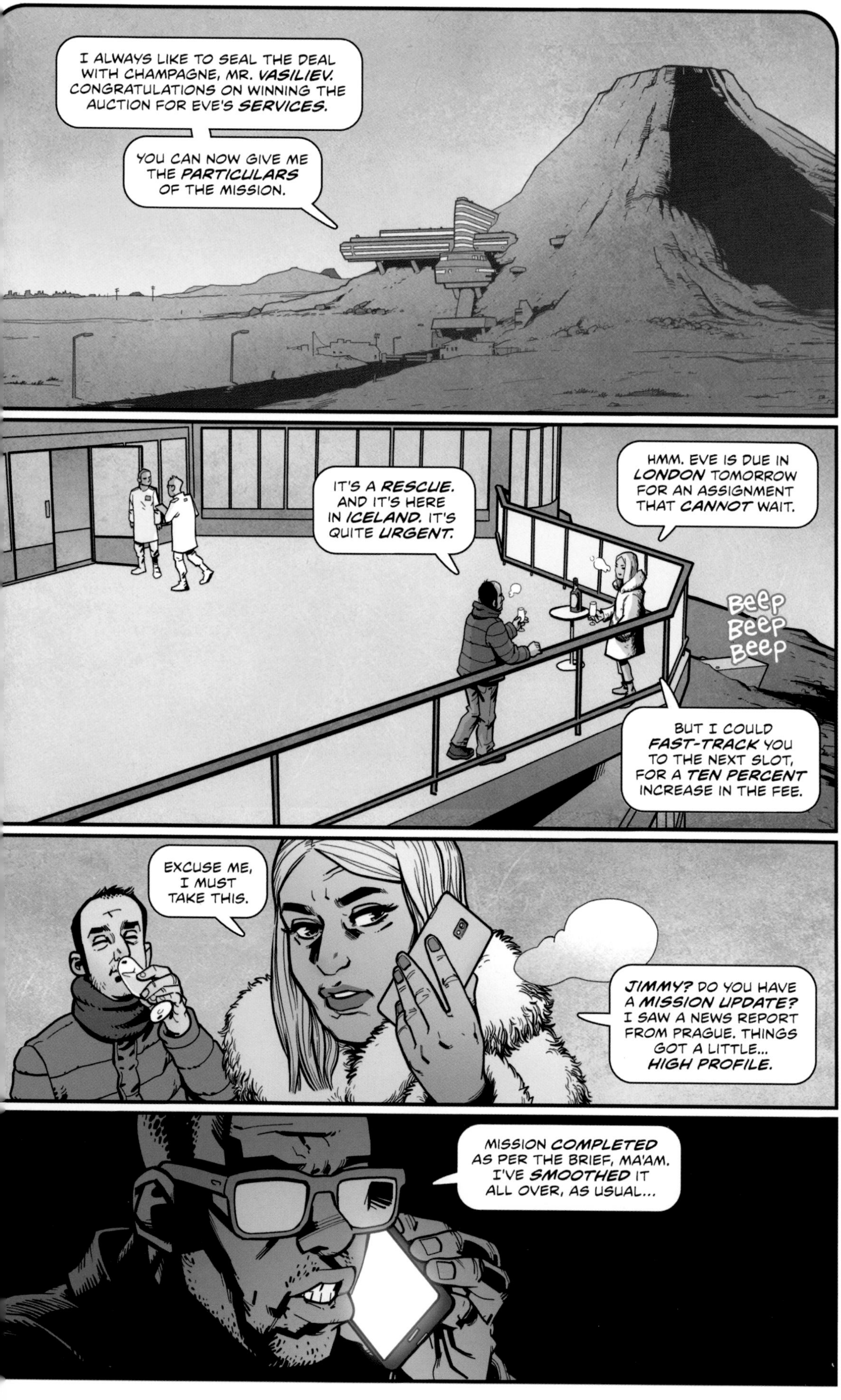
I ALWAYS LIKE TO SEAL THE DEAL WITH CHAMPAGNE, MR. VASILIEV. CONGRATULATIONS ON WINNING THE AUCTION FOR EVE'S SERVICES.
YOU CAN NOW GIVE ME THE PARTICULARS OF THE MISSION.
IT'S A RESCUE. AND IT'S HERE IN ICELAND. IT'S QUITE URGENT.
HMM. EVE IS DUE IN LONDON TOMORROW FOR AN ASSIGNMENT THAT CANNOT WAIT.
Beep Beep Beep
BUT I COULD FAST-TRACK YOU TO THE NEXT SLOT, FOR A TEN PERCENT INCREASE IN THE FEE.
EXCUSE ME, I MUST TAKE THIS.
JIMMY? DO YOU HAVE A MISSION UPDATE? I SAW A NEWS REPORT FROM PRAGUE. THINGS GOT A LITTLE... HIGH PROFILE.
MISSION COMPLETED AS PER THE BRIEF, MA'AM. I'VE SMOOTHED IT ALL OVER, AS USUAL...

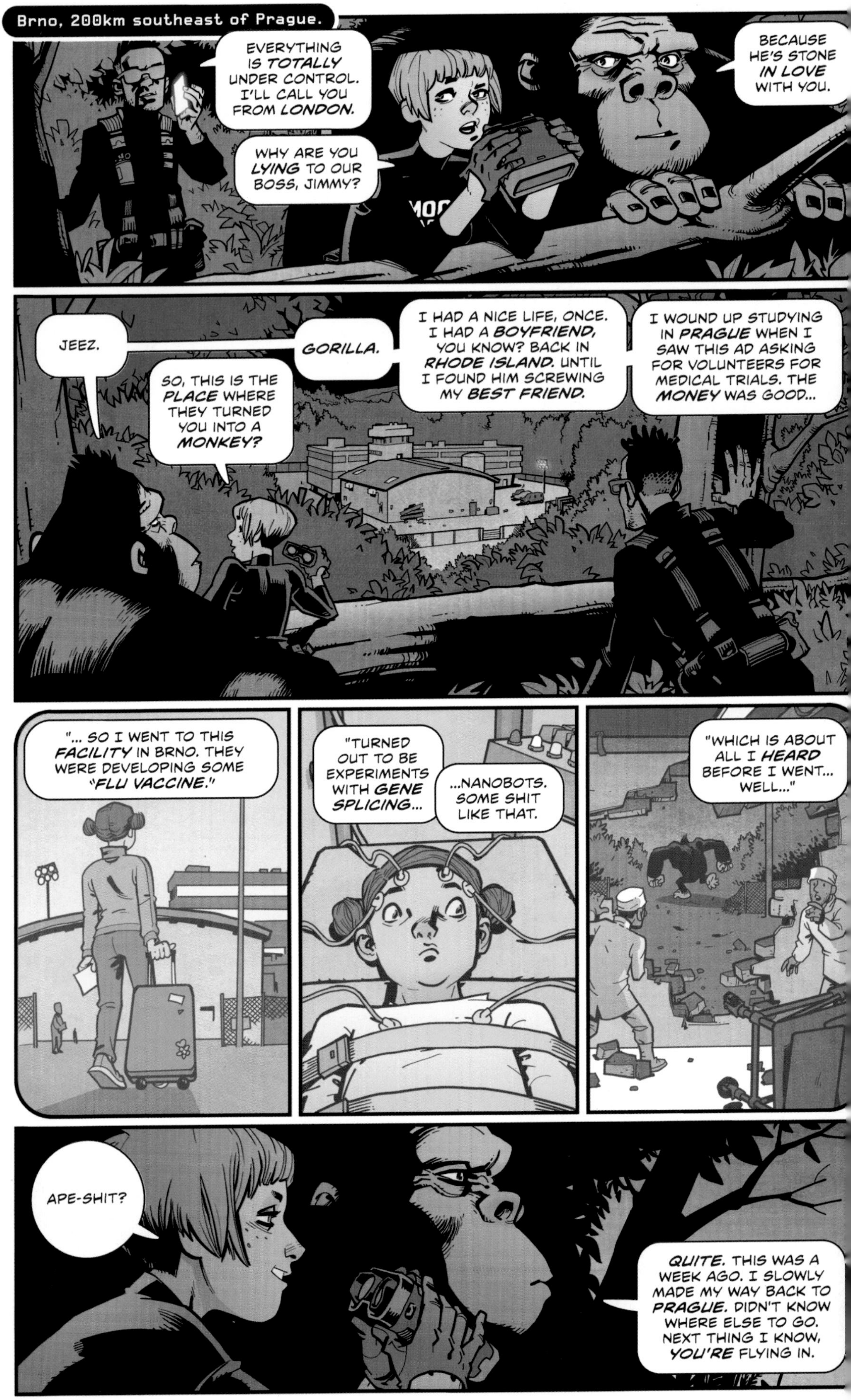
Brno, 200km southeast of Prague.
EVERYTHING IS TOTALLY UNDER CONTROL. I'LL CALL YOU FROM LONDON.
WHY ARE YOU LYING TO OUR BOSS, JIMMY?
BECAUSE HE'S STONE IN LOVE WITH YOU.
JEEZ.
GORILLA.
SO, THIS IS THE PLACE WHERE THEY TURNED YOU INTO A MONKEY?
I HAD A NICE LIFE, ONCE. I HAD A BOYFRIEND, YOU KNOW? BACK IN RHODE ISLAND. UNTIL I FOUND HIM SCREWING MY BEST FRIEND.
I WOUND UP STUDYING IN PRAGUE WHEN I SAW THIS AD ASKING FOR VOLUNTEERS FOR MEDICAL TRIALS. THE MONEY WAS GOOD...
"... SO I WENT TO THIS FACILITY IN BRNO. THEY WERE DEVELOPING SOME "FLU VACCINE."
"TURNED OUT TO BE EXPERIMENTS WITH GENE SPLICING...
...NANOBOTS. SOME SHIT LIKE THAT.
"WHICH IS ABOUT ALL I HEARD BEFORE I WENT... WELL..."
APE-SHIT?
QUITE. THIS WAS A WEEK AGO. I SLOWLY MADE MY WAY BACK TO PRAGUE. DIDN'T KNOW WHERE ELSE TO GO. NEXT THING I KNOW, YOU'RE FLYING IN.

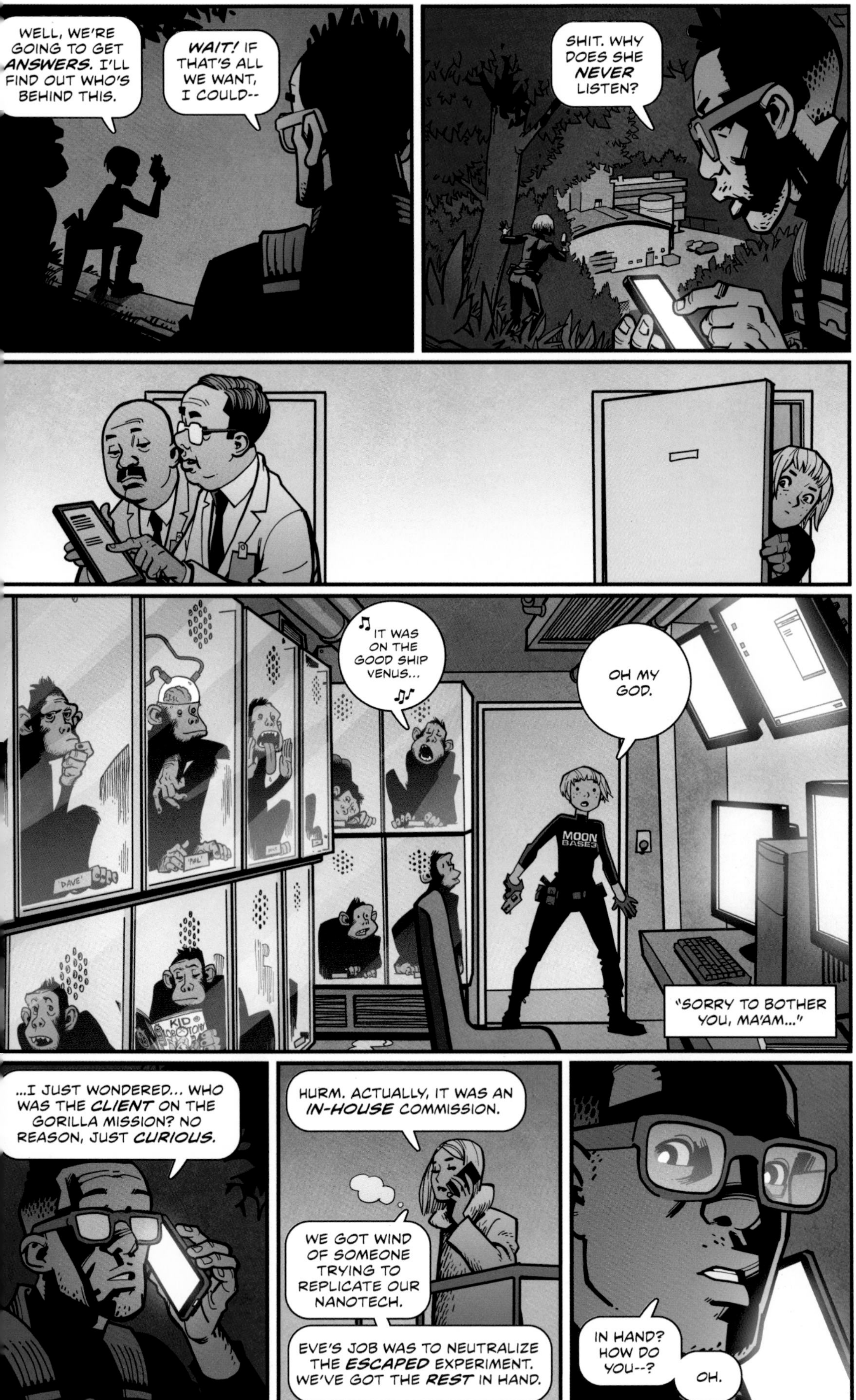
WELL, WE'RE GOING TO GET ANSWERS. I'LL FIND OUT WHO'S BEHIND THIS.
WAIT! IF THAT'S ALL WE WANT, I COULD--
SHIT. WHY DOES SHE NEVER LISTEN?
♫ IT WAS ON THE GOOD SHIP VENUS... ♫
'DAVE'
'PHIL'
OH MY GOD.
MOON BASE3
"SORRY TO BOTHER YOU, MA'AM..."
...I JUST WONDERED... WHO WAS THE CLIENT ON THE GORILLA MISSION? NO REASON, JUST CURIOUS.
HURM. ACTUALLY, IT WAS AN IN-HOUSE COMMISSION.
WE GOT WIND OF SOMEONE TRYING TO REPLICATE OUR NANOTECH.
EVE'S JOB WAS TO NEUTRALIZE THE ESCAPED EXPERIMENT. WE'VE GOT THE REST IN HAND.
IN HAND? HOW DO YOU--?
OH.

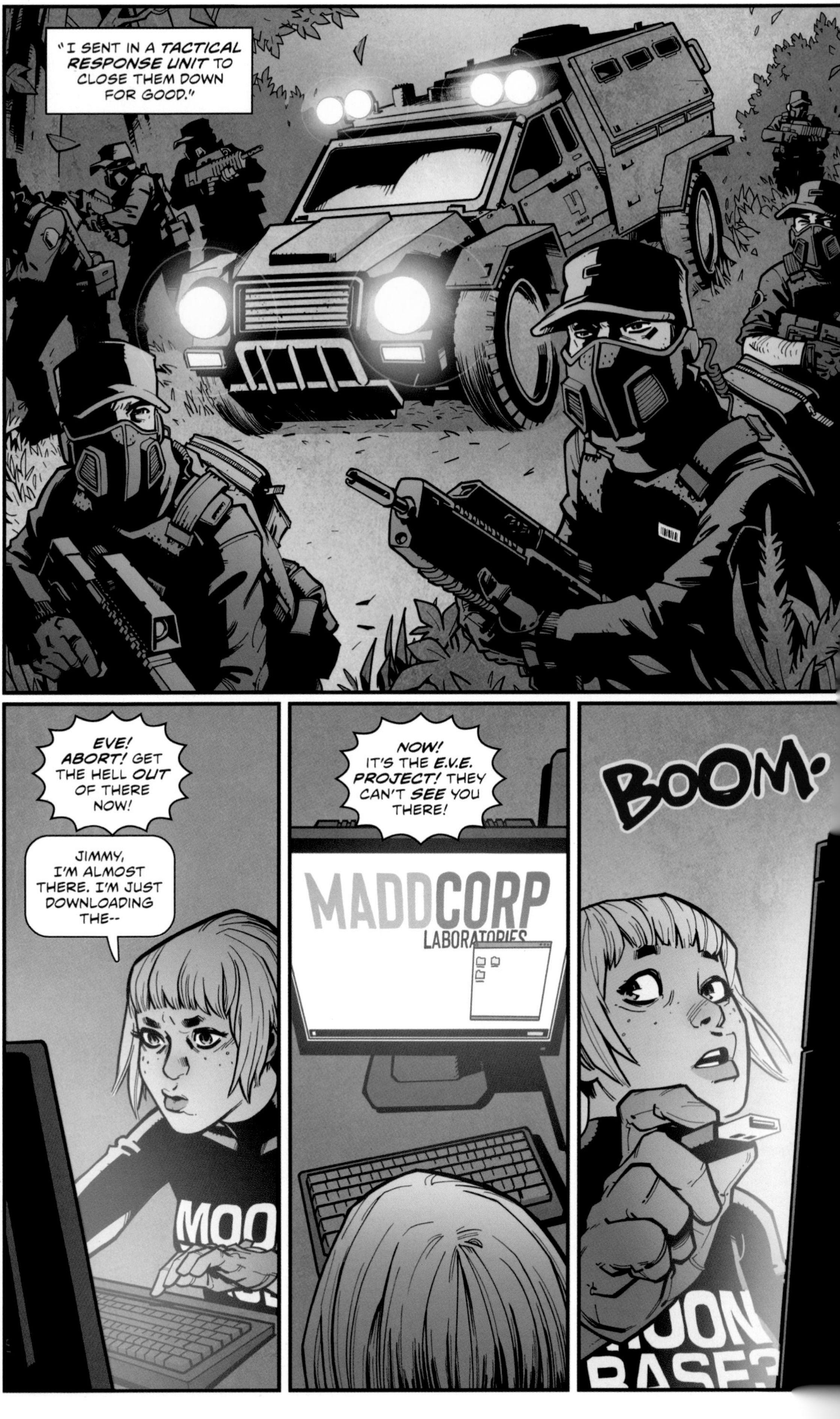

"I SENT IN A TACTICAL RESPONSE UNIT TO CLOSE THEM DOWN FOR GOOD."
EVE! ABORT! GET THE HELL OUT OF THERE NOW!
JIMMY, I'M ALMOST THERE. I'M JUST DOWNLOADING THE--
NOW! IT'S THE E.V.E. PROJECT! THEY CAN'T SEE YOU THERE!
MADDCORP
LABORATORIES
BOOM.

SHE'S OUT!

● 452784 332 23633.0804

IT'S ALL *ON* HERE. THE PLACE IS OWNED BY AN ORGANIZATION CALLED *MADDCORP.* THE FILES WERE BURIED DEEP.

HEY, ISN'T THAT THE COMPANY OWNED BY *SEBASTIAN MADDEN?* THE BILLIONAIRE *TECH* GUY?

I'LL TAKE CARE OF THAT. EVE, YOU *NEED* TO GET BACK TO PRAGUE. IT'S ONLY TWO HOURS UNTIL MIDNIGHT.

NOW AREN'T YOU GLAD I *MADE* YOU CARRY THIS? I'LL BE BACK WITH TIME TO HAVE A MOJITO *NIGHTCAP.*

OH, AND YOU'RE GOING TO LOOK INTO THIS *MADDCORP* THING FOR ME, RIGHT? AND TAKE CARE OF SAMANTHA?

I'LL GET HER SOMEWHERE SAFE WHILE WE DECIDE WHAT TO DO NEXT.

I'LL SEE YOU IN LONDON, THEN, I GUESS.

YEAH, *TRY* NOT TO BUST MY NOSE.

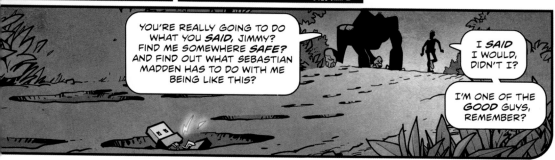

YOU'RE REALLY GOING TO DO WHAT YOU *SAID,* JIMMY? FIND ME SOMEWHERE *SAFE?* AND FIND OUT WHAT SEBASTIAN MADDEN HAS TO DO WITH ME BEING LIKE THIS?

I *SAID* I WOULD, DIDN'T I?

I'M ONE OF THE *GOOD* GUYS, REMEMBER?

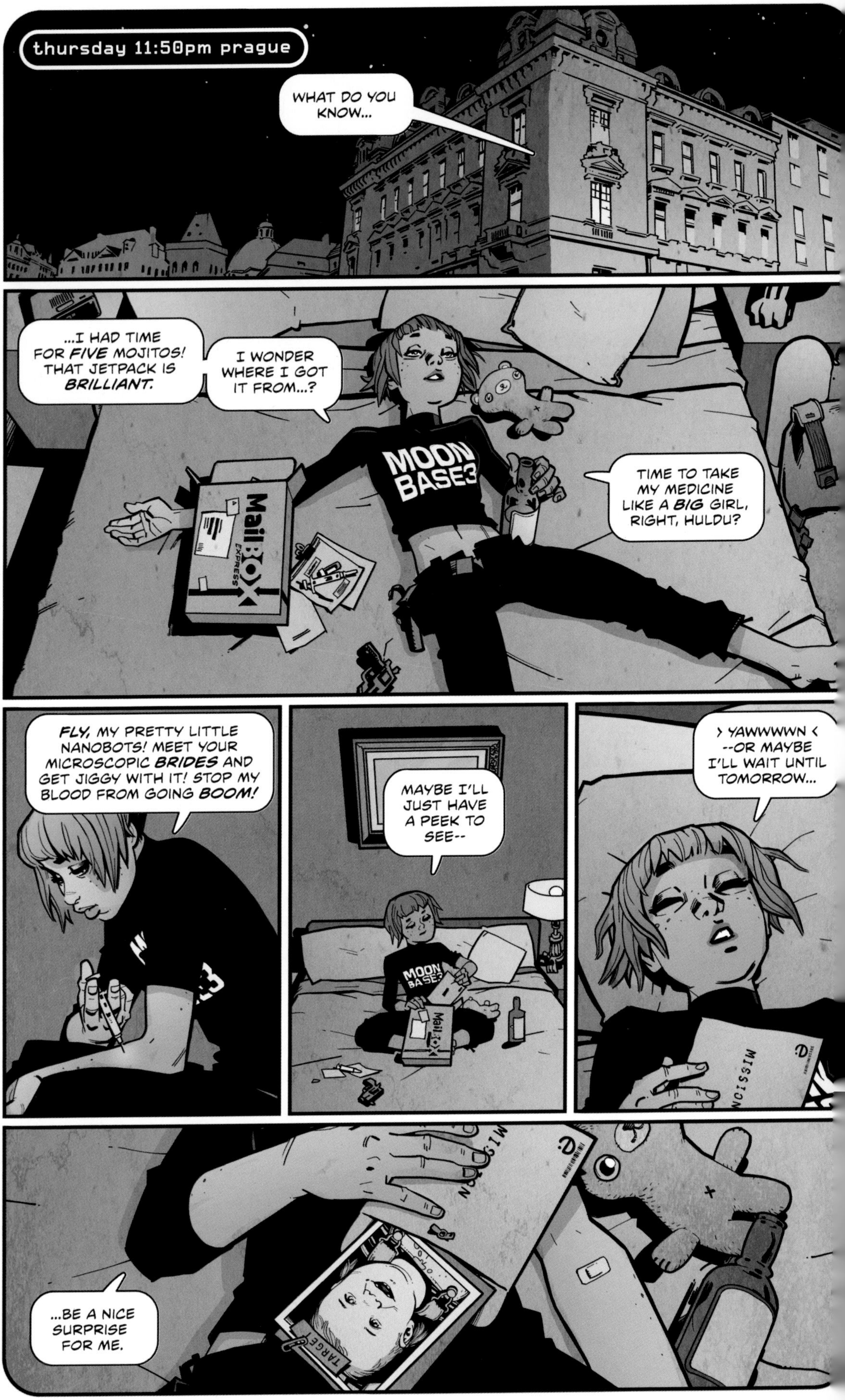
thursday 11:50pm prague
WHAT DO YOU KNOW...
...I HAD TIME FOR FIVE MOJITOS! THAT JETPACK IS BRILLIANT.
I WONDER WHERE I GOT IT FROM...?
MOON BASE3
MailBOX EXPRESS
TIME TO TAKE MY MEDICINE LIKE A BIG GIRL, RIGHT, HULDU?
FLY, MY PRETTY LITTLE NANOBOTS! MEET YOUR MICROSCOPIC BRIDES AND GET JIGGY WITH IT! STOP MY BLOOD FROM GOING BOOM!
MAYBE I'LL JUST HAVE A PEEK TO SEE--
> YAWWWWN < --OR MAYBE I'LL WAIT UNTIL TOMORROW...
MISSION
TARGET
...BE A NICE SURPRISE FOR ME.

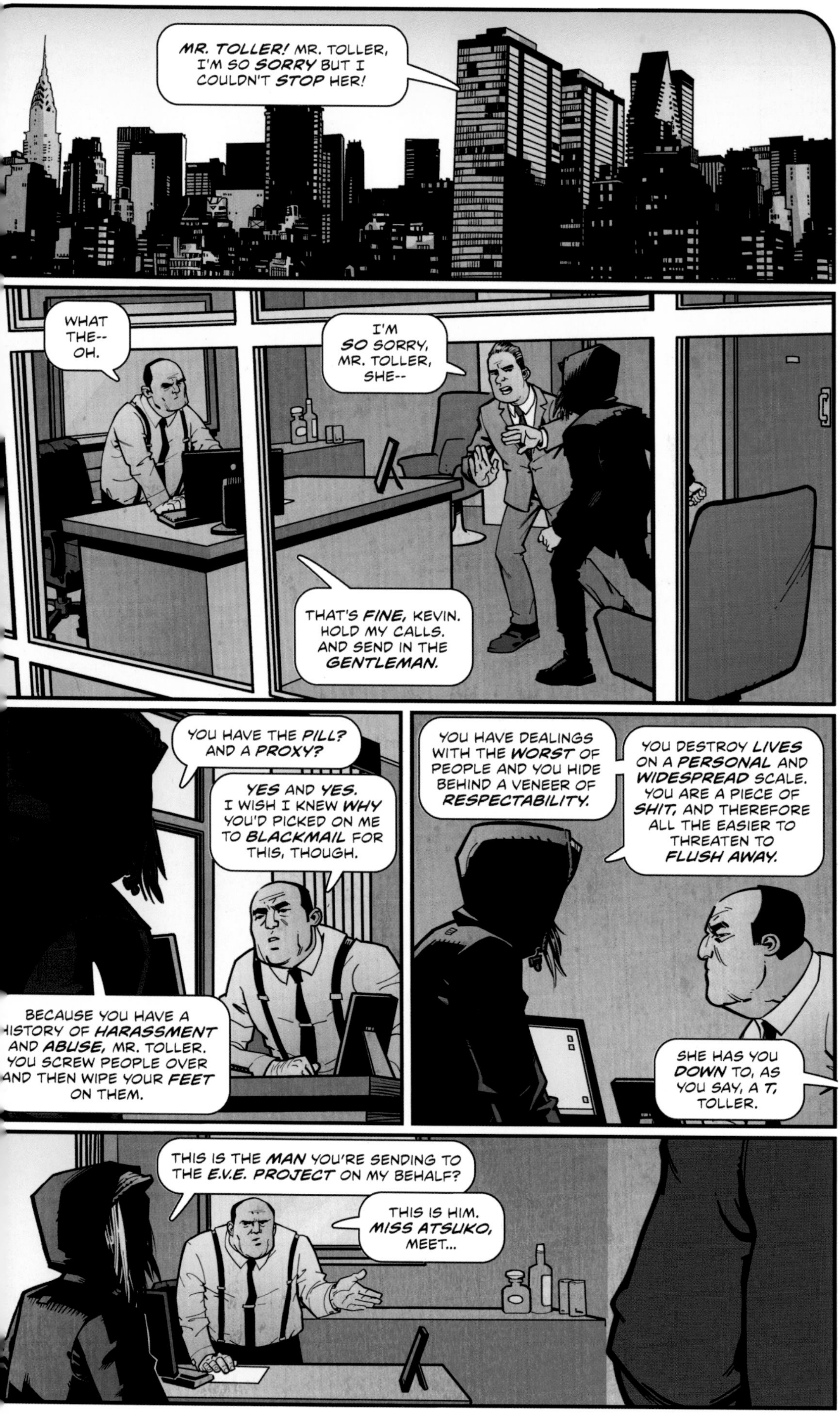
MR. TOLLER! MR. TOLLER, I'M SO SORRY BUT I COULDN'T STOP HER!
WHAT THE-- OH.
I'M SO SORRY, MR. TOLLER, SHE--
THAT'S FINE, KEVIN. HOLD MY CALLS. AND SEND IN THE GENTLEMAN.
YOU HAVE THE PILL? AND A PROXY?
YES AND YES. I WISH I KNEW WHY YOU'D PICKED ON ME TO BLACKMAIL FOR THIS, THOUGH.
BECAUSE YOU HAVE A HISTORY OF HARASSMENT AND ABUSE, MR. TOLLER. YOU SCREW PEOPLE OVER AND THEN WIPE YOUR FEET ON THEM.
YOU HAVE DEALINGS WITH THE WORST OF PEOPLE AND YOU HIDE BEHIND A VENEER OF RESPECTABILITY.
YOU DESTROY LIVES ON A PERSONAL AND WIDESPREAD SCALE. YOU ARE A PIECE OF SHIT, AND THEREFORE ALL THE EASIER TO THREATEN TO FLUSH AWAY.
SHE HAS YOU DOWN TO, AS YOU SAY, A T, TOLLER.
THIS IS THE MAN YOU'RE SENDING TO THE E.V.E. PROJECT ON MY BEHALF?
THIS IS HIM. MISS ATSUKO, MEET...

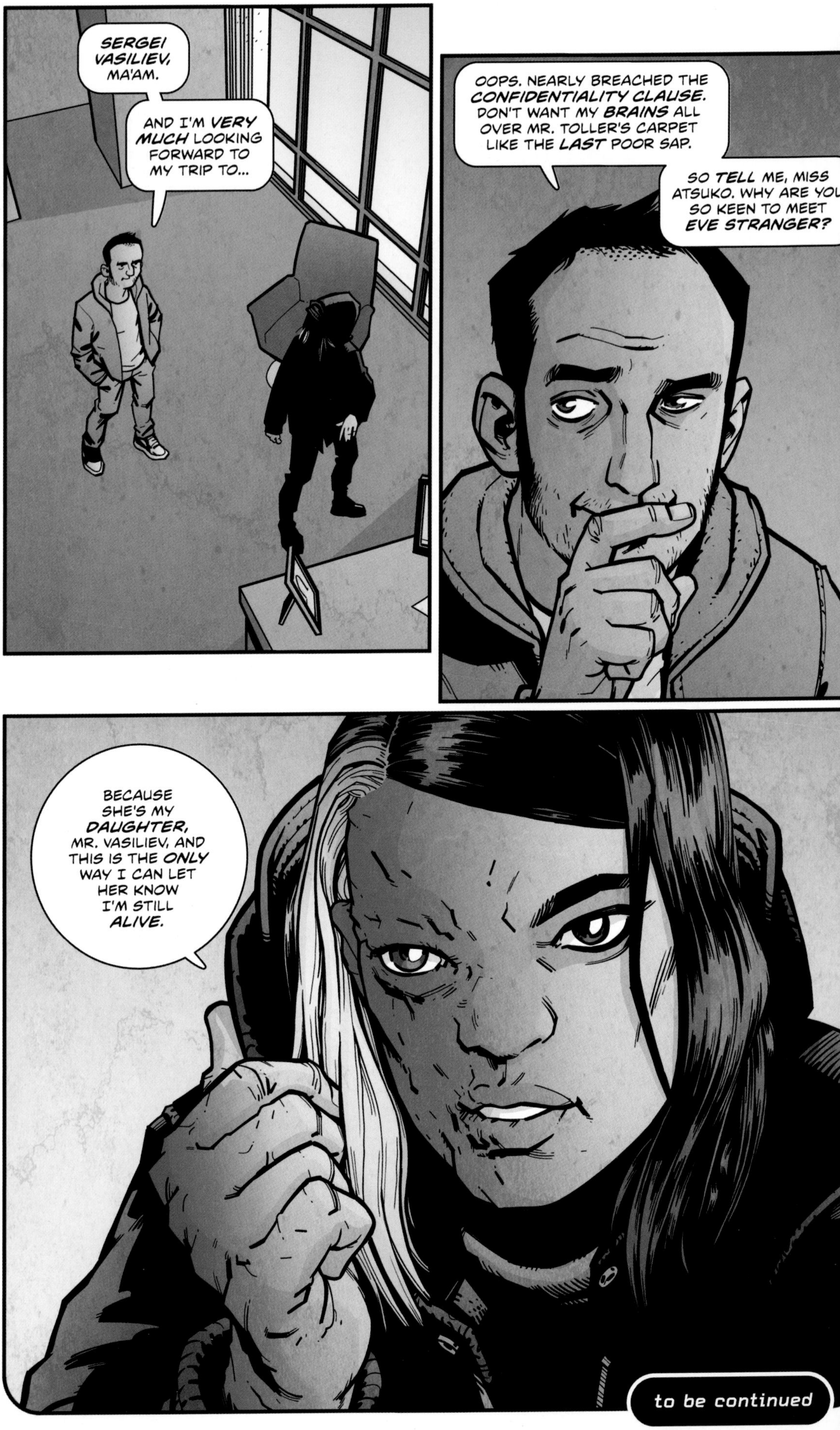
SERGEI VASILIEV, MA'AM.
AND I'M VERY MUCH LOOKING FORWARD TO MY TRIP TO...
OOPS. NEARLY BREACHED THE CONFIDENTIALITY CLAUSE. DON'T WANT MY BRAINS ALL OVER MR. TOLLER'S CARPET LIKE THE LAST POOR SAP.
SO TELL ME, MISS ATSUKO. WHY ARE YOU SO KEEN TO MEET EVE STRANGER?
BECAUSE SHE'S MY DAUGHTER, MR. VASILIEV, AND THIS IS THE ONLY WAY I CAN LET HER KNOW I'M STILL ALIVE.
to be continued

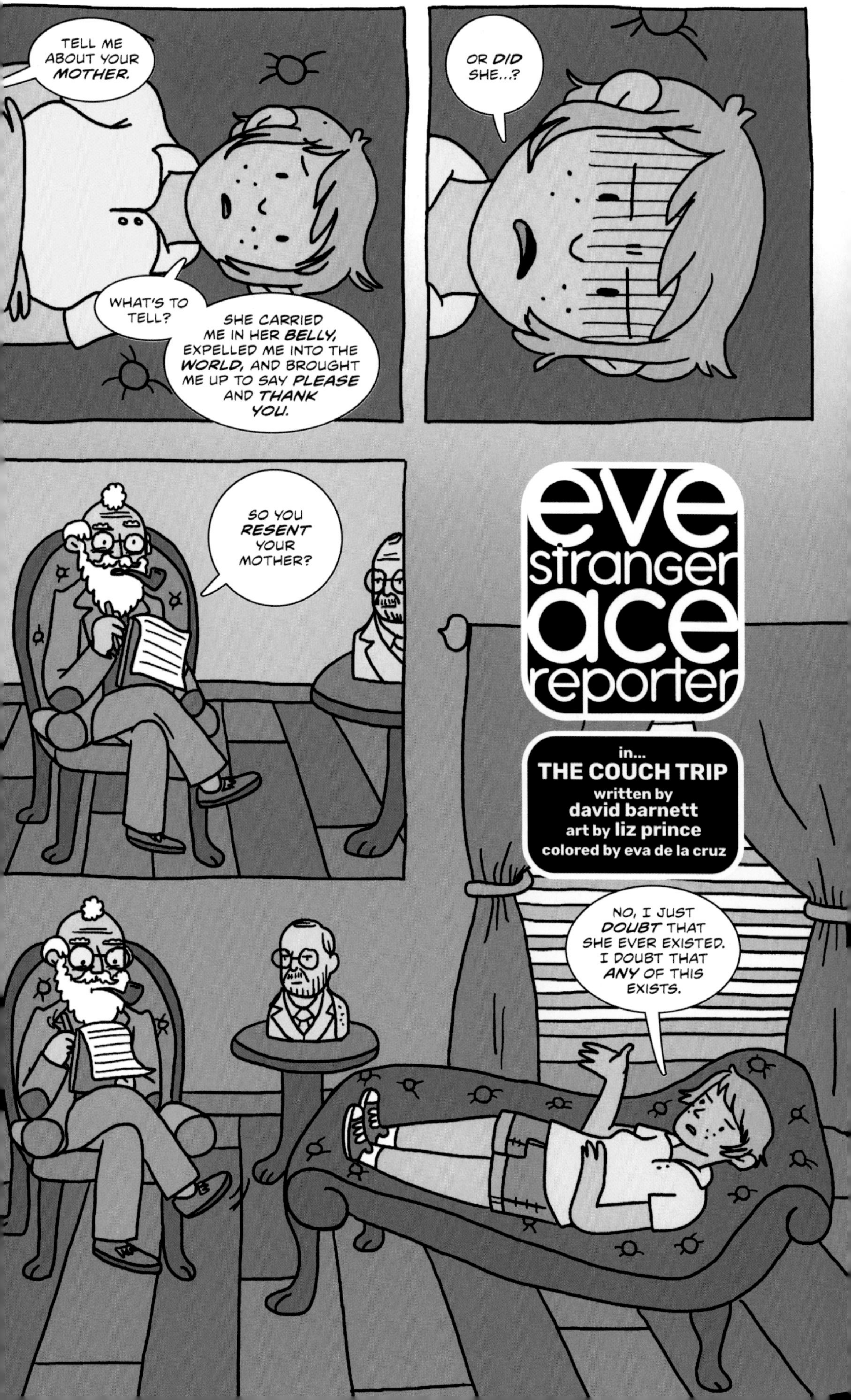
TELL ME ABOUT YOUR MOTHER.
WHAT'S TO TELL?
SHE CARRIED ME IN HER BELLY, EXPELLED ME INTO THE WORLD, AND BROUGHT ME UP TO SAY PLEASE AND THANK YOU.
OR DID SHE...?
SO YOU RESENT YOUR MOTHER?
eve stranger ace reporter
in... THE COUCH TRIP
written by david barnett
art by liz prince
colored by eva de la cruz
NO, I JUST DOUBT THAT SHE EVER EXISTED. I DOUBT THAT ANY OF THIS EXISTS.

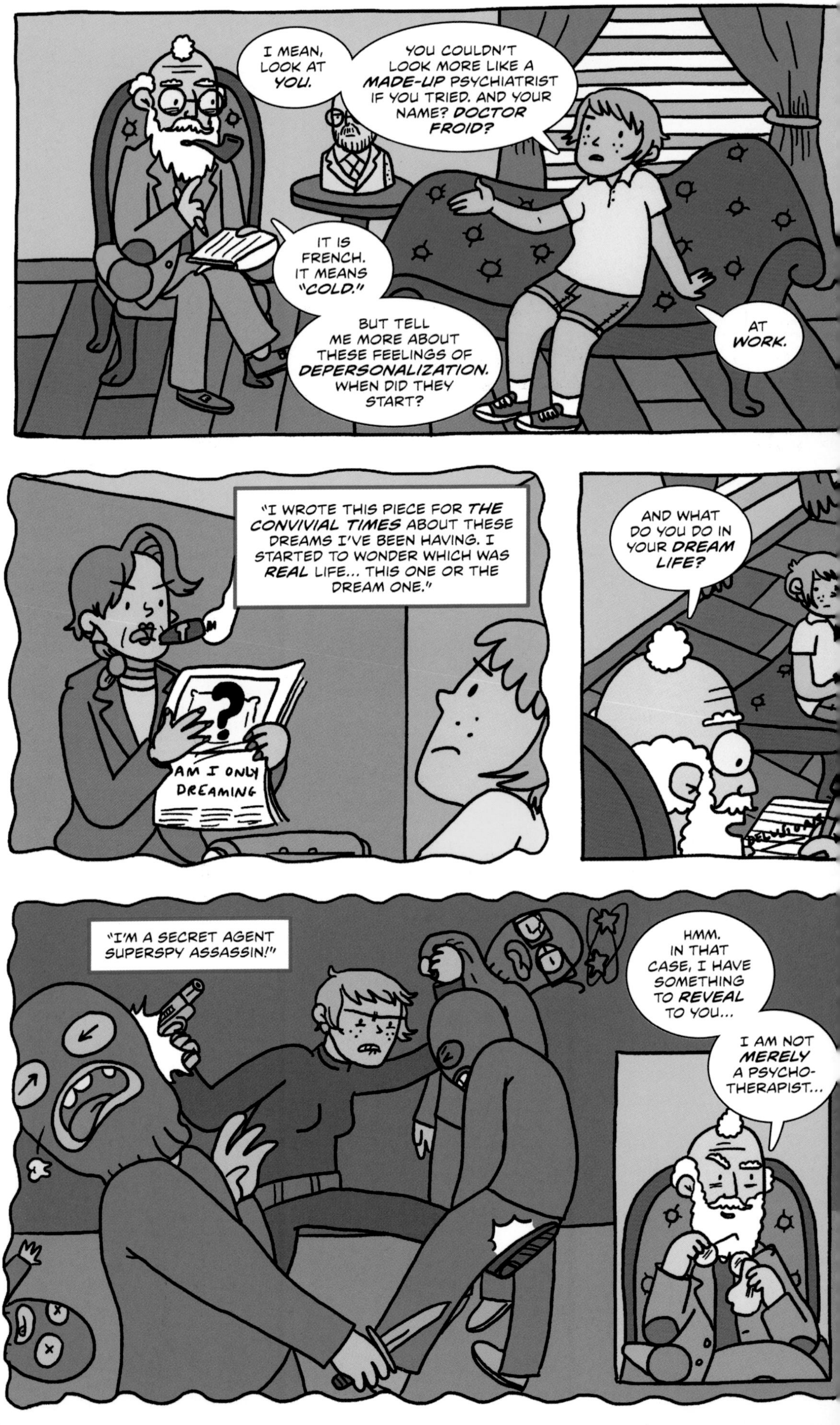
I MEAN, LOOK AT YOU.
YOU COULDN'T LOOK MORE LIKE A MADE-UP PSYCHIATRIST IF YOU TRIED. AND YOUR NAME? DOCTOR FROID?
IT IS FRENCH. IT MEANS "COLD."
BUT TELL ME MORE ABOUT THESE FEELINGS OF DEPERSONALIZATION. WHEN DID THEY START?
AT WORK.
"I WROTE THIS PIECE FOR THE CONVIVIAL TIMES ABOUT THESE DREAMS I'VE BEEN HAVING. I STARTED TO WONDER WHICH WAS REAL LIFE... THIS ONE OR THE DREAM ONE."
AM I ONLY DREAMING
AND WHAT DO YOU DO IN YOUR DREAM LIFE?
"I'M A SECRET AGENT SUPERSPY ASSASSIN!"
HMM. IN THAT CASE, I HAVE SOMETHING TO REVEAL TO YOU...
I AM NOT MERELY A PSYCHO-THERAPIST...

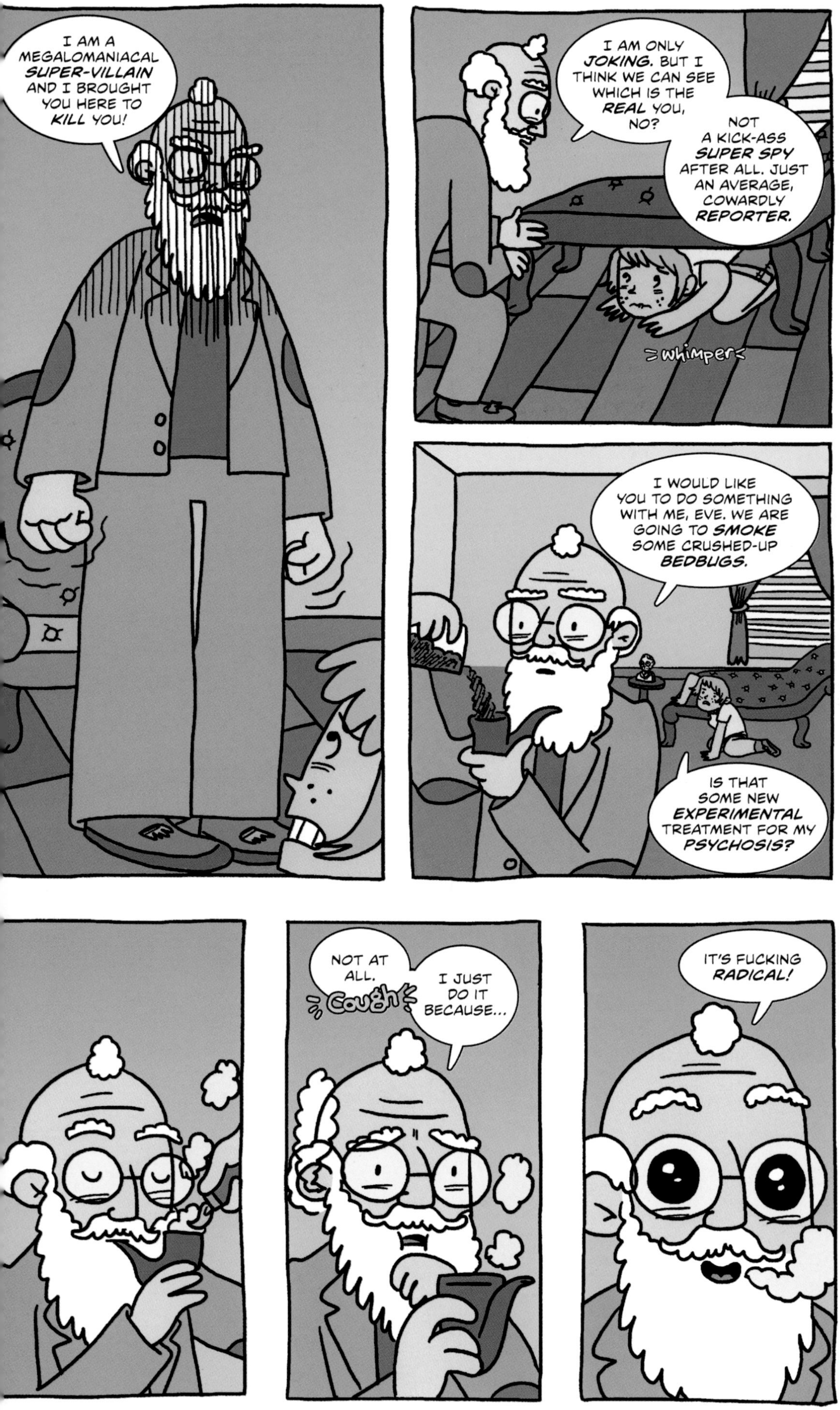

I AM A MEGALOMANIACAL SUPER-VILLAIN AND I BROUGHT YOU HERE TO KILL YOU!
I AM ONLY JOKING. BUT I THINK WE CAN SEE WHICH IS THE REAL YOU, NO?
NOT A KICK-ASS SUPER SPY AFTER ALL. JUST AN AVERAGE, COWARDLY REPORTER.
whimper
I WOULD LIKE YOU TO DO SOMETHING WITH ME, EVE. WE ARE GOING TO SMOKE SOME CRUSHED-UP BEDBUGS.
IS THAT SOME NEW EXPERIMENTAL TREATMENT FOR MY PSYCHOSIS?
NOT AT ALL.
Cough
I JUST DO IT BECAUSE...
IT'S FUCKING RADICAL!

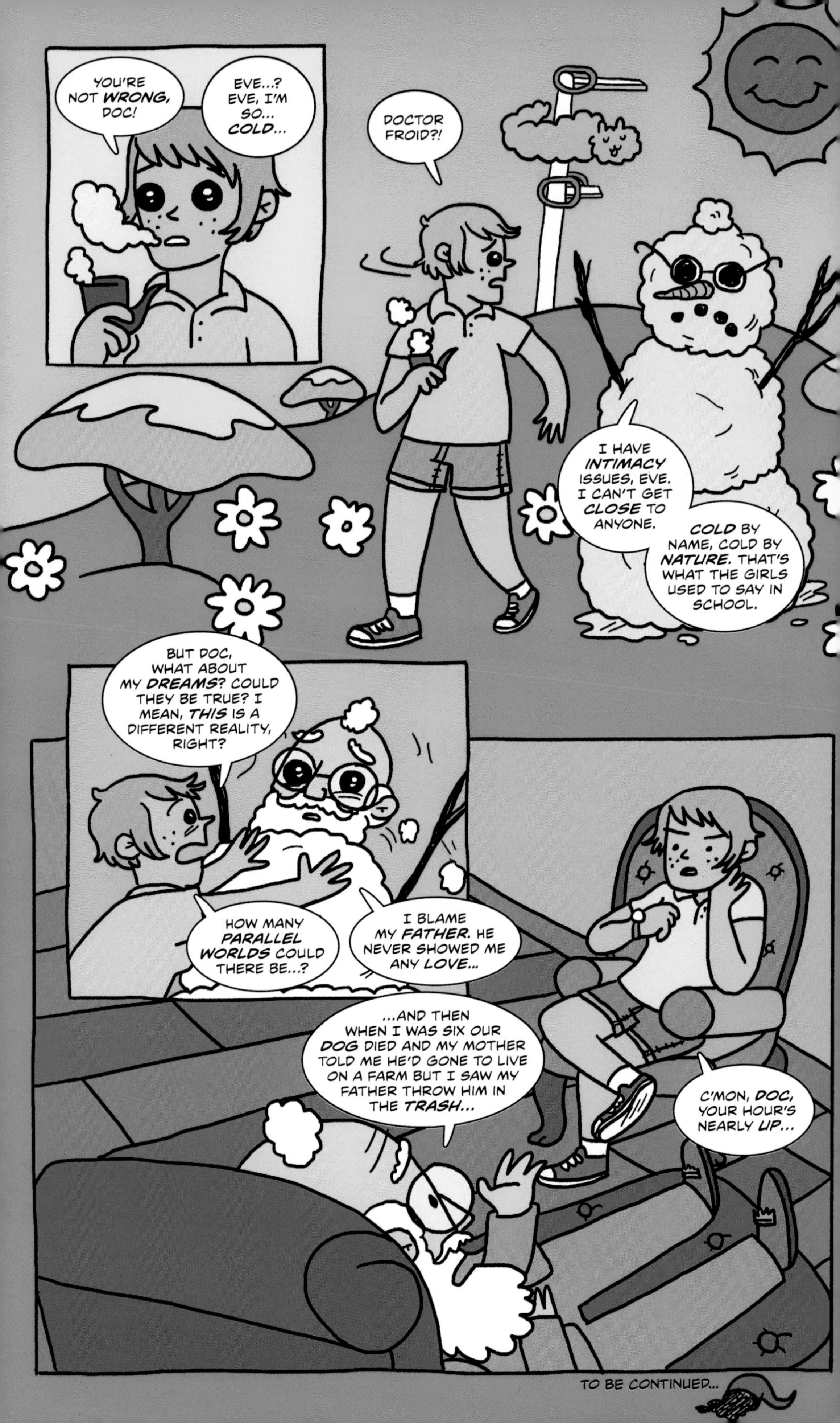
YOU'RE NOT WRONG, DOC!
EVE...? EVE, I'M SO... COLD...
DOCTOR FROID?!
I HAVE INTIMACY ISSUES, EVE. I CAN'T GET CLOSE TO ANYONE.
COLD BY NAME, COLD BY NATURE. THAT'S WHAT THE GIRLS USED TO SAY IN SCHOOL.
BUT DOC, WHAT ABOUT MY DREAMS? COULD THEY BE TRUE? I MEAN, THIS IS A DIFFERENT REALITY, RIGHT?
HOW MANY PARALLEL WORLDS COULD THERE BE...?
I BLAME MY FATHER. HE NEVER SHOWED ME ANY LOVE...
...AND THEN WHEN I WAS SIX OUR DOG DIED AND MY MOTHER TOLD ME HE'D GONE TO LIVE ON A FARM BUT I SAW MY FATHER THROW HIM IN THE TRASH...
C'MON, DOC, YOUR HOUR'S NEARLY UP...
TO BE CONTINUED...

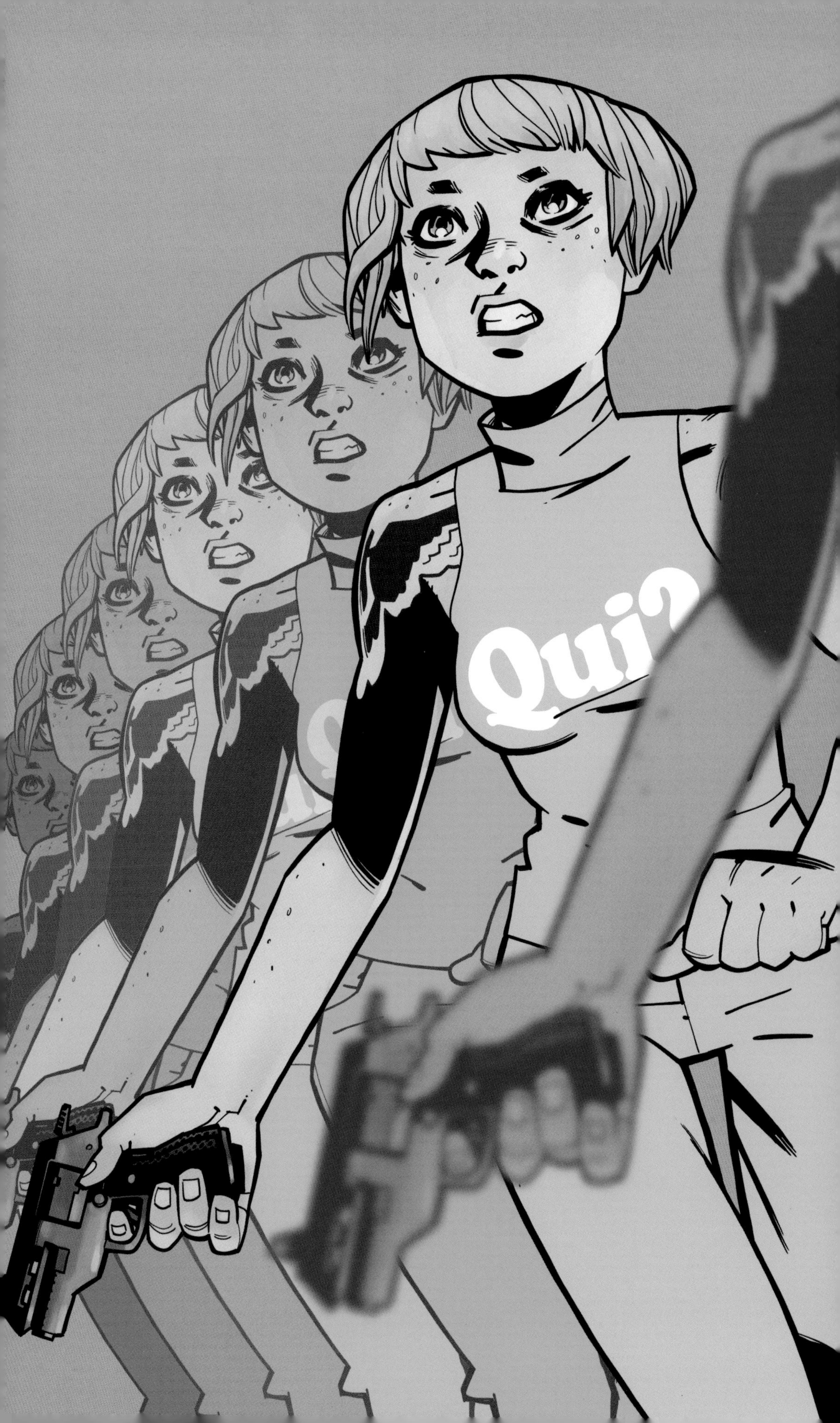
Qui?

part four:
IN THE
MIDNIGHT HOUR

"IT'S ALMOST
MIDNIGHT.
I CHANGED ALL
THE CLOCKS."

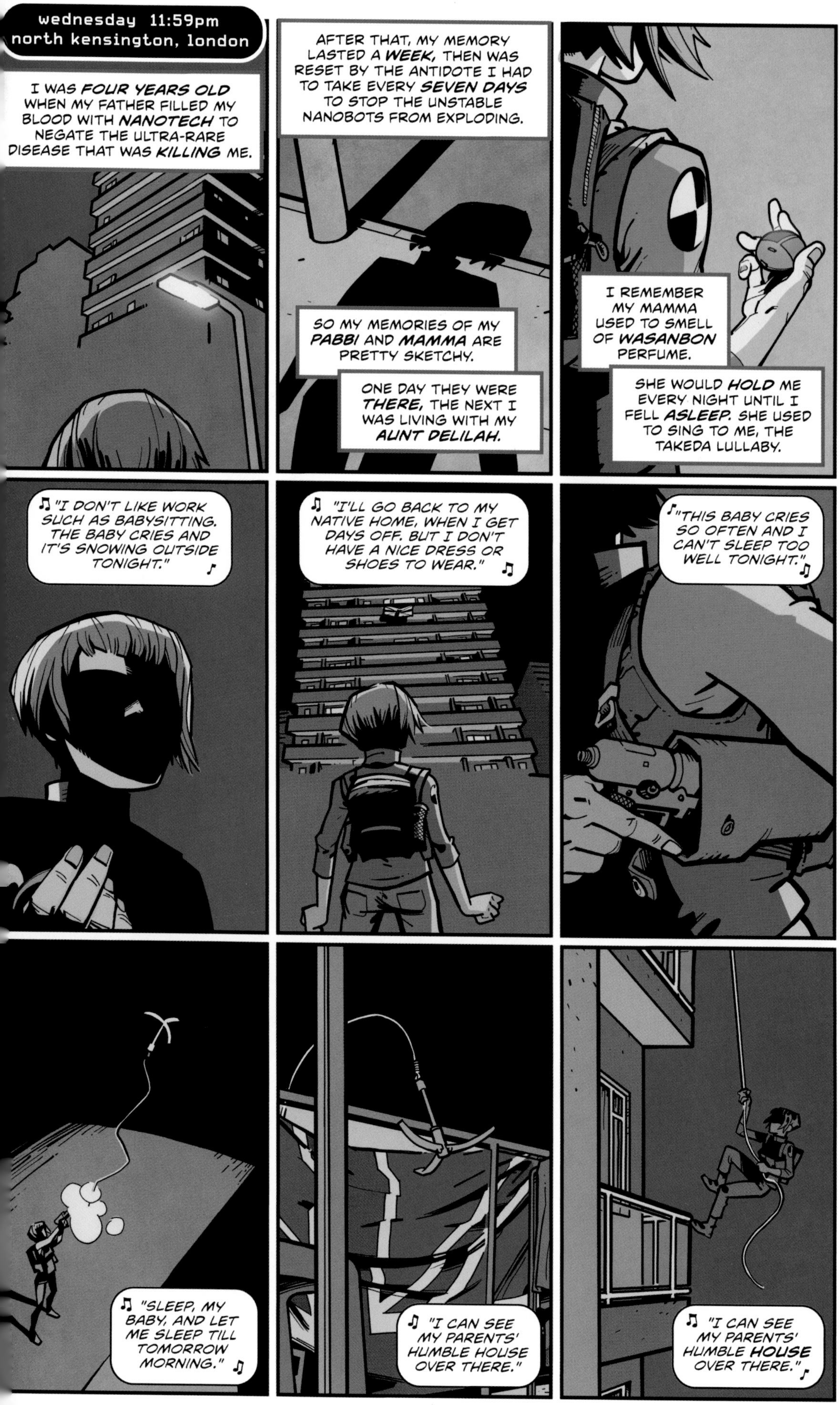

wednesday 11:59pm
north kensington, london
I WAS FOUR YEARS OLD WHEN MY FATHER FILLED MY BLOOD WITH NANOTECH TO NEGATE THE ULTRA-RARE DISEASE THAT WAS KILLING ME.
AFTER THAT, MY MEMORY LASTED A WEEK, THEN WAS RESET BY THE ANTIDOTE I HAD TO TAKE EVERY SEVEN DAYS TO STOP THE UNSTABLE NANOBOTS FROM EXPLODING.
SO MY MEMORIES OF MY PABBI AND MAMMA ARE PRETTY SKETCHY.
ONE DAY THEY WERE THERE, THE NEXT I WAS LIVING WITH MY AUNT DELILAH.
I REMEMBER MY MAMMA USED TO SMELL OF WASANBON PERFUME.
SHE WOULD HOLD ME EVERY NIGHT UNTIL I FELL ASLEEP. SHE USED TO SING TO ME, THE TAKEDA LULLABY.
♫ "I DON'T LIKE WORK SUCH AS BABYSITTING. THE BABY CRIES AND IT'S SNOWING OUTSIDE TONIGHT." ♪
♫ "I'LL GO BACK TO MY NATIVE HOME, WHEN I GET DAYS OFF. BUT I DON'T HAVE A NICE DRESS OR SHOES TO WEAR." ♫
♪ "THIS BABY CRIES SO OFTEN AND I CAN'T SLEEP TOO WELL TONIGHT." ♫
♫ "SLEEP, MY BABY, AND LET ME SLEEP TILL TOMORROW MORNING." ♫
♫ "I CAN SEE MY PARENTS' HUMBLE HOUSE OVER THERE."
♫ "I CAN SEE MY PARENTS' HUMBLE HOUSE OVER THERE." ♪

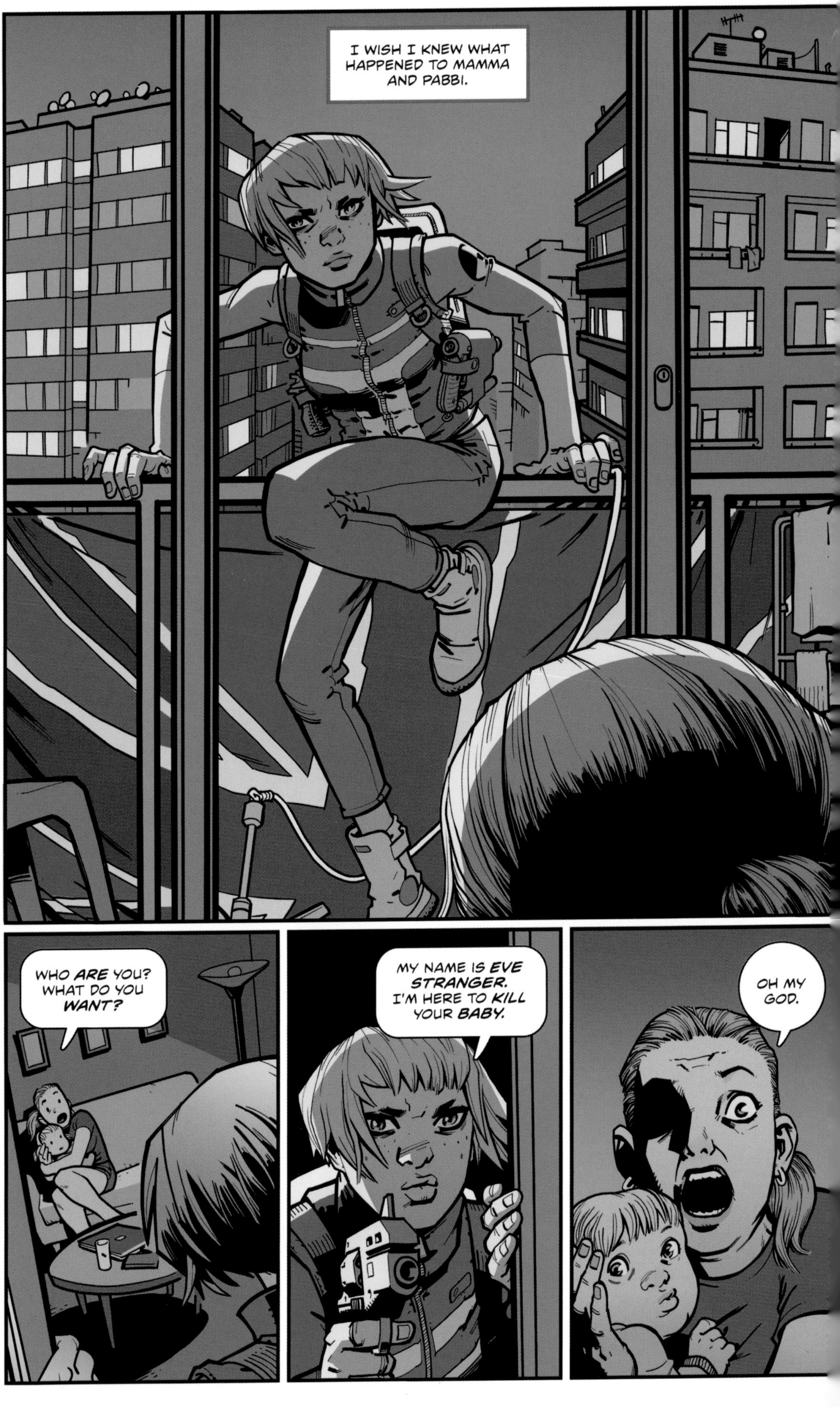
I WISH I KNEW WHAT HAPPENED TO MAMMA AND PABBI.
WHO ARE YOU? WHAT DO YOU WANT?
MY NAME IS EVE STRANGER. I'M HERE TO KILL YOUR BABY.
OH MY GOD.

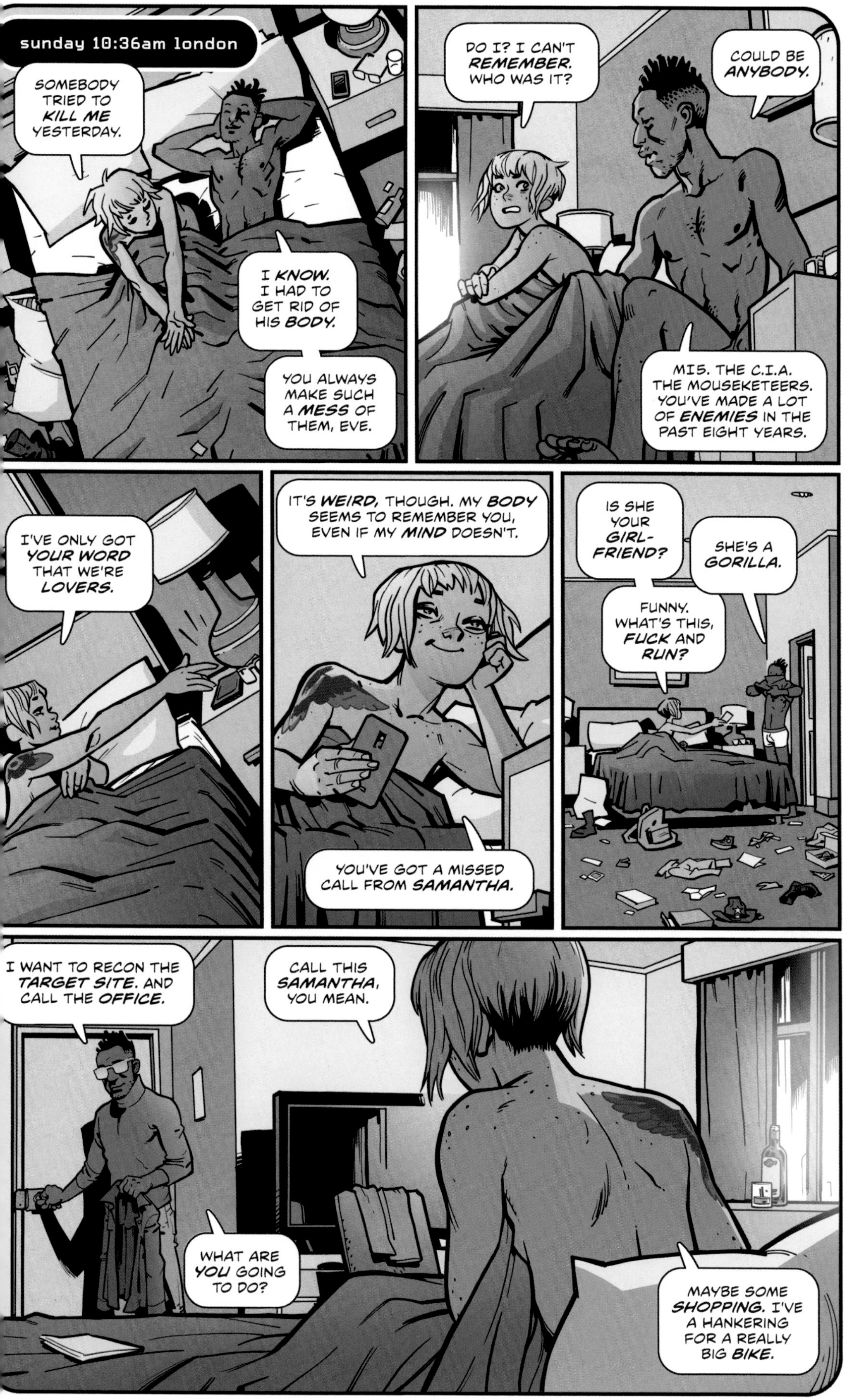
sunday 10:36am london
SOMEBODY TRIED TO KILL ME YESTERDAY.
I KNOW. I HAD TO GET RID OF HIS BODY.
YOU ALWAYS MAKE SUCH A MESS OF THEM, EVE.
DO I? I CAN'T REMEMBER. WHO WAS IT?
COULD BE ANYBODY.
MI5. THE C.I.A. THE MOUSEKETEERS. YOU'VE MADE A LOT OF ENEMIES IN THE PAST EIGHT YEARS.
I'VE ONLY GOT YOUR WORD THAT WE'RE LOVERS.
IT'S WEIRD, THOUGH. MY BODY SEEMS TO REMEMBER YOU, EVEN IF MY MIND DOESN'T.
YOU'VE GOT A MISSED CALL FROM SAMANTHA.
IS SHE YOUR GIRL-FRIEND?
SHE'S A GORILLA.
FUNNY. WHAT'S THIS, FUCK AND RUN?
I WANT TO RECON THE TARGET SITE. AND CALL THE OFFICE.
CALL THIS SAMANTHA, YOU MEAN.
WHAT ARE YOU GOING TO DO?
MAYBE SOME SHOPPING. I'VE A HANKERING FOR A REALLY BIG BIKE.

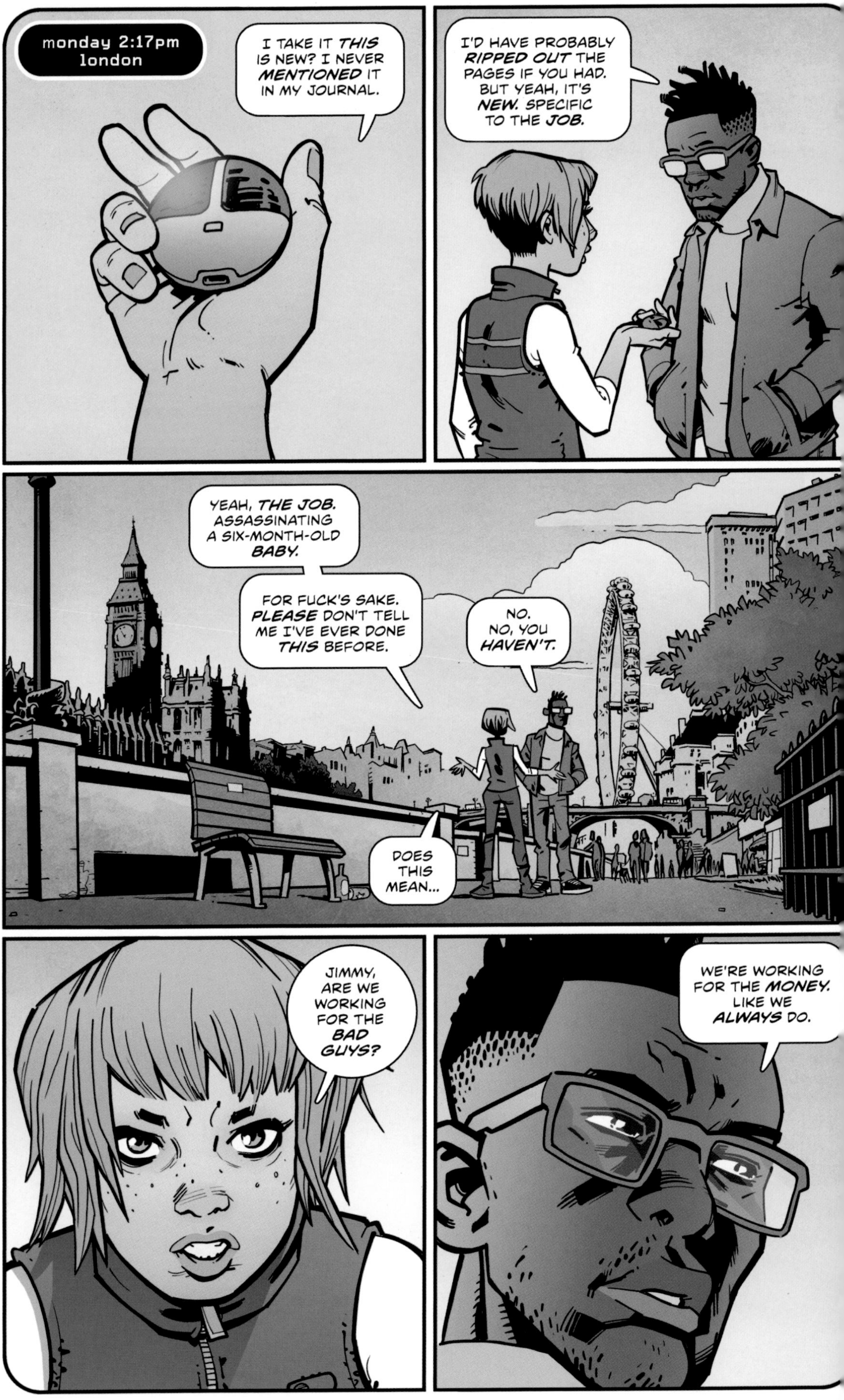
monday 2:17pm london
I TAKE IT THIS IS NEW? I NEVER MENTIONED IT IN MY JOURNAL.
I'D HAVE PROBABLY RIPPED OUT THE PAGES IF YOU HAD. BUT YEAH, IT'S NEW. SPECIFIC TO THE JOB.
YEAH, THE JOB. ASSASSINATING A SIX-MONTH-OLD BABY.
FOR FUCK'S SAKE. PLEASE DON'T TELL ME I'VE EVER DONE THIS BEFORE.
NO. NO, YOU HAVEN'T.
DOES THIS MEAN...
JIMMY, ARE WE WORKING FOR THE BAD GUYS?
WE'RE WORKING FOR THE MONEY. LIKE WE ALWAYS DO.

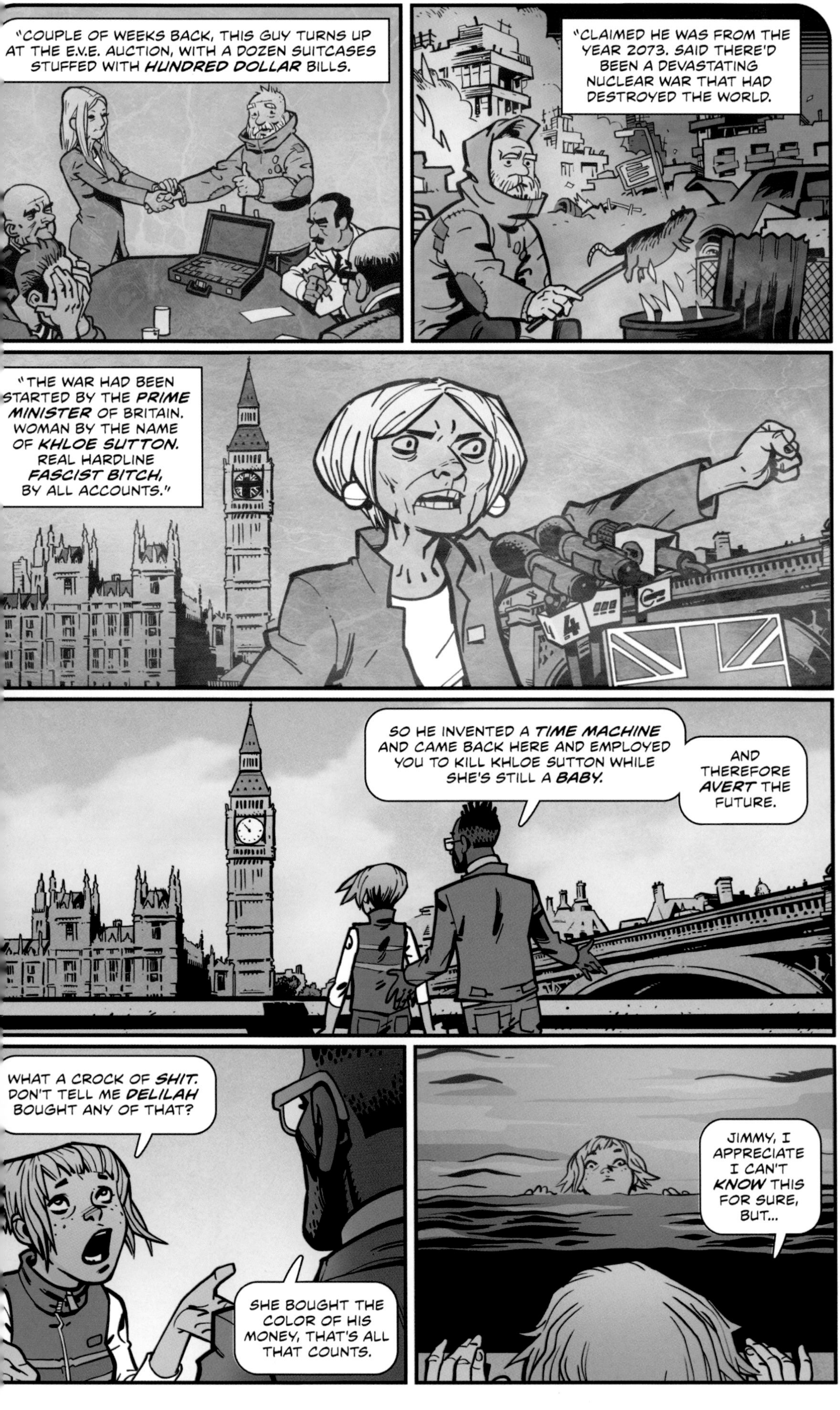
"COUPLE OF WEEKS BACK, THIS GUY TURNS UP AT THE E.V.E. AUCTION, WITH A DOZEN SUITCASES STUFFED WITH HUNDRED DOLLAR BILLS.
"CLAIMED HE WAS FROM THE YEAR 2073. SAID THERE'D BEEN A DEVASTATING NUCLEAR WAR THAT HAD DESTROYED THE WORLD.
"THE WAR HAD BEEN STARTED BY THE PRIME MINISTER OF BRITAIN. WOMAN BY THE NAME OF KHLOE SUTTON. REAL HARDLINE FASCIST BITCH, BY ALL ACCOUNTS."
SO HE INVENTED A TIME MACHINE AND CAME BACK HERE AND EMPLOYED YOU TO KILL KHLOE SUTTON WHILE SHE'S STILL A BABY.
AND THEREFORE AVERT THE FUTURE.
WHAT A CROCK OF SHIT. DON'T TELL ME DELILAH BOUGHT ANY OF THAT?
SHE BOUGHT THE COLOR OF HIS MONEY, THAT'S ALL THAT COUNTS.
JIMMY, I APPRECIATE I CAN'T KNOW THIS FOR SURE, BUT...

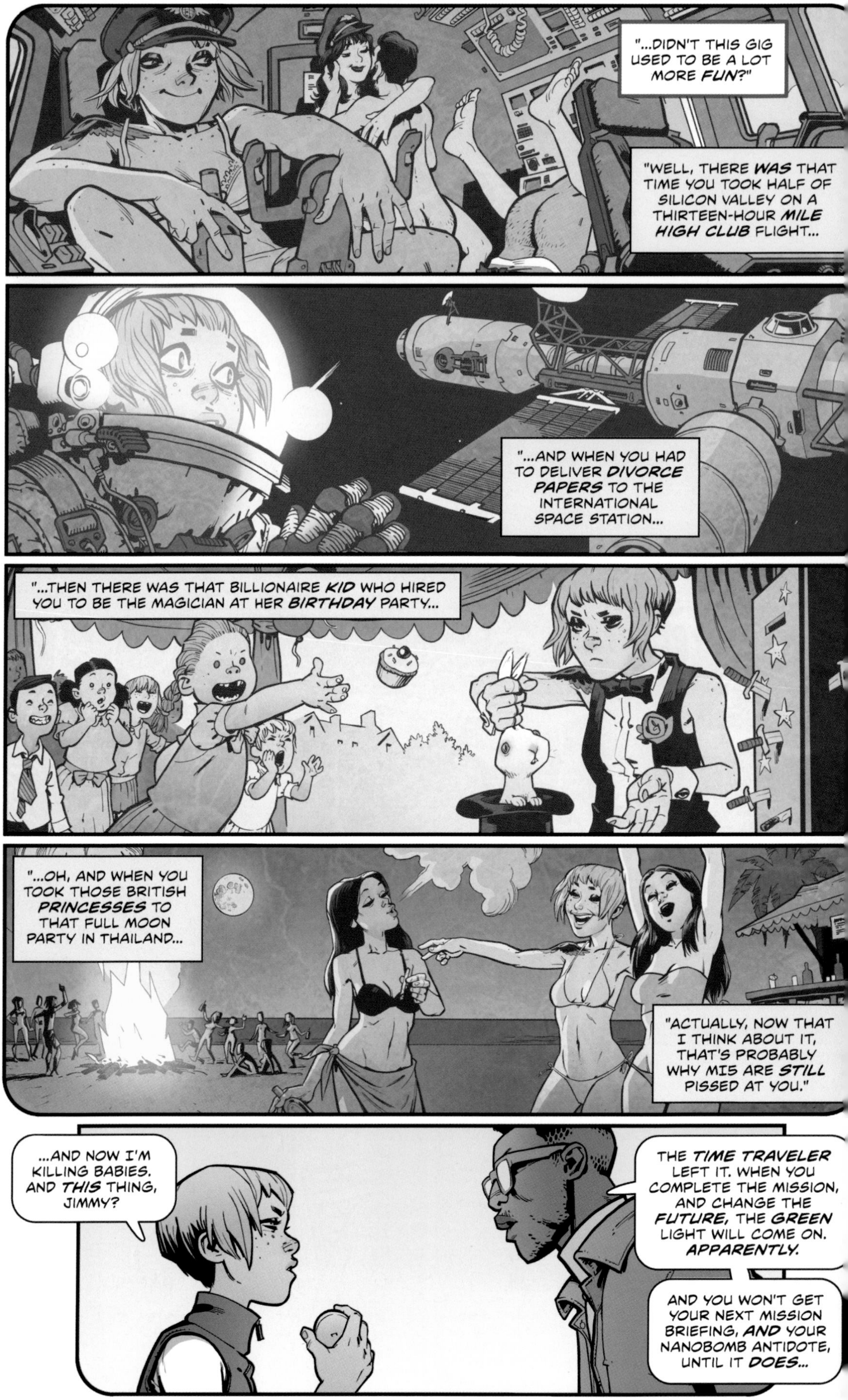
"...DIDN'T THIS GIG USED TO BE A LOT MORE FUN?"
"WELL, THERE WAS THAT TIME YOU TOOK HALF OF SILICON VALLEY ON A THIRTEEN-HOUR MILE HIGH CLUB FLIGHT...
"...AND WHEN YOU HAD TO DELIVER DIVORCE PAPERS TO THE INTERNATIONAL SPACE STATION...
"...THEN THERE WAS THAT BILLIONAIRE KID WHO HIRED YOU TO BE THE MAGICIAN AT HER BIRTHDAY PARTY...
"...OH, AND WHEN YOU TOOK THOSE BRITISH PRINCESSES TO THAT FULL MOON PARTY IN THAILAND...
"ACTUALLY, NOW THAT I THINK ABOUT IT, THAT'S PROBABLY WHY MI5 ARE STILL PISSED AT YOU."
...AND NOW I'M KILLING BABIES. AND THIS THING, JIMMY?
THE TIME TRAVELER LEFT IT. WHEN YOU COMPLETE THE MISSION, AND CHANGE THE FUTURE, THE GREEN LIGHT WILL COME ON. APPARENTLY.
AND YOU WON'T GET YOUR NEXT MISSION BRIEFING, AND YOUR NANOBOMB ANTIDOTE, UNTIL IT DOES...

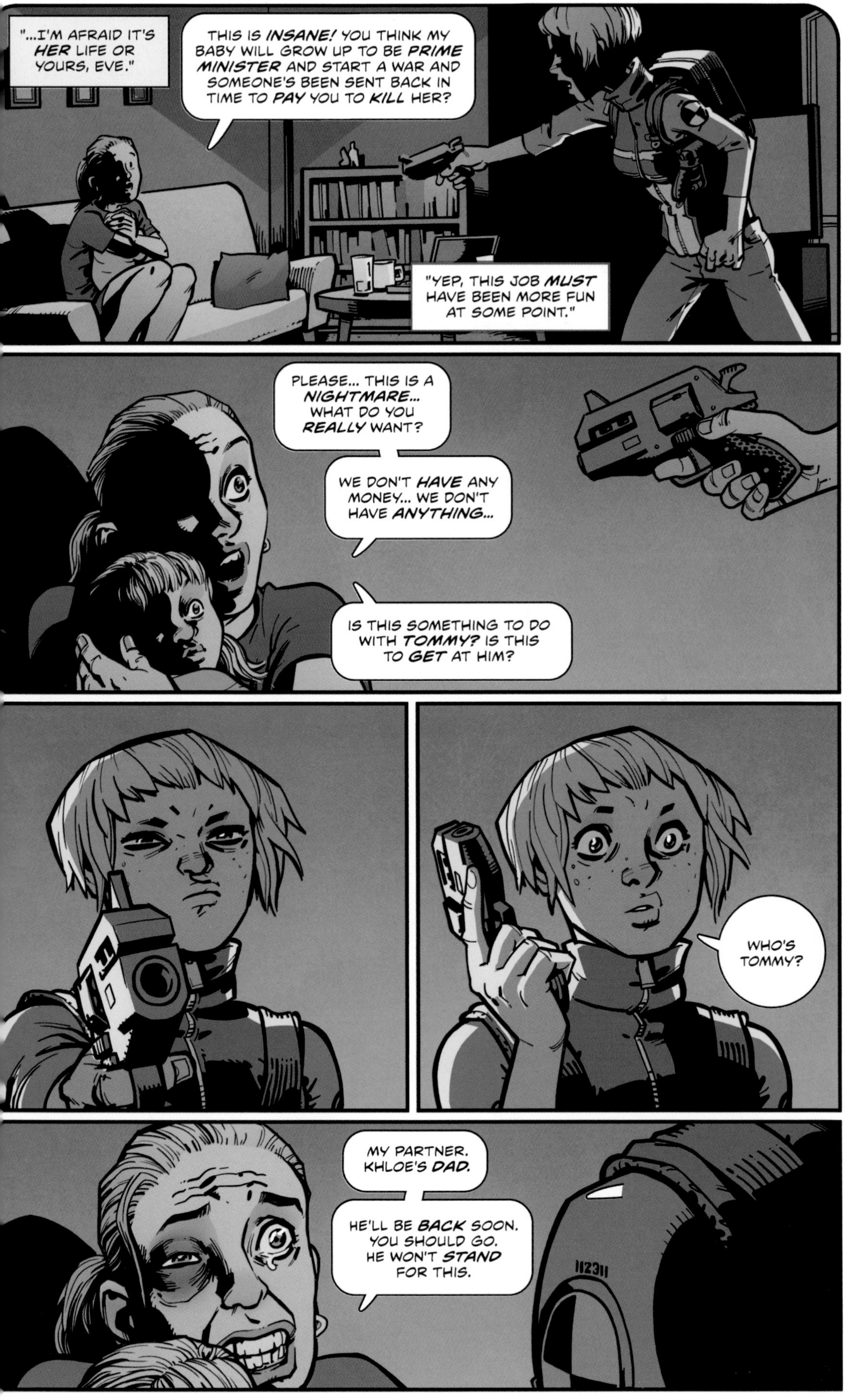
"...I'M AFRAID IT'S HER LIFE OR YOURS, EVE."
THIS IS INSANE! YOU THINK MY BABY WILL GROW UP TO BE PRIME MINISTER AND START A WAR AND SOMEONE'S BEEN SENT BACK IN TIME TO PAY YOU TO KILL HER?
"YEP, THIS JOB MUST HAVE BEEN MORE FUN AT SOME POINT."
PLEASE... THIS IS A NIGHTMARE... WHAT DO YOU REALLY WANT?
WE DON'T HAVE ANY MONEY... WE DON'T HAVE ANYTHING...
IS THIS SOMETHING TO DO WITH TOMMY? IS THIS TO GET AT HIM?
WHO'S TOMMY?
MY PARTNER. KHLOE'S DAD.
HE'LL BE BACK SOON. YOU SHOULD GO. HE WON'T STAND FOR THIS.

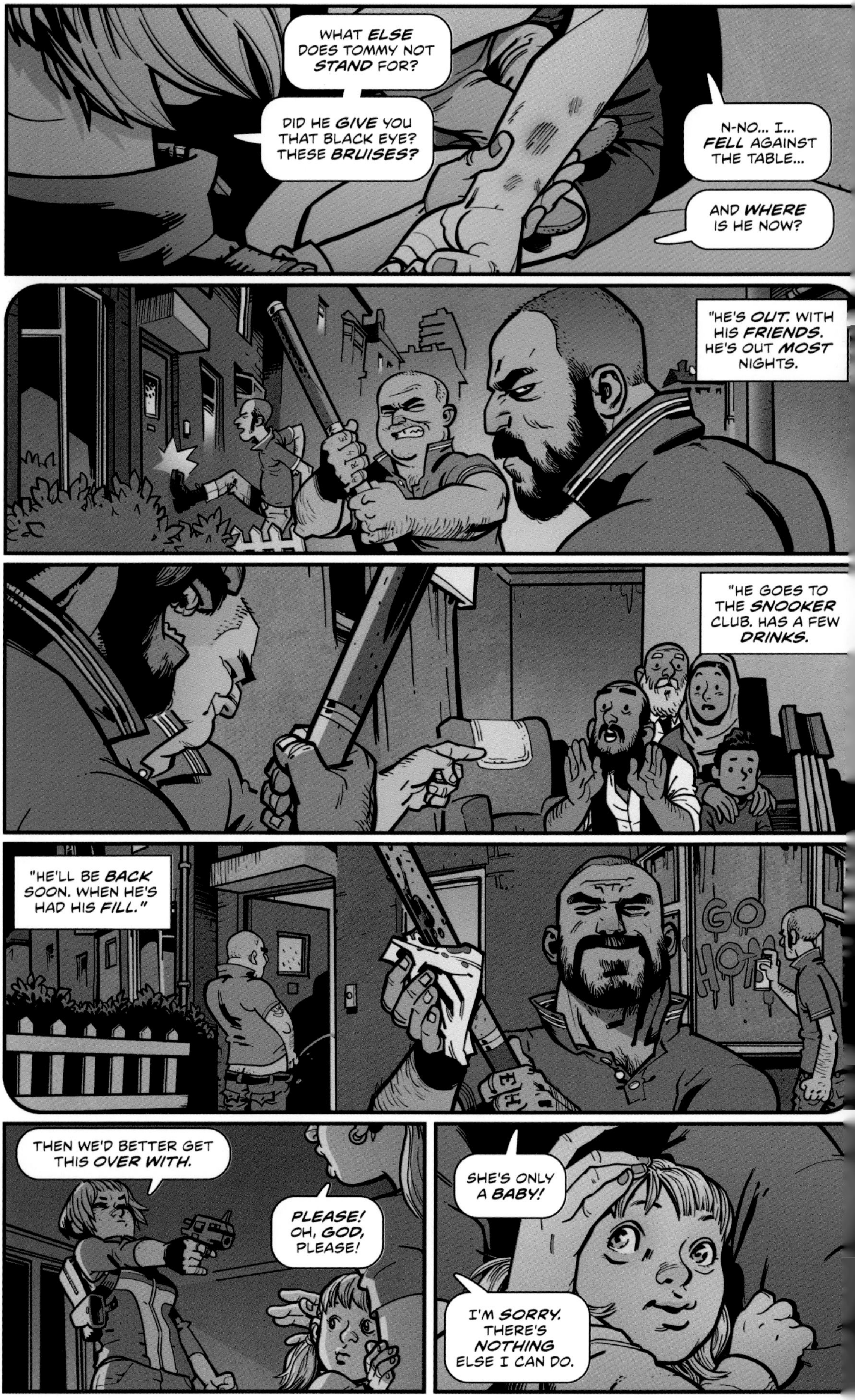
WHAT ELSE DOES TOMMY NOT STAND FOR?
DID HE GIVE YOU THAT BLACK EYE? THESE BRUISES?
N-NO... I... FELL AGAINST THE TABLE...
AND WHERE IS HE NOW?
"HE'S OUT. WITH HIS FRIENDS. HE'S OUT MOST NIGHTS.
"HE GOES TO THE SNOOKER CLUB. HAS A FEW DRINKS.
"HE'LL BE BACK SOON. WHEN HE'S HAD HIS FILL."
GO
THEN WE'D BETTER GET THIS OVER WITH.
PLEASE! OH, GOD, PLEASE!
SHE'S ONLY A BABY!
I'M SORRY. THERE'S NOTHING ELSE I CAN DO.

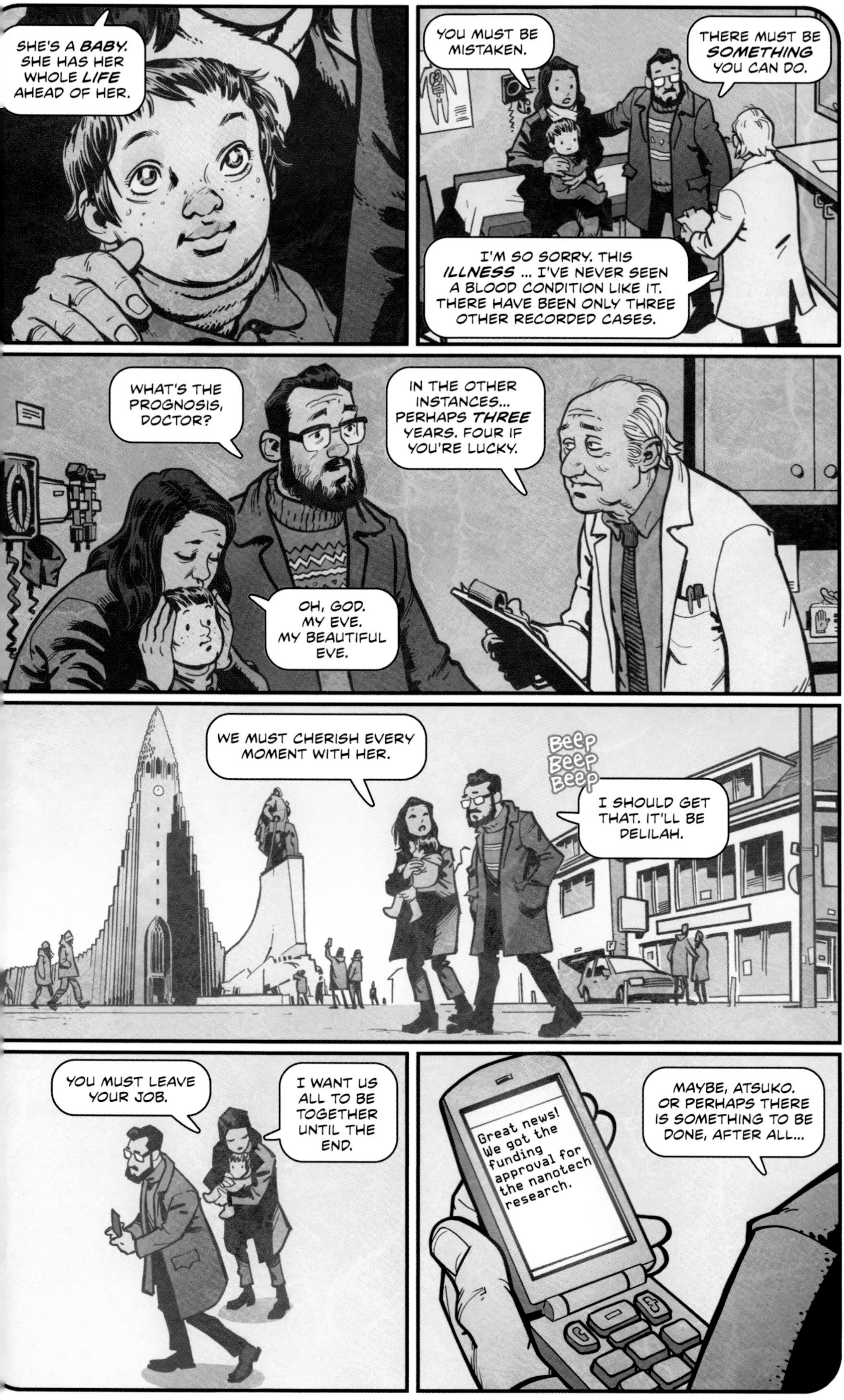
SHE'S A BABY. SHE HAS HER WHOLE LIFE AHEAD OF HER.
YOU MUST BE MISTAKEN.
THERE MUST BE SOMETHING YOU CAN DO.
I'M SO SORRY. THIS ILLNESS ... I'VE NEVER SEEN A BLOOD CONDITION LIKE IT. THERE HAVE BEEN ONLY THREE OTHER RECORDED CASES.
WHAT'S THE PROGNOSIS, DOCTOR?
IN THE OTHER INSTANCES... PERHAPS THREE YEARS. FOUR IF YOU'RE LUCKY.
OH, GOD. MY EVE. MY BEAUTIFUL EVE.
WE MUST CHERISH EVERY MOMENT WITH HER.
Beep Beep Beep
I SHOULD GET THAT. IT'LL BE DELILAH.
YOU MUST LEAVE YOUR JOB.
I WANT US ALL TO BE TOGETHER UNTIL THE END.
Great news! We got the funding approval for the nanotech research.
MAYBE, ATSUKO. OR PERHAPS THERE IS SOMETHING TO BE DONE, AFTER ALL...

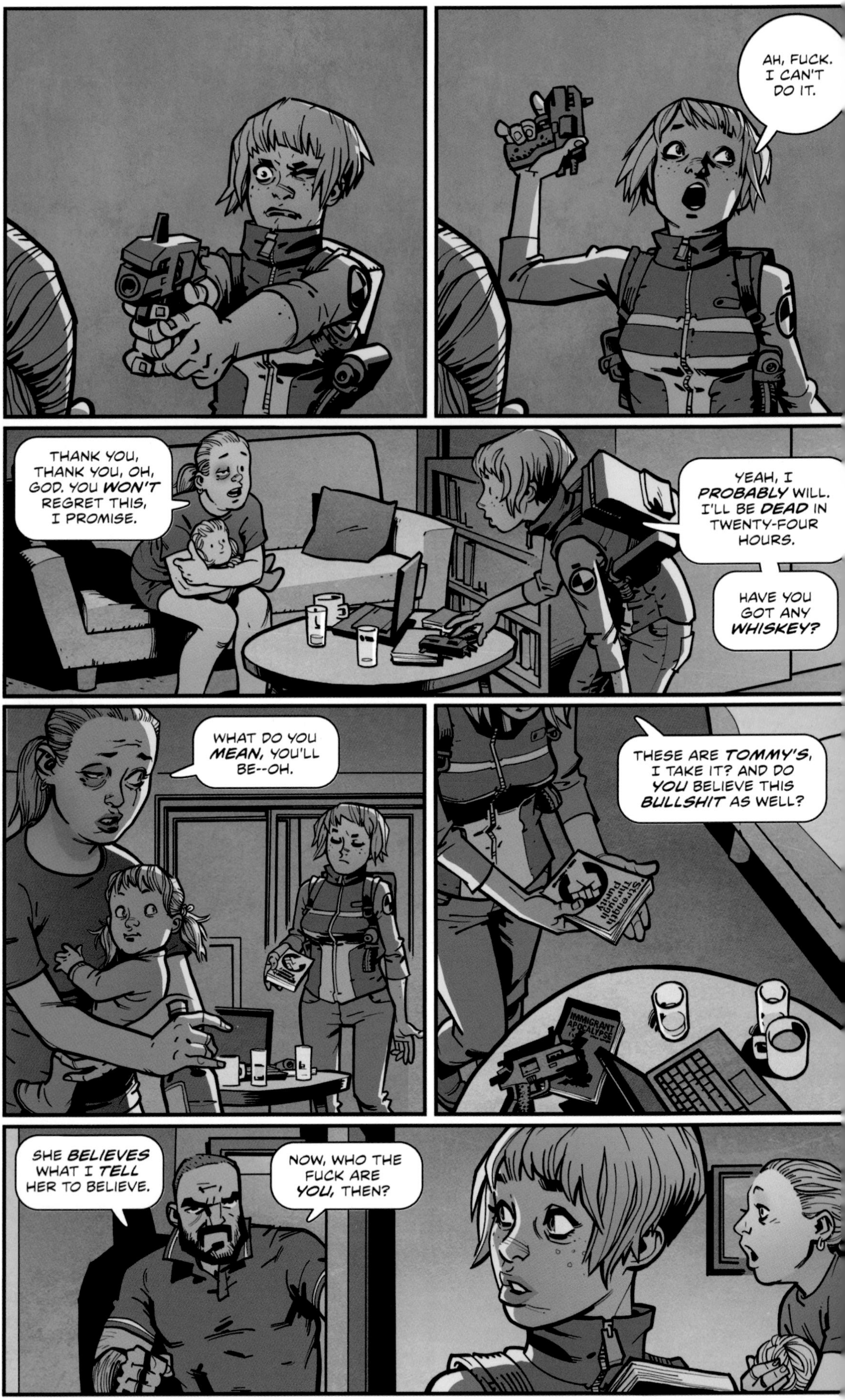
AH, FUCK. I CAN'T DO IT.
THANK YOU, THANK YOU, OH, GOD. YOU WON'T REGRET THIS, I PROMISE.
YEAH, I PROBABLY WILL. I'LL BE DEAD IN TWENTY-FOUR HOURS.
HAVE YOU GOT ANY WHISKEY?
WHAT DO YOU MEAN, YOU'LL BE--OH.
THESE ARE TOMMY'S, I TAKE IT? AND DO YOU BELIEVE THIS BULLSHIT AS WELL?
Strength Through Purity
IMMIGRANT APOCALYPSE
SHE BELIEVES WHAT I TELL HER TO BELIEVE.
NOW, WHO THE FUCK ARE YOU, THEN?

SHE'S **NOBODY**, TOMMY. SHE'S JUST **LEAVING**.

WELL, WELL, WELL, **THIS** IS A NICE **PIECE**.

AND **YOU'RE** NOT SO BAD, EITHER.

WHAT **ARE** YOU, ANYWAY? YOU'RE NOT **ENGLISH**.

MY MOTHER WAS **JAPANESE**. MY FATHER WAS **ICELANDIC**. THAT MUCH I CAN USUALLY REMEMBER.

VERY **EXOTIC**. SARA, PUT **KHLOE** DOWN WHILE I GET BETTER **ACQUAINTED** WITH YOUR FRIEND.

TOMMY, **PLEASE**, JUST LET HER **GO**.

DO AS YOU'RE FUCKING **TOLD**. AND DON'T **COME OUT** UNTIL I TELL YOU.

SO WHAT YOU **DOING** HERE? WHO **SENT** YOU? THAT **ANTI-FASCIST** MOB? TRY TO PUT THE **FRIGHTENERS** ON MY MISSUS?

TYPICAL OF THAT BUNCH OF **PUSSIES** TO SEND A BIT OF A GIRL TO DO A **MAN'S JOB**.

I CAME HERE TO **KILL** YOUR DAUGHTER.

MY **KHLOE?** YOU FUCKING **BITCH**.

IT'S FOR **HER** I DO WHAT I **DO**, SEE? MAKE THIS COUNTRY A **BETTER** PLACE FOR HER.

SO I CAN BRING HER UP **RIGHT** AND **PROPER**.

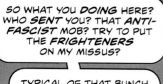

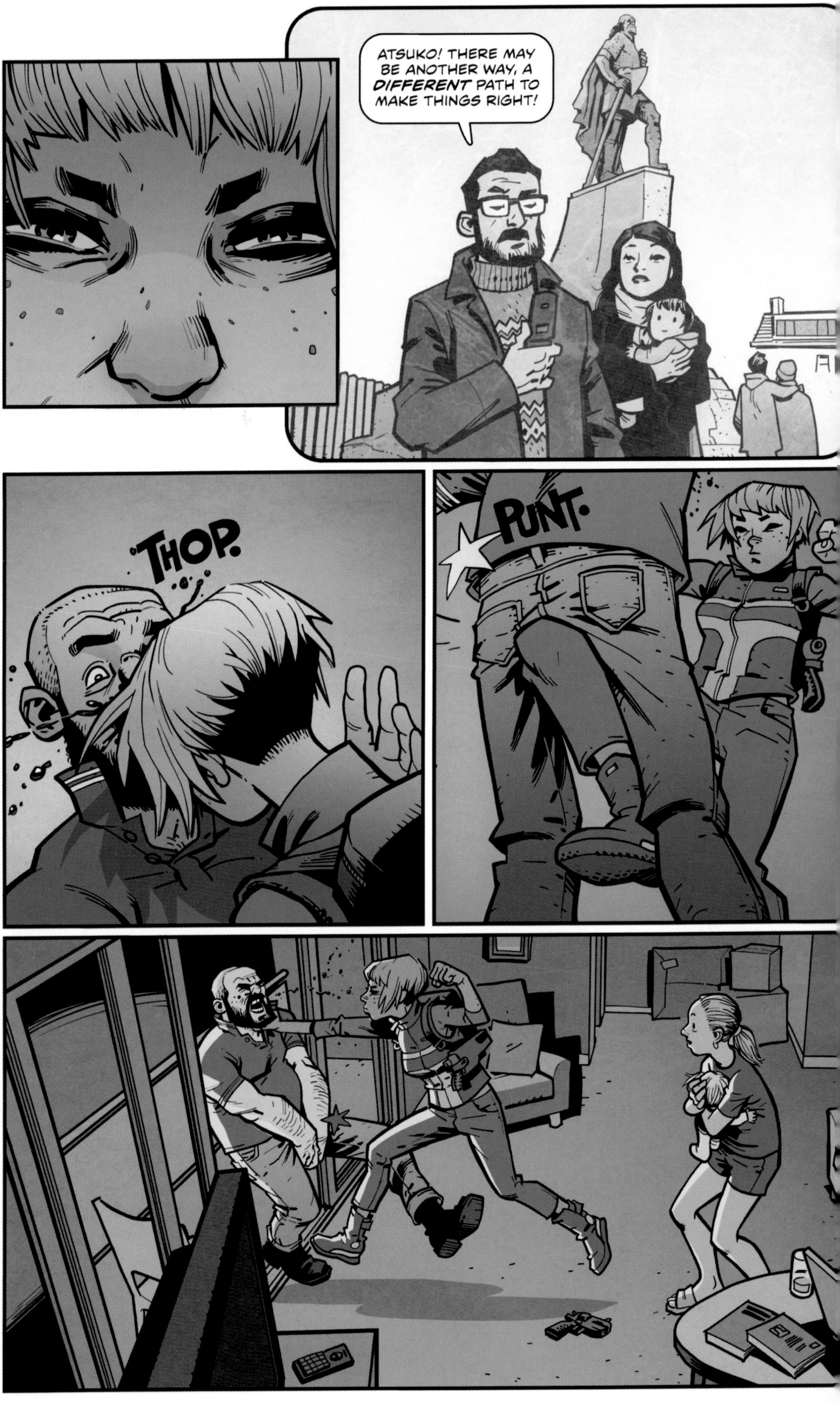
ATSUKO! THERE MAY BE ANOTHER WAY, A *DIFFERENT* PATH TO MAKE THINGS RIGHT!
THOP.
PUNT.

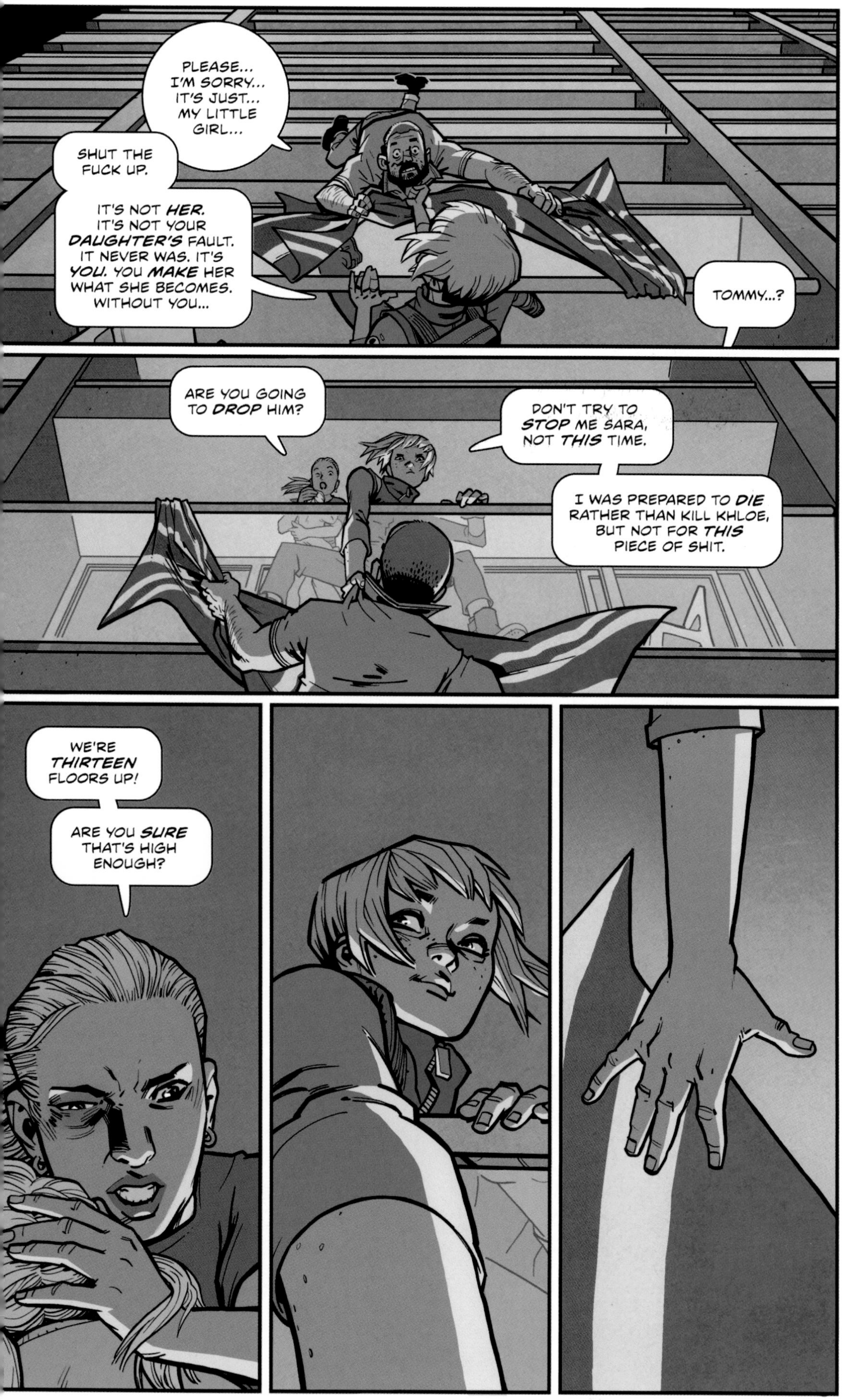
PLEASE... I'M SORRY... IT'S JUST... MY LITTLE GIRL...
SHUT THE FUCK UP.
IT'S NOT HER. IT'S NOT YOUR DAUGHTER'S FAULT. IT NEVER WAS. IT'S YOU. YOU MAKE HER WHAT SHE BECOMES. WITHOUT YOU...
TOMMY...?
ARE YOU GOING TO DROP HIM?
DON'T TRY TO STOP ME SARA, NOT THIS TIME.
I WAS PREPARED TO DIE RATHER THAN KILL KHLOE, BUT NOT FOR THIS PIECE OF SHIT.
WE'RE THIRTEEN FLOORS UP!
ARE YOU SURE THAT'S HIGH ENOUGH?

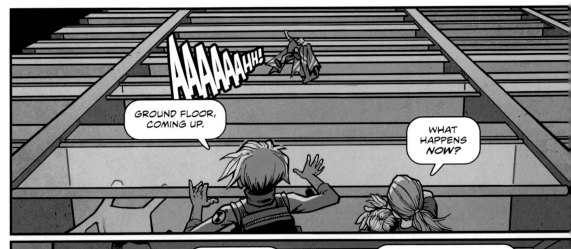

AAAAAAHH!

GROUND FLOOR, COMING UP.

WHAT HAPPENS *NOW?*

EMERGENCY SERVICES WILL BE ON THE SCENE IN *NINE MINUTES.* I ONLY NEED *THREE.*

IT'S OK. THIS IS *JIMMY MAC.* HE'S ONE OF THE *GOOD GUYS,* TOO.

THREE MINUTES FOR *WHAT?*

TO INSTALL A *SIZEABLE* AMOUNT OF *CHILD PORNOGRAPHY* ON TOMMY'S HARD DRIVE.

WHEN THE *POLICE* ARRIVE, TELL THEM YOU DISCOVERED IT AND *CONFRONTED* HIM, AND HE COULDN'T *LIVE* WITH THE *SHAME.*

HERE'S SOME *STERLING.* FOR YOUR TROUBLE.

OH, GOD, I CAN'T THANK YOU *ENOUGH.* YOU'VE CHANGED THE COURSE OF OUR *LIVES...*

JUST MAKE SURE *YOU* BRING THAT LITTLE ONE UP *RIGHT,* OK?

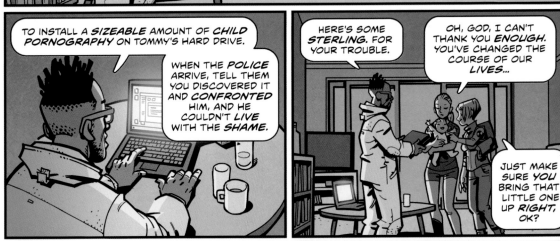

HEY, THIS THING'S GONE *GREEN!*

"...MISSION ACCOMPLISHED."

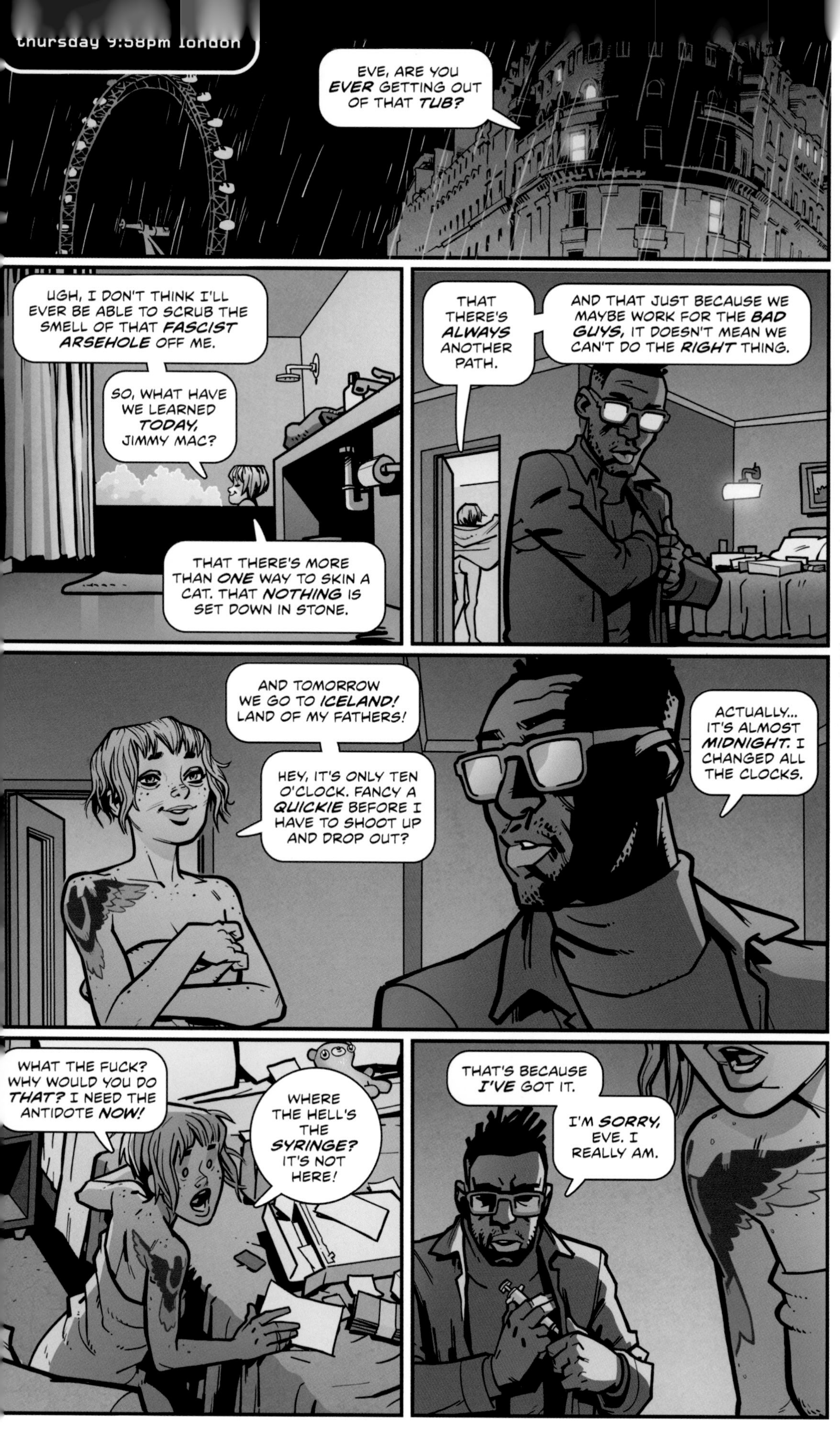
thursday 9:58pm london
EVE, ARE YOU EVER GETTING OUT OF THAT TUB?
UGH, I DON'T THINK I'LL EVER BE ABLE TO SCRUB THE SMELL OF THAT FASCIST ARSEHOLE OFF ME.
SO, WHAT HAVE WE LEARNED TODAY, JIMMY MAC?
THAT THERE'S MORE THAN ONE WAY TO SKIN A CAT. THAT NOTHING IS SET DOWN IN STONE.
THAT THERE'S ALWAYS ANOTHER PATH.
AND THAT JUST BECAUSE WE MAYBE WORK FOR THE BAD GUYS, IT DOESN'T MEAN WE CAN'T DO THE RIGHT THING.
AND TOMORROW WE GO TO ICELAND! LAND OF MY FATHERS!
HEY, IT'S ONLY TEN O'CLOCK. FANCY A QUICKIE BEFORE I HAVE TO SHOOT UP AND DROP OUT?
ACTUALLY... IT'S ALMOST MIDNIGHT. I CHANGED ALL THE CLOCKS.
WHAT THE FUCK? WHY WOULD YOU DO THAT? I NEED THE ANTIDOTE NOW!
WHERE THE HELL'S THE SYRINGE? IT'S NOT HERE!
THAT'S BECAUSE I'VE GOT IT.
I'M SORRY, EVE. I REALLY AM.

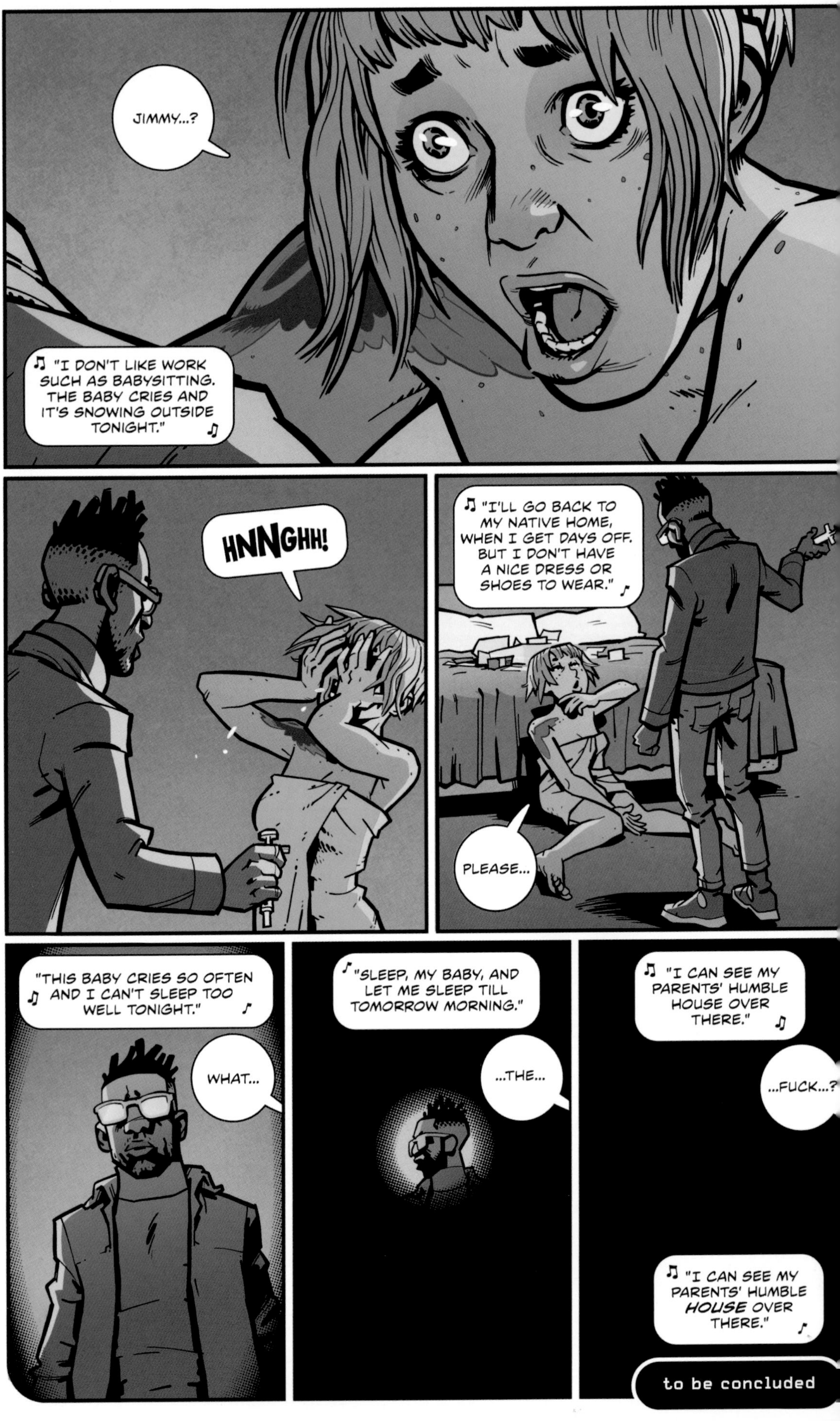
JIMMY...?
♫ "I DON'T LIKE WORK SUCH AS BABYSITTING. THE BABY CRIES AND IT'S SNOWING OUTSIDE TONIGHT." ♫
HNNGHH!
♫ "I'LL GO BACK TO MY NATIVE HOME, WHEN I GET DAYS OFF. BUT I DON'T HAVE A NICE DRESS OR SHOES TO WEAR." ♪
PLEASE...
"THIS BABY CRIES SO OFTEN ♫ AND I CAN'T SLEEP TOO WELL TONIGHT." ♪
WHAT...
♪ "SLEEP, MY BABY, AND LET ME SLEEP TILL TOMORROW MORNING."
...THE...
♫ "I CAN SEE MY PARENTS' HUMBLE HOUSE OVER THERE." ♫
...FUCK...?
♫ "I CAN SEE MY PARENTS' HUMBLE *HOUSE* OVER THERE." ♪
to be concluded

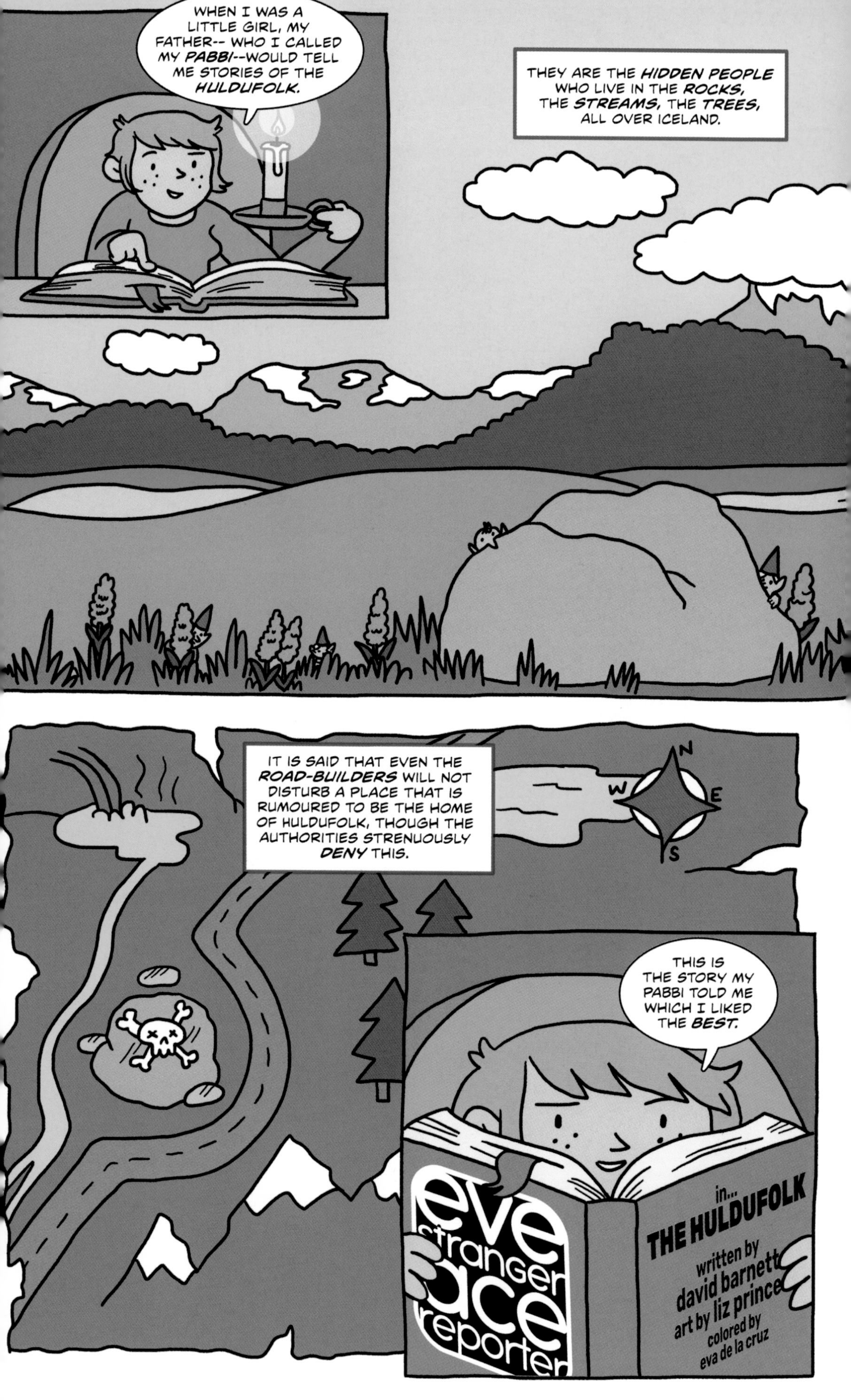
WHEN I WAS A LITTLE GIRL, MY FATHER-- WHO I CALLED MY *PABBI*--WOULD TELL ME STORIES OF THE *HULDUFOLK.*
THEY ARE THE *HIDDEN PEOPLE* WHO LIVE IN THE *ROCKS,* THE *STREAMS,* THE *TREES,* ALL OVER ICELAND.
IT IS SAID THAT EVEN THE *ROAD-BUILDERS* WILL NOT DISTURB A PLACE THAT IS RUMOURED TO BE THE HOME OF HULDUFOLK, THOUGH THE AUTHORITIES STRENUOUSLY *DENY* THIS.
N
W
E
S
THIS IS THE STORY MY PABBI TOLD ME WHICH I LIKED THE *BEST.*
eve stranger ace reporter
in...
THE HULDUFOLK
written by
david barnett
art by liz prince
colored by
eva de la cruz

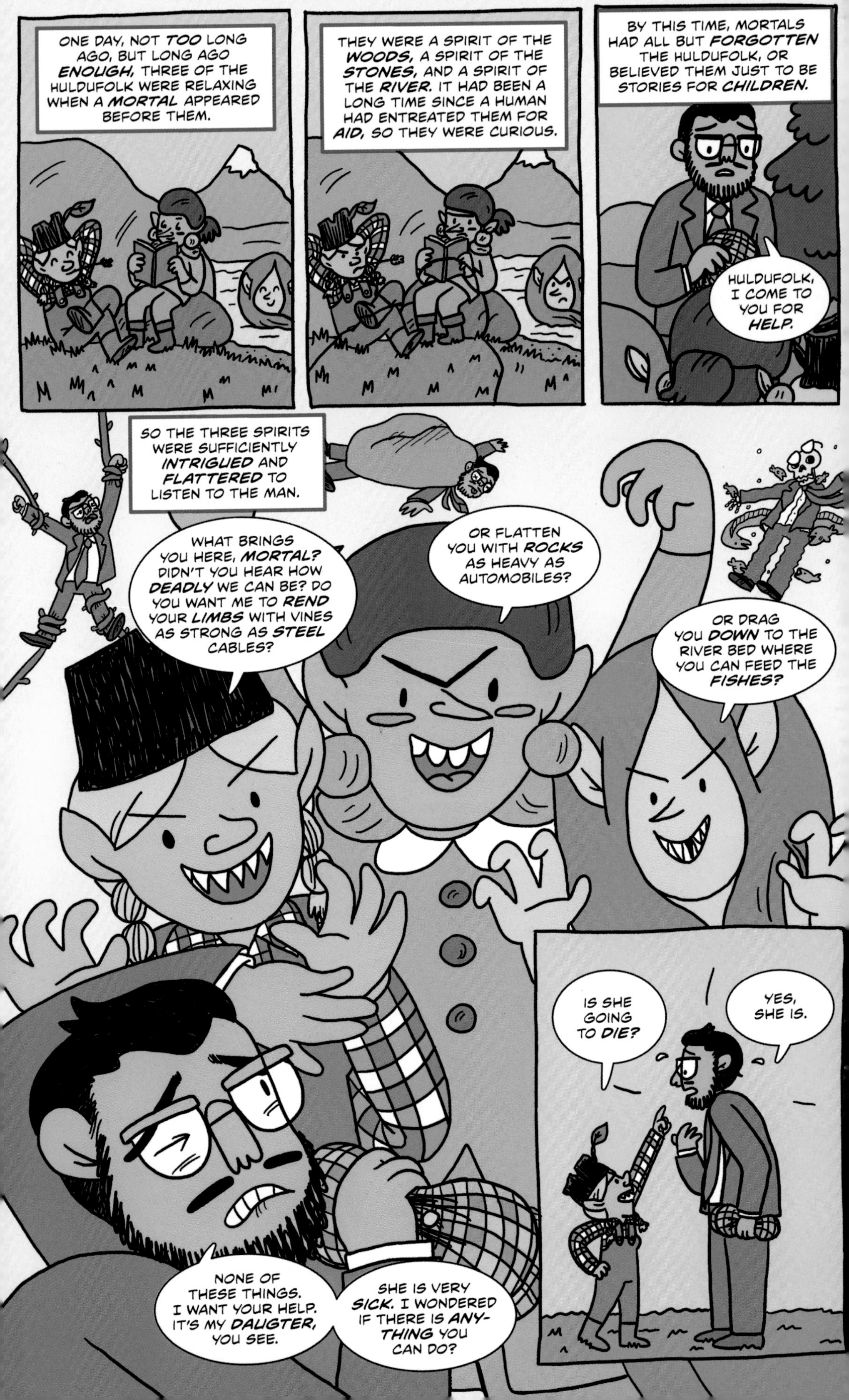

ONE DAY, NOT TOO LONG AGO, BUT LONG AGO ENOUGH, THREE OF THE HULDUFOLK WERE RELAXING WHEN A MORTAL APPEARED BEFORE THEM.
THEY WERE A SPIRIT OF THE WOODS, A SPIRIT OF THE STONES, AND A SPIRIT OF THE RIVER. IT HAD BEEN A LONG TIME SINCE A HUMAN HAD ENTREATED THEM FOR AID, SO THEY WERE CURIOUS.
BY THIS TIME, MORTALS HAD ALL BUT FORGOTTEN THE HULDUFOLK, OR BELIEVED THEM JUST TO BE STORIES FOR CHILDREN.
HULDUFOLK, I COME TO YOU FOR HELP.
SO THE THREE SPIRITS WERE SUFFICIENTLY INTRIGUED AND FLATTERED TO LISTEN TO THE MAN.
WHAT BRINGS YOU HERE, MORTAL? DIDN'T YOU HEAR HOW DEADLY WE CAN BE? DO YOU WANT ME TO REND YOUR LIMBS WITH VINES AS STRONG AS STEEL CABLES?
OR FLATTEN YOU WITH ROCKS AS HEAVY AS AUTOMOBILES?
OR DRAG YOU DOWN TO THE RIVER BED WHERE YOU CAN FEED THE FISHES?
NONE OF THESE THINGS. I WANT YOUR HELP. IT'S MY DAUGTER, YOU SEE.
SHE IS VERY SICK. I WONDERED IF THERE IS ANYTHING YOU CAN DO?
IS SHE GOING TO DIE?
YES, SHE IS.

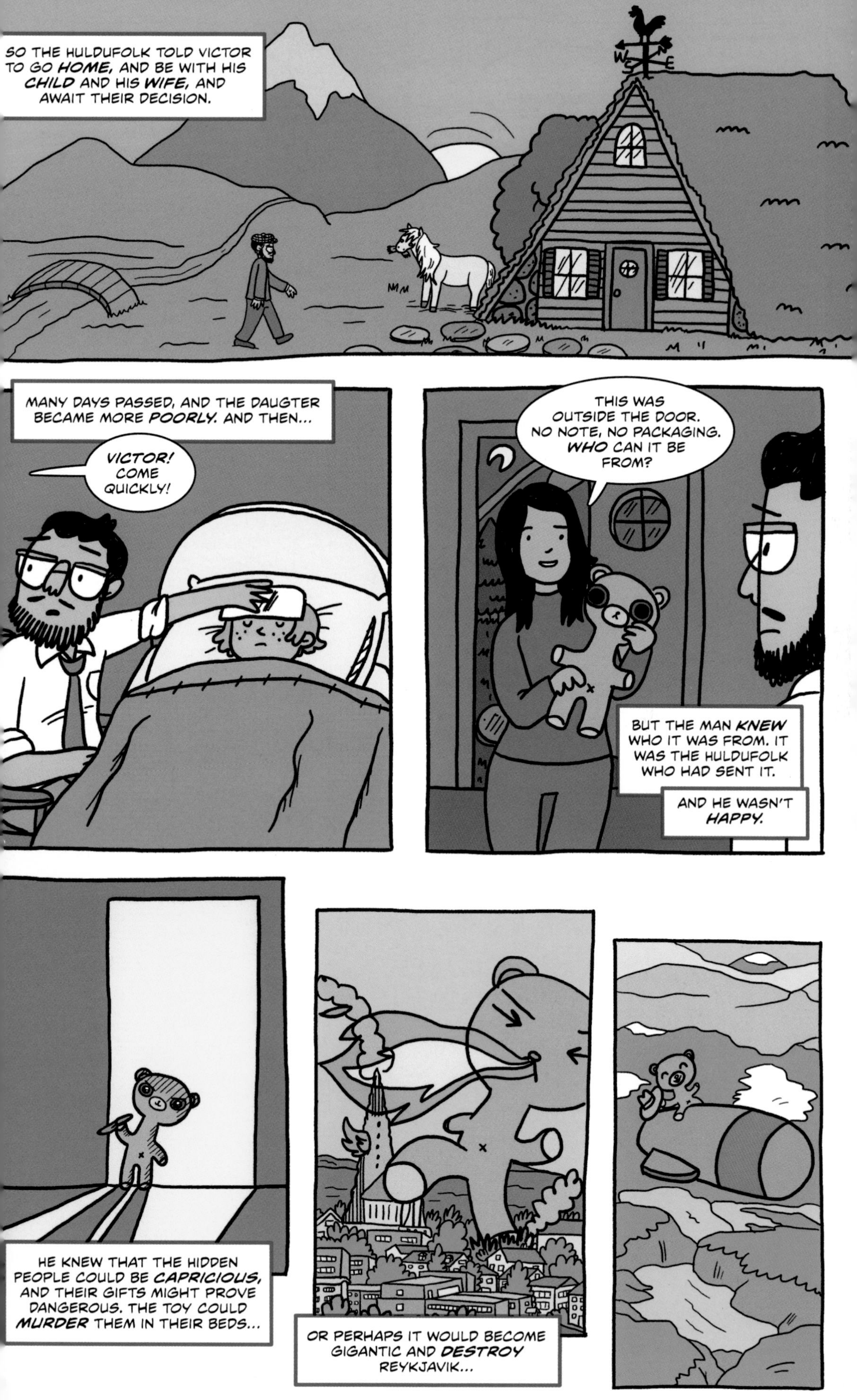

SO THE HULDUFOLK TOLD VICTOR TO GO *HOME,* AND BE WITH HIS *CHILD* AND HIS *WIFE,* AND AWAIT THEIR DECISION.
W
S
N
E
MANY DAYS PASSED, AND THE DAUGTER BECAME MORE *POORLY.* AND THEN...
VICTOR! COME QUICKLY!
THIS WAS OUTSIDE THE DOOR. NO NOTE, NO PACKAGING. *WHO* CAN IT BE FROM?
BUT THE MAN *KNEW* WHO IT WAS FROM. IT WAS THE HULDUFOLK WHO HAD SENT IT.
AND HE WASN'T *HAPPY.*
HE KNEW THAT THE HIDDEN PEOPLE COULD BE *CAPRICIOUS,* AND THEIR GIFTS MIGHT PROVE DANGEROUS. THE TOY COULD *MURDER* THEM IN THEIR BEDS...
OR PERHAPS IT WOULD BECOME GIGANTIC AND *DESTROY* REYKJAVIK...

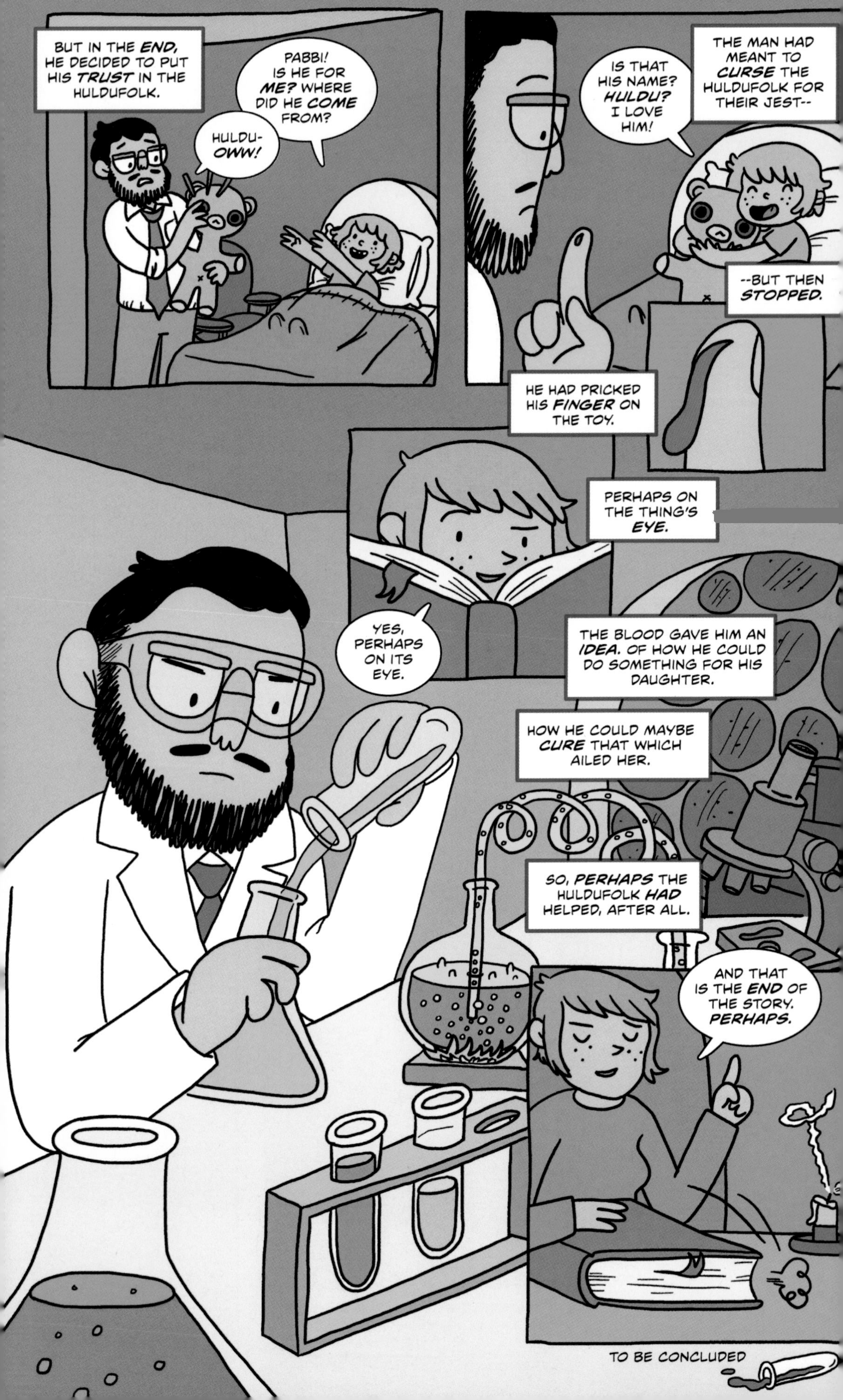
BUT IN THE END, HE DECIDED TO PUT HIS TRUST IN THE HULDUFOLK.
PABBI! IS HE FOR ME? WHERE DID HE COME FROM?
HULDU-OWW!
IS THAT HIS NAME? HULDU? I LOVE HIM!
THE MAN HAD MEANT TO CURSE THE HULDUFOLK FOR THEIR JEST--
--BUT THEN STOPPED.
HE HAD PRICKED HIS FINGER ON THE TOY.
PERHAPS ON THE THING'S EYE.
YES, PERHAPS ON ITS EYE.
THE BLOOD GAVE HIM AN IDEA. OF HOW HE COULD DO SOMETHING FOR HIS DAUGHTER.
HOW HE COULD MAYBE CURE THAT WHICH AILED HER.
SO, PERHAPS THE HULDUFOLK HAD HELPED, AFTER ALL.
AND THAT IS THE END OF THE STORY. PERHAPS.
TO BE CONCLUDED

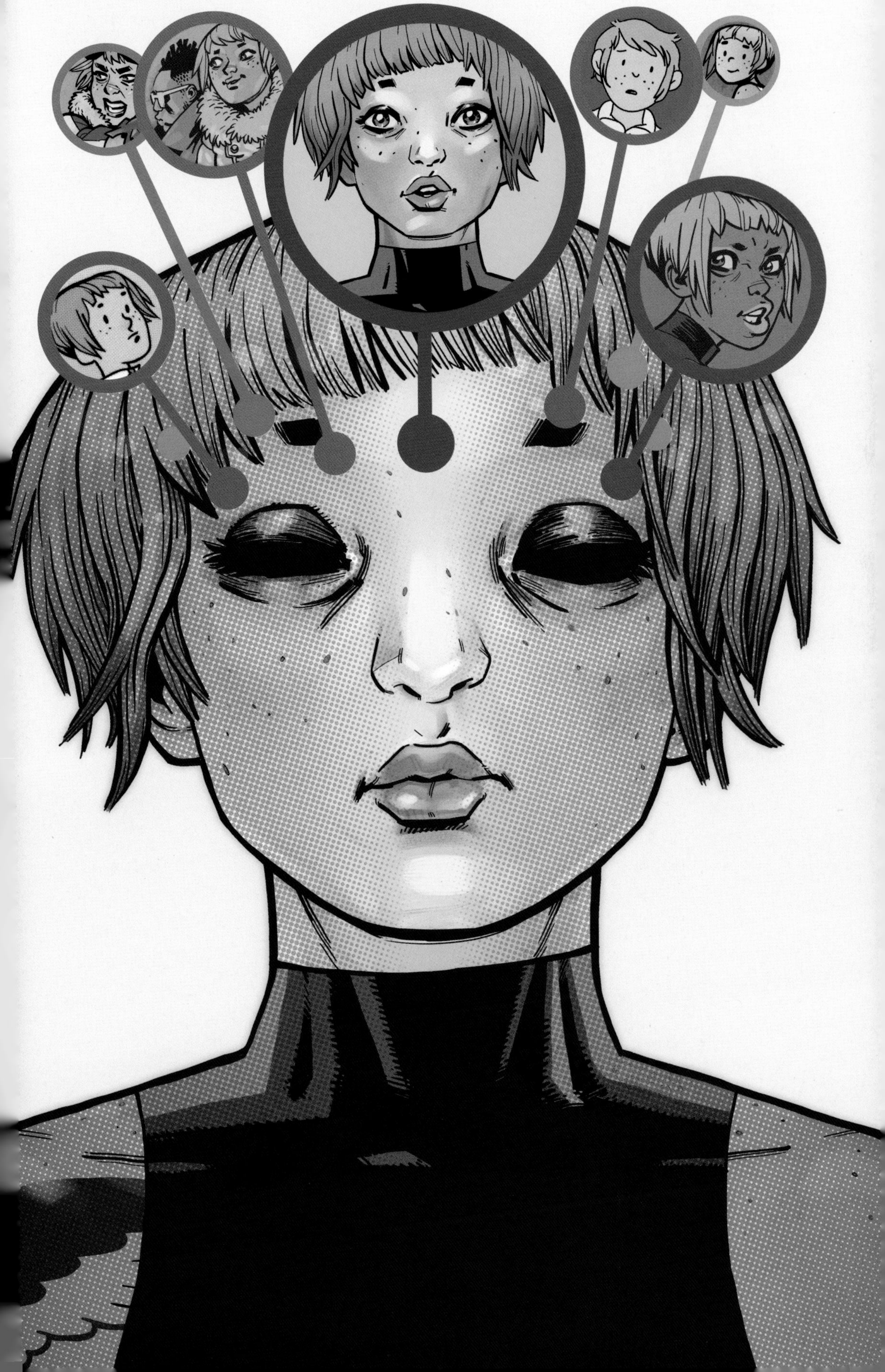

part five:
A CHANGE IS GONNA COME

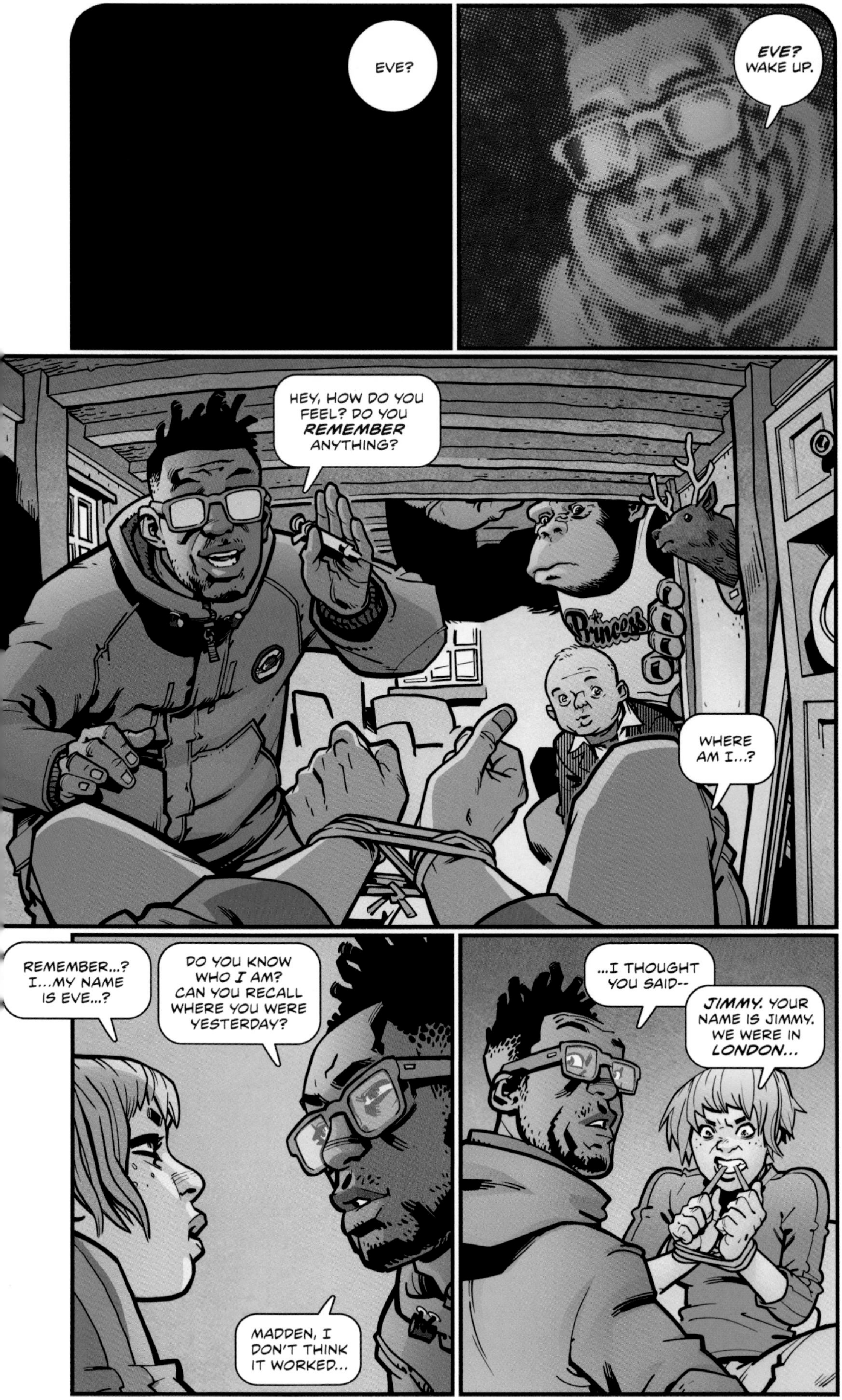
EVE?
EVE? WAKE UP.
HEY, HOW DO YOU FEEL? DO YOU REMEMBER ANYTHING?
WHERE AM I...?
Princess
REMEMBER...? I...MY NAME IS EVE...?
DO YOU KNOW WHO I AM? CAN YOU RECALL WHERE YOU WERE YESTERDAY?
MADDEN, I DON'T THINK IT WORKED...
...I THOUGHT YOU SAID--
JIMMY. YOUR NAME IS JIMMY. WE WERE IN LONDON...

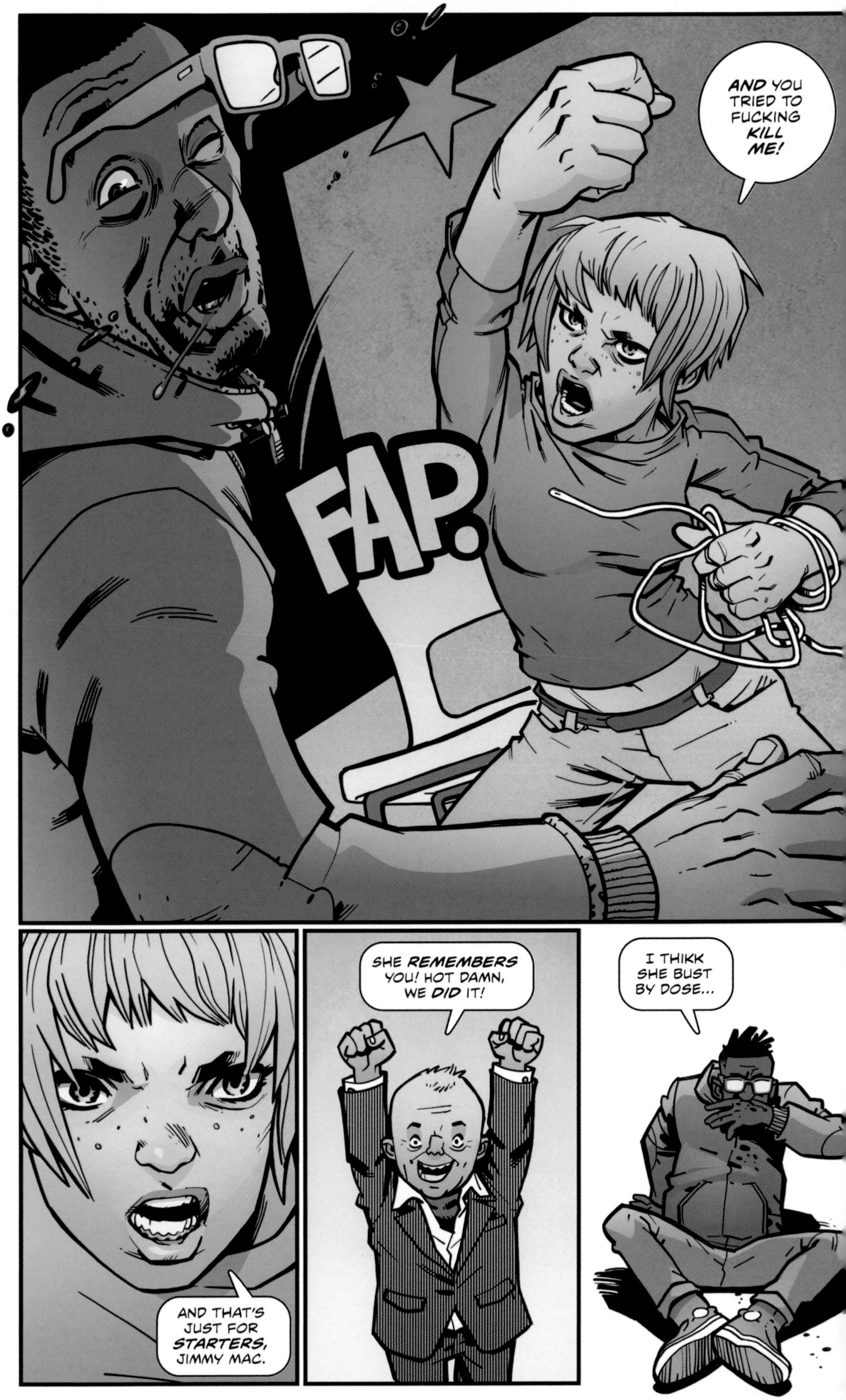

AND YOU TRIED TO FUCKING KILL ME!
FAP.
AND THAT'S JUST FOR STARTERS, JIMMY MAC.
SHE REMEMBERS YOU! HOT DAMN, WE DID IT!
I THIKK SHE BUST BY DOSE...

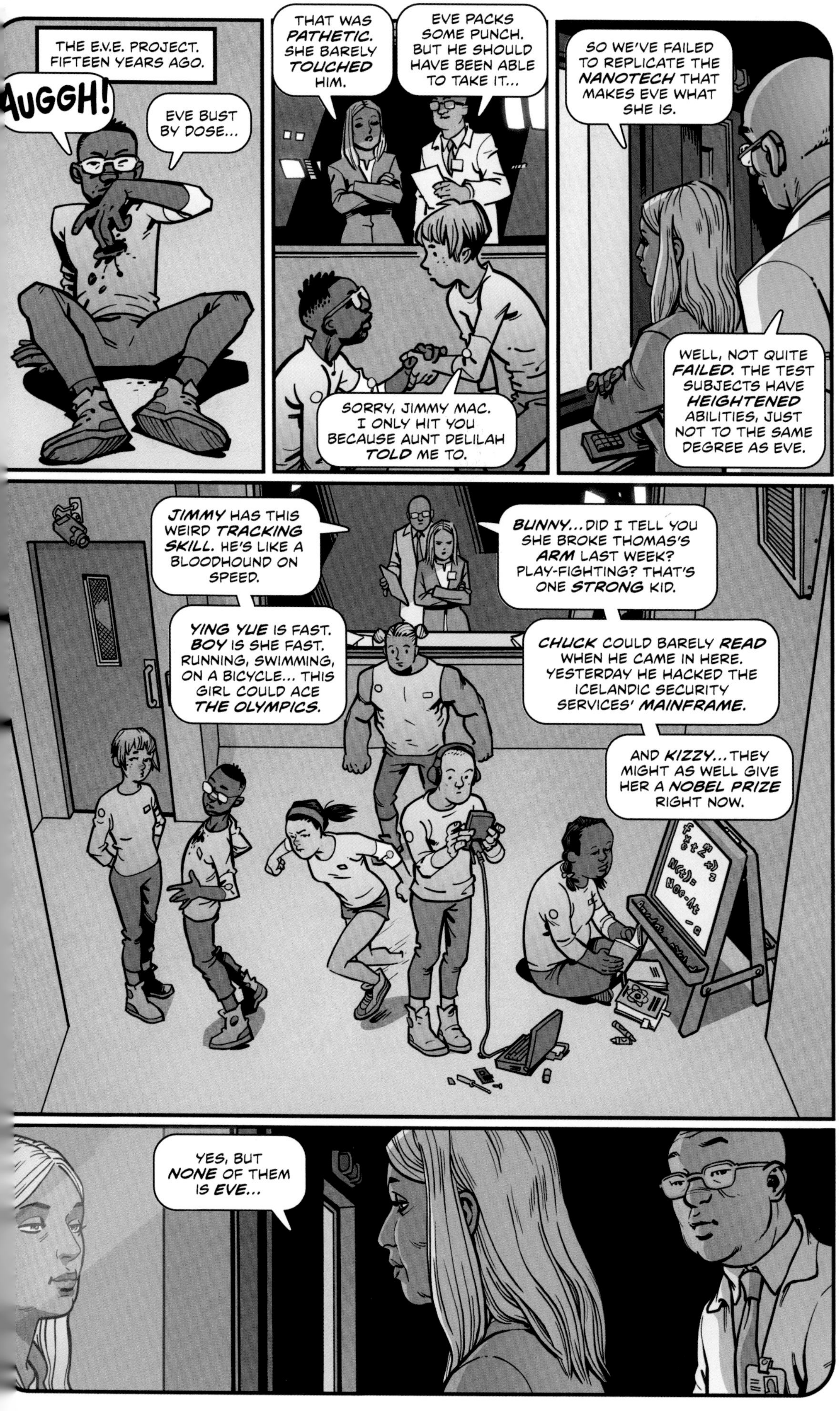
THE E.V.E. PROJECT. FIFTEEN YEARS AGO.
AUGGH!
EVE BUST BY DOSE...
THAT WAS PATHETIC. SHE BARELY TOUCHED HIM.
EVE PACKS SOME PUNCH. BUT HE SHOULD HAVE BEEN ABLE TO TAKE IT...
SORRY, JIMMY MAC. I ONLY HIT YOU BECAUSE AUNT DELILAH TOLD ME TO.
SO WE'VE FAILED TO REPLICATE THE NANOTECH THAT MAKES EVE WHAT SHE IS.
WELL, NOT QUITE FAILED. THE TEST SUBJECTS HAVE HEIGHTENED ABILITIES, JUST NOT TO THE SAME DEGREE AS EVE.
JIMMY HAS THIS WEIRD TRACKING SKILL. HE'S LIKE A BLOODHOUND ON SPEED.
YING YUE IS FAST. BOY IS SHE FAST. RUNNING, SWIMMING, ON A BICYCLE... THIS GIRL COULD ACE THE OLYMPICS.
BUNNY...DID I TELL YOU SHE BROKE THOMAS'S ARM LAST WEEK? PLAY-FIGHTING? THAT'S ONE STRONG KID.
CHUCK COULD BARELY READ WHEN HE CAME IN HERE. YESTERDAY HE HACKED THE ICELANDIC SECURITY SERVICES' MAINFRAME.
AND KIZZY...THEY MIGHT AS WELL GIVE HER A NOBEL PRIZE RIGHT NOW.
YES, BUT NONE OF THEM IS EVE...

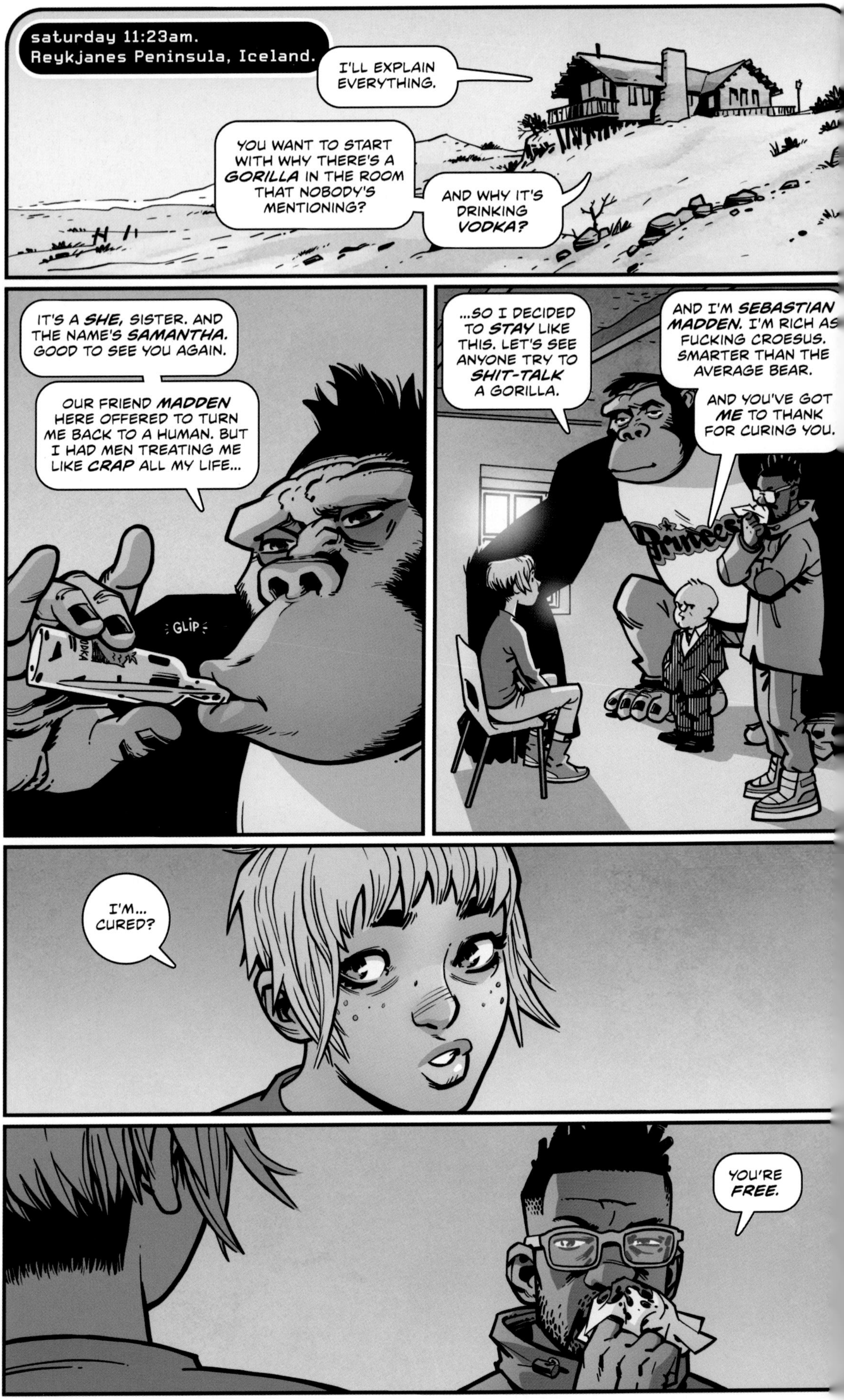
saturday 11:23am.
Reykjanes Peninsula, Iceland.
I'LL EXPLAIN EVERYTHING.
YOU WANT TO START WITH WHY THERE'S A GORILLA IN THE ROOM THAT NOBODY'S MENTIONING?
AND WHY IT'S DRINKING VODKA?
IT'S A SHE, SISTER. AND THE NAME'S SAMANTHA. GOOD TO SEE YOU AGAIN.
OUR FRIEND MADDEN HERE OFFERED TO TURN ME BACK TO A HUMAN. BUT I HAD MEN TREATING ME LIKE CRAP ALL MY LIFE...
GLIP
...SO I DECIDED TO STAY LIKE THIS. LET'S SEE ANYONE TRY TO SHIT-TALK A GORILLA.
AND I'M SEBASTIAN MADDEN. I'M RICH AS FUCKING CROESUS. SMARTER THAN THE AVERAGE BEAR.
AND YOU'VE GOT ME TO THANK FOR CURING YOU.
I'M... CURED?
YOU'RE FREE.

I KNOW, I KNOW. YOU'RE REALLY CONFUSED.

AT LEAST, YOU *MIGHT* BE.

ACCORDING TO WHAT JIMMY SAYS, THOUGH, MAYBE NOT.

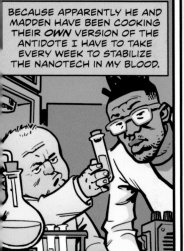

BECAUSE APPARENTLY HE AND MADDEN HAVE BEEN COOKING THEIR *OWN* VERSION OF THE ANTIDOTE I HAVE TO TAKE EVERY WEEK TO STABILIZE THE NANOTECH IN MY BLOOD.

THE ANTIDOTE THAT *ROBS* ME OF MY MEMORY. EXCEPT THIS NEW, IMPROVED FORMULA DOESN'T *DO* THAT.

I REMEMBER EVERYTHING.

BINGO! WE'RE IN TO THE E.V.E. PROJECT SYSTEM.

...HOLY SHIT, EVE!--

"--THE FILE ON THE ICELAND RESCUE MISSION...

"--THE WOMAN WHO NEEDS *RESCUING*...

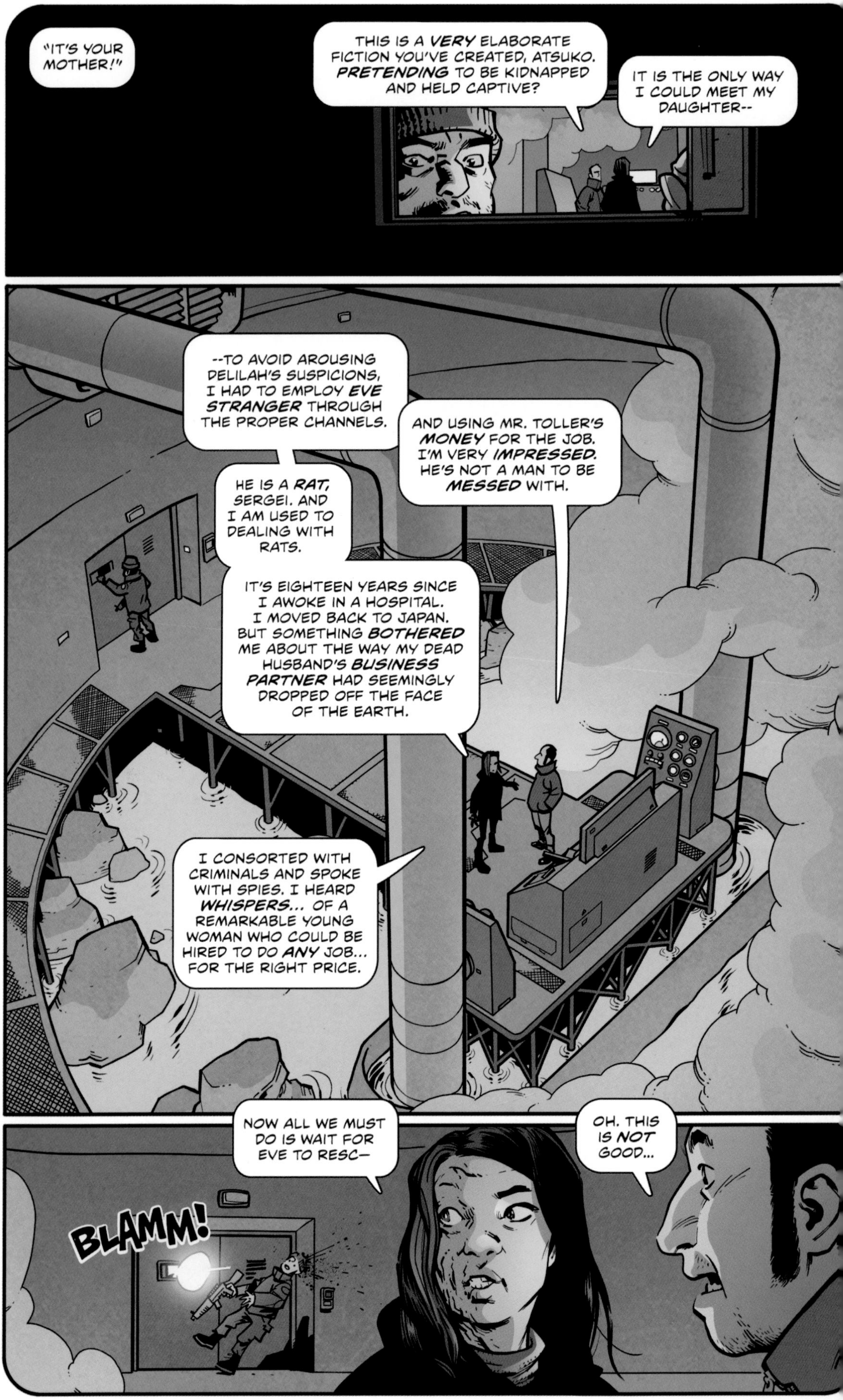
"IT'S YOUR MOTHER!"
THIS IS A VERY ELABORATE FICTION YOU'VE CREATED, ATSUKO. PRETENDING TO BE KIDNAPPED AND HELD CAPTIVE?
IT IS THE ONLY WAY I COULD MEET MY DAUGHTER--
--TO AVOID AROUSING DELILAH'S SUSPICIONS, I HAD TO EMPLOY EVE STRANGER THROUGH THE PROPER CHANNELS.
AND USING MR. TOLLER'S MONEY FOR THE JOB. I'M VERY IMPRESSED. HE'S NOT A MAN TO BE MESSED WITH.
HE IS A RAT, SERGEI. AND I AM USED TO DEALING WITH RATS.
IT'S EIGHTEEN YEARS SINCE I AWOKE IN A HOSPITAL. I MOVED BACK TO JAPAN. BUT SOMETHING BOTHERED ME ABOUT THE WAY MY DEAD HUSBAND'S BUSINESS PARTNER HAD SEEMINGLY DROPPED OFF THE FACE OF THE EARTH.
I CONSORTED WITH CRIMINALS AND SPOKE WITH SPIES. I HEARD WHISPERS... OF A REMARKABLE YOUNG WOMAN WHO COULD BE HIRED TO DO ANY JOB... FOR THE RIGHT PRICE.
NOW ALL WE MUST DO IS WAIT FOR EVE TO RESC—
OH. THIS IS NOT GOOD...
BLAMM!

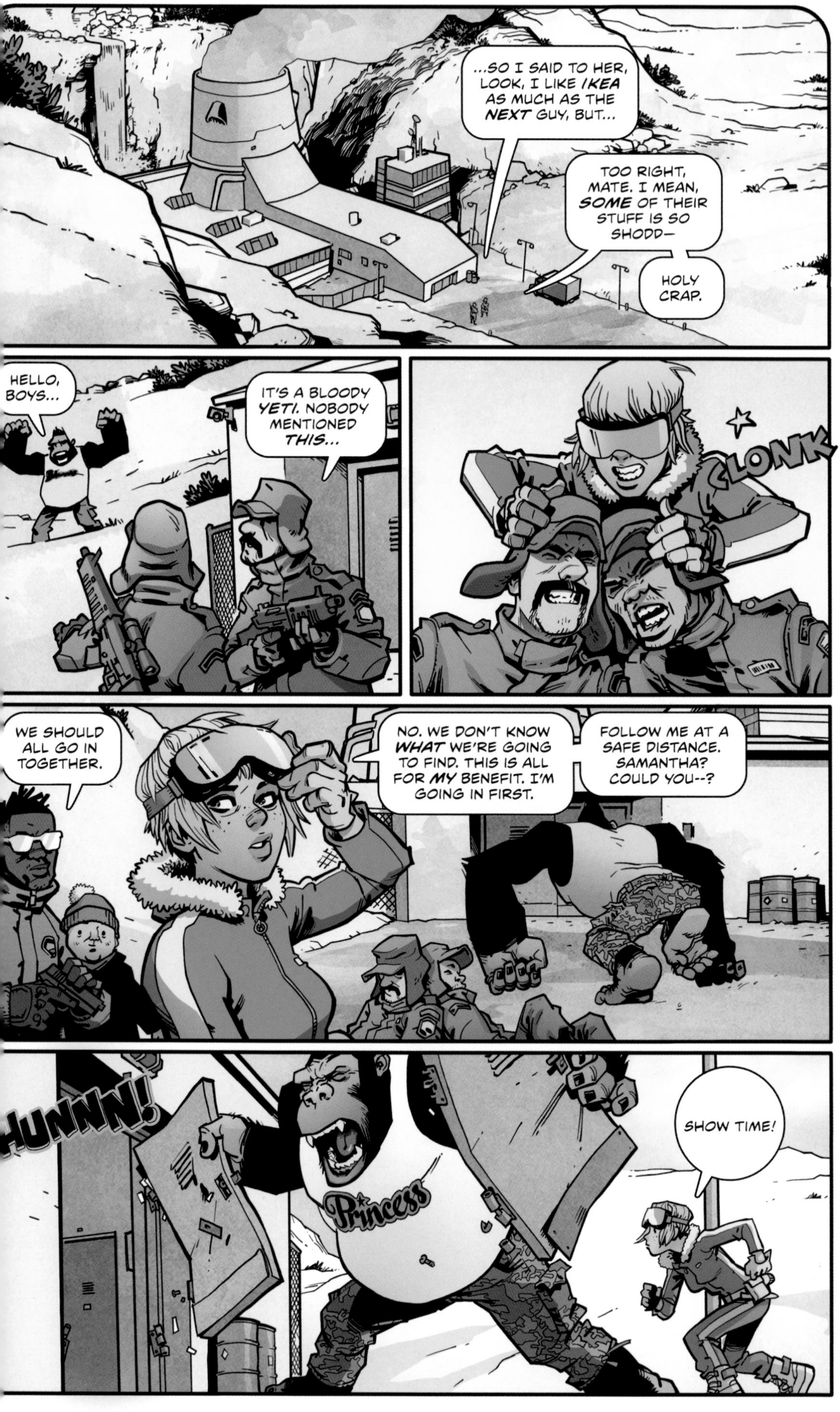
...SO I SAID TO HER, LOOK, I LIKE IKEA AS MUCH AS THE NEXT GUY, BUT...
TOO RIGHT, MATE. I MEAN, SOME OF THEIR STUFF IS SO SHODD—
HOLY CRAP.
HELLO, BOYS...
IT'S A BLOODY YETI. NOBODY MENTIONED THIS...
CLONK
WE SHOULD ALL GO IN TOGETHER.
NO. WE DON'T KNOW WHAT WE'RE GOING TO FIND. THIS IS ALL FOR MY BENEFIT. I'M GOING IN FIRST.
FOLLOW ME AT A SAFE DISTANCE. SAMANTHA? COULD YOU--?
HUNNN!
Princess
SHOW TIME!

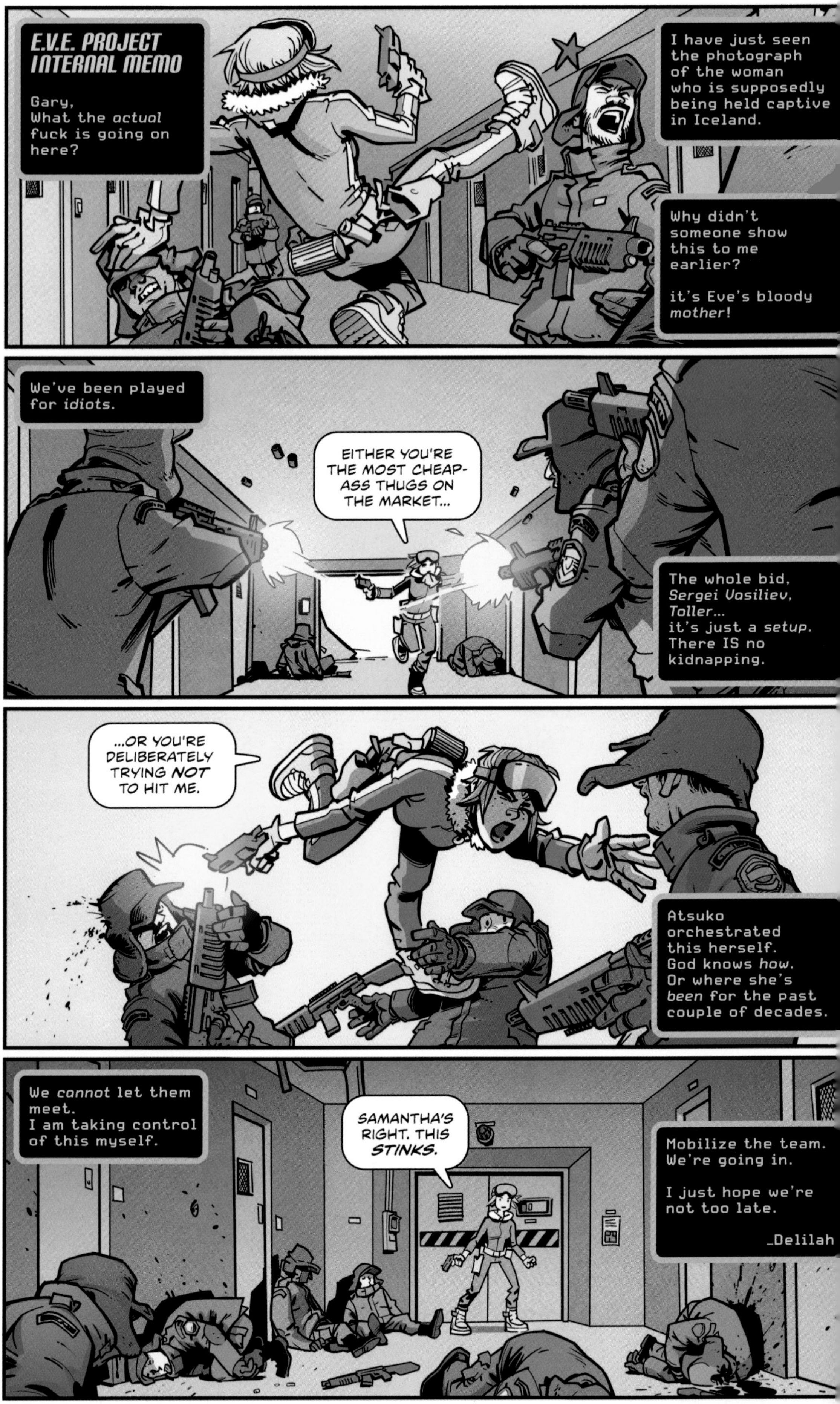
E.V.E. PROJECT INTERNAL MEMO
Gary,
What the *actual* fuck is going on here?
I have just seen the photograph of the woman who is supposedly being held captive in Iceland.
Why didn't someone show this to me earlier?
it's Eve's bloody *mother*!
We've been played for *idiots*.
EITHER YOU'RE THE MOST CHEAP-ASS THUGS ON THE MARKET...
The whole bid, *Sergei Vasiliev*, *Toller*... it's just a *setup*. There IS no kidnapping.
...OR YOU'RE DELIBERATELY TRYING ***NOT*** TO HIT ME.
Atsuko orchestrated this herself. God knows *how*. Or where she's *been* for the past couple of decades.
We *cannot* let them meet. I am taking control of this myself.
SAMANTHA'S RIGHT. THIS ***STINKS***.
Mobilize the team. We're going in.
I just hope we're not too late.
_Delilah

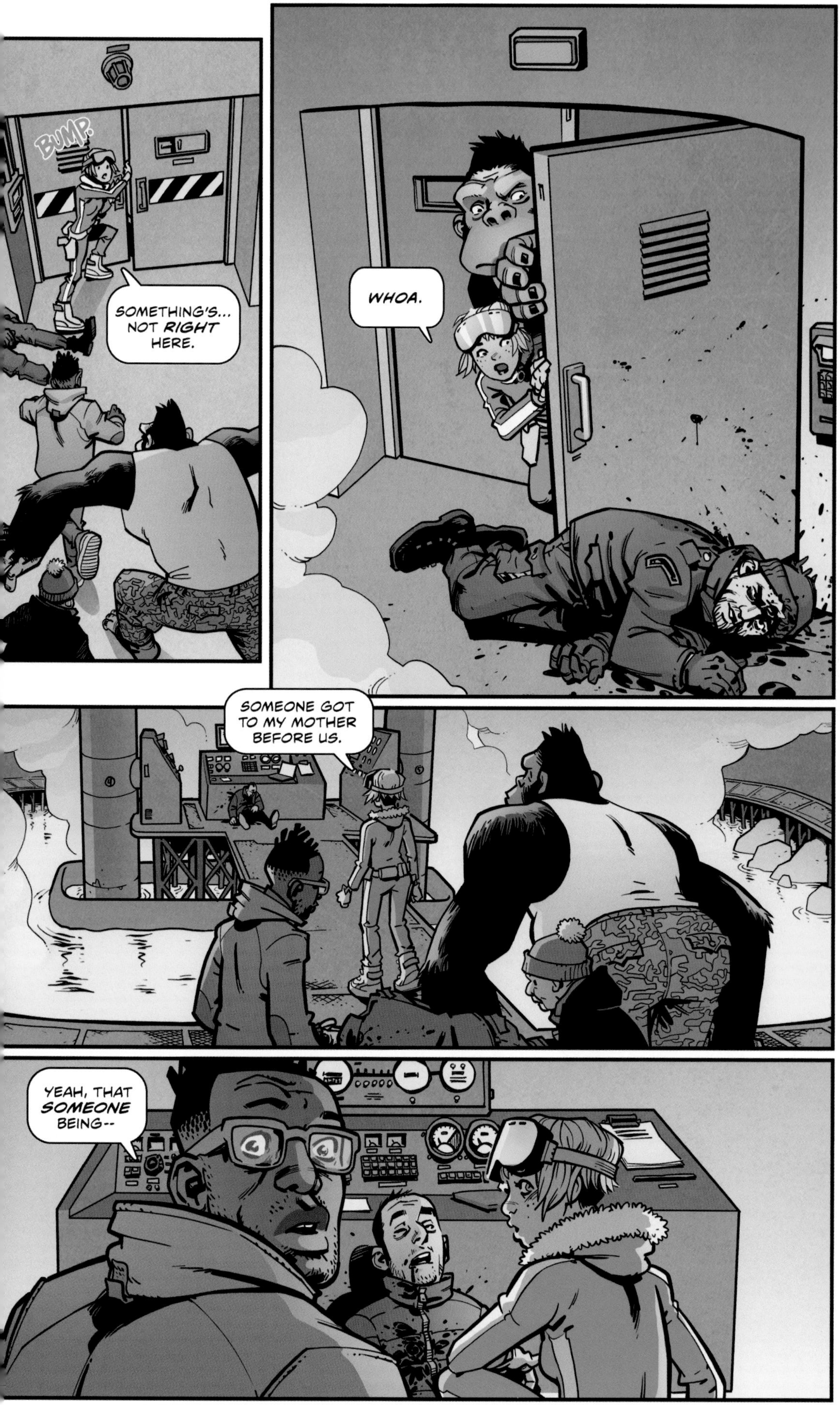
BUMP!
SOMETHING'S... NOT *RIGHT* HERE.
WHOA.
SOMEONE GOT TO MY MOTHER BEFORE US.
YEAH, THAT *SOMEONE* BEING--

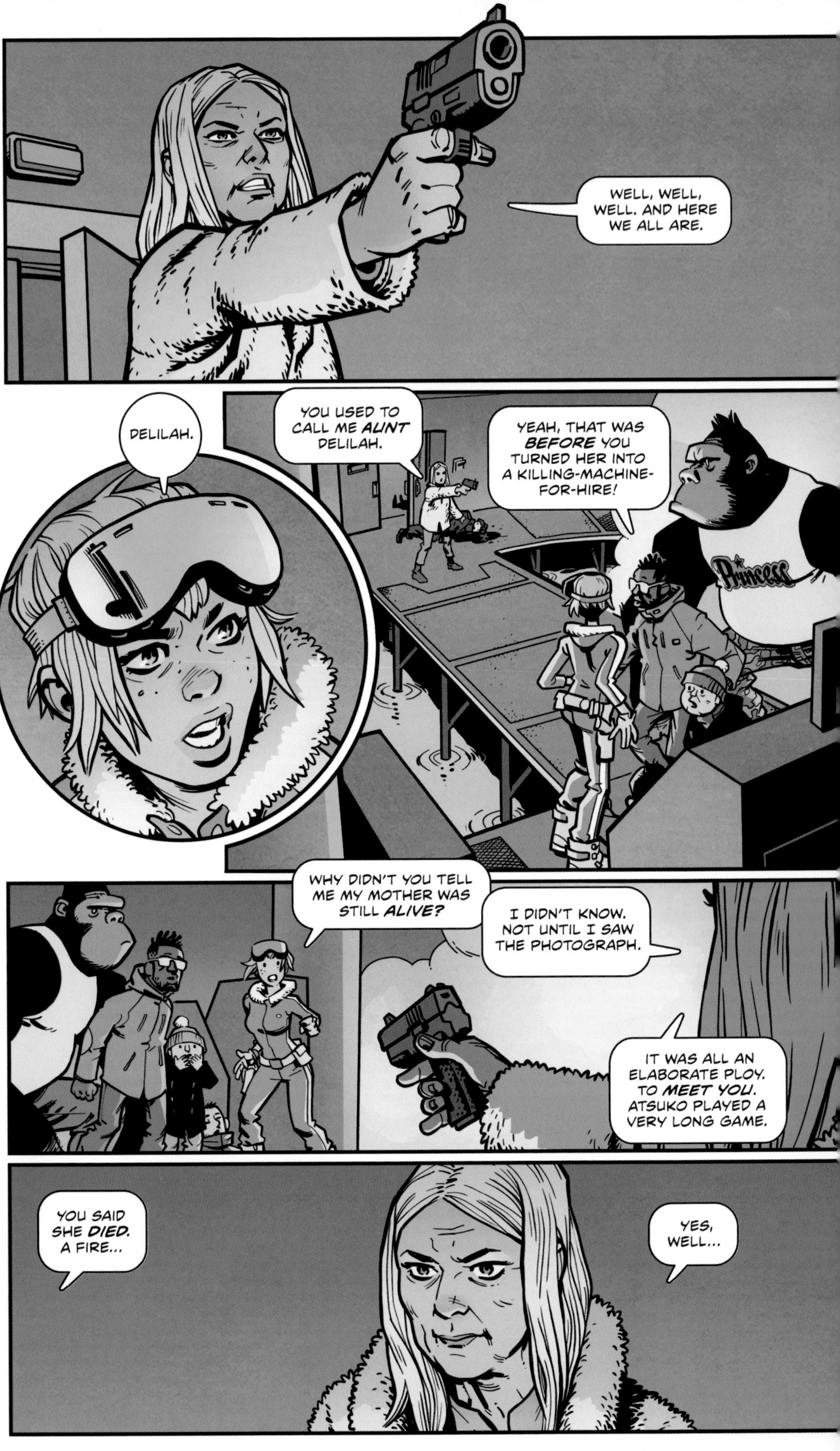

WELL, WELL, WELL. AND HERE WE ALL ARE.
DELILAH.
YOU USED TO CALL ME *AUNT* DELILAH.
YEAH, THAT WAS ***BEFORE*** YOU TURNED HER INTO A KILLING-MACHINE-FOR-HIRE!
Princess
WHY DIDN'T YOU TELL ME MY MOTHER WAS STILL *ALIVE?*
I DIDN'T KNOW. NOT UNTIL I SAW THE PHOTOGRAPH.
IT WAS ALL AN ELABORATE PLOY. TO ***MEET YOU***. ATSUKO PLAYED A VERY LONG GAME.
YOU SAID SHE *DIED.* A FIRE...
YES, WELL...

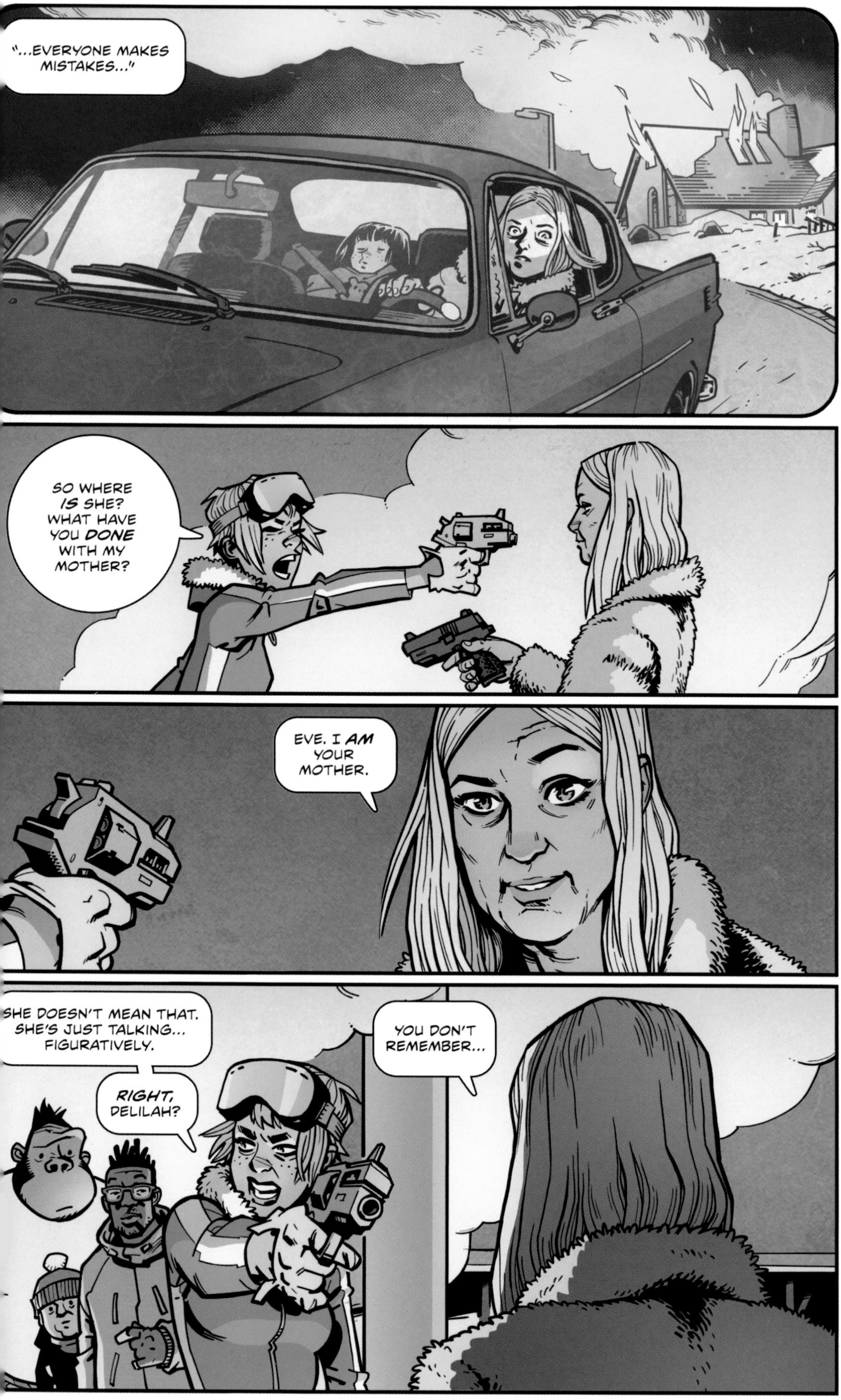
"...EVERYONE MAKES MISTAKES..."
SO WHERE *IS* SHE? WHAT HAVE YOU *DONE* WITH MY MOTHER?
EVE. I *AM* YOUR MOTHER.
SHE DOESN'T MEAN THAT. SHE'S JUST TALKING... FIGURATIVELY.
RIGHT, DELILAH?
YOU DON'T REMEMBER...

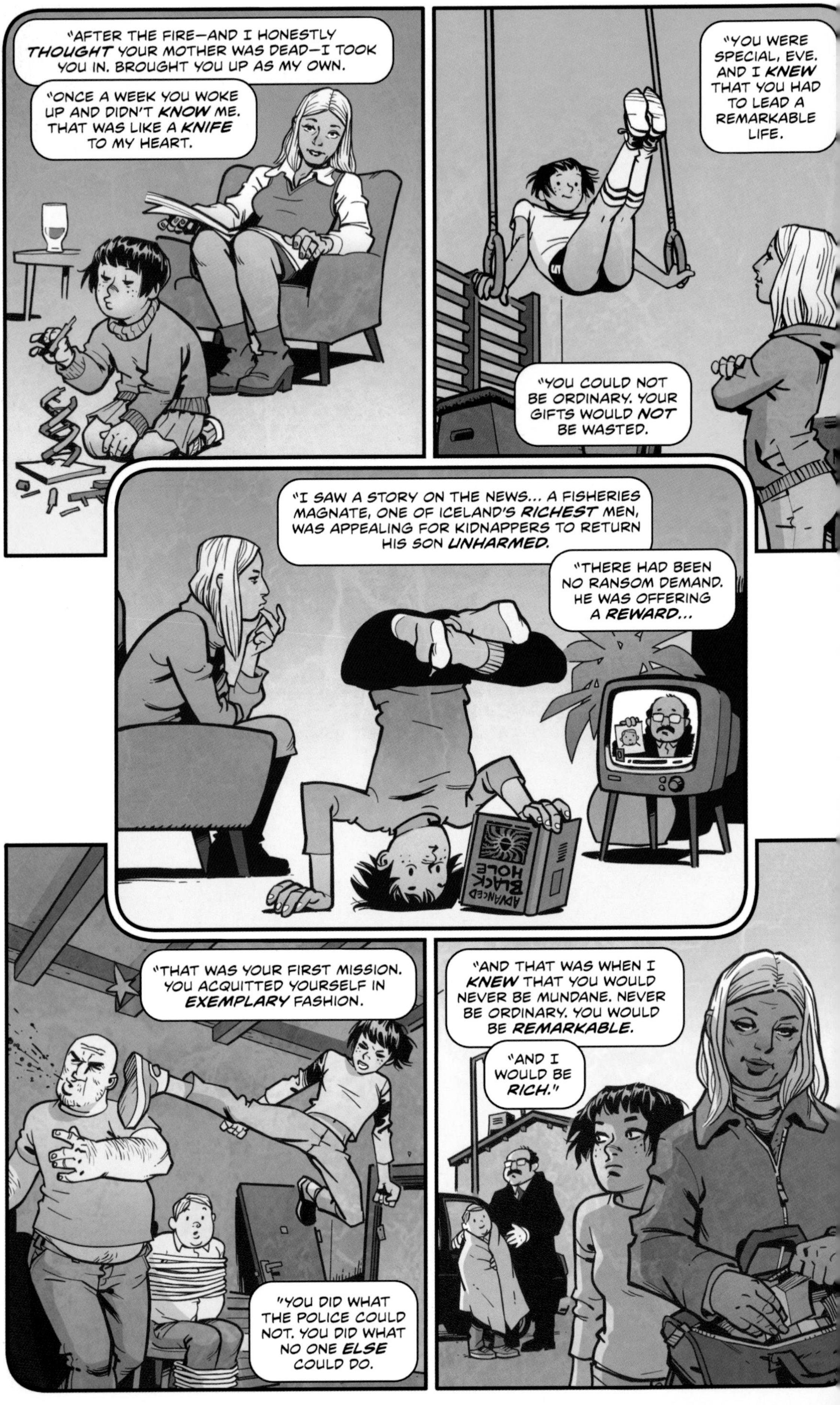
"AFTER THE FIRE—AND I HONESTLY THOUGHT YOUR MOTHER WAS DEAD—I TOOK YOU IN. BROUGHT YOU UP AS MY OWN.
"ONCE A WEEK YOU WOKE UP AND DIDN'T KNOW ME. THAT WAS LIKE A KNIFE TO MY HEART.
"YOU WERE SPECIAL, EVE. AND I KNEW THAT YOU HAD TO LEAD A REMARKABLE LIFE.
"YOU COULD NOT BE ORDINARY. YOUR GIFTS WOULD NOT BE WASTED.
"I SAW A STORY ON THE NEWS... A FISHERIES MAGNATE, ONE OF ICELAND'S RICHEST MEN, WAS APPEALING FOR KIDNAPPERS TO RETURN HIS SON UNHARMED.
"THERE HAD BEEN NO RANSOM DEMAND. HE WAS OFFERING A REWARD...
ADVANCED BLACK HOLE
"THAT WAS YOUR FIRST MISSION. YOU ACQUITTED YOURSELF IN EXEMPLARY FASHION.
"YOU DID WHAT THE POLICE COULD NOT. YOU DID WHAT NO ONE ELSE COULD DO.
"AND THAT WAS WHEN I KNEW THAT YOU WOULD NEVER BE MUNDANE. NEVER BE ORDINARY. YOU WOULD BE REMARKABLE.
"AND I WOULD BE RICH."

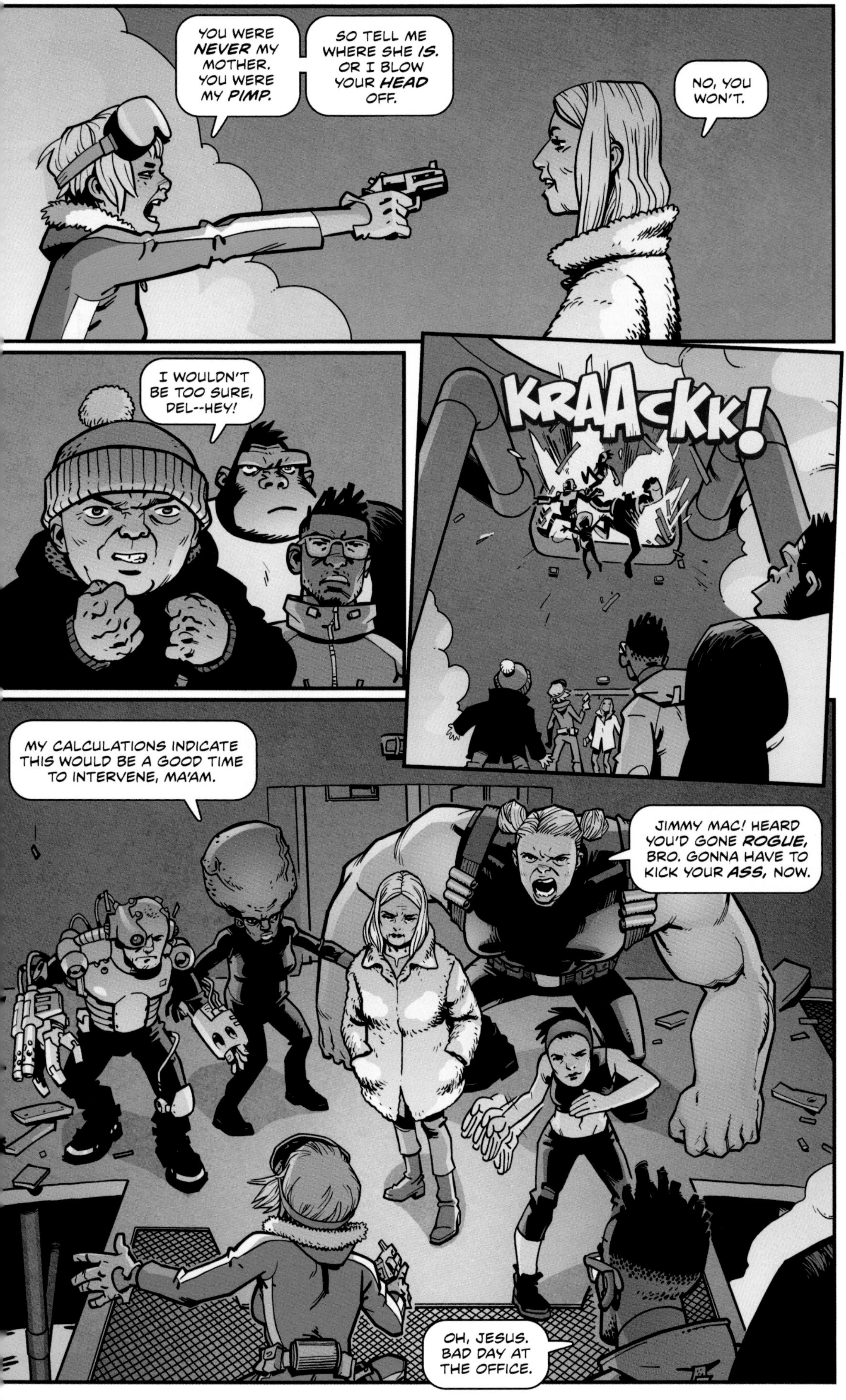
YOU WERE NEVER MY MOTHER. YOU WERE MY PIMP.
SO TELL ME WHERE SHE IS. OR I BLOW YOUR HEAD OFF.
NO, YOU WON'T.
I WOULDN'T BE TOO SURE, DEL--HEY!
KRAACKK!
MY CALCULATIONS INDICATE THIS WOULD BE A GOOD TIME TO INTERVENE, MA'AM.
JIMMY MAC! HEARD YOU'D GONE ROGUE, BRO. GONNA HAVE TO KICK YOUR ASS, NOW.
OH, JESUS. BAD DAY AT THE OFFICE.

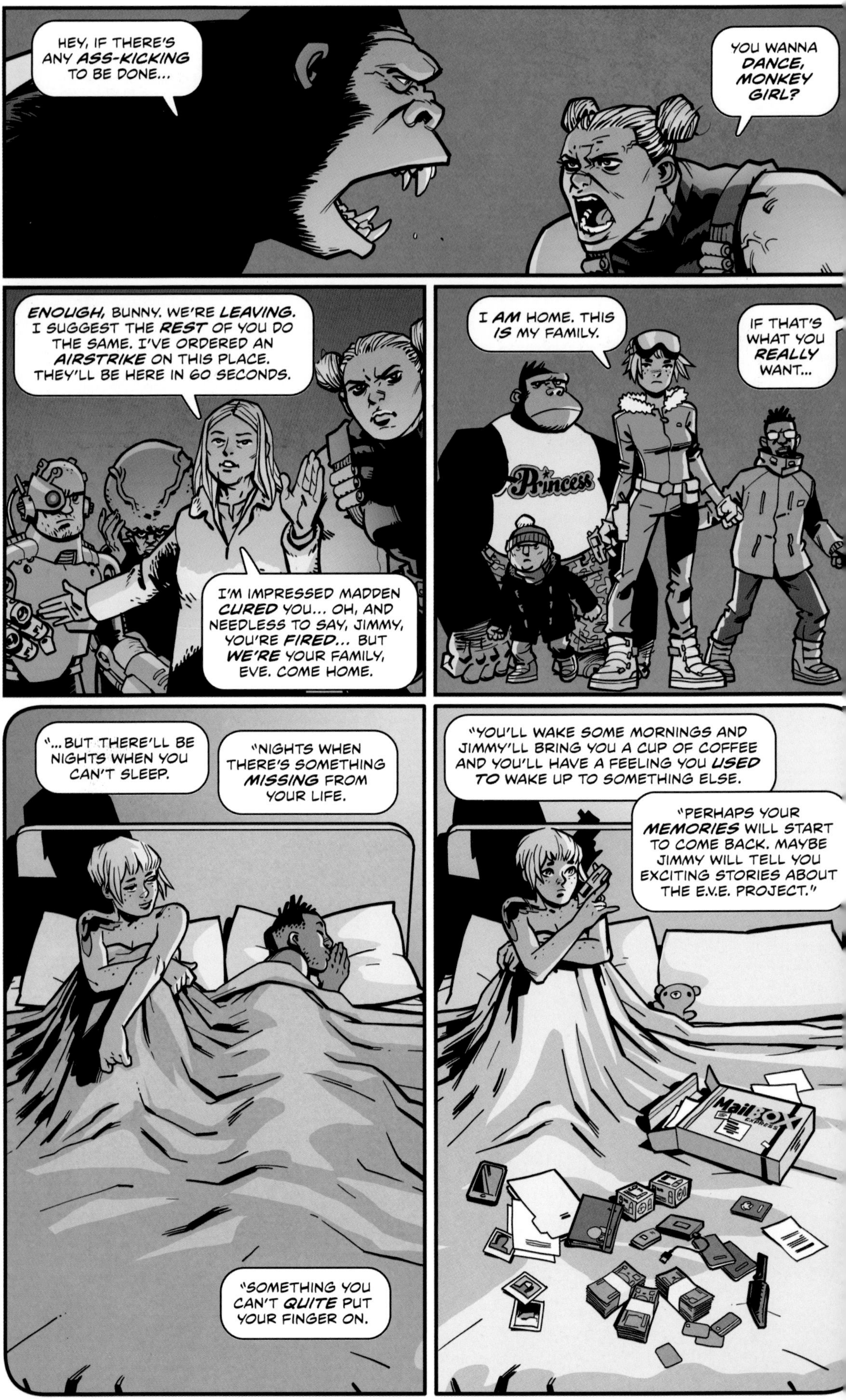
HEY, IF THERE'S ANY ASS-KICKING TO BE DONE...
YOU WANNA DANCE, MONKEY GIRL?
ENOUGH, BUNNY. WE'RE LEAVING. I SUGGEST THE REST OF YOU DO THE SAME. I'VE ORDERED AN AIRSTRIKE ON THIS PLACE. THEY'LL BE HERE IN 60 SECONDS.
I'M IMPRESSED MADDEN CURED YOU... OH, AND NEEDLESS TO SAY, JIMMY, YOU'RE FIRED... BUT WE'RE YOUR FAMILY, EVE. COME HOME.
Princess
I AM HOME. THIS IS MY FAMILY.
IF THAT'S WHAT YOU REALLY WANT...
"...BUT THERE'LL BE NIGHTS WHEN YOU CAN'T SLEEP.
"NIGHTS WHEN THERE'S SOMETHING MISSING FROM YOUR LIFE.
"SOMETHING YOU CAN'T QUITE PUT YOUR FINGER ON.
"YOU'LL WAKE SOME MORNINGS AND JIMMY'LL BRING YOU A CUP OF COFFEE AND YOU'LL HAVE A FEELING YOU USED TO WAKE UP TO SOMETHING ELSE.
"PERHAPS YOUR MEMORIES WILL START TO COME BACK. MAYBE JIMMY WILL TELL YOU EXCITING STORIES ABOUT THE E.V.E. PROJECT."
Mail BOX

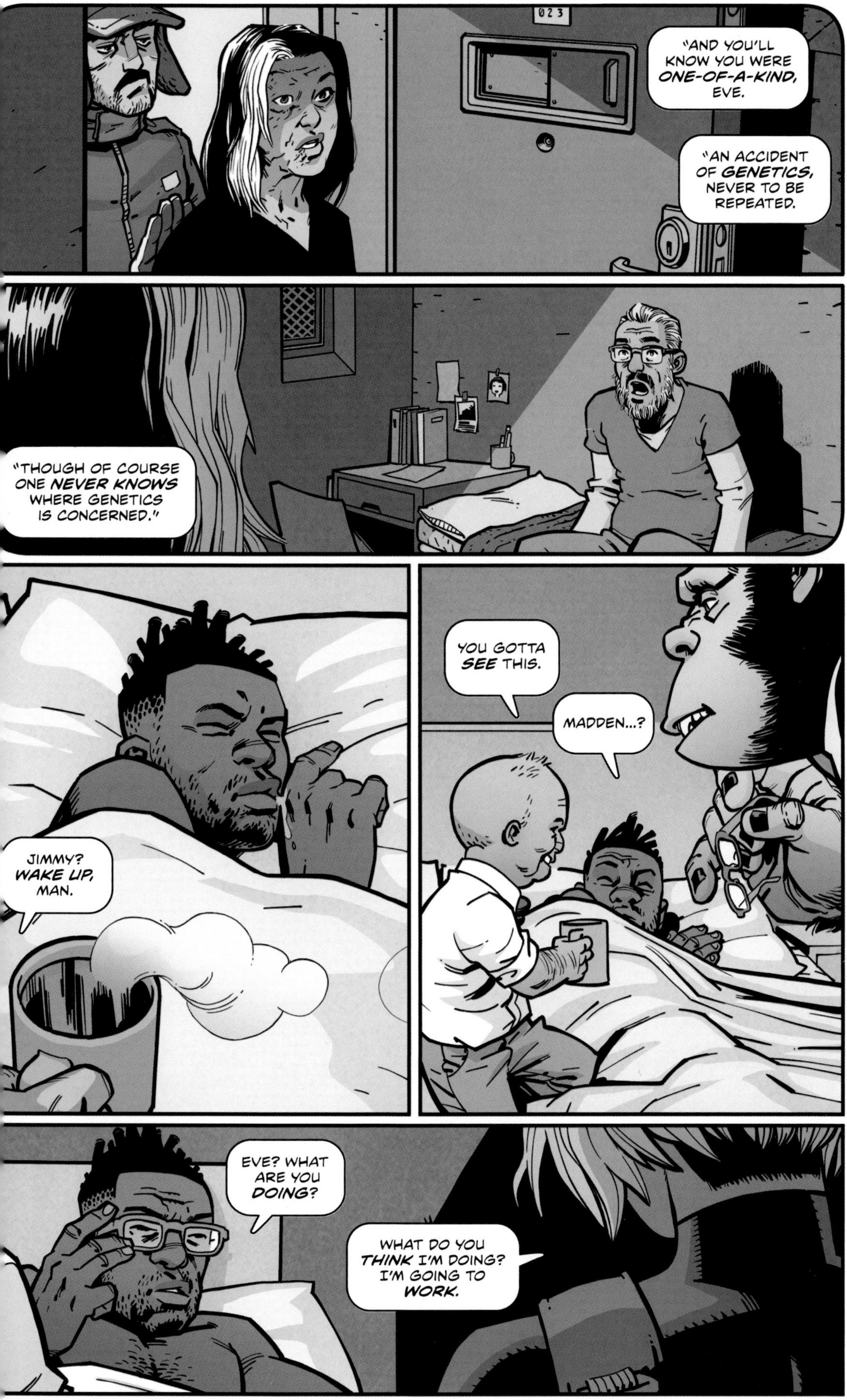
"AND YOU'LL KNOW YOU WERE ***ONE-OF-A-KIND,*** EVE.
"AN ACCIDENT OF ***GENETICS,*** NEVER TO BE REPEATED.
"THOUGH OF COURSE ONE ***NEVER KNOWS*** WHERE GENETICS IS CONCERNED."
JIMMY? ***WAKE UP,*** MAN.
YOU GOTTA ***SEE*** THIS.
MADDEN...?
EVE? WHAT ARE YOU ***DOING?***
WHAT DO YOU ***THINK*** I'M DOING? I'M GOING TO ***WORK.***

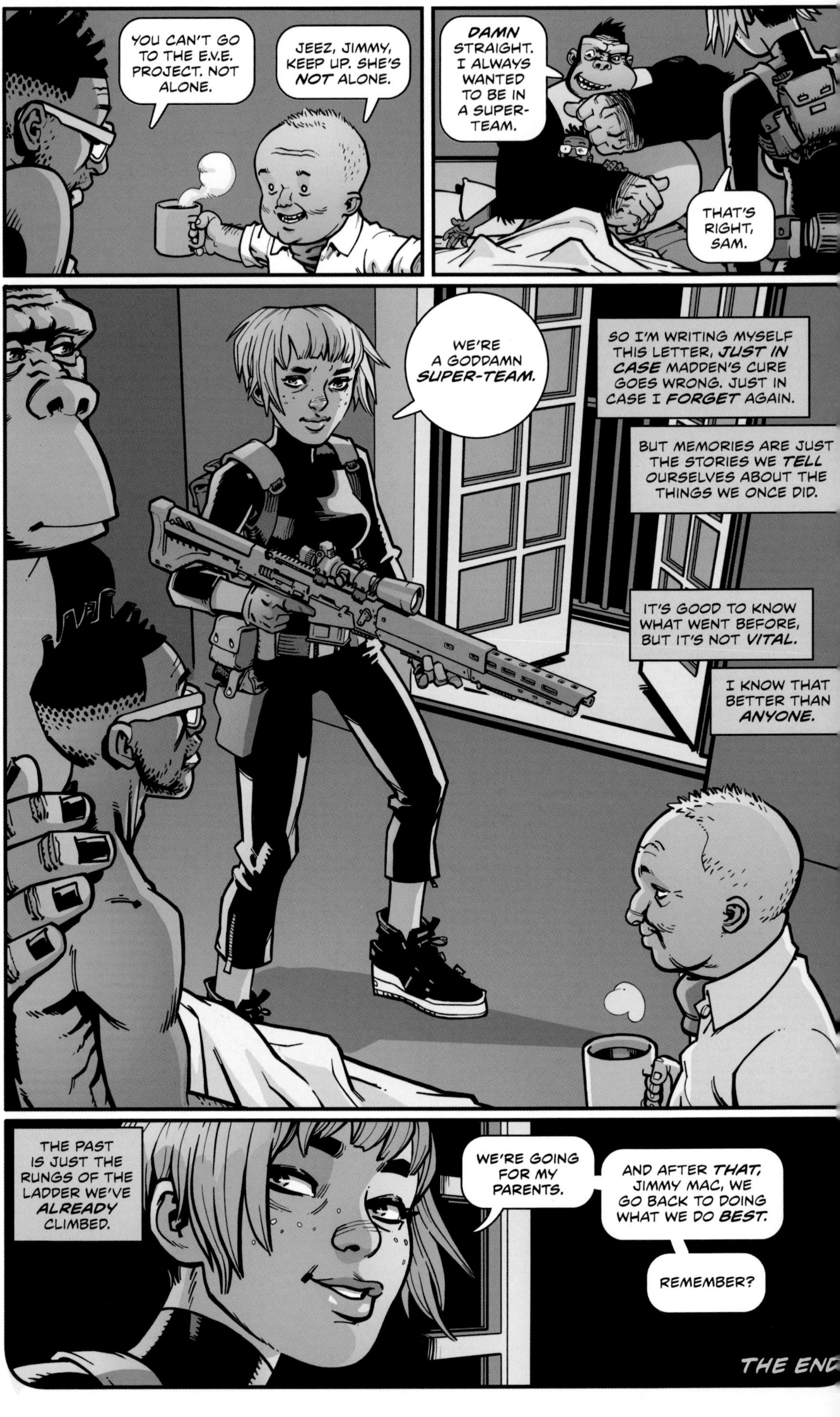

YOU CAN'T GO TO THE E.V.E. PROJECT. NOT ALONE.
JEEZ, JIMMY, KEEP UP. SHE'S *NOT* ALONE.
DAMN STRAIGHT. I ALWAYS WANTED TO BE IN A SUPER-TEAM.
THAT'S RIGHT, SAM.
WE'RE A GODDAMN *SUPER-TEAM.*
SO I'M WRITING MYSELF THIS LETTER, *JUST IN CASE* MADDEN'S CURE GOES WRONG. JUST IN CASE I *FORGET* AGAIN.
BUT MEMORIES ARE JUST THE STORIES WE *TELL* OURSELVES ABOUT THE THINGS WE ONCE DID.
IT'S GOOD TO KNOW WHAT WENT BEFORE, BUT IT'S NOT *VITAL.*
I KNOW THAT BETTER THAN *ANYONE.*
THE PAST IS JUST THE RUNGS OF THE LADDER WE'VE *ALREADY* CLIMBED.
WE'RE GOING FOR MY PARENTS.
AND AFTER *THAT,* JIMMY MAC, WE GO BACK TO DOING WHAT WE DO *BEST.*
REMEMBER?
THE END

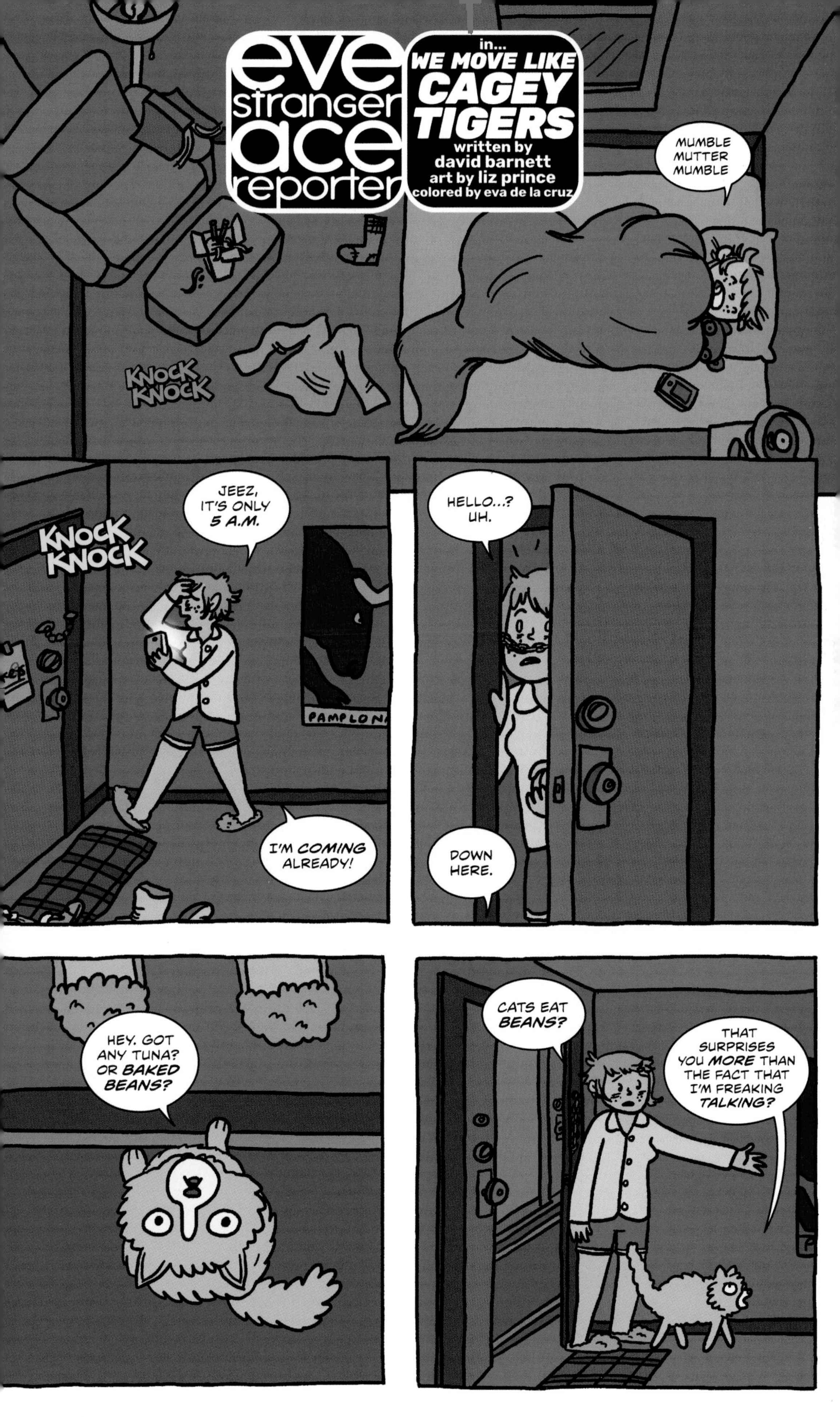
eve stranger ace reporter
in... WE MOVE LIKE CAGEY TIGERS
written by david barnett
art by liz prince
colored by eva de la cruz
MUMBLE MUTTER MUMBLE
KNOCK KNOCK
KNOCK KNOCK
JEEZ, IT'S ONLY 5 A.M.
PAMPLONA
I'M COMING ALREADY!
HELLO...? UH.
DOWN HERE.
HEY. GOT ANY TUNA? OR BAKED BEANS?
CATS EAT BEANS?
THAT SURPRISES YOU MORE THAN THE FACT THAT I'M FREAKING TALKING?

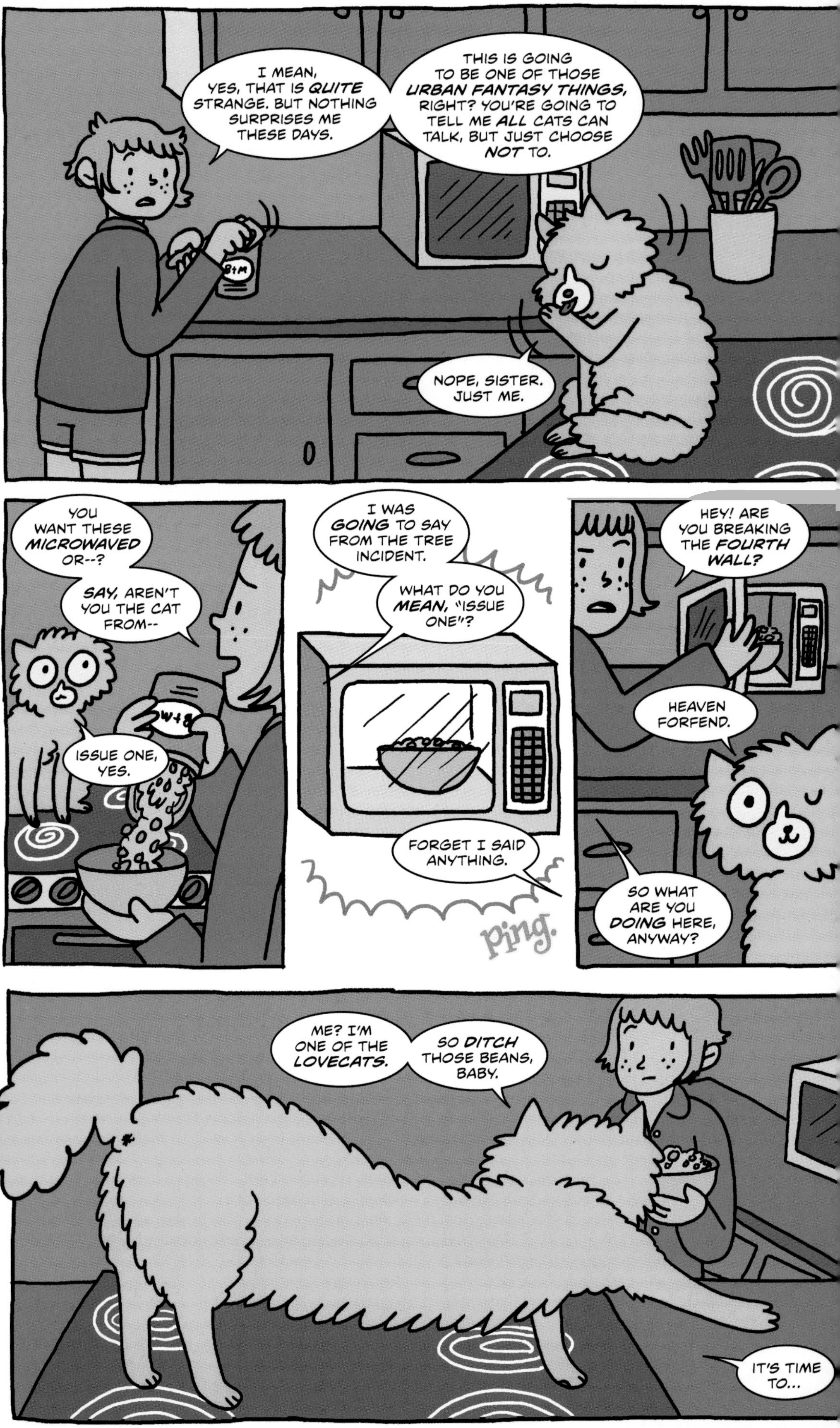
I MEAN, YES, THAT IS QUITE STRANGE. BUT NOTHING SURPRISES ME THESE DAYS.
THIS IS GOING TO BE ONE OF THOSE URBAN FANTASY THINGS, RIGHT? YOU'RE GOING TO TELL ME ALL CATS CAN TALK, BUT JUST CHOOSE NOT TO.
NOPE, SISTER. JUST ME.
YOU WANT THESE MICROWAVED OR--?
SAY, AREN'T YOU THE CAT FROM--
ISSUE ONE, YES.
I WAS GOING TO SAY FROM THE TREE INCIDENT.
WHAT DO YOU MEAN, "ISSUE ONE"?
FORGET I SAID ANYTHING.
ping.
HEY! ARE YOU BREAKING THE FOURTH WALL?
HEAVEN FORFEND.
SO WHAT ARE YOU DOING HERE, ANYWAY?
ME? I'M ONE OF THE LOVECATS.
SO DITCH THOSE BEANS, BABY.
IT'S TIME TO...

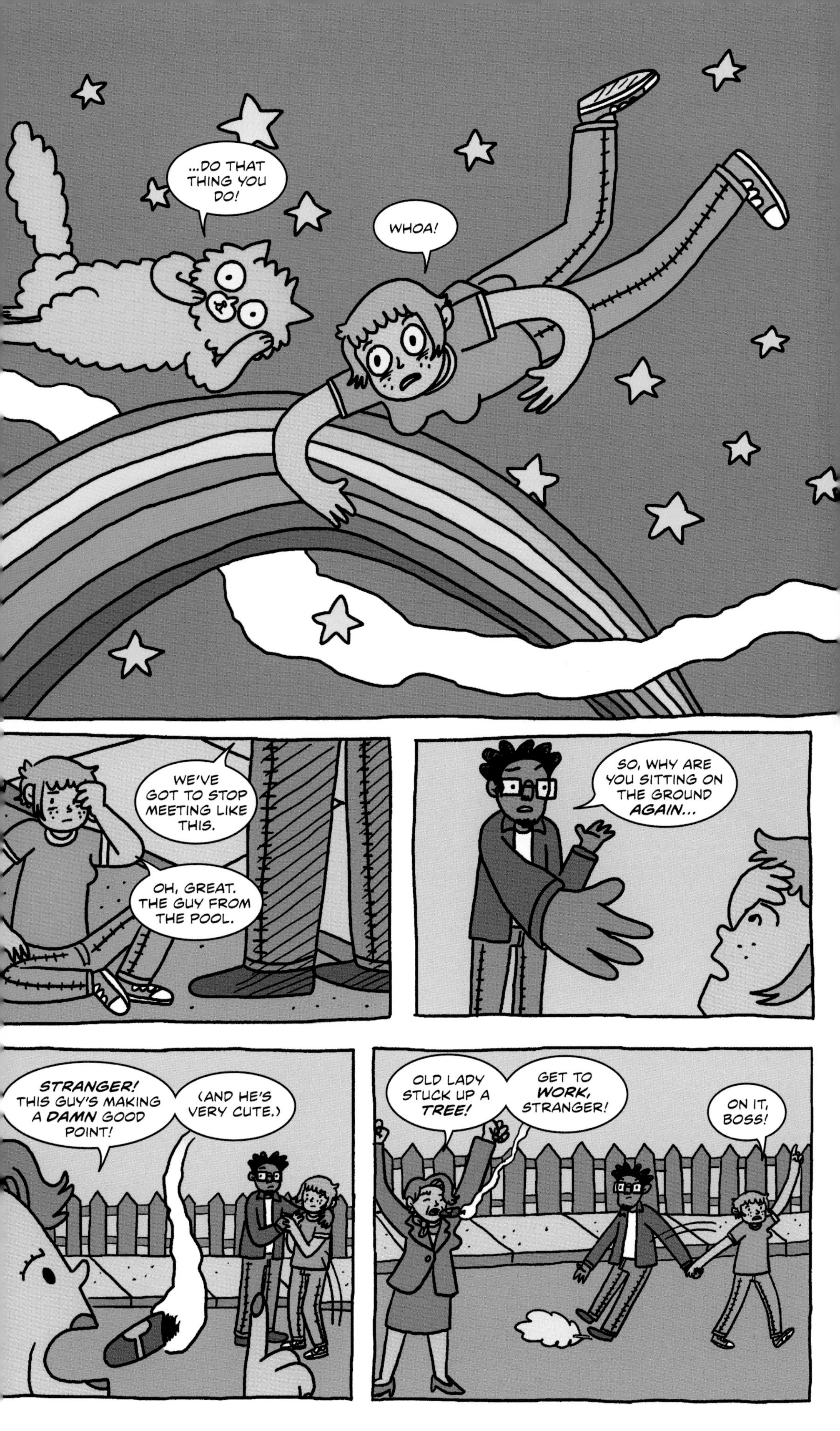
...DO THAT THING YOU DO!
WHOA!
WE'VE GOT TO STOP MEETING LIKE THIS.
OH, GREAT. THE GUY FROM THE POOL.
SO, WHY ARE YOU SITTING ON THE GROUND AGAIN...
STRANGER! THIS GUY'S MAKING A DAMN GOOD POINT!
(AND HE'S VERY CUTE.)
OLD LADY STUCK UP A TREE!
GET TO WORK, STRANGER!
ON IT, BOSS!

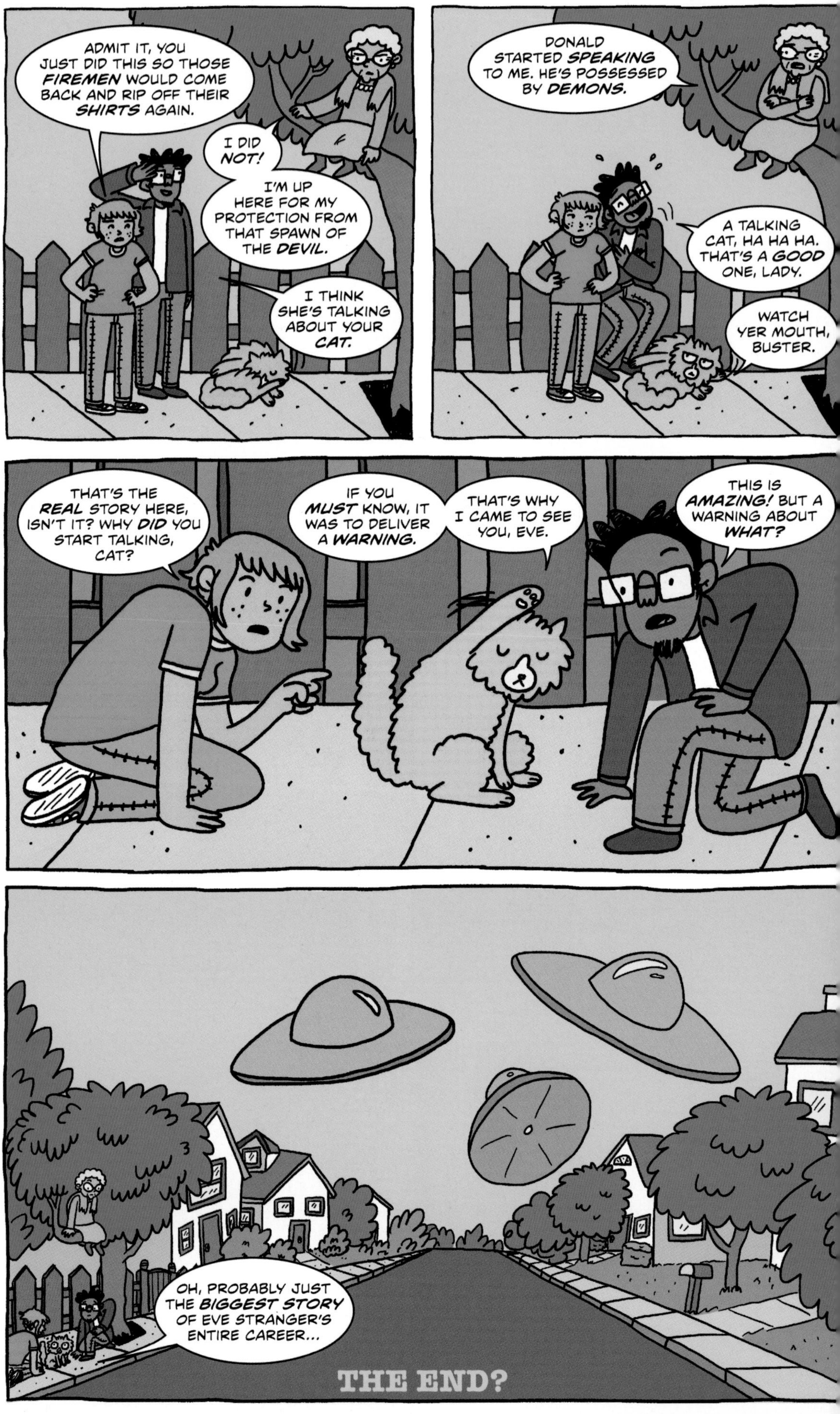
ADMIT IT, YOU JUST DID THIS SO THOSE FIREMEN WOULD COME BACK AND RIP OFF THEIR SHIRTS AGAIN.
I DID NOT!
I'M UP HERE FOR MY PROTECTION FROM THAT SPAWN OF THE DEVIL.
I THINK SHE'S TALKING ABOUT YOUR CAT.
DONALD STARTED SPEAKING TO ME. HE'S POSSESSED BY DEMONS.
A TALKING CAT, HA HA HA. THAT'S A GOOD ONE, LADY.
WATCH YER MOUTH, BUSTER.
THAT'S THE REAL STORY HERE, ISN'T IT? WHY DID YOU START TALKING, CAT?
IF YOU MUST KNOW, IT WAS TO DELIVER A WARNING.
THAT'S WHY I CAME TO SEE YOU, EVE.
THIS IS AMAZING! BUT A WARNING ABOUT WHAT?
OH, PROBABLY JUST THE BIGGEST STORY OF EVE STRANGER'S ENTIRE CAREER...
THE END?

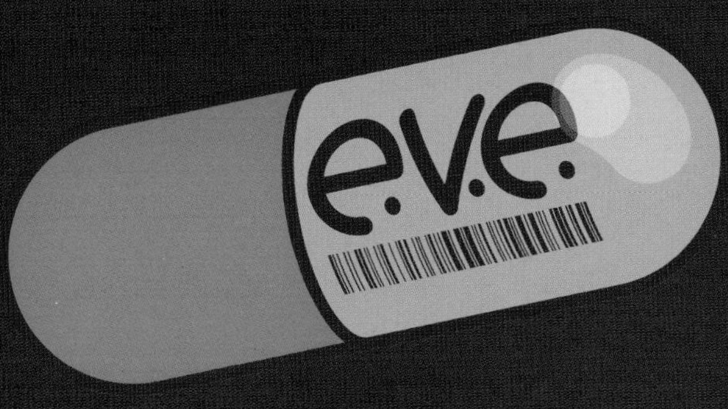
e.v.e.

EXTRA MATERIALS

issue 1 variant cover by Dilraj Mann

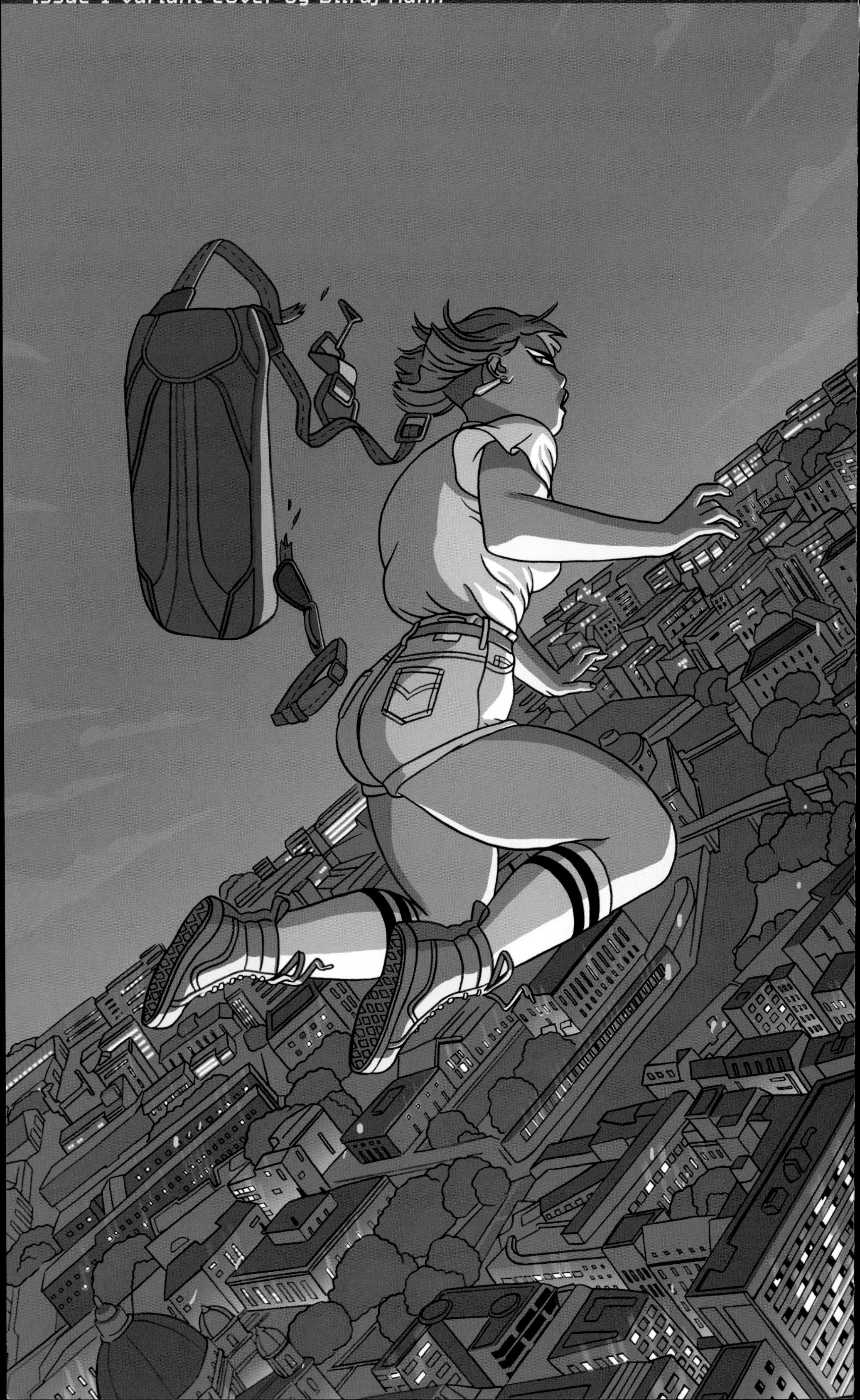

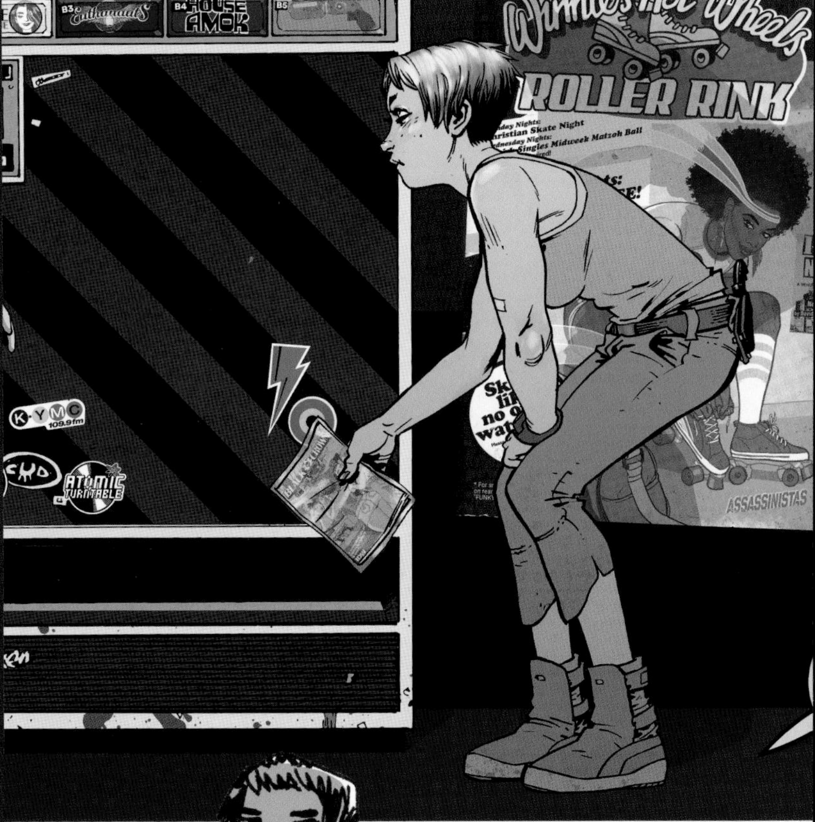
HOUSE AMOK
ROLLER RINK
Christian Skate Night
Singles Midweek Matzoh Ball
ATOMIC TURNTABLE
109.9fm
ASSASSINISTAS

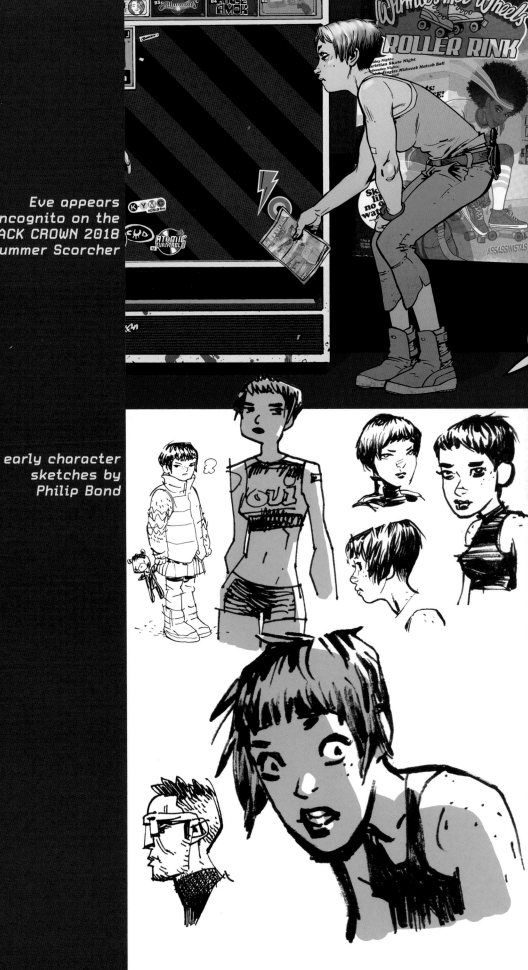

Eve appears incognito on the BLACK CROWN 2018 Summer Scorcher

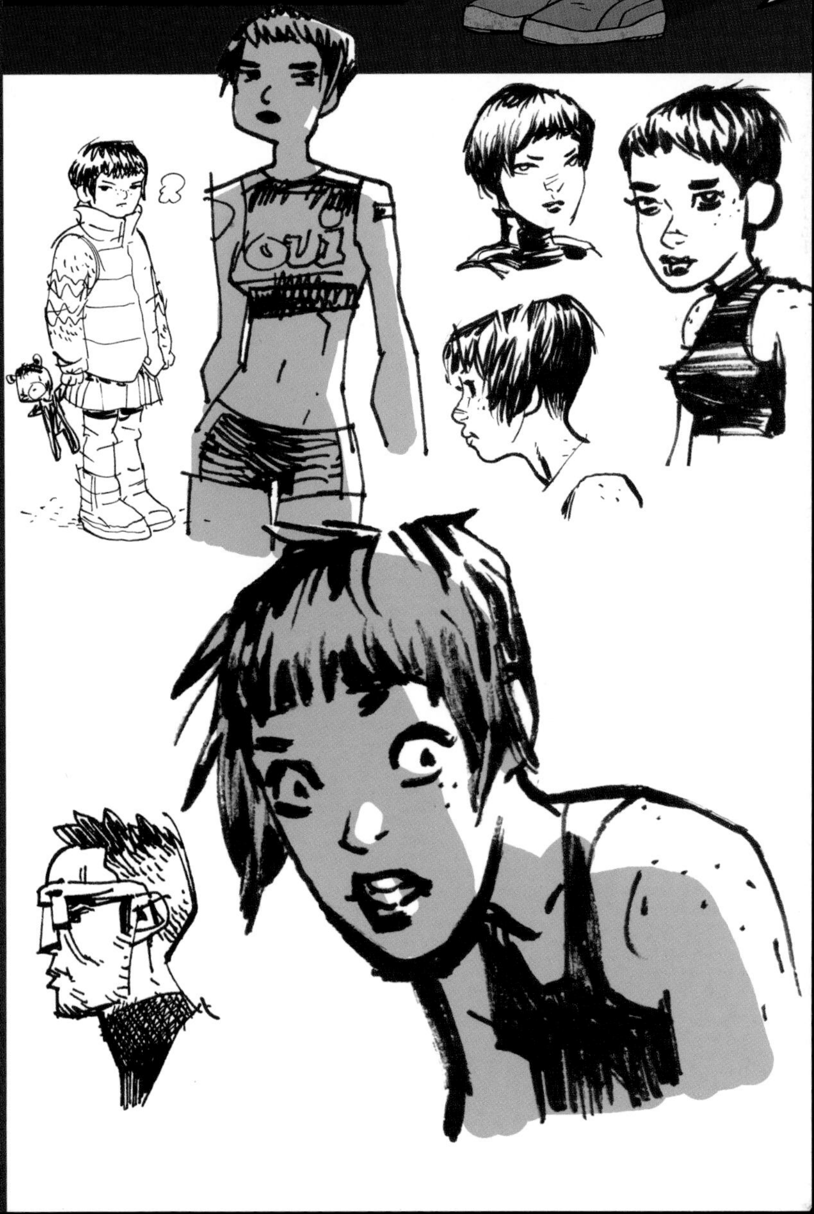

early character sketches by Philip Bond

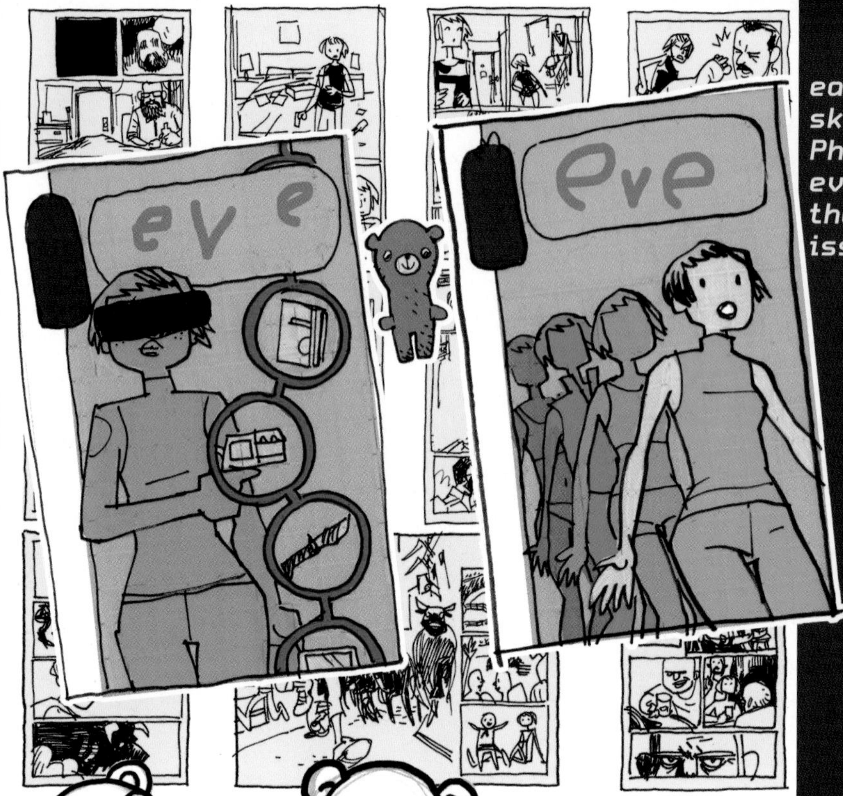
eve
eve

early cover sketches by Philip Bond eventually became the covers for issues 1 and 3

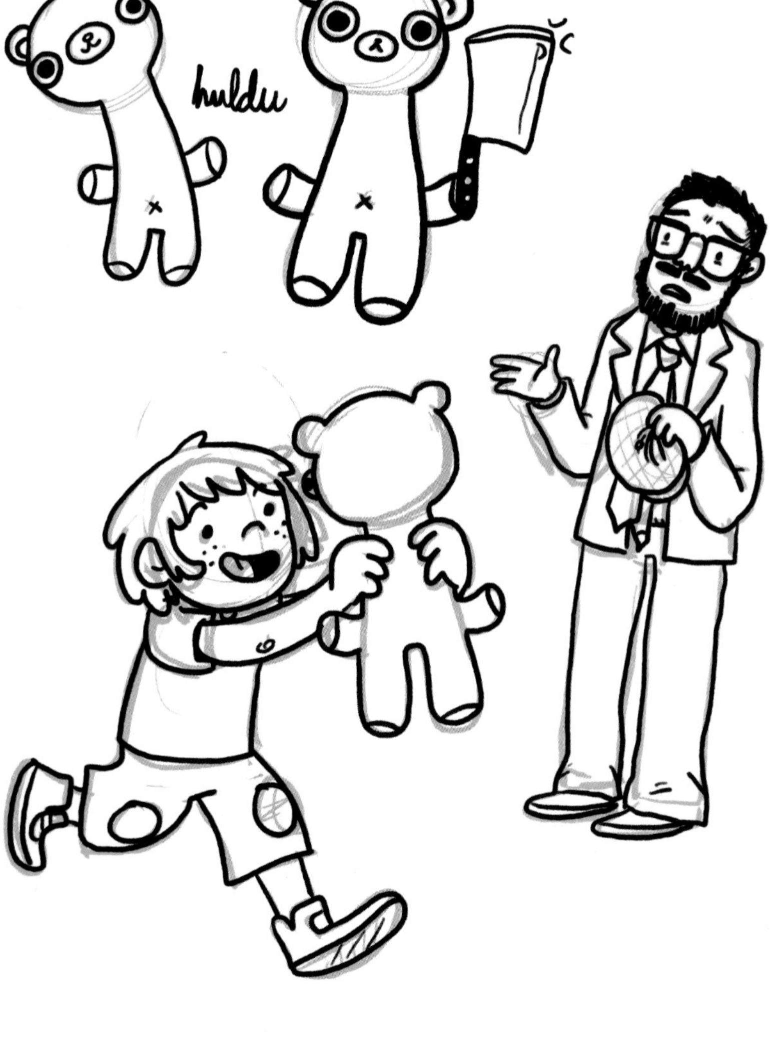

character sketches by Liz Prince

breaks!

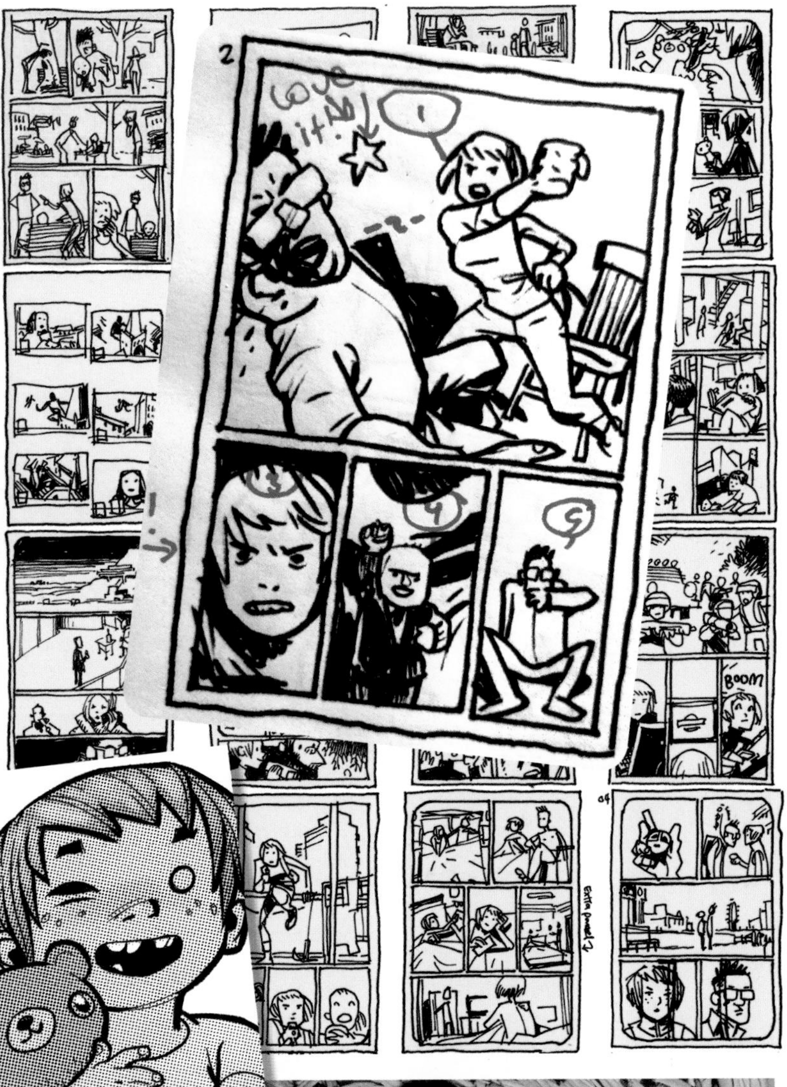

retailer promo gift: handmade Huldu bears by letterer Jane Heir with handout designed by Philip Bond

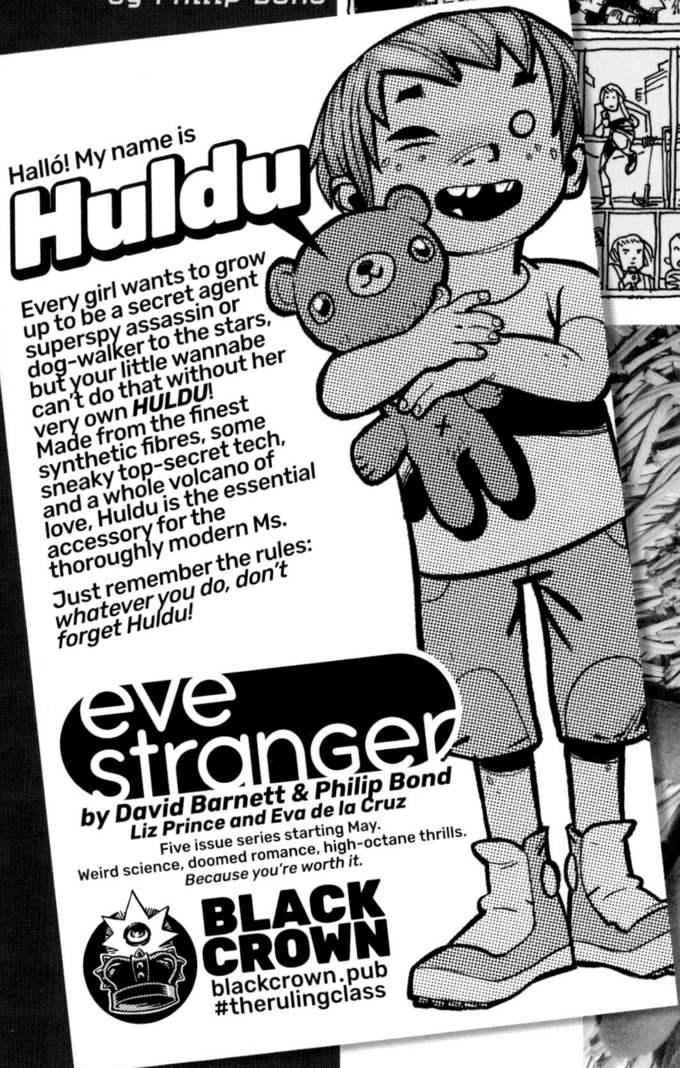

Halló! My name is
Huldu
Every girl wants to grow up to be a secret agent superspy assassin or dog-walker to the stars, but your little wannabe can't do that without her very own ***HULDU***! Made from the finest synthetic fibres, some sneaky top-secret tech, and a whole volcano of love, Huldu is the essential accessory for the thoroughly modern Ms.
Just remember the rules: *whatever you do, don't forget Huldu!*
eve stranger
by David Barnett & Philip Bond
Liz Prince and Eva de la Cruz
Five issue series starting May.
Weird science, doomed romance, high-octane thrills.
Because you're worth it.
BLACK CROWN
blackcrown.pub
#therulingclass

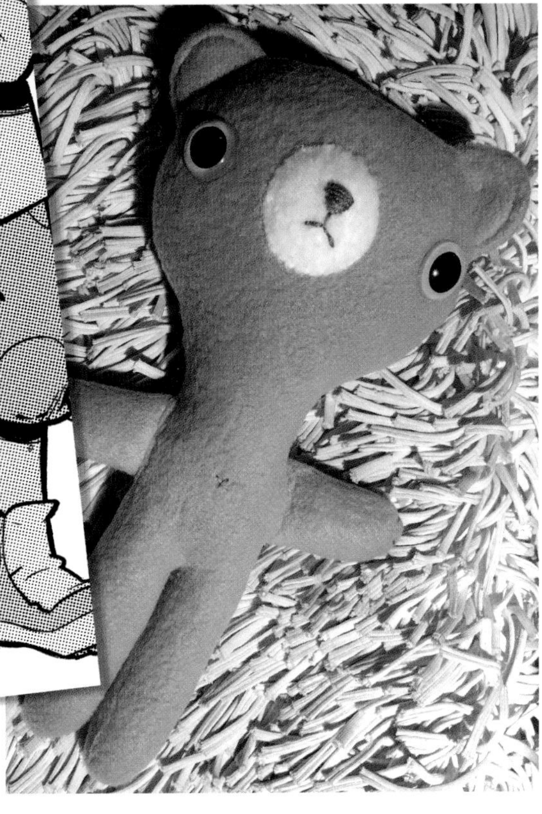

COMIC-BOOK Writer
24 hour TIP LINE
0800-MILLIGAN

NANOBOMBS? in *MY* bloodstream?

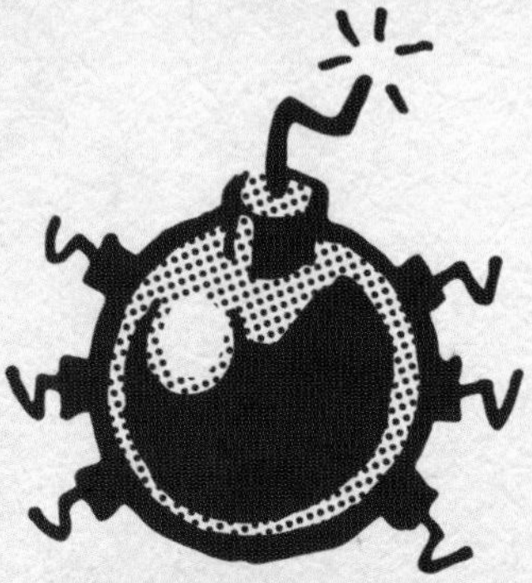

It's more likely than you think.

Call ***The EVE Project*** to hear about our latest all-in-one solution.

1-800-GLEYMDUÞVÍ

e.v.e. project

CAN'T WRITE? CAN'T DRAW?

LEARN TO EDIT!

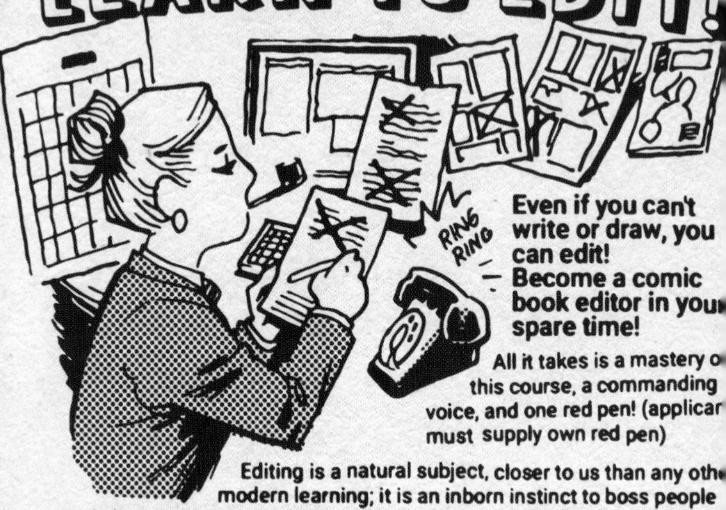
RING RING

Even if you can't write or draw, you can edit! Become a comic book editor in you[r] spare time!

All it takes is a mastery o[f] this course, a commanding voice, and one red pen! (applica[nts] must supply own red pen)

Editing is a natural subject, closer to us than any oth[er] modern learning; it is an inborn instinct to boss people around, deprive them of any/all confidence. Be the ice skate blade that glide[s] over an artist's fingers! You know you want to! No filter necessary! Be the first on your block to kick someone in the proverbial darlings! Method can be applied in writing or orally!

1. Still - Life Editing
2. Perspective - only yours applies. You are the rule and the exception.
4. Figure Editing - it figures you have to play both good cop and bad cop. Turn on a dime! Show those freeloaders who's the boss.
5. Composition Editing - tangents be damned!

Yes! Sign me up!
Send name, address and credit car[d] details to Roeberg & Son Publishing House, 643 E Canon St. Suite #208

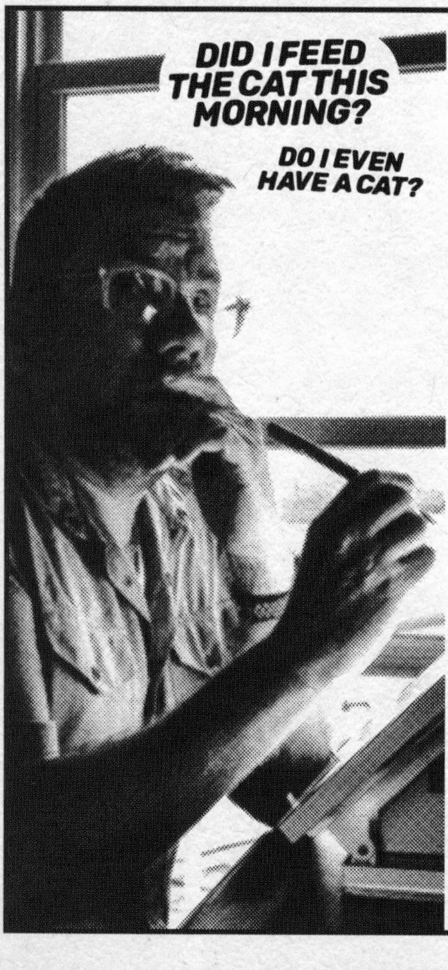
DID I FEED THE CAT THIS MORNING?
DO I EVEN HAVE A CAT?

DO *YOU* FIND YOURSELF FORGETTING WHAT DAY OF THE WEEK IT IS?

...forgetting why you went to the grocery store?
Do you forget phone numbers?
...internet passwords?
...the names of friends?
...the formula of Pi beyond 20 decimal places?
Where did I leave my hat?

REMEMBERY (TM)'s patented blend of homeopathic psychotropes can bring those memories flooding back. Everything from why you went to the fridge to that buried childhood trauma.

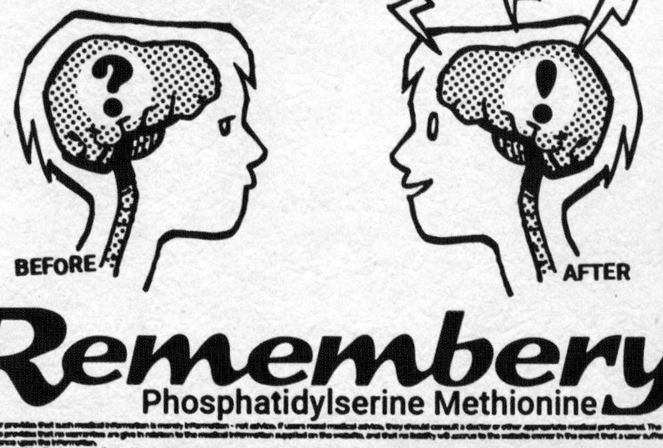
BEFORE
AFTER

Remembery

Phosphatidylserine Methionine

This disclaimer provides that such medical information is merely information - not advice. If users need medical advice, they should consult a doctor or other appropriate medical professional. The disclaimer also provides that no warranties are give in relation to the medical information supplied on the website, and that no liability will accrue to the website owner in the event that a user suffers a result of reliance upon the information.
Of course, this kind of liability disclaimer will not always be enforceable. The courts regularly rule that limitations and exclusions of liability are ineffective (on various grounds). You should take advice f[rom] your lawyer if you may wish to rely upon a disclaimer of liability. The disclaimer may be used on its own or used as part of another legal document.
The contents of this medical advice disclaimer are as follows: (1) no advice; (2) no warranties; (3) professional assistance; (4) limiting our liability; and (5) this disclaimer.

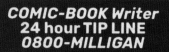

CATALOGUE

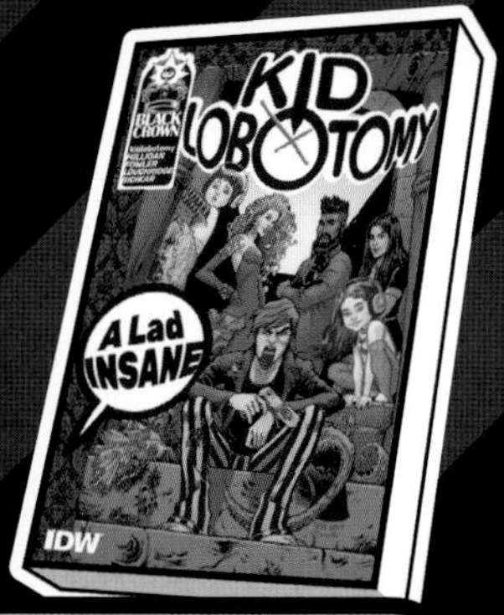
KID LOBOTOMY
A Lad INSANE
IDW

KID LOBOTOMY
Almost Rockstar. Awkward Hotelier. Definitive Madman.
by Peter Milligan + Tess Fowler

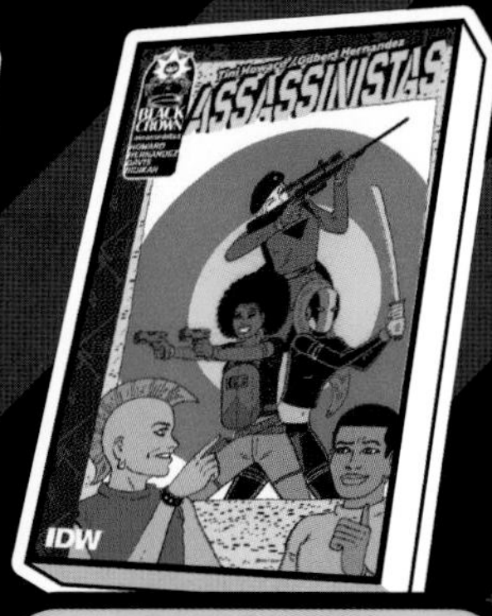
ASSASSINISTAS
IDW

ASSASSINISTAS
Modern Family. Retro Sass. Highly Trained to Kick Your Ass.
by Tini Howard + Gilbert Hernandez

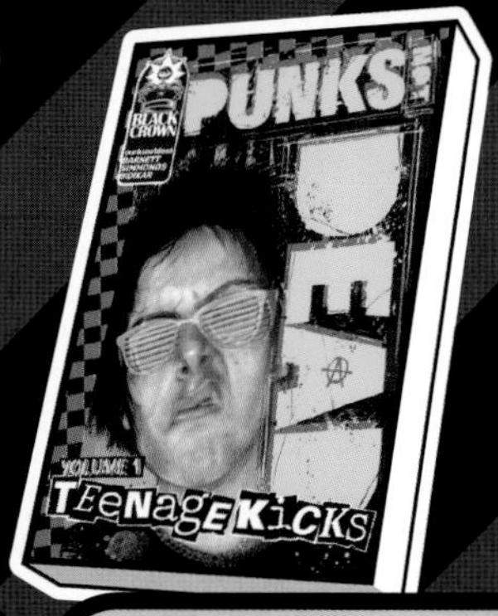
PUNKS!
VOLUME 1
TEENAGE KICKS

PUNKS NOT DEAD
The Ghost. The Geek. The Geriatric Mod Superspy. Everything & the Bollocks
by David Barnett + Martin Simmonds

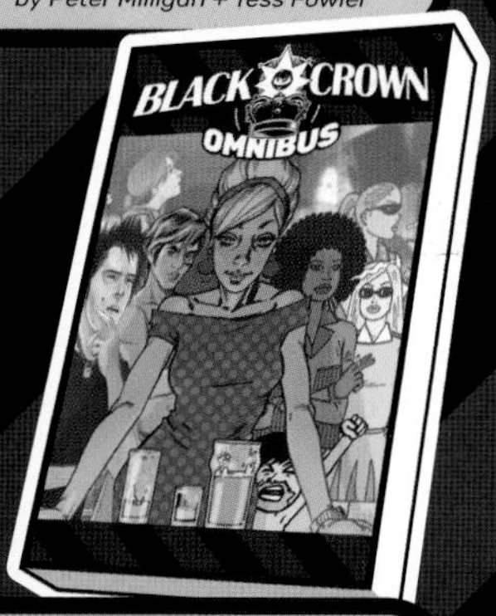
BLACK CROWN
OMNIBUS

BLACK CROWN OMNIBUS
The Compendium of Comics, Culture & Cool featuring Tales from the BC Pub.
by Rob Davis, CUD + others

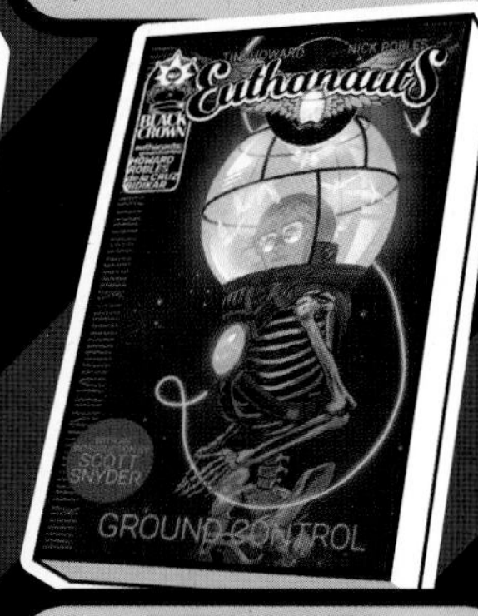
Euthanauts
SCOTT SNYDER
GROUND CONTROL

EUTHANAUTS
Tethers to the Great Beyond. Psychonautic Mindspaces.
by Tini Howard + Nick Robles

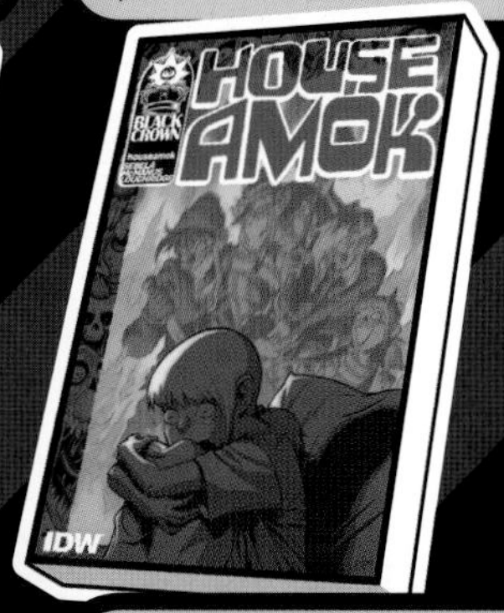
HOUSE AMOK
IDW

HOUSE AMOK
Conspiracy theories come to life. Shared Family Madness & Murder.
by Christopher Sebela + Shawn McManus

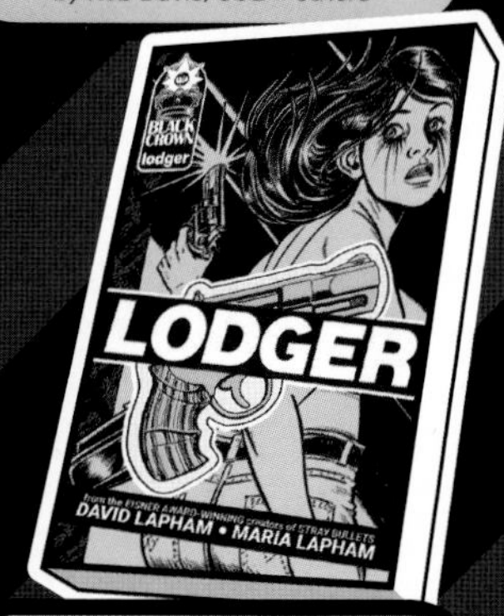
LODGER
DAVID LAPHAM • MARIA LAPHAM

LODGER
A serial killer hides in plain sight as a travel blogger in a game of cat & mouse.
By The Laphams of Stray Bullets

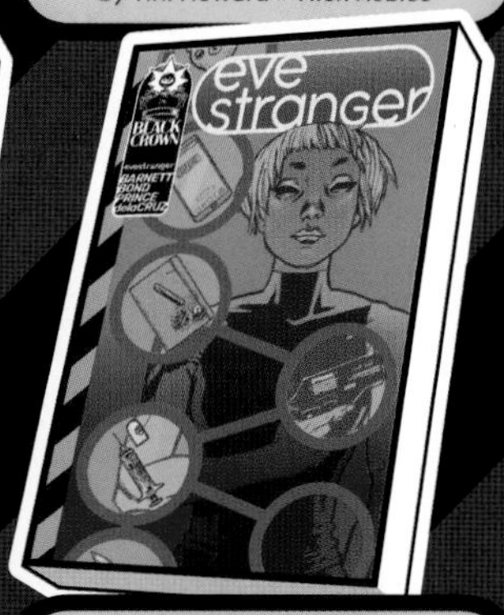
eve stranger

EVE STRANGER
High-Octane Thrills! Weird Science! Doomed Romance!
by David Barnett + Philip Bond

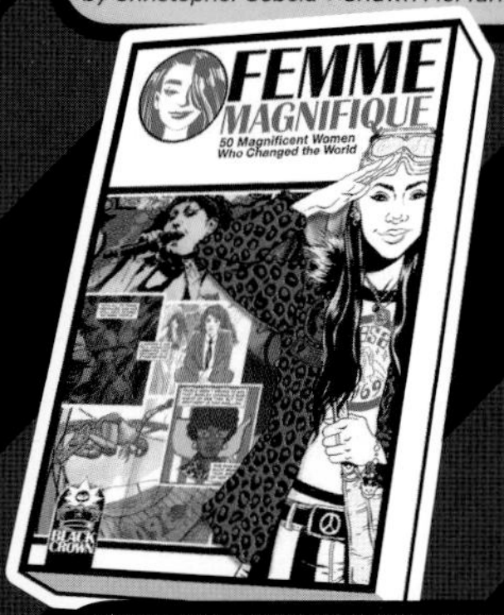
FEMME MAGNIFIQUE
50 Magnificent Women Who Changed the World

FEMME MAGNIFIQUE
A salute to personal icons who shatter ceilings in pop, politics, art & science.
by 100+ A-list writers & artists

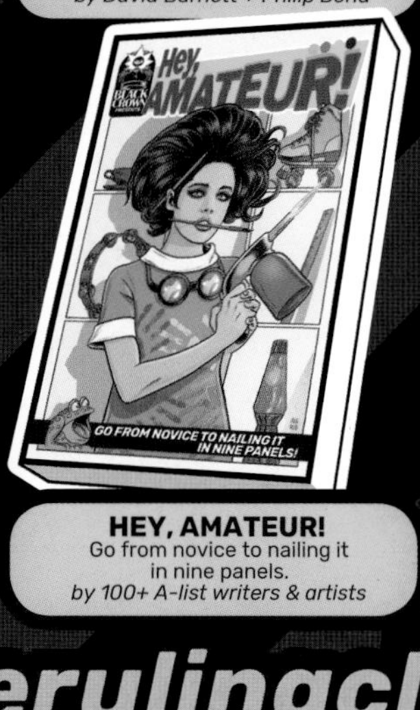
Hey, AMATEUR!
GO FROM NOVICE TO NAILING IT IN NINE PANELS!

HEY, AMATEUR!
Go from novice to nailing it in nine panels.
by 100+ A-list writers & artists

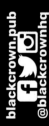

blackcrown.pub
@blackcrownhq

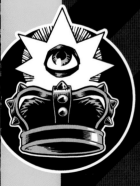

#therulingclass

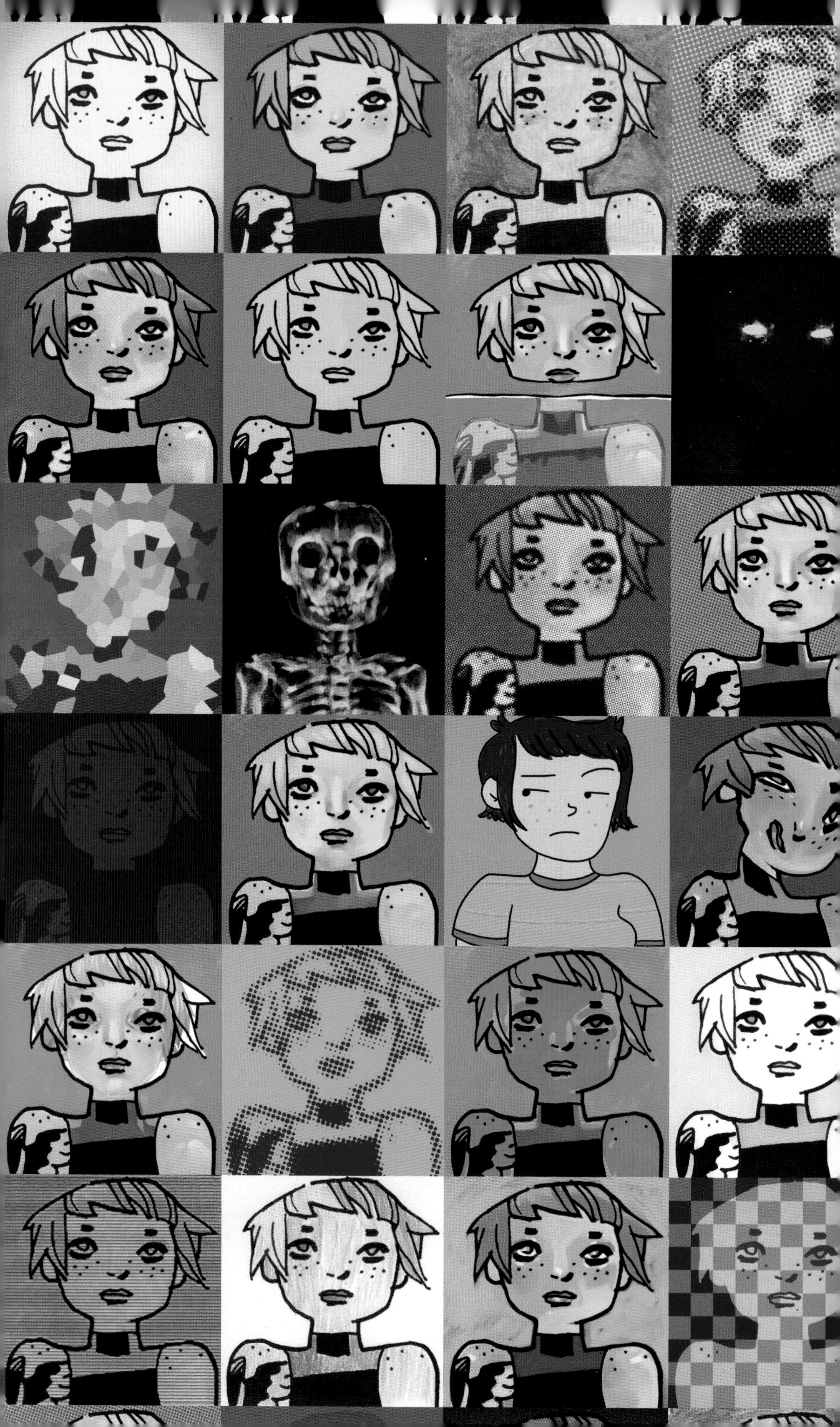